ENIGMA

In the middle was a symmetrical grassy mound, fenced by poles which raised into the pouring rain skulls marked with broad red stripes. Everyone stopped, prisoners bunching together, cops looking around as if expecting an ambush. De Ramaira touched the boy's shoulder. "The aborigines?"

"Something my father found."

"I can't remember anything like this described in Webster." Anger and excitement fizzed in de Ramaira's blood. Anger because the boy wouldn't have told anyone about the place if a life had not been in danger; excitement because of the implications, the possibilities. . . .

By Paul J. McAuley
Published by Ballantine Books:

FOUR HUNDRED BILLION STARS

OF THE FALL

OF THE FALL

FALL

Paul J. McAuley

A Del Rey Book
BALLANTINE BOOKS • NEW YORK

A Del Rey Book
Published by Ballantine Books

Copyright © 1989 by Paul J. McAuley

Library of Congress Catalog Card Number: 88-92823

ISBN 0-345-36056-7

Printed in Canada

First Edition: June 1989

Cover Art by Don Dixon

But els in deep of night when drowsiness
Hath lockt up mortal sense, then listen I
To the celestial Siren's harmony . . .
Such sweet compulsion doth in music ly,
To lull the daughters of *Necessity*,
And keep unsteedy Nature to her law,
And the low world in measur'd motion draw
After the heavenly tune, which none can hear
Of human mold with grosse unpurged ear.

John Milton, *Arcades*

To every ω-consistent recursive class of *formulae* there correspond recursive *class-signs* r, such that neither v Gen r nor Neg (v Gen r) belongs to Flg κ (where v is the *free variable* of r.)

Kurt Gödel, *On Formally Undecidable Propositions in Principia Mathematica and Related Systems I*

CONTENTS

PROLOGUE

Understanding the Aliens

The shoulder of the last valley shrugged free of the forest and at last the three riders gained the high plain, an empire of red grass sparely punctuated by clumps of wind-sculpted thornbush. Eastward, the Trackless Mountains rose above a colorless haze, snowcapped peaks reflecting chiseled planes of sunlight.

David de Ramaira reined in his horse and stretched in the saddle. Despite therapy, he had not quite regained muscle tone lost during years of coldcoffin sleep. A tall, slim, brown-skinned man, he looked around with a delighted grin, his heart quickening as it had when he had first woken in the reception center and realized that he had made it. *Another world.*

"Magnificent," he said. "Magnificent country." To his eyes, the plain of red grass glowed with surrealistic intensity beneath the cloudless indigo sky, something to do with the spectrum of Tau Ceti perhaps, the soft orange sun so different from the star of Earth.

The guide from Broken Hill, Jonthan Say, shrugged. "Soil too thin to farm," he said.

"How far is the village?" de Ramaira asked.

Jonthan pointed out a gleaming line that in the heat seemed to be layered between red grasses and dark sky. "That there's the lake. The abo village is a ways around the shore." His hair, a halo of spun brass, was matted with sweat; and sweat glistened on his bare chest, darkened the thighs of his faded jeans where he gripped the saddle of the bay mare. Fifteen, sixteen years old (they still measured age by the years of Earth, here), imbued with coltish adolescent grace. When he noticed de Ramaira's stare, he jogged the mare and rode on to catch up with Lieutenant McAnders, who as usual couldn't be bothered to wait. The boy's dog circled wide through dry red grass. After a moment, de Ramaira flicked the reins of his own horse, a stolid gelding, and followed the others toward the lake.

While Jonthan Say pitched camp, de Ramaira walked around the reed-fringed shore of the lake to the village, eager for his first glimpse of the Elysian Aborigines. Lieutenant McAnders insisted on coming with him, and for all that he had wanted the moment to himself, de Ramaira kept his peace. After all, she was head of the Office of Aboriginal Affairs and so, by extension, head of the expedition. As they pushed through crackling grasses she gestured at the case he carried and said scornfully, "You won't learn anything new, even with those things."

"We'll see," de Ramaira said evenly.

"Well, hell," the lieutenant said. "You know it all, right?" She was a stocky woman, dressed like de Ramaira in the white coveralls of the Port Authority cops (but with a pistol in the power holster at her hip), hair of no particular color cut in a bristling crewcut, mouth pursed around the dead butt of a cheroot. De Ramaira was beginning to learn to hate her.

Toiling through long grass, they skirted a marshy arm of the lake and a skimpy line of thornbushes. And there, suddenly, was the village, round huts topping a gentle rise like a random arrangement of boulders. As he came closer, de Ramaira began to make out a faint, furious high-pitched buzz, like wasps trapped in a bottle. He stopped, set down his case and looked at the cluster of domed roofs. The restless buzzing of the aborigines hung in the hot, still air. De Ramaira wanted to deploy his remotes there and then, but the lieutenant had other ideas.

"Hell, you ought to see them face to face. Maybe then you'll get the idea that they aren't worth the trouble. Lord knows I tried to tell you." She pushed on through the grass and de Ramaira sighed and picked up his case and followed.

The huts were surrounded by a wide band of bare earth. The buzzing stopped as soon as the two humans set foot upon this margin, as if at the throw of a switch. In his sudden rush of exhilaration de Ramaira hardly noticed: he had seen his first aborigine.

It stood a little way from the first of the huts, a good deal taller than de Ramaira's own two meters, and terribly thin. Its hide, mottled tan and black, shrinkwrapped its long limbs, closely modeling bulbous double joints, contoured arrow-head-shaped ribs running from narrow pelvis to neck, the long unsutured skull. De Ramaira cautiously circled the crea-ture. Apart from the restless stirring of finely divided fronds packed in its nasal cavity, it was quite motionless, paralyzed by human presence just as Webster had described. Its eyes were round and wholly black, its mouth wide and lipless as a frog's. It gave off a faint, fishy reek.

"Keep at that long enough and it'll drop dead," the lieu-tenant said.

"Is that really true?"

The woman spat out the butt of her cheroot. "Sure. They last maybe two hours and then their nervous systems burn out." She stepped up and rapped the aborigine's low fore-head. De Ramaira winced, although the creature did not move. "Know what's going on in there? Almost zero, that's what. I'll show you the Source Cave when you're ready, but there isn't anything to see there, either. This isn't the breed-ing season, and it's too dangerous to go in when it is, the hatchlings go for anything that moves. As Webster found to his cost. You want the truth, my father thought Webster was a damned romantic."

"His work is well regarded on Earth." In defending Web-ster, a scientist sent especially to Elysium to study the abo-rigines, de Ramaira was also defending himself, a phylogenist sent to describe and classify Elysium's biota.

The lieutenant shrugged, and lighted another of her evil-smelling cheroots.

Nettled, de Ramaira added, "If Webster had had more support, he might have been able to give a definite answer to the question of the aborigines' intelligence." He looked up into the enigmatic eyes of the aborigine, pupilless black holes pitted deep in the mask of its face, and wondered if its immobility was due to terrified denial of the existence of humans, of things completely outside its world-picture, or if there was a deeper reason. An expression of irreconcilable distaste, perhaps. He was vain enough to nurture the small hope that he could somehow break this fugue, reach out and make contact.

The lieutenant led de Ramaira around the dozen or so widely spaced huts, pointing out bowls made of grass stems woven so tightly that they could hold water, crude stone-tipped spears, bone knives lying beside the flayed carcass of a mire boar. The huts themselves were identical, four or five meters in diameter and half as high at the apex of their domed roofs, built of mud-plastered panels of plaited grass and reeds. Here and there, the village's inhabitants stood or squatted like so many skeletal statues. The lieutenant ignored their presence, and when de Ramaira asked if there were any children she said dismissively, "The little fuckers run off into the grass. They're not worth the trouble of tracking down."

"There are a few hours of daylight left. I'd like to see if the children come back, get an idea of the way these creatures move. They will return to normal, once we've gone?"

The lieutenant assured him that he'd soon have his fill of the aborigines' normal behavior, and left him alone to play, as she put it, with his remotes. De Ramaira lay in the long grass outside the village until sunset, interfaced with a comp-sim so that he could send one of the little machines buzzing about the huts at will, the pictures of the aborigines that its avid camera eyes transmitted blooming one after the other on the inside of his eyelids like the giddy distortions of a bad trip.

As the lieutenant had promised, the aborigines soon began to move once they had been left alone, jerking out of their paralysis and resuming their communal buzz all at the same moment. They walked with a curious stiffly bending gait, long arms hanging loosely, narrow head tilted back. It reminded de Ramaira of something, but it was a while before he made the connection. The rigid gait of the aborigines was like that of the figures of ancient Egyptian friezes. They even looked a little like something dug up from some sandy grave, long dead and dried out and . . . distorted.

De Ramaira watched as two aborigines butchered the mire boar carcass with almost ritualistic elaboration, squatting close to their work so that the double joints of their knees bent above their heads. Meanwhile, children, exact miniatures of the immature adults, played at chipping pebbles or bones, or chased each other among the huts; while the only aborigine which could be easily distinguished from its fellows, by a ridged web of scars at its crotch, sat cross-legged at the center of the village. Like a dried-up spider, de Ramaira thought. Webster, noting the presence of one of these mutilated aborigines in every village, had called them shamans. Really, he had not been strictly objective in many of his interpretations.

The orange sun sank lower, deepening the shadows of the huts. At last de Ramaira recalled the remote and returned to the camp. A fire had been lit in a hearth of pebbles and the lieutenant sprawled beside it reading a book. It was the book de Ramaira had brought with him: a leather-bound volume with its title, *The Report of a Reconnaissance of the Trackless Mountains, 2057*, stamped in gold on its cover. Printed books, like smoking tobacco and marijuana, had been revived during the colony's first years; unlike smoking, however, they had quickly lapsed into a curiosity.

The lieutenant, not at all embarrassed at having been caught with evidence of having gone through de Ramaira's kit, said, "There's some odd stuff in here."

"Odder to me than to you, surely." De Ramaira dumped the metal case which housed the remotes. "Where's Jonthan?"

"Hunting for his dog's supper."

"And you're not hunting with him?" Twice on the ride up from Broken Hill, the lieutenant had broken away to fruitlessly pursue some beast or other through the tangled valley forests.

She smiled and said, "He's some catch, right?"

"That's not what I meant," de Ramaira said, stung by the implication. The lieutenant would have read his file as a matter of course, but he didn't like to be reminded of it. "If you've quite finished with my book, I'd like to check up on a couple of things."

The lieutenant closed the heavy volume, but made no move to hand it over. "Why did you bring this, Doctor? This is as close to the Trackless Mountains as you'll get."

"Is it? I'd like to explore them one day, and see what's beyond them, too. I'm an ambitious man, Lieutenant. Describing the plants and animals of this little peninsula is nothing to the chance of exploring a whole world."

"Ambition is all very well," the lieutenant said, "but there are limits." She looked at him. "I wondered why you insisted on coming out this far when there are abo villages nearer the city."

"Well," de Ramaira said, "this was the first Webster had fully described." That was only part of the reason. While he had been recuperating from years of coldcoffin sleep he had pored over maps of the peninsula—about the size of California, it was the only part of Elysium settled so far—determining how far he could travel without breaking Port of Plenty's prohibitions. He had wanted to get a good idea of the world as quickly as possible, and the week-long journey had not disappointed him. Out of Port of Plenty on a little coastal packet which had hugged a bleak sandy shore to Freeport, a settlement of low white buildings either side of a broad river, hemmed by cave-riddled limestone cliffs. Then up the river to Broken Hill on a slow steam-launch with a raked funnel, and then by horseback to the high grass plains at the foot of the Trackless Mountains. Every day he had gloried in the simple thrill of apprehension—*another world!*—but he couldn't tell the lieutenant about that thrill. She would refuse to understand. She would sneer. This was nothing to her, no more than another pointless trip into the boondocks. He said,

"Look, I know that Port of Plenty prohibits movement of people beyond the peninsula, but I don't see why that should apply to me. I don't intend to start an illegal settlement, after all."

"Some would call you a separatist if they heard talk like that. If the city didn't regulate the settlers they'd be all over the continent inside a century."

De Ramaira had already had conversations like this, and asked the question only to needle the lieutenant. "Would that be such a bad thing?"

"My people were here first, built Port of Plenty years before the colonyboats started arriving. We didn't ask to have more people dumped on us. We have a right to see that our world isn't raped. Keep quiet about your plans in Port of Plenty, or you might never be allowed out again." She crossed to the neat cache of supplies, sorted out two cans and tossed one to de Ramaira. "Let's eat. God knows when the boy will be back."

Jonthan Say didn't return until long after sunset. De Ramaira was reading his book by the light of an electric lantern while on the other side of the campfire the lieutenant fiddled with her transceiver, the tip of her cheroot brightening and dimming like a fitful star. The boy, his dog trotting at his heels, hailed them cheerfully. He had the carcass of something like a fat blunt-headed lizard slung over one shoulder. Long tail tipped with heavy spines; the oval scales which lapped its body tufted with bright red hair. Jonthan allowed de Ramaira to perform a rough dissection—three-chambered heart and single ramifying lung, a string of half-formed eggs coiled in the abdomen like a pearl necklace—then dressed the carcass and tossed half of it to the dog. As he opened a tin for himself, Jonthan asked, "I always wondered, Doctor, why we weren't modified so we could eat the native plants and animals."

"On Earth it's illegal, anti-evolutionary, to modify human stock. Besides, gene-melding can only be done on the ovum before the first division horizon, not on the people who come to settle Elysium.''

Across the fire, the lieutenant looked up from the transceiver. ''You spend time out here, Jonthan, but you have to go home eventually. That's how it has to be.''

The boy said without rancor, ''That's how the city sees it, that we can be controlled if we have to rely on our farms and the chemicals we must buy from the city to help the crops grow. If we could live off the land . . . Is it true there are escaped rabbits living wild around the city?''

''They're all over the Outback,'' de Ramaira said. ''Something should be done, before they screw up the native ecosystem.''

''Don't give the boy ideas,'' the lieutenant said, taking out her earplug speaker. ''He knows what happens to people who go dingo. Right, Jonthan?''

The boy shrugged, began to spoon up his stew.

''Remember those people who took off from Horizon, last year? Word's on the air that they've been captured; the party'll be passing us by in a couple of days, on the way to the prison mines. Watch and learn, boy. Anyway, I'm turning in, don't wait up long, okay?''

De Ramaira, his fingernails biting into the blisters on his palms, watched the lieutenant strut toward the tent. He had heard cops joking about *droit du seigneur*, but until now he hadn't believed it.

''Got to keep on the right side,'' Jonthan said softly to de Ramaira, ''or my travel permit might get held up come renewal. Doesn't happen all that often anyhow. But usually women more than men.''

''Men have asked you too?'' It was out before he knew it.

''Sometimes girls are guides, I didn't properly explain. I suppose it's worse for them because women prefer to make their own choice.'' After a while, he added, ''It's almost worth it, to be in-country again.''

''I wish I knew it better.''

''You'll learn, if you want. My father was from Earth, he knew it best of anyone in Broken Hill. He used to spend weeks out here, you know? When I was old enough, sometimes I'd go with him. But he really liked to be alone."

"I'd like to talk with him, if I could."

"He died," the boy said simply. "Happened two years ago. He loved this world, see, but things in it kept making him ill. Sam's all the family I've left."

There was a silence, broken only by twigs popping in the fire, in which de Ramaira thought of and rejected various formulations of polite apology. The larger of Elysium's two moons hung low above the mountain peaks. The first stars were out, tremblingly enlarged in the soft night air.

At last Jonthan stood. His dog looked up at once and said, " 'On't, Jonthan."

"Stay there, Sam, look after Dr. de Ramaira. My rifle's just there, Doctor, by my saddle, but you shouldn't need it." Jonthan wouldn't meet de Ramaira's eyes. "Well, good night."

"Good night," de Ramaira echoed as the boy crossed to the tent and lifted its flap. A ray of light shot across trampled grass as he stooped inside. The flap fell. The light went out.

The dog, Sam, said, "No goo', yah?"

De Ramaira reached over and picked up Jonthan's hunting rifle. "Know how this works?"

"Manthing. I juss a 'og, ry?"

"Well, keep a good lookout, then."

"Ry. 'ucking well ry." The dog bared his teeth. De Ramaira couldn't tell if it was meant as a smile or a display of strength.

That night, de Ramaira dreamed that he was back on the colonyboat, that his coldcoffin had somehow failed and he had woken in transit. Naked, he arose and walked the aisles between the other coldcoffins, row upon row. Inside each was the masked, skeletal figure of an aborigine, but somehow this didn't seem strange. A tremor went through the pod, the fusion motor cutting in. It was the midpoint of the voyage.

He awoke with a start to the neon orange of Tau Ceti's

dawn. Jonthan Say looked up from tending the ashy campfire and said, ''There's coffee.''

''Made from some native crap.'' The lieutenant was buckling her pistol belt around her wide hips.

''Well, I'd like to try it,'' de Ramaira said, and rolled out of his thermoblanket. The air was the exact temperature of his skin. It was going to be another hot day.

The drink was tan and tart, not much like coffee. ''If that stuff poisons you, don't look to me to carry you back to Broken Hill.'' The lieutenant stalked off to saddle her horse.

''She wants to go hunting,'' Jonthan said. ''If you need help I will be here, Doctor.''

''You could come and watch the aborigines with me.''

The boy knuckled the springy helmet of his hair. ''I've seen them,'' he said, after a moment.

''Even the goddamn settlers know the abos aren't worth the trouble,'' the lieutenant said, and grunted as she pulled the cinch of the saddle's bellyband tight around her horse.

''Why must you always denigrate the aborigines, Lieutenant?'' de Ramaira asked. ''After all, your job is to represent their interests.''

The lieutenant spat out the dead butt of her cheroot. ''I'll do just that when they tell me what their interests are, instead of freezing as soon as they set eyes on me or anyone else. Listen, the only reason I got this job was because my father had it before me. My younger brother started at the bottom, and already he's aide to Senator O'Hara—who may well make governor eventually—while I sit in my crummy office or make trips into the stinking wilderness.'' Her small eyes fixed de Ramaira as if calculating a trajectory. ''You look all you want, Earthman. I've got better things to do.'' She swung up into the saddle, then added gratuitously, ''You watch your ass, Jonthan, while I'm away.''

De Ramaira spent the whole day at the village, lying in long grass with his eyes closed, watching pictures relayed via the compsim interfaced to his nervous system from the remotes which stitched their trajectories among the mud and grass huts like so many inquisitive mosquitoes. As near as he could judge (apart from the mutilated shaman, sitting in the center of the village, the aborigines were almost impossible to tell apart—even their black and tan markings were almost identical) there were about three dozen immature adults in the village, about half that number of children. According to Webster there would be at least as many roaming the land, following paths that webbed a territory up to a hundred kilometers in diameter, overlapping with those of half a dozen other villages. They might leave their home village as soon as they were large enough to be independent, six or seven years old, might not return until they had gone through their two or three years as a sexually active male and matured into a female. But always they would return, and in the fall mate with as many males who would accept them before going to what Webster called the Source Cave (another romantic anthropomorphism) to lay their fertilized eggs and die, and be consumed by the hatchlings.

All of the quasimammalian species on Elysium had some sort of variant on that life cycle. Mire boars did not lay their eggs but went into a kind of hibernation and were consumed from within by their children; sabertooths, the biggest predators on the continent, laid their eggs in the flesh of paralyzed prey, and so on. Webster theorized that the necrogenetic life cycles were adaptations to the dryer, colder contemporary climate by animals which had evolved in the swampy, tropical world which Elysium had once been and would be again in some distant era, when inconstant Tau Ceti burned hotter once more. It was a theory de Ramaira intended to test more rigorously, in time. He had plenty of that, at least, the rest of his life. In the meantime, there were the aborigines, and although he was loathe to admit it, he was beginning to tire of simply watching them. He lacked the patience of an ethologist. Already he'd identified more than a dozen activities, and all corresponded closely to the descriptions given by Webster. As if the aborigines were no more than programmed robots, or like ants and bees, their seemingly purposeful activity merely blind instinct butting at a task until it was done. Only the young showed any semblance of free will. De Ramaira had fantasies of stealing a hatchling, raising it to intelligence. Perhaps it would imprint on him, like Lorenz's goslings. Well, he'd satisfied himself about the veracity of Webster's painstakingly detailed observations, but he'd discovered nothing new.

At last he recalled his remotes and returned to the camp. The boy was sprawled in the shade of the tent; Sam roused himself to say, "McAn'ers no' ba', so we slee'."

"She's been gone a long time, hasn't she?"

"Yeah. Goo' an' long," Sam growled, and settled back to sleep.

The sun had bled into the western horizon, Jonthan had relit the campfire and he and de Ramaira had eaten, but still the lieutenant had not returned. Jonthan squatted by the fire and watched the darkness. The firelight playing over his bare, lean torso made him look like something by Michelangelo, de Ramaira thought, glancing up now and then as he read in his book, rummaging through terse descriptions: *Twenty days beyond the first foothills we reach a high plain. Lame horse slaughtered for meat. Cold driving rain.*

De Ramaira did not ask what the boy was thinking. He had hardened his heart, the only defense against the affair. He was an observer, nothing more. But at last Jonthan stood and picked up his rifle and said, "I'm going to look for her. You better come too, Doctor."

Although the big moon had risen above the Trackless Mountains, its cold radiance laid such a tangle of deceptive shadows over the grassland that darkness would have been preferable. De Ramaira's horse, stolid enough by day, kept shying at nothing its rider could see, or stumbling heavily on the uneven ground. Ahead, Jonthan's torch threw a nervous oval of yellow light which only occasionally revealed the rustling track Sam pushed through tall grass as he searched out the lieutenant's faint trail. Once, he lost it for more than ten minutes, and in the hiatus Jonthan, his patience worn out by concern, lost his temper. "Wanna 'racker, ge' a 'ucking blu'houn'," the dog grumbled as he cast about. But at last he rediscovered the trail and they set off again.

And ten minutes later found the lieutenant's horse standing patiently in the moonlight, reins flipped over its head. Finding the lieutenant took longer, even with Sam's help. De Ramaira was about to suggest that the horse could have run off after she had fallen somewhere else, when Sam barked. A moment later Jonthan gave an inarticulate cry.

The lieutenant lay in a kind of nest of dry grass, her face and arms marred by dead white swellings, her eyelids so puffy that she could scarcely open them. As the boy and de Ramaira tended her, she roused enough to mumble fragments of her story. She had disturbed a mire boar in the bottom of a dry ravine and chased it through dense banks of thornbush until her horse would go no further, getting her legs badly scratched up in the process. Then, on the way back to the camp, some kind of fever had taken hold in her, weakening her muscles until she could ride no further.

Jonthan helped her drink a little water, and then he and de Ramaira lifted her over the saddle of her horse. As they slowly rode back, de Ramaira asked about the cause of the lieutenant's fall. "Are the thornbushes poisonous, then?"

The boy, leading the lieutenant's horse with one hand and guiding his own with the other, said, "Almost all wild plants are poisonous if you eat a piece of them, but I never did hear of anyone being poisoned by a thornbush scratch. I guess she could be more sensitive than most. Like my father."

"Allergic, then, not poisoned. We'll give her some antihistamines, back at the camp."

But the camp was a long way off, the going slow. The lieutenant, by now delirious, kept slipping off her saddle. Every ten minutes or so they would have to stop and heave her up again. The third time it happened Jonthan cried out, "She could fucking well *die* out here!"

It was the woman's own damn silly fault, but de Ramaira could hardly tell the boy that. He was about to suggest that they tie her across the saddle when the dog said, "Something ow there. Liss'n."

But the humans saw it before they heard anything. No more than a fitful spark at first, far out beneath the huge starry sky, suddenly resolving into twin headlight beams. And then the sound of a cushiontruck came to them, small and clear. The boy grabbed his rifle, pointed it straight up and fired, swore as he fumbled to eject the spent cartridge and insert a new one. But there was no need. His signal had been heard. The truck was turning toward them.

Kneeling in the flat glare of the cushiontruck's headlights, de Ramaira inexpertly swabbed the lieutenant's swollen forearm and jabbed home the ampoule of antihistamine.

Jonthan, watching him closely, asked, "Will that do any good?"

"I'm not that sort of doctor. We'll have to see."

The leader of the three cops who had come to their rescue, a rangy young man called Sinclair, scratched at his sunbleached mop of hair and said disdainfully, "In-country's no place for keyboarders. You don't know it, you can get hurt bad." One of his companions, a woman, said, "No lie," and laughed. Sinclair added, "You finished now, get her in back. Your camp close by? Lucky for you we were heading for it."

The loadbed of the cushiontruck was pitchblack beneath its canvas roof. Something shifted in the darkness as de Ramaira and Jonthan lifted the lieutenant into it, and Sinclair shone his torch briefly, showing half a dozen people huddled on a bench. "Can't let you ride with these, you sit up front with me. Mueller will bring your horses along with the ones we took off of these shiteaters." Behind them, the woman cop laughed again. It was not a friendly sound.

When de Ramaira quit the tent at the lakeside camp, he found Sinclair overseeing the unloading of the prisoners. He had eased an antipyretic pill down the lieutenant's throat and left Jonthan dabbing water on her dry lips, an intimacy that made him uneasy. Now, watching the prisoners as they clumsily clambered down, hobbled by short ankle chains, he asked Sinclair, "Is that really necessary?"

"Weren't for the chains they'd be over the Trackless Mountains soon as we turned our backs. They know they're for the mines." The blond cop was amused. "Listen, how did you all get in such a mess?"

Wearily, de Ramaira told Sinclair what he knew about the lieutenant's accident. The woman cop, Mueller, went from prisoner to prisoner, linking their ankle chains to a staked line. The third member of the patrol, a taciturn man named Kelly, brewed coffee.

When de Ramaira had finished, Sinclair grinned, showing yellow teeth crowded in a narrow jaw. "She wanted hunting she shoulda come with us," he said, and eagerly related how he and his companions had tracked down the illegal homestead in a valley high in the mountains, of the ambush which had trapped the runaway settlers. The cops were due to share out the prisoners' possessions in addition to a credit bonus, and the lieutenant's misadventure only added to their *schadenfreude*. They stayed up late, drinking coffee and passing around fat reefers which de Ramaira politely refused, joking in loud voices about their little clean-up action.

Jonthan stayed in the tent with the lieutenant, Sam sprawled watchfully outside. That night, de Ramaira slept fitfully, waking often on the hard ground beside the ashy fire to see the lamp still burning in the tent, outlining the boy's figure as he bent in an attitude of devotion.

Toward dawn, de Ramaira untangled himself from his silvery cocoon and went over to the tent. Jonthan was asleep at last, face smooth and untroubled, fists doubled in his groin. The lieutenant breathed raggedly beside him, still unconscious, the reaction blisters on her arms inflamed. De Ramaira gave her another shot of antihistamine and patched a glucose drip into a vein inside her elbow. The boy awoke and instantly asked, "Is she any better?"

"She's fighting it. How are you?"

The boy shrugged, then touched the lieutenant's brow. "She's so hot."

"You can leave her long enough to get some breakfast,"

de Ramaira said. "If you're going to look after her, you must look after yourself."

"I shouldn't have let her go off alone," the boy said.

"Eat. Then you can wallow in guilt all you want."

Their water sack was empty, so they set off for the lake together. One of the prisoners was awake, a burly man with a bald pate and the longest white beard de Ramaira had ever seen, a gaze as fierce as a hawk's. All around, the sea of red grass stretched silent and still. When they had pushed through the reeds which fringed the lakeshore, Jonthan pointed to ominous black clouds towering over the mountains and said that there was a storm coming down.

"Well, I suppose we'll be back in Broken Hill soon enough."

"I guess," Jonthan said, and bent to fill the sack.

The three cops were up and about by the time de Ramaira and Jonthan returned to the camp. "We've plenty of clean water in the truck," Sinclair called out, but the boy ignored him and went on toward the prisoners. Sinclair said sharply, "They drink when we've done. Go look to your keyboarder, kid."

De Ramaira said, "There's no need—"

Sinclair pushed hair from his eyes. His stare was hard and mean. "They're my prisoners, friend. Go on, boy."

All the prisoners were awake now, the old man with the patriarchal white beard, another man about de Ramaira's age, and two women and three children, the oldest a girl of twelve or so with a dirty bandage around her head. The patriarch caught de Ramaira's eye, then deliberately spat on the ground between his boots, looked up again. De Ramaira tried and failed to match his fierce proud gaze and turned away, ashamed.

It took the cops more than an hour to feed the prisoners and load them onto the truck, and by the time they set off a fine rain had begun to fall. De Ramaira sat in the cab of the cushiontruck, turning to watch the aborigine village dwindle into the landscape. Kelly whistled tunelessly as he steered the vehicle along the narrow track. Sinclair and Mueller were following on horseback, leading the string of spare mounts, and Jonthan Say rode with them; Sinclair hadn't allowed him to ride in the back of the truck with the prisoners and Lieutenant McAnders. The rain fell harder, sweeping across empty red grassland. Lightning flickered like whips at the level horizon.

After a while, de Ramaira ventured, "Will this get worse?"

"Maybe so."

And a little later: "This reminds me of Kansas, you know. On Earth."

"Yeah? Fancy."

After that riposte, de Ramaira abandoned any attempt at conversation and simply watched rain and grass trawl past, thinking of the aborigines and his failure to understand them. Perhaps they are only animals after all, he thought, but it gave him no comfort. He was beginning to understand the frustration which had driven Webster to his extravagant fantasies of shamans and Source Caves and secret underground rituals.

The convoy began to descend into the first of the forested valleys, following a narrow trail made treacherous by the rain that poured straight down between the towering trees. At last Sinclair rode up to the cab and yelled through the side window, "Go on before it gets worse, Kelly. Mueller and the kid and me, we'll catch up."

Kelly instantly gunned the cushiontruck and it leaped forward. De Ramaira watched with helpless fascination as large bare trunks whipped past scant centimeters from the sides of the truck. The windscreen was blinded by the rain. The truck scythed over a swollen stream at the bottom of the valley, crested the ridge beyond. And then the trail vanished in a tangle of boulders and mud and uprooted trees. Kelly blew air from the truck's skirt but there was no way to stop in time. Sliding sideways, the truck slammed into a fallen tree, spun nose-first into another. De Ramaira pitched forward, banged his head on the windscreen. Then there was only the sound of rain and running water.

"Fuck," Kelly said succinctly.

They had fetched up at the edge of a spreading lake, penned by the landslip and visibly rising. De Ramaira and Kelly checked on the prisoners and the lieutenant, and were examining the buckled side of the truck when Sinclair and the others rode up.

Sinclair walked around the truck, then shook his head and ordered the prisoners out. A wind was getting up, raising a chop on the water, blowing rain sideways. Jonthan and de Ramaira lifted the lieutenant down and rigged a shelter with a waterproof poncho while Sinclair started the truck and tried to back it out of the jam of boulders and tree trunks. For a moment it seemed as if he might succeed, but then the damaged skirt blew out in a spray of air and mud and the truck sat down with abrupt finality.

As the prisoners unloaded their looted possessions, Sinclair told de Ramaira and the boy, "We'll walk out, follow the river back until we can cross it safely."

Jonthan said, "It would be quicker to go downstream."

"So we'd be caught when that pile of rock goes? It isn't going to last much longer, I reckon. Save your advice for keyboarders, boy. I was working in-country way before you got hair on your balls." Sinclair indicated Lieutenant Mc-Anders, unconscious on her stretcher beneath the orange poncho. "Better figure out a way of carrying her," he said, and strode off to harangue the prisoners.

Jonthan slung a blanket between two of the horses, stiffened by stays taken from the truck's canvas roof. When the lieutenant had been lifted onto this improvised stretcher the party set off through the storm.

Sinclair's plan to keep close to the flooded river until they found a crossing place was soon abandoned. Floodwater was steadily undermining the sides of the valley, exposing a reticulated net of roots which seemed to connect each tree with every other. Trees at the edge of the flood had already fallen, dragging others with them and pulling up ragged tangles of root. The cops could have picked a way through the muddy wreckage on their own perhaps, but not the shackled prisoners or the horses. So, in single file, the party climbed higher and higher up the steep slopes of the valley, people slipping and horses foundering in earth turned to mud by the relentless rain.

At last Sinclair called a halt. Everyone hunkered down as best they could, soaked through and exhausted. All around, tall trees groaned under the lash of the wind. Gusts of rain blew between them like shot, obscuring anything more than a few meters away.

De Ramaira, cold and soaked through despite his poncho, bruised forehead throbbing, boots filled with mud, leaned against a buttress root of one of the tall trees and wondered vaguely what would happen. It came to him that they could all die here. He pushed the thought around in his head, but it didn't seem particularly relevant. Exhaustion flattened his perception to *here*, to *now*, the cold rain blowing into his face, the hard wet shape of the tree root against his back.

Jonthan left the horses which were carrying the lieutenant and came over to de Ramaira. Sam slunk miserably beside him. "She'll die if we don't get out of this," Jonthan said. "I've got to do something."

De Ramaira wiped cold rain from his face; more blew over him an instant later. One of the prisoners' children sat crying in the mud a little way off, picking at the shackles around his ankles. De Ramaira said, "Those cops were crazy to try and get that truck down the trail, and now we're headed off in the wrong direction. Do you think they'll listen to you?"

"I know a place where we can shelter."

Sam growled, "No goo'."

Jonthan shook his head. His curly hair was plastered to his skull. He looked twice, three times his age. "There's no other way," he said.

"The Source Cave?" de Ramaira asked.

"That's kilometers to the north. This is something else."

"No goo'," the dog insisted, but Jonthan went over to Sinclair and bent to confer with him. They talked a long time. At last the cop stood, rain streaming from his white poncho, and called to his two companions. "Kelly, Mueller! Get the cattle moving. We just might have a place out of this fucking storm!"

With Jonthan at the head of the party, leading the horses which carried the lieutenant's stretcher, they crossed the ridge and descended into another valley, following the line of a low cliff. Trees leaned out above them, giving a little shelter from the rain. They had not gone very far when de Ramaira realized that they were following a definite path. Then the path turned from the cliff, descending into a wide, tree-circled clearing.

In the middle was a symmetrical grassy mound, fenced by poles which each raised into the pouring rain a skull marked with a broad red stripe. Everyone stopped, prisoners bunching together, cops looking around as if expecting an ambush. De Ramaira went past them to Jonthan, touched the boy's shoulder. "The aborigines?"

"Something my father found."

"I can't remember anything like this described in Webster." A mixture of anger and excitement fizzed in de Ramaira's blood. Anger because he was certain that the boy wouldn't have told anyone about this place if the lieutenant's life had not been in danger; excitement because of the implications, the possibilities. . . .

Jonthan said, "The aborigines don't use this place very often. My father—" He broke off as Sinclair stalked up.

The cop asked, "What is this shit? Where's that shelter you promised?"

"Just up ahead."

In the shadow of the hood of his poncho, Sinclair's face was congested with blood. He thrust his face close to Jonthan's. "So show us, for Christ's sake!" he said hoarsely, then spun on his heel and began to shout at the prisoners.

"Ba'," Sam said. "Ver' ba'."

A narrow path led out of the clearing, so narrow that the lieutenant's stretcher had to be unshipped from the horses and carried by two of the prisoners. It climbed and turned, revealing the stream in the valley below, and then widened into another clearing, this one in the embrace of a sheer cliff. A narrow cave entrance broke the cliff face, its arch smoke-blackened, and in front of the cave were neat rows of plants so unexpectedly familiar that it was several seconds before de Ramaira could put a name to them: potatoes.

The cave was long, dry and sandy-floored, a rubble slope in back rising up into darkness. Jonthan reached into a crevice and fetched out a lantern, lighted it and held it above the lieutenant's wet white face as the prisoners set her down. De Ramaira shucked his poncho and checked the lieutenant's pulse and temperature.

Mueller herded the prisoners to the back of the cave, began to link them to an alarm wire. "Cuff the kid too," Sinclair said.

Sam rose, his wet hair bristling in points, but Jonthan muttered, "Easy." Sinclair and Kelly had both unholstered their pistols.

"I had to," Jonthan said to the dog. He looked at de Ramaira, gave a little shrug, as of resignation, and sat down on the sandy floor.

De Ramaira started to protest, but subsided when Sinclair glared at him. Might, here, was right. The cops broke out self-heating cans and passed them around. While they ate just outside the cave entrance, sheltered from the rain by the lip of an overhang and passing a flagon of wine back and forth (loot from the homesteaders), de Ramaira sat with the boy and the other prisoners.

De Ramaira had little appetite. With one eye on the cops, he asked Jonthan about the raised mound, the skulls.

"My father found it," the boy explained. "He followed them here just as Webster followed them to the Source Cave. They have places all over their territory, he used to say, like we have rooms in our houses. But he never told me what they did. I think it's something to do with the scarred one."

"The shaman."

"Maybe they initiate a new one here when the old one dies. Most aborigines only live a dozen or so years, but the scarred ones live much longer. Those skulls have been there as long as I can remember, and there are piles of them downslope, I guess the old ones are thrown out when the place is used again. An aborigine will come by now and then, put up any poles that have fallen over, clear back the grass. I do that too, when I can.''

"A ritual, a ceremony, for a specific purpose. Do you understand what it means, Jonthan? It could prove that the aborigines really are intelligent. Your father told no one?''

"Only me. And he didn't tell me very much. Maybe if Webster had been around my father would have told him, but Webster died before Broken Hill was founded. He used to live out here sometimes, my father—he loved this place, Doctor. I buried him here, flowers on the grave, from Earth. They don't need to be tended like the potatoes because his body in the ground keeps off the native plants.''

"Why are you telling me this?''

"You can leave the city whenever you want, can't you? I thought maybe you could come here once in a while. Check it over.''

"Well, I'd like to help—''

De Ramaira was interrupted by the hoarse whisper of the white-bearded patriarch. "You'd like to help?'' He and the other prisoners, even the children, were looking at de Ramaira. The man repeated, "You like to help, I know a way.''

"I don't even have a knife, let alone a gun,'' de Ramaira was whispering too. "Are you crazy?''

"We aren't talking violence,'' the man said. "Just feel in my pocket, the left one. It's okay, the cops aren't looking. Just be casual. Okay, you got it?''

A twist of paper. De Ramaira unfolded it, spilled a dozen black, slippery seeds onto his palm.

The man told de Ramaira, "Was saving those in case things got too bad. Want you to put one in that wine of ours the cops are drinking.''

"You are crazy.'' De Ramaira turned his hand over, tipping the seeds to the floor. "See that, now. I won't be a party to murder. Not even of those three.''

"We aren't talking murder. Just one in all that wine will knock them out, is all. We won't do anything to them after, just slip away. I've never told a lie in my life, and I don't aim to start now. You don't mind knocking those fools out a while, right? Or you want the boy to go to the mines? Not a nice place, Earthman."

" 'ucking well righ'," Sam growled.

De Ramaira asked Jonthan, "You want to take a chance on this?"

The boy looked at the lieutenant, looked back at de Ramaira. "The man is right, about the mines."

De Ramaira sighed, then began to pick the seeds from the sandy floor. The patriarch smiled.

When de Ramaira sat beside Sinclair, the cop clapped his shoulder and said, "We're about to have a goddamn shooting contest! You shoot?" The wine had made him loose and foolish. Beside him, Mueller was thumbing fat cartridges into the breech of a hunting rifle.

De Ramaira moved from under Sinclair's hand and said, "I'll leave the shooting to the professionals." He could feel the shape of the seeds in his clenched hand.

Outside, the rain had gentled. The storm was almost over. Out in the middle of the potato patch, Kelly was setting the last skull on its uprooted pole. Strung out in a line, the vacant grins of the skulls glimmered through the settling dusk. De Ramaira started to protest about the desecration, but Sinclair only said, "If the abos did stick them up, they can always find plenty more." He pushed the jug of wine toward de Ramaira. "Go ahead, take a drink. It's okay, we shook it up with a Sterilin tablet."

The wine's thick sweet taste was cut by a burning chlorine tang. Sinclair and Mueller were watching Kelly finish his work. Quickly, guiltily, de Ramaira thumbed a seed into the narrow neck of the jug, set it down and said that he ought to check on the lieutenant.

Sinclair shrugged, and took the rifle from Mueller. "One gets you five if I don't hit it first time," he told her, then yelled, "Goddamnit, Kelly, move your body out of the way!" and without waiting loosed a single round. Echoes of the discharge rolled around the high cliff. Kelly had dropped to the ground; now he picked himself up, smiling. None of the skulls had been touched.

As Mueller took the rifle for her turn, de Ramaira went back and sat beside Jonthan. The patriarch leaned over and asked, "You did it?"

"I did it. You're sure it won't kill them?"

"Probably not. What are they shooting at? The horses?"

De Ramaira jerked around as Mueller fired two shots in quick succession. "They set up those skulls we saw along the trail. Some sort of game."

"You see?" one of the women whispered to Jonthan. "You see how it is?"

The lieutenant was still unconscious, but her fever had burned out. De Ramaira settled beside her and waited for the seed to do its work, while the cops took potshots and passed the jug of wine back and forth. He didn't remember falling asleep, but suddenly Sam was tugging at his sleeve.

"Come see," the dog said, when he saw that de Ramaira was awake. "Come see. They slee' like 'ucking babes."

Sinclair was curled around the almost empty wine jug just inside the cave, snoring loudly. Kelly and Mueller sprawled on wet grass a little way beyond. Moonlight flooded the clearing, made luminous the few skulls which still stood on their poles among the potato plants. His heart beating in his throat, de Ramaira bent over Mueller and pulled the keyring from her belt.

Once freed, Jonthan went straightaway to the lieutenant. The patriarch looked over the sleeping cops while the others stretched and rubbed their chafed ankles, murmuring to each other and glancing sidelong at de Ramaira. The other man said, "Thanks for this, Earthman. We'll be on our way, now."

"May I ask where you are going?"

One of the women laughed softly, gathering the youngest child to herself. "Well," she said, "you may *ask*."

The patriarch returned, stooping under the low cave roof. "We'll take the horses and the rest of our stuff, though the truck will have to stay where it is. Then we go back to where we hid our stock, and after that I hope you don't mind if I don't tell you. But we won't be staying this side of the mountains. Leave that cop, boy. She'll live or die without you. You come with us."

"I'm no part of your thing," Jonthan said. "This is my place."

"The mine will be your place, you stay."

"He's right," a hoarse voice said. It was the lieutenant.

De Ramaira's heart stumbled. How much had she heard? How long had she been awake? He was no longer the cool observer, no longer separate, aloof. Because he cared so much for the boy he had floundered into something he didn't understand.

The lieutenant raised herself on her elbows. Her face was a puffy mask bleached by harsh lamplight. When she smiled, bloody cracks opened in her lips. She said, "I'm not going to stop you people. It's not my place to say anything, except to Jonthan. Listen, boy, I know this is your place, and your father's, but you won't serve his memory in the mines. Take it in your heart and go. I'll look to his grave, though I can't promise to do it regularly. And don't worry, Doctor, I won't tell on your part."

The patriarch put away the pistol he had taken, and told his people to get the horses ready. "Why are you doing this?" de Ramaira asked the lieutenant.

"You live here long enough, you'll understand." Her grin was ghastly. "Now listen," she told the patriarch, "I can fake I've been under all the time, but the doctor here can't. He doesn't get any blame, you should take care of him. See what I mean?"

"Sure," the man said, and with a sudden motion swung his arm at de Ramaira's head. He had wrapped a set of ankle cuffs around his big fist. De Ramaira barely had time to flinch.

* * *

De Ramaira and Lieutenant McAnders returned to the aborigine village two months later. The fall rains were over and the grass of the plain had turned, a flawless green sea now, stirring in the cold wind which blew from the Trackless Mountains. De Ramaira dismounted when they were in sight of the village, and drew the wrapped package from his saddlebag.

As he walked toward the village, the unraveling seeding heads of the grasses brushing the hem of his jacket, de Ramaira felt a quickening nervousness. But he couldn't leave it undone; he owed it to Jonthan.

The aborigines were motionless as he walked between their huts to the center of the village where the shaman sat, a crooked wire-thin statue marred at the forking of its folded legs. "I brought this to show you what had been done, to show you what needs to be replaced," de Ramaira said. "I'm sorry, for what has happened."

He laid the package on the ground and unrolled it to show the pieces of shattered bone. Some were still touched with red. "I'm sorry," he repeated, and waited, his whole skin tingling, for some token of understanding.

A move.

A sound.

A blow.

Anything.

But the aborigine sat as still as ever, and after a while de Ramaira left the village and walked empty-handed through the long grass to the waiting woman.

"I don't think I'll ever know about them," he said as they rode off, "nor ever really know if they're intelligent. When I saw the mound, what Jonthan told me, I thought I knew then. Now . . . well, it could have been set up by Jonthan's father, for all I know."

"That's a crock of shit and you know it," the lieutenant said. She twisted to spit out the butt of her cheroot, wiped her mouth on her wrist. "Never thought I'd say this, David, but who can tell with those critters. We'll break through to them, talk with them. Maybe not soon. But eventually. I can feel it.''

"I don't think I'll ever understand *you*, Lieutenant, let alone the aborigines," de Ramaira said, and laughed. "All I know for certain is that you're all of you aliens. I don't think I'll ever understand any of you."

He was wrong, but more than a dozen years would pass before he finally learned the truth.

PART ONE

1. The Body in the Beach

When the helicopter rounded the point of the bay, Miguel had barely enough time to grab his pack and reach the cover of a patch of quaking vine, in a deep saddle which broke the ridge of the dunes. He was settling himself among white flowers and shivering loops of leaves when the helicopter turned sharply, almost standing on its nose above the sea's chop, the bubble of its cabin flaring with Tau Ceti's last light. The cops had seen the overlander, all right.

In another moment the helicopter was skimming over the dunes, circling twice before finally settling near the overlander. The helicopter had an egg-shaped cabin, much clear plastic webbed by black steel, and a long narrow tail with flared air vents to stabilize it. The wash of its rotors sent tidewrack fluttering out to sea, enveloped Miguel in torn petals and a gritty sandstorm. He was still cleaning sand from his face and whiskery beard when the two cops ducked out of the helicopter and sprinted down the beach to the overlander.

Miguel crouched lower, leaves trembling around him.

The cops walked around the big white vehicle, ducking to look under its tracks, peering up at its curved windscreen.

Then they went up the ladder onto its roof and one pulled up the hatch while the other clambered inside, reappearing a minute later to say something that was lost in the roar of the surf. Both cops scrambled down and quickly quartered the beach, their white coveralls ghostly in the last light. At last, one returned to the helicopter, leaning into the plastic bubble of the cabin to talk to the radio.

Miguel watched the other cop poke around at the foot of the dunes. They knew he was hiding from them, he thought. The goddamn cops, you didn't stand a chance against them when they got on your tail. He should have run when he had had the chance. He could have been a kilometer away by now.

The cop by the dunes bent, began to scoop away sand with both hands. A boot appeared, then part of a bloated leg. The cop turned away, pinching the wings of his nostrils with finger and thumb. A dozen meters away, Miguel caught a whiff of corruption over the dusty scent of the quaking vine. He was shivering with anticipatory fear now, nerving himself to make a run for it. So much for charity. He should have left the body where he had found it, propped up against the over-lander with the back of its head spattered all over the tracks. Now the cops wouldn't rest until they found out who had buried the body; and because the body's head was spoiled they might take Miguel's instead, if they caught him, turn him into a machine the way they did to all their dead people.

As both cops bent to the unpleasant task of exhuming the corpse from its shallow sandy grave, Miguel slowly wriggled backward, tendrils clutching at his clothing, catching in his matted hair. When he was out of sight of the beach he stood, dusting sand from his red trousers. Then he shouldered his pack and broke into a run, feet flying over close-cropped turf, the scooped mouths of rabbit burrows, dancing around loops of briar and vine. He ran through the maze of the dunes until he was winded and then he walked on, holding his aching side, shadows gathering around him. Some time later he heard the angry buzz of the helicopter. It circled above the dunes for half an hour, searchlight blazing, before giving up and turning away, heading west.

Miguel had taken cover in a hollowed clump of thornbush. Even after the helicopter had gone he sat still, fearing some trick, so still that, first one, then two, then a dozen more, rabbits emerged from their burrows and began to nibble at the turf. When Miguel finally stood, they dived for safety in frantic crisscross trajectories of white scuts.

Miguel walked back the way he had come.

The overlander was still there, but the hatch in its roof had been locked. Miguel pried at it in a halfhearted way, then sat on his heels. He thought, I should have taken as much as I could at the beginning and gone on. He'd spent too much time here, bumping his head on a mystery not for him. And now the goddamned cops would be after him, really, specifically after him. . . .

Miguel pulled a heavy foil envelope from inside his over-jacket, scraped off a sliver of the gummy stuff inside with a fingernail, put it under his tongue. Numbness spread from the cavern of his mouth, weighting his tongue, his jaw, suffusing his face. His fear did not go away, but it no longer seemed important.

There was little light now. Only the small inner moon was up, a chipped fleck of light not much brighter than the first stars. But as the drug took hold, things seemed to gain their own luminescence, as if every object shadowed a spectral inner light. The unraveling lines of foam far down the beach continually renewed lacy patterns of phosphorescence; and the curved beach itself held a heavy glow flecked with small furtive flickers of life. Each leaf of the quaking vine, every recurved blade of grass, glistened as if coated with frost. Only the overlander was unchanged, a dead shadow in the landscape of living light.

Miguel rubbed his bristly chin, chuckling to himself, then dropped to the sand and crossed to the empty grave. The long, shallow hole held a deep, dusty green radiance, as if lined with moldering velvet. Miguel urinated into it, his water gouging crusty shadows in the green glow. Piss on it all, on everything that came out of the city. He climbed the steep dune face and stood at the rim for a moment, a stocky, ragged figure silhouetted against the starry sky.

And stepped down, was gone.

2. The Dingo

On a desk-sized platform of mesh high above the baking Outback, in the shade of the reaching dish of the relay station's ten-meter antenna, Richard Damon Florey looked out across dry red grassland at the shimmering horizon while the machines talked to each other. He held a compsim in his right hand, one input jacked into the guidance computer, the other into the cuff, wrapped loosely around his left wrist, which interfaced with his nervous system via a subdermal implant. It turned him into the active link, the mediator, between the relay station and Constat, the one point eight megacee computer in Port of Plenty (he imagined microlaser impulses jittering back and forth along the buried cable like quantum fireflies). But unless Constat found something wrong, there would be nothing else for him to do.

Bored with the scenery, Florey took another peek at the operation: an endless array of figures scrolling across his vision, the manifestation of Constat's interrogation of the billion or so elements and innumerable shifting pathways of the guidance computer. Briefly, Florey shifted deeper, but encountered only Constat's calmly floating colophon, a skeletal sketch in vivid electric blue of four interlocking pyramids hanging before the unsettling sense of dark seething vastness, as if an information-dense yet insubstantial mountain had somehow rooted in his mind. This intimation of Constat's power gave him a chill despite the sweltering heat. So different from the idiot savant mind of his compsim, icon-accessed subroutines worn smooth with familiarity. Thinking about accessing Constat was like contemplating a dive into a sea of churning razors.

He uncoupled and found himself staring into the sun, his glasses darkened to an opaque black. Afraid of losing his balance and falling from his precarious perch, he looked away and, one hand holding the compsim, the other the platform's flimsy railing, stood quite still while the sensitive molecules in the lenses depolarized.

Although tricked out in the coveralls of the Port Authority cops, even to the recoilless pistol in the power holster at his hip, Rick Florey looked bemused and defenseless: a sparely built technician marooned with his machinery in anarchic nature. As his sunglasses cleared, the shimmering plain became visible once more, but there was little to interest him out there. Open tracts of red grass, a few clumps of twisted leafless trees, perhaps the dark slash of a river canyon. Directly below were the remnants of the research post, bleached shells of half a dozen abandoned shacks scattered on a weedy apron of concrete and ringed round with a sagging wire fence, and the white overlander where the two cops who had escorted Rick out to the relay station sat in air-conditioned comfort. Orange sunlight flared on the curved windscreen; Rick couldn't see if the cops were watching him or not.

He peeked again. The compsim was still parading numbers.

With his wrist, Rick wiped sweat from his forehead and yawned. This routine inspection was horribly tedious, despite the importance of the relay station. A century ago it had received an unending stream of news and advice from a laser transmitter beyond Neptune's orbit, but the government which had built and funded the transmitter had long ago fallen from power in the United States. Now that only colonyboats linked Earth and Elysium, the relay station served to pick up their femtowatt signals as they decelerated at the edge of Tau Ceti's gravity well. Not that warning of another arrival was needed—after a century, the rhythm of arrival, once every three point six three terrestrial years, was a tradition as invariable as celestial mechanics—but the signals contained information about the type of cargo and supercargo to expect. Revivification of the cargo of new settlers was one of Port of Plenty's major industries, while the supercargo of technological wizardry, automat tapes, and cultural ideology insured that the city retained its necessary edge over the settlements.

Important, yes, though in Rick's opinion this routine inspection was hardly important enough to warrant the personal attention of the University's only lecturer in Communications Engineering, despite the imminent arrival of the latest colonyboat. But although the research station had been abandoned, the relay tower was still the property of the University, and the inspection tours were the only way of insuring continued control. And so, although the assignment was an annoying interruption of his routines, Rick had not been able to refuse it. That would have been a conspicuous act of defiance. In the city, with his ambitions, such acts were to be avoided. Besides, the task was almost certainly some kind of test of his loyalty. So he had publicly declared that it would be an honor; and both Cath and Professor Collins had agreed that it was. Privately, though, Rick just wanted to get on with his research into the radio-reflecting properties of Elysium's turbulent ionosphere. He had begun to miss the cubbyhole of his office even before the overlander had swung out of the city's fenced limits toward the vast unconquered emptiness of the Outback.

There was a kind of soundless detonation in his head, and Constat's colophon appeared in his vision, seeming to float just beyond the tip of his nose. The computer's quiet baritone, intimate as God's own voice, announced, "Analysis complete. All components are functioning within acceptable limits. Thank you for assisting in this interesting problem.''

For any other computer on Elysium, this would have been no more than a mechanical nicety ground out in obedience to some programmer's whim. But Constat was a megacee computer, and therefore had self-direct consciousness of at least a limited sort—even philosophers were agreed on that. The fact that the overhaul of part of the interstellar communications system was of especial interest to the unimaginably abstract workings of Constat would have been at the very least suspicious, if not outright alarming, to most people. But to Richard Damon Florey, his mind on the experiments that he wanted to fit into the payload of a high altitude balloon, it meant nothing.

Nothing at all.

Overnight, Miguel's snares had yielded a brace of rabbits, not bad for a river canyon in the middle of the Outback. He had skinned and gutted and spitted them, and now they were roasting over a slow, smokey fire while he sprawled atop a mossy boulder at the edge of the river, once again fiddling with the little machine he had stolen from the dead man's overlander.

Miguel had been in the wilderness for two-thirds of his life now, mostly alone. So long that he had to think hard to remember his own name. *Miguel Lucas. Mickey.* His father's hoarse soft voice. Miguel could remember his father's voice but not his face; in memory it was always in the shadow of the wide-brimmed hat the tall, tired, stooped man used to wear, even around the house. Miguel remembered his father as being an old man, but now he was himself older than his father had been when he had died. Alone for more than thirty years, two-thirds of his life.

Going dingo, the settlers called it. Half of the original colonists had been from Australia, a sop to nationalist pride when that continent had finally ceded independence to become the largest of all the United States. They had named the dry grasslands after the empty heart of their birthplace, just as they had given the indigenous semi-intelligent inhabitants of Elysium the name of the long-lost original inhabitants of Australia. Going dingo was to drop out of society, to try and make it alone: usually one or two families striking off to carve a living out of the wilderness east of the Trackless Mountains; less often someone who could no longer bear to be among people. In either case it was illegal.

Miguel Lucas had been one of identical twins, but his brother had been afflicted by some toxin or other while still in the womb, had lived less than a day after the long, hard delivery which had killed their mother. Miguel grew up a shy, solitary child. Sometimes he fancied that his dead brother was with him, swollen head bent close to his ear, eyes shut by a translucent membrane, whispering words Miguel only just failed to hear, the secrets of the hearts of others. Although he couldn't catch the words, Miguel was often overwhelmed by the feelings behind them, especially the dizzying depths of lust and hate which even the mildest of grown-ups concealed. Miguel would be weak and feverish for days after one of these visitations, and he soon learned that it was best to stay away from other people.

Miguel's father was something of a loner, too. They lived at the edge of the settlement in a ramshackle cabin filled with the carcasses of junked machines from which Miguel's father cannibalized parts to repair the broken gadgets which the settlers brought to him. "We don't need people," Miguel's father would say. "You understand, Mickey. People are just a world of hurt to our family, always have been." Sometimes he showed Miguel faded holograms of people posed stiffly in strange old-fashioned clothes, though Miguel had been more interested in the background glimpses of Earth than his ancestors. "See there," his father would say, "that's your great-grandfather, Mickey, you're named after him. He made a living guessing what was in people's minds, only one of us who ever did any good with it."

Sometimes it seemed to Miguel that there was a cap pressing down on his skull, a pressure relieved only when he took himself away from his father, the settlement. He learned to live wild, searching out the few plants that were edible—for most were poisonous, as were all of the native animals, the same kind of poison which had crept into his mother's womb and warped his brother's growth into something monstrous. When his father died from cancer, Miguel continued to live in the cabin at the edge of the settlement, although he didn't take up his father's trade and eventually the tools and stocks of parts were confiscated. Miguel didn't mind. Weeds tangled in the once neat vegetable garden. Dust thickened on the crude wooden furniture and the dismantled machines, muffled the hemp carpets and blinded the windows. Sometimes Miguel helped at harvest, or weeded the fields alone at night, by the light of the larger moon. The people of the settlement regarded him as touched, but still one of their own. Sometimes little parcels of food were left for Miguel to find on his doorstep the next morning. He spent more and more time away from the settlement, and at last he went out into the wilderness and didn't return.

He had had little time for the doings of humankind since, except to trade pelts or wild spices and herbs for small luxuries and cast-off clothing. But when he had found the dead man slumped against the overlander on the beach, his curiosity had been stirred. Who would drive all the way out into the wilderness just to kill himself? It was like a sign to Miguel, if only he could understand it.

So while he waited for the rabbits to cook, he fiddled with the little machine, numbers and word-strings flickering in a ghostly block of light above its control pad as he ransacked its functions. Like the gun he'd also taken, he hoped to sell it to some settlement or other, but before he did he wanted to crack its memory open, extract the kernel of an explanation.

So far he had had no luck, perhaps because he couldn't plug into it directly. He remembered the first time he'd seen one of these things, at the hip of one of the cops who came once a year to audit the settlement, collect records of births and deaths and survey the boundaries of the fields to make sure that they were within the limits stipulated by the city. A tank on his back, Miguel had been helping his father spray rice seedlings, the wand of the sprayer fanning a rainbow film over brown water pricked by rows of vivid green shoots. The cop had driven along the embankment in his truck, dust blowing out in a great cloud when it stopped. Miguel had watched as the man made sightings with a hand-held theodolite, the shaft wobbling in mysterious obedience to true vertical, its little laser light sparkling like a fragmented ruby. The white coveralls. A gun in a bulky holster riding one hip, a smooth black shape clipped to the belt at the other, connected by a looped cable to a band wrapped around the cop's wrist. When the cop had gone, Miguel's father had spat into the water in which they stood up to their knees, and said that Miguel should never say anything to one of those bastards unless he was asked, and to make sure that he never *was* asked. Miguel remembered that clearly, the stinging scent of the spray, the sun softened by mist which coiled along the wide river valley, the whistling *chirrs* of hopper larvae calling each to each as they writhed through the soft mud at the foot of the embankment, waiting for their legs to grow. Remembered it all but his father's face.

Now he pecked at function keys, calling up encrypted file headings and scrolling through them as if hoping to catch some clue that would unlock them. A word. A number. It must be there, but it continued to elude him.

At last he set the machine aside and went to the fire, turned the rabbit joints. Dripping fat sizzled on glowing coals. Above, orange light danced through etched outlines of interlaced branches. The sun was in the last quarter of the sky.

Miguel went to the edge of the river and splashed his face before going down on his sadly slack belly and lapping up stingingly cold water, washing away the little knot of frustration. Later, as he sat among glossy tongue ferns, tearing succulent flesh from a rabbit haunch, fingers greasy to the knuckles, it came to him that he was happy. He was on the right way, mystery or not. But there was no one to share the moment with.

* * *

The sun was in the last quarter of the sky, rouging the roostertail of dust which the overlander raised as it ploughed the dry grassland. In the cool, humming cave of its cabin, behind the two cops, Rick was plugged into his compsim, concentrating on some setting-up exercises for optimizing the payload of his experiments, when the overlander made a sudden turn. He unplugged and looked up. They had turned off the arrow-straight track, toward the uneven green line which marked some canyon's course.

Rick asked what was happening, and the blond sergeant who was driving told him that she'd seen some smoke. "Don't worry about it, Dr. Florey. We just have to take a look is all."

"Probably just some abos," her companion said, rubbing his face and yawning.

"The aborigines don't light fires," Rick said.

The sergeant said sharply, "You let us worry about that. You're just the passenger here, remember?"

The overlander brushed through the last bunches of grass and bumped across bare ground to the canyon's edge. The sergeant parked it at a prudent distance from the drop and cracked the hatch. Orange light struck into the cabin like a lance. When Rick followed the cops out, hot air enveloped him, dry as baked dust. Sweat ribboned his back and chest even before he had clambered from the ribbed roof.

Sandstone cliffs dropped to green masses of feathery foliage. The smoke trickled up from somewhere in the center of this sunken line of trees, a thick white rope that rose a long way in the hot still air.

"You wait here for us," the sergeant told him. Sweat shone on her round, pockmarked face. She shaded her eyes to stare at the smoke, and Rick asked her who she thought was down there.

"I don't think anything."

"Standard procedure," her companion said smoothly. "You look after the overlander, okay?"

Rick stood at the edge and watched as the two cops scrambled down unhandily. Their flip dismissal rankled. He'd grown up in-country—he probably knew more about it than any cop. The cliffs slumped into talus slopes about half a kilometer away, and Rick walked until the drop didn't look so bad, lowered himself over the edge and let go. Something snagged his coveralls and he landed sprawling on loose scree, breath knocked out of him. He stood and dusted his tingling hands, looking up at deeply grooved sandstone, the indigo sky. Rock shards clattered under his boots. Already he was worried about getting back.

Somewhere in the middle of the canyon, cutting between the trees that lifted from the slopes, there was a river. Rick listened to the distant chuckling rush and suddenly realized how hot and sticky he was. Well, it wouldn't do any harm, he thought, and went on down through the trees. Delicate foliage pressed closely overhead; rich mold cushioned his steps. Whenever he brushed one of the slim green boles, clouds of gnats dropped from quivering branches and got into his hair and eyes. Some distant bird or animal was making a repetitive, knocking sound, muffled pulse of the wood's secret heart.

The cops out there were chasing down some poor fellow who only wanted to be left alone. Tension was centered between Rick's shoulderblades, the expectation of hearing shouts of pursuit, or a shot as final as a full stop.

The trees gave way to shingle sloping down to the river. An irregular curb of boulders rimmed the water's edge, so overgrown with moss and tongue-fern that they resembled unkempt green pillows. Rick knelt on a mossy shelf of rock and drank, scooping cold water to his mouth with a cupped hand. It had a gritty mineral taste the filtered city water lacked, the taste of the earth, its bed, something he hadn't tasted since he'd gone to the city for good.

Growing up in the circumscribed world of Mount Airy, the Californian Substantivist settlement three hundred kilometers east of Port of Plenty, his mother and father most often working in their smithy, his sister and two brothers a dozen or more years older, Rick had often run off with the half-dozen children of his age through the forest which surrounded the clutter of concrete buildings and stony fields. There was freedom in the forest, freedom from the strict rules of the grown-ups, a chance to run and shout. But the children's noise was soon swallowed by the steadfast silence of the trees through which they ran. At last, intimidated, they walked home in a close group, whispering warily. There were strange things in the forest, wild animals, maybe even abos—though the nearest abo village was a good day's walk away. Certainly, there were piles of stones here and there which some people said were the remains of structures built by the abos an age ago, long before humankind had come to Elysium. Rickey and the other children always gave these revenants a wide berth, scaring each other with stories of what might still live deep underground.

Now, sitting beside the rushing river in the green shadows of the canyon, Rick felt a touch of that old unease, and began to wish that he had stayed beside the overlander after all. Only a crazy person or a criminal would build a fire out here. He stood, ready to go back, and saw a flicker of color in the distance, a patch of red among feathery sunlit green. His heart gave a little leap, pure anticipation, as he crouched beside one of the boulders.

Dressed in bright red trousers and a dirty overjacket, the man came along the shingle bank with a kind of hunched lope. When Rick stood, the man stopped, a hand at the wide belt which bunched the waist of his trousers. He said, "Man, what are you doing here?"

"I might ask you the same question," Rick said. "I just came down to the river to cool off, is all. I've been checking out the relay station. The one which receives laser pulses from the colonyboats."

"Oh yeah?" The man looked to be about fifty, twice Rick's age, thickening into an ungraceful end to middle-age. Broken capillaries speckled his cheeks above an unkempt beard; his throat sagged in three folds. Yet he had an air of authority, of power. "Look here," he said, "I never meant any harm. I was just doing the decent thing." What he had his hand on was a sheathed knife.

"I'm no cop, if that's what you think." Sweat rolled down Rick's chest, rib by rib. He could feel the weight of the pistol holstered at his side, but didn't dare move his hand toward it.

The man spat black phlegm toward the river. There was something wadded in his cheek, Rick saw; and there was something funny about his eyes too, the irises no more than thin rims around wide black pupils. The man said, "I don't aim to hurt anyone out here. I just want to be left alone."

"If that's all you want," Rick said, "I guess there isn't any harm to it. I won't tell the cops, if that's what you're worried about." He wanted to run, but didn't dare. He said, "I mean, is that okay with you?"

The man shrugged.

"Okay, if that's how you want it," Rick said, and turned to start up the steep shingle bank. Then a heavy blow sent him sprawling: shock, titanic galvanism, struck down his spine. The man's body pressed his in an obscene embrace, legs mixed clumsily together, weight pivoting on his back, hot breath hissing by his ear. Rick remembered the knife and managed to jerk up an elbow, felt it connect with something solid. The weight rolled away and Rick kicked out, catching the man just below his knee so he went over backward, sprawling among glossy loops of fern.

Rick scrambled to his feet, clumsy and slow, breath digging a raw pit in his throat, backed away as the man got up on one knee, glaring up through his tangled fringe. For an instant, Rick saw into those eyes. Then the spell snapped, and he could run.

Panting hard, Rick gripped the hot metal ladder and pulled himself onto the overlander's ribbed roof. Beyond the canyon, far out across the plain, the sun was an amorphous blur within a bank of haze on the horizon. The bare sandstone at the edge of the canyon glowed like red-hot iron; the sunken slopes of vegetation ribboned away beneath the darkening sky. There was no sign of the cops.

Rick's muscles thawed to a spasmodic trembling. There

was no smoke now, nothing to show that anything had happened down there. He reached to finger the power holster, reflecting wryly that he had had nothing to fear . . . and discovered only the edge of the clip that had held it to his belt: shattered, empty. He looked around as fresh panic unfolded, the world seeming to slip askew. And saw the two cops coming toward the overlander, luminous as angels in their white coveralls.

3. In the System

Teep. Tip-tip. Teep. The timer's plaintive cry dragged Rick from the clamorous depths of REM sleep to the edge of consciousness. Beside him, Cath rolled onto her stomach, clutching a pillow to her face. He reached out to touch the cut-off, focused on the glowing green figures: 0716. Shit. What kind of time was that?

He was still not properly awake, did not remember that he had an appointment at the police headquarters. He relaxed back into the softness of the bedplate and a fugitive dream fragment overtook him instantly. Someone was whispering urgently and he strained to catch the meaning, knowing that it was desperately important . . . but the whisper faded to a dribbling susurrus, dismal universal hiss, and he was falling, falling over a darkling land, nothing into nothing—

The timer went off again. Rick shut it off and sat up. Exhaustion was a gritty veil in his eyes; memory of the madman and of his own panic smoldered behind it. No. Remember instead the amnesty he and Cath had achieved late last night. She was still asleep, or pretending to be, black hair tangled over the raised planes of her shoulderblades.

Rick left her to sleep on—after all, she had waited for him
until his return just before midnight, and through the debacle
that had followed—and padded into the bathroom. Its bright
light, slickly reflected from glass and plastic surfaces, gave
him a sudden sense of urgency. He urinated and perfunctorily
scrubbed at his face and hands, then went back into the suspended half-light of the bedroom and quickly dressed,
choosing somber clothes for the interview which lay ahead.
Gray pants with only narrow pleating, a white half-sleeved
shirt, sandals.

In the kitchen, the treacher delivered his customary breakfast of milk-drenched oatcakes and milky tea. One of Bach's
violin concertos murmured in the air. A summer morning
beyond the picture window, gold light pricking through levels of wide cedar branches, beginnings of heat.

He pulled on his asymmetric linen jacket and stepped outside, the door rolling shut at his back. In the kitchen, the
treacher shut its hatch on the soiled dishes and retracted into
the wall with a smug click. Elsewhere, a small homeostatic
mechanism uttered a brief staccato of clicks and was silent.
The canopy over the fanlight of the sunken bedroom tilted
half a degree to admit a little more light. Below, on the cool
bedplate, Cath murmured and reached out.

The houses of the University staff were strung around a
sculptured hill above the sprawling campus, half-sunken into
the earth and hidden by landscaping and clumps of trees.
Cedar and pine, oak and elm, chestnut and sycamore: all
raised from cell templates carried by the two arks which had
originally colonized Elysium. Aisles of green calm, artfully
contrived clearings and banks of shrubbery. You had to look
carefully to make out the line of a pastel wall or the jut of a
roof, the flash of light on a window.

Absorbed, Rick walked down a gravel path scattered with
spiked fruit fallen from the chestnut trees into the awakening
campus. Lawns and long low buildings, their flat roofs cluttered with antennae masts, windmill generators, and solar
collectors. The flow tubes and racked mirrors of the exper-

imental hydroponics farm glittering in the early morning
sunlight. Rick could have taken a bicycle from one of the
public racks, but he wanted to walk. He had been sent for,
and resented it, knowing that at best his time would be wasted
in a reshuffling of the facts he had recited the previous night,
at worst . . . but he didn't want to think about that.

He passed the Neo-Bauhaus Architecture building, with
its rust-stained concrete panels, polyhedral decking and steel-
framed windows, and climbed the grassy ridge at the boundary of the campus. A road ran beyond the downslope, its far
side bounded by the high stone walls of the estates of the
rich, the quaintly peaked roofs of their sprawling houses is-
landed in the trees which stepped away down the hillside.
Beyond were the domes of the bubble-suburbs, embraced on
either side by the enigmatic native forest, crowding toward
the packed roofs of the old quarter at the edge of the silty
waters of the estuary. A hundred thousand people down there,
and most would never be affected by anything he did. Suburban culture was deep into the gifts of Earth: body aug-
mentation, reality structuring, wholetime art, cultism, trash
aesthetique. Science was not relevant. The citizens of Port
of Plenty looked inward, took advice from the stored personality matrices of their dead relations rather than make
their own decisions, turned their backs on the vast unknown
continent.

Yet still the city sang a seductive siren song to Rick. There
was no other place in the world where he could pursue his
research, no other place where he could live long enough to
pursue it properly—only a year into his lectureship, he had
had his blood purged of toxins twice already, and with citizenship came full medical and the chance to live on after
death in the cool matrix files. So long as he kept to the path
Professor Collins had mapped out for him it would all be his
. . . but how easy it was to stray from that path! If he had
not gone down into the river canyon he would not have lost
the pistol, would not have been called to account for it now.

Rick crossed the road and began the long walk to the police headquarters. The stone walls of the estates gave way to

faceted domes, each screened by burgeoning evergreen
shrubs, that year's horticultural fad; and these in turn yielded
to rooming houses built of native limestone. No more gardens. A steady stream of cyclists flowed toward offices, automats, or the docks. Rick passed the brightly lit windows
of the marts at the edge of the commerce sector, waited while
a procession of cushiontrucks slid through the intersection at
Market and 5th. Produce from Arcadia, the nearest and oldest settlement: soft fruit, wine, and other foodstuffs difficult
to synthesize. Rick had once watched his own settlement's
trucks leave for the city, had wanted to ride with them to
discover the terrible secrets that lay at the end of their journey.

Unbelievably, he had arrived already. He checked the timetab on the cuff of his jacket—0814—and crossed the parking
lot. The statue of the first governor of Port of Plenty, gesturing over ranks of bicycles and police cruisers and overlanders, had been daubed with red paint by the separatists, the
third time in as many weeks. Out of warm morning sunlight
into shadow. The police headquarters was, of course, the
tallest building in the spreading city.

A bored sergeant in the reception area clipped a tag to
Rick's linen jacket and gave him a direction card. Unes-
corted, Rick rode an elevator down one floor. The basement
corridors were decorated in the natural style of a decade past.
Sourceless lighting glistened on imitation grass matting,
rough chalk walls. Every intersection was an excuse for an
arbor of fake flowering shrubs. Vendors glittered among
dusty stands of bamboo, machines submitting to Nature's
relentless growth.

The direction card guided Rick to a door at the end of a
blind corridor. There was no nameplate, not even a number.
When he knocked, the door swung in and across the small
room the man behind the desk looked up.

"Come right in, Dr. Florey. My name is Savory."

Rick turned to close the door. But it was already shut. The
man was smiling now. He wasn't wearing the uniform cov-

eralls of a cop, but a lightweight suit and a white high-collared shirt, a luminous white echoed in his smile.

Rick perched on the chair before the desk. His scalp prickled, charged with blood. Tentatively, he said, "I understand—"

Savory's smile switched off like a light. "One moment," he said, and turned to his desk compsim.

Rick felt another surge of embarrassment and looked away. The small room was almost bare. No decoration but a print of Dürer's *Melencolia*, hung in the precise center of one green wall; the desk and two chairs the only furniture.

Savory angled the compsim away slightly, as if he suspected that Rick was trying to peek. The compsim was as big as a portable trivee, its manual mode display, from Rick's point of view, a luminous blur over the gull-wing of its projector. Such machines, cannibalized from the arks, were more complex and efficient than colonially manufactured models, and in fantastically short supply. The head of Rick's department had one, but Rick did not.

Rick looked at the print again. Behind the scowling angel was a four-sided magic square. Reason behind divine wrath. *Is he trying to make me nervous with this waiting?* At that moment, Savory's voice startled him.

"Sorry about that, Dr. Florey." Savory was smiling again. His bushy blond hair was thinning back from a freckled forehead; his eyes, hooded with heavy pink lids, were set close together over a snub nose. This face was somehow familiar, as if Rick had seen it in passing every day.

"If this is about my report, I've already gone over that with your people. They pulled me straight back after the interview I did. See here, I was told that there would be no trouble over losing the pistol. It was hardly my fault."

"Now, Dr. Florey, you haven't gone over it with me. I'm not a cop, but a member of the City Board. I have my office here for the moment, that's all."

Perfectly shocked, Rick said, "I don't see why the Board should be interested."

Savory linked his hands at the edge of his desk. "I can

assure you that it is. Not about the pistol, exactly, but about the circumstances of its loss. You aren't a citizen, are you?''

"Not yet. But I hope to be. My loyalty isn't in question, is it?''

"I don't think so. How long have you been at the University?''

"Three years as an undergraduate, four as a doctoral candidate. This academic year is my first as a lecturer.''

"And are you happy with your work?''

"Sure.'' Passively, he waited to see where Savory wanted to go.

"Now, you were asked to interface the computer at the relay station with Constat. Everything went right. Yes?''

"I did what I was asked to do, even to the little charade on the trivia.''

"Charade?''

"Well,'' Rick said, beginning to sweat, "I mean I was asked to give certain replies to the questions asked of me. I don't know the truth of what I was asked to say.'' Careful, he thought, careful.

"You were asked to say that the colonyboat was approaching on schedule,'' Savory said briskly. "Surely that follows from your successful mission at the relay station. Now, after that, on your way back to the city, smoke was seen over a river canyon. Your police escort investigated, and you took it into your head to follow them, and got yourself in trouble with a dingo.''

"He just . . . jumped me.'' The memory was painfully vivid. "We didn't fight, exactly.''

Savory's gaze was intent.

Compelled, Rick said, "Surely you've read the report. I put all that I could remember into it. Look, Mr. Savory, that isn't why you had me come here, is it?''

"It has everything to do with it, Dr. Florey. Constat has a flag routine to call in anyone who reports a contact such as yours. I'm sorry your call came so early in the morning, but the priority rating is high.''

"You mean that he was some sort of criminal?''

Savory nodded gravely. "Something like that."

"Has there been an escape from the mines?" Rick remembered the man's knife, and felt a cold wave travel over his entire skin.

Savory said, "Not as of yesterday. Actually, simply by being out there, without a permit, he is violating enough laws to be sent to the mines, just as we send those families who think that they can make their own little kingdoms in the wilderness. However, Dr. Florey, a man may intend to commit a crime and if that intention is discovered, why he is then a criminal. There are certain factions, I'm sure you know, who think to gain by harming the city."

Remembering the defaced statue in the parking lot, Rick said flatly, "You think he's a separatist."

"Perhaps. Now, Dr. Florey, I'm going to show you a picture of someone. I want you to tell me if he looks anything like your dingo. But remember that the man in the picture is probably better groomed."

Rick leaned forward as Savory turned the compsim.

"Well, Doctor?"

After the thrill of recognition, Rick laughed. "How could he be!"

"The question, Dr. Florey."

"Of course he isn't. What is this, Mr. Savory? A ghost hunt?"

"As I told you, Dr. Florey, there's nothing to worry about. I'm simply checking something out. I'm sorry to have troubled you."

Behind Rick, the door swung open.

The interview with Savory colored the rest of Rick's day. He muddled through his auditing of a couple of lectures and then settled in his office to read a paper pertinent to his project. But the pattern of sense underlying the words refused to come together. Burning more brightly was the puzzle of just what Savory had wanted of him. Also, his application to send up a high altitude balloon was still neither approved nor refused.

Suppose the University Senate had realized that he was

embarked on a program of pure research? He was beginning to doubt whether he could continue to evade that central issue, although of course no one could ever predict what would turn out to be of practical value. He had skewed the present project, for instance, to emphasize its potential for developing better weather prediction systems, just as his thesis work on the nonlinear dynamics of atmospheric scintillation and interference levels touched on the problem of radio reception. Well enough, but Rick was interested in global systems not local problems. He wanted to understand the deep mechanisms of the world's climate, not just the weather of the little part which humans had colonized.

The thing to do was to keep his head down. He resisted the temptation to put out an inquiry and turned to grading problem sheets instead. At least that required no real thought. But it seemed that the world would not leave him be.

His first visitor was Max Rydell, a materials engineer who played jai alai with Rick. The stocky, gruffly self-important man came into Rick's little office without knocking and said with his usual briskness, "I suppose I can confirm you for two tickets, right?"

"Tickets?"

"For Landing Day." Rydell tapped his compsim. "I'm organizing seating in the amphitheater this year; you're almost the last fish I need to net. You'll want two, I guess."

"Oh. Yes, of course."

Rydell plugged into his compsim. "I saw your interview last night. Not bad. Except you sounded a little impatient."

"Well, I'd had a long day."

Rydell's eyes unfocused for a moment. Then he pulled the interface band from his hairy wrist and shut the compsim's case with a flourish. "I heard that you should always pause for a second or two before answering. That way you seem to be giving each question proper consideration," he said. And then he was gone, the door banging shut behind him.

Rick returned to his grading, but toward the end of the afternoon Professor Collins, the head of the Department of Communications Engineering, knocked on his door. "I've come to see if all is well with you," Collins said, after they had exchanged pleasantries.

"You think something's wrong?"

"Not exactly." Sitting upright in the office's worn armchair, Professor Collins smoothed first one, then the other, of his gray sideburns. As always, he was impeccably dressed, in an up-to-the-minute asymmetric suit of an iridescent lightweight synthetic; but then nothing looked ridiculous on his slim, straight-backed figure. He said in mild rebuke, "You didn't come to tell me, but I understand that your mission was successful."

"Well, there was nothing wrong with the relay station," Rick said cautiously. He was always intimidated by Collins's smooth, worldly style, and memory of his encounter was a fresh node of guilt that he wanted to keep hidden. He added, "It was the debriefing that caused the problems."

"Ah, the toils and coils of bureaucracy." Professor Collins smiled. "I know all about that, I'm afraid. I hope that the experience has not harmed your position with the Board."

"Why would the Board be interested in me?"

"It's not always easy to earn your citizenship," Collins said enigmatically. "Well now. The reason I came to see you is that I received a call from a Mr. Savory."

"Jesus. What did he want?" Rick had the sudden, unsettling sensation that he was sinking into something that was nothing to do with him at all.

"He asked my opinion of you. I told him, of course, about your impeccable work here. You're sure that everything is all right?"

"Savory interviewed me this morning, but I wasn't sure what he was after."

Professor Collins smiled winningly. "Please, Richard, don't be afraid to come to me for support. It's what I'm here for, after all. And do let me know if you hear anything more from Mr. Savory. He has not been very supportive of the University in the past, and I wouldn't like to see you getting out of your depth."

After that, there was no question of Rick's doing more

work. He locked his office and went to see David de Ramaira.

The biologist was in his laboratory, hunched at a binocular
microscope on the central bench. The monitor was display-
ing a false-color outline of the slowly rotating specimen,
overlaid with columns of rapidly changing readouts. It looked
like a curled-up thumb-sized fish. "Take a seat," de Ramaira
said without looking around. "I just have to finish this."

Rick found a stool, watched as de Ramaira delicately
flensed away thin sheets of muscle to reveal the little specimen's internal organs. The odors of preserving alcohol,
formaldehyde, and dusty dried specimens began to calm
Rick's jittery nerves.

The benches around three sides of the cluttered room and
the shelves above them were crammed with samples of Elysium's biota. Dissected packrats, bellies flayed to show pale
organs, paws held out as if in entreaty, were sunken in yellow
fluid; a series of jars held the complete sequence of the on-
tological recapitulation through which a mire boar toiled after hatching, from necrogenetic larvae equipped with rasping
suckers to a miniature of the bristle-hided, porcine adult.
Trays held ranks of glittering, carefully labeled insects. There
were tottering stacks of papers with plants pressed between
them, varnished fossils, the mud bell of a kraalmouse's nest
sectioned to show the convoluted chambers. Tiny iridescent
parabirds gathered dust next to shrunken specimens of the
pitcher plants with which they were symbiotic; the meter-
long peg-toothed skull of an amphibian sat behind them like
a revenant. Faded holograms of the heads of aborigines
glowed along one wall like a row of hollow-eyed masks; a
whiteboard took up most of another, covered in double-
barreled Latin names joined one to another by arrows—half
the arrows had been hastily rubbed out.

De Ramaira's laboratory was unique in the University, an
evergrowing monument to research which had no practical
applications at all. Consequently, he was regarded with the
same loathing as the least idea of a physicist or pure mathe-

matician, tolerated only because he had arrived with an interdict from the Seeding Council. There was little the other lecturers could do but snub the Wombworlder; for fifteen years de Ramaira's only social contacts in the University had been a few of his students. But now there was Richard Florey, who in his own opinion at least was as much a scientist as de Ramaira. With de Ramaira, Rick could lose himself in discussions that soared far above the muddy buttresses of technology, forget about his prosaic duties for a while. Even so, the sidelong glances of staff who saw him with de Ramaira, loaded with unguessable appraisal, were beginning to make him uncomfortable.

At last, de Ramaira logged the data on the screen and switched off the microscope. Despite his long-limbed, almost adolescent gawkiness, his movements had a deft economical grace. "Sorry," he said, "but I've been waiting a week to look at that. Guess what it is."

"Well, I suppose it isn't a fish."

"Indeed not. It's the larval stage of a sabertooth, just prior to hatching. Someone shot a pregnant female over at Cooper's Hill. The rest of the eggs are in there." De Ramaira kicked the pail at his feet—half a dozen jelly spheres, each as big as a doubled fist, rocked in cloudy water—then looked narrowly at Rick. "You know, when you first came in you looked as if your grant application had just been kicked out of court."

"I guess I won't hear about that until after Landing Day now. No, it's just that I had a bad start to the day, and it went on from there. You know how it is."

"Indeed. It varies directly with the number of my fellow lecturers I see before my first class." De Ramaira got up and filled a beaker with water, set it on a hotplate. "So, how was your trip into the wilderness?"

Hesitantly at first, then with growing confidence, Rick sketched his encounter with the dingo, the loss of the pistol, the subsequent interview with Savory. "Well now," de Ramaira said, when Rick had finished. He went to the hotplate and began the ritual of filtering coffee. "I doubt that you've heard the last of that. They are hardly going to let what could be Lindsay's murderer slip away. Here.''

Rick sipped scalding coffee. "You're kidding."

De Ramaira sighed. "The problem with this utterly two-dimensional teaching system is that the only people taught anything at all about the synthesis of ideas are the cops.''

"Well I guess you're going to have to explain it to me," Rick said, smiling.

There was this thing about de Ramaira: he delighted in attempting to puzzle out a logical explanation for anything, no matter how absurd, and deliver it in clear terms. As a consequence, he was addicted to conspiracy theories, the more baroque the better.

He said, ''If you remember, Lindsay was supposed to have committed suicide out in the wilderness, although why he ran from his position is anyone's guess. His brains had been blown out days before the cops found him, no way to read anything into the matrix. And when the cops did find his body, it had been buried near the overlander—and some of his stuff was missing, too. The newscasts started to make a big play about that, until the cops clamped down. And then there was a drive against the separatists, although nothing's come of that so far.''

"I know he could have been murdered. You think by that guy I met out there? Jesus.'' The knife. The heavy weight of the man's body pressing his own into the dirt. Not a day ago.

"Perhaps, perhaps not. It's more likely the Constitution-alists are hoping to turn inquiries about whatever scandal Lindsay ran from into a murder hunt. And I bet it's a pretty deep scandal. I mean, it's hardly normal for the Board member in charge of colonyboat affairs to run off a couple of weeks before Landing Day, let alone commit suicide. It's the only way they can hope to keep ahead in the next election, and your fellow provides a nicely helpless suspect. One, two, three. If you hadn't been brainwashed by this educational establishment for dial readers, you would have seen it yourself.''

"Maybe so. But I really don't have that kind of morbid curiosity."

De Ramaira worried at his wiry hair. "But don't you think the politics interesting?"

"I don't find any politics interesting—or particularly relevant to what I'm doing. Let people like Collins take care of that. I'll get on with my own work."

De Ramaira chided gently, "Politics are important. Besides, I'm interested in everything."

For a dizzy moment Rick felt as if the bindings of his old doubts had been loosened, the doubts he'd had when, after the death of his parents, he had taken the course away from Mount Airy and wondered if he was doing the right thing or simply running away. No, that belonged in the past. It was too late now.

De Ramaira leaned back against the bench. "Don't take it to heart, anyhow. You're just a very small piece in the game. You've done your part."

"You think so? I wish I could believe it." Rick put down his half-empty cup of coffee. "Thanks for the talk, David, but I should be getting home."

Rick found Cath lying on her back in a shaft of sunlight at the far end of the sunken living room. She was plugged into her compsim, long black hair fanned around her white face, eyes closed. Rick gazed at her for a long moment, feeling the tumult of the day's events fade, calmed by the familiar sight of her.

They had met at the University, of course. Cath, working in the computer center, had been taking an advanced programming course and, in the third year of his doctorate, Rick had shared some of her classes. Cath had introduced him—a gangling, slightly awkward, over-intelligent settler, but capable of a certain ingenious patter, possessed of a quaint intimacy with classical music—into her nebulous social crowd. Soon they had begun a casual affair, Rick's first, dizzying him with the realization that sex could be for something other than procreation or affirmation of a solemn vow, its own fulfillment. At the beginning of his tenure, it had seemed a natural move for them to share one of the houses especially built for the University staff, an eight-room arcology on the hill. Rick couldn't have afforded it on his own, and the alternatives were both unpalatable, either senior residency in a student dorm or, more ignominiously, an apartment down in the old quarter of the city. But increasingly his and Cath's lives touched only tangentially, for all that Rick was a little in love with her: a love he dared not declare, for love did not yet figure in Cath's plans.

As if Rick's gaze had penetrated the flow of data behind her eyelids, Cath slowly opened her eyes, turned her head to look at him. Rick spread his arms, asked, "Am I bleeding?"

She was slow to focus on his face. "What did the cops do?"

"They didn't *do* anything, it was more what was *said*. I was just about called a separatist."

"If that was all," Cath said, "I think you got off lightly. You did lose their gun, after all."

"The fellow I saw wasn't interested in that. He thought that the encounter I had out there was significant in some way, only he didn't bother to tell me just what he thought it meant. Want a drink?"

"Not while I'm working." She was still plugged into her compsim. In the beat of silence, Rick thought that she meant that he should leave, but then she asked, "Who interviewed you?"

"Someone called Savory," Rick said, and saw her reaction, thinking, why does everyone think he's important?

She said, "You *have* been seeing people. He's in line for assistant governor, if the Constitutionalists make the next election."

"Oh. De Ramaira said something like that as well."

"Look, you know if you go around with that Womb-worlder you'll get yourself in trouble, Rick. I know we agreed not to meddle in each other's lives, but it reflects on me, too!"

Rick shrugged, unsettled by her sudden change in mood.

He feared her temper. Sometimes she flared up uncontrollably, arms flailing, face pinched white, bloodless. He said, "If other people think they have to avoid him then that's their problem. But I don't have to be a part of that. You might not think that there's prejudice here, but I'm from a settlement, I've seen things differently."

"I'm from a settlement too."

"Arcadia isn't really a settlement, you know that."

"What was that you said about prejudice?" She was smiling now.

"I guess. Anyway, I did get two places in the amphitheater today, so it wasn't a total loss. Is that all right?"

"Of course! I asked you about that weeks ago. You know I've always wanted to see the Landing from there. My father has tried over and over to get into it, but never has yet."

"Not even this time?" Cath's father was halfway through his first term on Arcadia's public committee.

"Arcadia isn't really part of Port of Plenty, despite what the other settlers think." She smiled, perhaps at the thought of outreaching her father's small ambition. "Daddy used to say that the City Board and the University had it sewn up between them. We got to see it from the beach, of course, but it isn't the same. It's really good of you, Rick. Are you over your day, now? I really have to get this work finished."

Rick sighed. "I guess. You want I should program dinner for you?"

"Oh, I'm going out later," she said, closing her eyes.

De Ramaira called early in the evening. "I've a small discovery to announce," he told Rick.

"Go ahead."

"I looked up the details of Lindsay's so-called suicide in the back files of the newscast service, then got out my maps. It turns out that the relay station is almost in a straight line between the city and the place on the coast where the cops found his body. So he could have called at the station first, to perpetrate whatever damage you were called out to repair."

"But he didn't. There was nothing wrong with the station."

"You're sure?"

"I was kitted out like Eljar Price, given a police escort and driven fifty kilometers into the Outback, and all Constat told me was thanks for nothing. If Lindsay was at the station, he didn't do anything."

De Ramaira worried at his hair. "So much for that, then. You might have told me before."

"You didn't ask. You just went galloping off—"

"Tilting at what turns out to be a radio telescope in full working order. Well, I suppose that whatever it was that Lindsay ran from will surface of its own accord eventually. Check you."

"Good night," Rick said, and switched off.

Later, alone in bed—Cath had not yet returned—Rick found that sleep eluded him, a space over which his active mind lightly skimmed. His thoughts turned about the encounter in the Outback, the dislocated sense of the man's talk, the knife, struggle as nauseously intimate as rape. He tried to counter this with the thought that he was safe in the harbor of home, returned to reassuring routine, the prospect of his research. Things hold, blind faith. But repetition soon devalued this to a meaningless groove from which his mind skipped, circling his central fear once more.

He must have fallen asleep, for Cath's return woke him. In the darkness he sat up expectantly, but she went past his door into her own room. Then silence. Rick lay back, and once more his thoughts began to circle.

Things had changed.

4. Rebels without a Pause

The dogs came racing up the track as Miguel neared Lake Fonda's perimeter fence, a half dozen big black-and-tan German Shepherds barking fierce imprecations. Miguel stood still as they circled him, hands held up so they could see he carried no weapon, meant no harm. One turned and ran off toward the settlement, and Miguel asked the others, "It's okay to sit, huh? Sun too much to stand in."

"No 'rouble," one of the dogs growled.

"I don't mean trouble to no one. Don't you remember me, huh? I was through here a year, two years ago." Slowly and carefully, Miguel sat in the dust. Presently, the dogs sat too, watching him alertly, pink tongues lolling from their black muzzles. It was a little past noon, the orange sun burning high in the deep, indigo sky. The wide ditches either side of the track were dry, and the turned earth between the endless rows of corn was like soft, bleached dust.

The escort from the settlement was a long time coming. Miguel thirsted for the flat insipid water in his canteen, but the canteen was in his pack, and he wasn't going to ask any goddamn dog for permission to get it out. So he sat and sweated in the relentless heat, thinking of the aborigine village he had passed the day before, the secret places scattered around it like rooms in the vast mansion of the landscape. He had plenty of time to think, a whole hour before someone came out to meet him.

He was taken to the settlement's commons, seated at one of the long tables and served bread and thin, cold beer while a woman and two men of the central committee, which was what the settlement of Lake Fonda called its governing body, asked about his travels.

He remembered the woman, iron-gray hair brushed back from her long face, from before, although she had been subordinate to old Ella Falconer then. The two men were new to him. One handled most of the talking, and seemed genuinely interested in what Miguel had to say; the other put on a show of disdainful boredom, and shook his head when Miguel started to talk about the aborigines.

"Only a guy like you would waste his time with those animals."

Miguel shrugged.

The woman said, "Get off his case, Hamilton. Where do you think he learned about the spices he sells? Right, Miguel?"

But Miguel wasn't sure if it were true or not. Sometimes, when he hid near a village, watching the aborigines go stiffly about their business among the round huts, things just seemed to pop into his head, out of the peace that descended as he let their continual buzz trance him out. Chewing the gummy snakeroot extract helped. In that state it was as if he could smell out the few wild plants that weren't poisonous to people. So far he hadn't made a mistake. But this was too complicated to explain even if he had wanted to, so he just shrugged and smiled nervously.

Hamilton shook his head again. The other man said, "Well, what do you have for us, Miguel?"

They spent a good hour dickering over various packets of seeds and powdered barks, dried leaves and flowers. When he had his price, Miguel reached into the bottom of the pack and took out the two guns, the one which he had taken from the dead man's hand on the beach, the other he'd pulled from the young, frightened cop in the river canyon a few days back. The reaction of the three settlers was all he had hoped for. "What'll you give me for these?" he asked.

The woman picked one up, hefted it in her big, callused palm. "Prophet's beard, Miguel, where did you find these?"

"I don't need them, figured you might, for the right price."

"Maybe so," the woman said, "but we've got to know their provenance. Understand me, Miguel? Hamilton, go get Bobby Richter, you think?"

"You don't want them, I can always go on to the next place," Miguel said.

"You're among friends, Miguel. Count on that. Go ahead, Hamilton."

Miguel took a swig of beer, trying to stay calm as the woman worked the actions of the guns, stripped out their ammunition clips, dry-fired each in turn and laid them down. "Very nice," she said.

The second man asked, "You been near the sea recently, Miguel? Down on a beach, maybe?"

"Listen, what are you, the cops or something?" Miguel smiled, but the settlers on the other side of the table didn't smile back. He was getting a bad, heavy feeling from them. "I should just walk out of here maybe," he said, and knew that they wouldn't let him. The long room was expectantly quiet. Miguel could hear the cries of children playing somewhere outside, the hum of a generator. He took another swallow of beer. Drink helped the pain, his father had said sometimes, though Miguel had never seen his father touch anything but coffee or water. The wine of the country: that was what his father had called water.

Miguel had finished his beer by the time Hamilton returned, accompanied by a tall young man in a rumpled black jerkin and black jeans. He looked at the guns but didn't touch them, looked at Miguel, bright blue eyes magnified by the round lenses of wire-rimmed glasses. "You want to sell these?"

"Look, I don't want trouble."

"I'll buy them, don't worry about that." The young man passed a hand over his close-cut hair; it rasped under his palm. "Have you talked about a price yet?"

"New clothes and boots. Medicines. One of my teeth in back sometimes hurts if I chew on it. Like that seen to."

The young man looked at the woman, who said, "No problem with us."

"That's all you want?" the young man asked.

Miguel hesitated, then reached into his pack. When he brought out the compsim Hamilton whistled sharply. The young man's gaze was steady. Miguel told him, "I need to be able to read in this. Need to plug into it."

"I knew that that was where he got the guns, didn't I say that—"

"Keep quiet," the woman told her companion. She said to Miguel, "You really want to be wired, comrade? What will you do with it? It's no toy."

"I know that."

Hamilton started to say something, and the young man, Bobby Richter, raised a hand. "Let me talk with him awhile, please."

"We need to know what we're getting into," the woman said. "You're only here under an obligation to the previous administration, don't forget that."

"Of course. You want to talk with me, Miguel?"

"You can give me what I want?"

"If you need it."

When the others had gone, Richter leaned back in his chair and smiled. "Jesus, these people. Hard to deal with, you know."

"Last time I was here there was another woman, older. She understood."

"Ella Falconer? There's been a rearrangement since then. A little extra kick in their perpetual revolution. You name it, they'll rebel against it, right?" Richter laughed. "Rebels without a pause. Yeah, well. Your friend is probably working the fields now. What was it she understood, Miguel? I hear you study the aborigines. That's what you meant?''

Miguel shrugged.

"I won't press too deeply. But that compsim you have, it could be important, Miguel, important for all the settlers. If it really is Lindsay's. You know the name?''

Something came together in Miguel's head. He saw that to get what he wanted he would have to tell the truth. He said, "The man was dead when I found him. Nothing on him to name him.''

"This was by the sea," Richter said. His glasses flashed when he leaned forward, hands flat on the table.

"Sure. I buried him in the sand there, said a few words over him.''

"And that's where you got the guns and the compsim.''

"Yeah. Well, one of the guns.'' The story came out in little pieces, the man dead on the beach against his overlander, the cops in the helicopter and the other cops who came after him in the river canyon, how he had managed to frighten off one of them, get his pistol. As he talked, Miguel felt a pressure easing inside him, a lightening of what he only now recognized was fear. He had been afraid ever since he had seen the helicopter coming in over the sea.

When Miguel had finished, Richter picked up the compsim, turning it end for end. Miguel asked, "You can fix it so I can use it? Wire me up?''

"I can arrange that, Miguel, but you would have to come with me to have it done. You know what it involves?''

Miguel wrapped his right hand around his left wrist. "They plug in here.''

"It's a little more complicated than that. There is an interface, yes, just beneath the skin. Little wires go from the interface into your brain, to your visual area just here—'' Richter touched the back of his head—"to the auditory and motor areas as well, so you can talk to the compsim or anything it's connected to, and so the compsim can talk to you and display data directly. You follow me? The interface grows these wires, organic electron paths, once it has been planted, but growth has to be guided. There has to be a computer checking and cross-matching every neuron path or at best you would receive nothing but garbage, at worst you'd end up an insane cripple. With supervision that hardly ever happens, even with the bootleg equipment we have to use. But it can't be done here, Miguel. They don't even have the interfaces, let alone the transplanting hardware. I must be the only one with an interface in the whole settlement here, and I'm just a visitor.''

"I know what you are, man, don't worry.''

"Are you on our side, Miguel?'' the young man said softly. "Do you want to see the settlements free? An end to the city's imperialism?''

"I'm not against you. I just live my own life, you know. All I ever wanted.''

"That's what all of us want, in-country. The name I mentioned—Lindsay. It didn't mean anything to you, did it?''

Miguel shrugged.

"He was someone in Port of Plenty, someone important. Like Anna or Hamilton here. From what you say he killed himself; that's something the cops have been trying to prove was murder. Maybe they're after you, Miguel. Did you think of that?''

It was the root of his fear.

"We can help you, if you need it. There may be information in this compsim that can help our cause. Perhaps a clue to why Lindsay killed himself.''

"You plug in. Plug in and tell me that!''

"Is that why you want an interface? To find that out?''

"Yeah. And to use it. You tell me why he did that to himself, and you give me a plug too, okay?''

"There are compsims and compsims, Miguel. Different kinds. Most of them are made in Port of Plenty. But there are some that come from Earth. New settlers bring them on the colonyboats, and the city takes them. Steals them. Important people like Lindsay get them. This one is from Earth, and it is what's known as a transducer. It sets up patterns in the peripheral motor nerves, superimposes its own impulses. Into your hand say, up your arm, into your brain. You don't have to plug in to use this one, Miguel. You just need to hold it in your hand and know how to ask it the right questions. I can try to do that, if you'll let me. It's your responsibility, you see. We don't steal.''

"Yeah. Yeah." The words rasped in Miguel's throat. He reached across the table and grabbed Richter's hand. The young man looked up from the compsim, blue eyes round with surprise behind the round lenses of his glasses. "I want you to do that," Miguel told him. "And you teach me too. Teach me that stuff."

Miguel was left alone in the commons for an hour. Richter went off to talk the matter over with Lake Fonda's committee, and a guard was placed on the other side of the door. Miguel's eager expectation soon faded. He was unused to being shut in and paced up and down nervously, stared out of the narrow windows at the settlement's dusty, deserted main square, paced some more. By the time Richter returned, Miguel was almost ready to make a run for it, guard or no guard.

But the guard, a burly unsmiling man in dirty coveralls, followed Richter inside, and shut and locked the door. Richter straddled a bench and set two compsims on the polished wood of the long table, the one Miguel had taken and a smaller, battered machine. Miguel watched warily as Richter jacked them head-to-head. "Don't worry," the young man said, his glasses flashing as he looked up. "I won't hurt your prize. Go ahead, sit down, that's it." He rolled the interface cuff around his left wrist, plugged into his own compsim.

And then, eyes closed, Richter went away for a moment. Miguel sensed the withdrawal, and the sudden return. "All right," Richter said, opening his eyes. He smiled. "A real amateur, Miguel."

"You have done it?"

"It's on the way." Richter shook the cuff from his wrist. "Want to see what's happening? Just touch your compsim, on the plate on its side there. Trust me, it won't hurt."

Miguel trusted no one, but something, his woken curiosity perhaps, made him reach out and brush his fingertips against the shiny plate. Something instantly overlaid his sight, a glimpse of a silvery net melting into a complex surface of pure light. Miguel snatched back his hand and the vision was gone.

"If you really want to use that thing, you're going to have to get used to it," Richter said, smiling.

"All that light . . . it came from in there?"

"From inside your head, Miguel. The compsim induces patterned firing in the neurons inside the visual area of your cortex. Well, never mind. What you saw was my compsim interfacing with the files of your compsim, injecting a command string that will fish out the algorithm we need to unpack the data stored there. Lindsay really didn't deserve a machine like this, leaving it vulnerable to the simplest safecracker." Richter took off his spectacles and polished them on the knee of his black jeans. "It'll open any moment now," he said, hooking the spectacles back over his ears; and as if in obedience his own compsim emitted a beep and light gathered over the projection plate of the other compsim, a tiny, blurred image of a man's head.

"Lindsay," Richter said, and hushed Miguel's question with an upraised hand, for the little head had begun to speak.

It was a thin squeaking voice, the kind of voice an insect might have. Even so, Miguel could sense the fear that drove its every word.

"It's stronger, every day it's stronger. Taking over my head. Like the whole world is dissolving, becoming unreal. And the dreams . . . he's in all of them, all the ones I remember, angry, always angry, as if it's my fault. I can't make the ship talk, none of us can, but that's what he wants, and I think if he can't get what he wants he'll take it out on me. I should never have let him inside my head; I can feel him in there now, wanting to stop me saying this. Even if we heard from the ship he'd still—"

Richter had, with an abrupt motion, unjacked the compsims. "Hey!" Surprise clashed with outrage at the root of Miguel's tongue. "What are you . . . why did you do that, man?"

Richter grabbed both compsims and stood. Miguel stood too, really afraid now. He was out of his depth, water closing over his head. He reached across the table and Richter danced back just as someone, the guard, plucked Miguel's knife from his belt and jerked his arms back and up.

"I'm sorry," Richter said. "But it's for the greater good, if that's any consolation. This is like an explosive, Miguel, and in the right place it could blow away the city and the cops. We have to have it, and we'll have to keep you safe, too."

A small room, bare concrete walls, a tiny barred window, a cot with a stained mattress barely covered by a thin blanket, a bucket for a toilet. Miguel banged on the heavy door and shouted until he was hoarse, tested the bars at the window, probed the walls for a flaw he could widen into an escape hole. But there was no way out. Anyway, they had taken away his pack and his boots. He lay on the cot and must have fallen asleep, for when the door opened he jerked awake, blinking in the glare of the unshaded fluorescent light.

The old woman pressed a finger to her lips, and softly closed the door.

It was Ella Falconer, the one-time leader of the settlement. Her lined face was thinner than Miguel remembered, her hair wholly white. She wore baggy, stained coveralls, muddy sneakers.

"This is a whole pile of trouble you've stepped into, Miguel," she said, and threw him his boots. She held his pack in her other hand.

"That man, Richter, he's crazy," Miguel said. He was beyond surprise at this apparition.

"I always have supported the separatists, always will. But I don't hold with them locking up people like you, Miguel. Even if it is for the good of the cause. If you come with me straight away, I can get you out, across the dam."

"Go by myself. Safer for you."

"You know, I always did think there was something human about you, deep inside. Don't worry about me, the worst they can do is kill me right now, instead of waiting for me to drop dead out in the fields.'' She handed him his pack and said as he began to look through it, ''It's all there. Even the compsim.'' But only when he saw it did something inside Miguel relax. ''They locked it up in what used to be *my* office,'' Falconer told him. ''Not very forward-thinking of them. I put some food in there for you, too.''

''Why are you doing this?''

''Call it revenge, if you want,'' Ella Falconer said, smiling. ''Besides, you don't deserve to be locked up like this, Miguel. You're a free spirit, a genuine Elysian soul. Richter has the information to fire up his cause against the city, he doesn't need you as well. Come on, now.''

There were three dogs waiting outside. Falconer laid a restraining hand on Miguel's arm when he jerked back in fright. ''Don't worry. I still have a few loyal followers. This way. The committee are busy dickering with Richter over their reward, but they could take it into their heads to question you further, and you wouldn't like that. Things have taken a brutal turn here.''

The dogs loping ahead in the dusk, they hurried through the huddle of long buildings, took the dusty track between cornfields to the little dam which penned the still, black waters of the lake.

''Go on, now,'' Falconer said, when Miguel hesitated.

But he stayed a moment, and asked, ''What will happen?''

''You're not as crazy as they say, I always thought that. Just sensitive, I suppose. What will happen? War, maybe. Things will change, that's all I can say for certain. Now go on, before some courting couple finds us.''

Halfway across the dam, Miguel began to run. He thought he heard Falconer call something after him, but he didn't look back. His pack, the compsim safe inside it, banged at his hip as he headed out into the empty country.

5. Landing Day

Preparations for Landing Day had been going on for weeks, but with only a handful of days to go, they began to take a grip on everyday life in the city. The countdown in hours, minutes, and seconds was permanently projected in one corner of the newscast channel. Garlands were strung across streets and banners hung from windows, although, of course, the Wombworlders would not see these decorations. They would be ferried through the city in their coldcoffins, still in the grip of their long sleep. The reception center had already been unsealed, its service cores powered up, but as usual the deadlines had been overrun, and crews were working around the clock to ready the machines that would help the new settlers ride out the multiple traumas of revivification. On the slope to the east of the city the lights of the center blazed at night like the checklights of a computer board.

The warm weather held, the sky an untroubled dome of purest indigo. Not the brutal heat of the Outback, but a lively warmth given zest by breezes off the ocean. Beyond the pontoon docks, barges that would transport the coldcoffins from the descent pod of the colonyboat to the shore maneuvered around the stripped shell of a previous arrival. Crews sweated under the high sun as they eased dummy containers into cradles, winched them into the barges which jostled beside the huge, calmly floating black cone. A few small sailcraft were always tacking back and forth beyond, red spinnakers bellying in the constant southerly breeze. Every day a small crowd gathered on the outermost wharves of the docks to watch.

The spirit of the impending Landing percolated into every part of city life. It even touched the routines of the University. For the students, it was a welcome pause before the killing grind toward the examinations at year's end. Rick couldn't blame them for lack of concentration in the classes he was auditing on the day before the colonyboat was due to enter orbit and send down its descent pod. He remembered well enough the previous Landing Day, in his third undergraduate year, when he had sat on the roof of the student dormitory with a dozen friends, sharing bottles of rough red wine to keep out the chill of the bleak winter day, cheering with everyone else when the cluster of orange parachutes, small and far, had blossomed in the iron sky.

This time, though, it seemed to Rick that there was a hollowness to the frenetic preparations, although the feeling was so vague that it vanished under the focus of definition. And on the surface, little troubled the established routine. There had been an asymptotic increase in separatist slogans, but that was only to be expected. And on Jones Beach someone had set up a huge deconstructed holo of Lindsay's face, fractured into a dozen planes. It took the cops all day to find where the little projector had been buried in the sand. Rick would have put his unease down to his lingering memories of his encounter in the Outback, had not de Ramaira agreed that something seemed wrong.

"It reminds me of a nest of packrats stirring about after their queen has died," he told Rick over lunch on that penultimate day. It was almost the end of the noon break, the seventy-two minute period between the twelve-hour halves of the day. Only a few people lingered in the common room.

Shafts of sunlight sank through the tall windows on the southern side, glowing on the sweep of small tables and the chairs around them.

Rick had been fiddling with the remains of his salad. Now he looked up, smiling at de Ramaira's remark. "Maybe that's it," he said. "Everyone is running around, making the usual preparations, but it's as if they don't know what they're preparing for. So they're working harder to cover it up, if you see what I mean."

"I was thinking of Lindsay's death—his suicide or murder, what you will—and the way Governor O'Hara is doing rather less than muddling through. But you do have a point." De Ramaira turned to watch the handful of people who were stapling, letter by letter, a banner message to the wall above the vendors. He smiled and added, "They're busy enough, anyhow. Do you know, even the identity of the new arrivals isn't known, in the sense of what group they are."

"That's never revealed anyway, until after Landing Day. I suppose you're going to tell me you have contacts in the right place."

"In revivification. They were rather miffed when I asked. All this secrecy has put their noses out of joint. You might think a band of positive undesirables is about to be unloaded on Elysium, and the Board's keeping shut until they have them safely in-country."

"Like the Collectivists, you mean?"

"Oh, you should hear ideas that are going around. If you're interested, perhaps you'd like to come with me tonight. The bars are full of the most interesting amateur politicians."

The thing Rick disliked most about de Ramaira was this casual patronizing contempt toward people more ordinary than himself. One day it might be turned upon Rick himself. "I don't think," Rick said, around a mouthful of lettuce, "that the Senate would approve of its lecturers barhopping downtown."

"No doubt," de Ramaira said casually. "But what can they do? They can't throw me out, and they already seem to have quite enough reasons to impede my work as much as they can. And my time is entirely my own, as yours should be."

"Still, it's not sensible," Rick said, uncomfortable now. After all, de Ramaira was more than twenty years his senior, even more in the strict Newtonian sense. "Anyway, Cath has arranged something this evening, we're going to a party."

"And how are you and Ms. Krausemann getting along, after a year of living together?"

"We just share the house," Rick said warily. He sometimes wondered about de Ramaira's sex life. There had to be something, but what? Pickups in bars, houses of ill-repute; he couldn't imagine.

"Well, it's a pity you won't come. I'd hate to see you ending like that bunch of decerebrated packrats over there." He gestured toward the people who were admiring the completed banner hung over the vendors, its message spelled out in clumsily aligned alternately red and blue letters: *Welcome to the new settlers, whatever they believe in.*

"Well, it certainly doesn't mean anything," Rick said. "One way or the other. Will I see you down at the beach tomorrow, David?"

De Ramaira held his hands a few centimeters apart in front of his face, as if taking the measure of something. His nails were yellow, shrunken and buckled. "Oh, I wouldn't miss it for the world. Elysium, that is."

Amplified music mingled strangely with the sound of waves breaking farther down the beach. Rick and Cath were dancing slowly in the translucent shade of a canvas awning, arms linked around each others' necks as they slowly revolved among the other couples. The fine white sand was stirred into little mounds and dimples. It made the soles of Rick's bare feet itch.

Cath's breath touched his neck. "I could do with another drink. With a whole *lot* of ice."

"Whatever you want." He let go with one arm and dropped the other to her waist. Linked, they walked out of the shade into level orange sunlight.

They had arrived at Jones Beach late in the afternoon, and now it was early evening. The crescent of Cerberus, the large outer moon, slanted in the dark sky. Five kilometers south of Port of Plenty, the beach faced the open ocean beyond the mouth of the estuary, where the descent pod of the colony-boat would splash down. It was crowded with people from the city, brought by a shuttle service of big ground-effect coaches which had begun early that morning.

A wide sandy meadow separated the beach from the native forest, and the amphitheater stood in the middle of the meadow. A space had been fenced off in front of it by a palisade of wired stakes. Rick and Cath had to show their tickets at the single gate. The VIP enclosure was almost empty. Most of those who would watch from the amphitheater hadn't arrived yet; rumor scheduled splashdown for some time after sunset.

A bar had been set up near the arched entrance to the stairs which led up to the amphitheater's tiered seats. Cath accepted her rum punch absentmindedly as she looked about.

"Over there," she said. "Most of the department must be here already!" She started across, and two of the half dozen terrifyingly elegant people by the fence turned to greet her. A swarthy, bare-chested man, hair swept back and woven into many braids, each braid tipped with a crystal bead, grinned as the tall woman beside him took Cath's arm.

Rick had hesitated a moment too long. Really, he didn't fit easily into Cath's social set anymore. He had felt mis-placed all through the noisy, informal lunch at the home of Cath's departmental head, and disliked the assumed superi-ority of most of the Computing staff. He and Cath were be-ginning to follow different paths, that much was clear. Yet he had shared moments of pure happiness with her today. On the coach ride, on the beach, dancing under the canvas awning. And he did admire her cool determination as she made her way in the world. It's not what she's making for herself that I don't like, he thought, it's the friends that she's picking up on the way. A small hollowness blooming in his chest, he turned and nearly collided with Max Rydell.

"Well, hell. Hello, Rick." Rydell lifted his hand from the top of his beer glass (foam ran the sides) and smiled. Sweat glistened on the pelt of his bare chest. He said, "This is sure something, huh? Must be the hottest Landing Day in memory."

"I guess. You're not working too hard, I hope. This is a holiday."

"I was in charge of the tickets, so I got all my organizing out of the way before this. But if I get on the entertainments committee you really will see me running around next time!"

"Sure." Rick drank off half his punch. He had a vision of Rydell thirty years on, as carefully groomed as Professor Collins, gruffly running his own department, chairing half a dozen committees.

"Did I see Cath with you? How is she?"

Rick glanced at the group over by the fence. The tall woman, her thin witchy face speckled with little black cuneiform marks, was rubbing a clear jelly into Cath's forearm. Focus. All the systems people did it, according to Cath. Rick told Rydell, "I guess she's enjoying it."

"Well," Rydell said seriously, "I wish I could say that about everyone. Have you seen David de Ramaira?"

"No. Should I?"

"Well, he seems to be trying to stir up trouble. Someone ought to be looking out for him. He doesn't seem to be able to look after himself. I've just come in from the beach, I had a glimpse of him out there. He looked half-drunk!"

Rick smiled and felt uncomfortable, remembering his conversation with de Ramaira the day before. He said, "I can't stop him being drunk, can I?"

"Well, no. I just thought you could maybe talk to him?"

"Is he fighting drunk or what?" Rick set his glass among the dreggy clutter in the bar's discard pan. "If he's really bothering people, maybe you should tell one of the stewards."

"Oh, he's just going around saying really stupid things. You know, inflammatory. I thought I'd save some bother if I had you reel him in."

"Okay." Rick thought that he knew what sort of things de Ramaira would be saying. "I'll see if I can find him. But I don't know if I can actually do anything."

As Rick went through the gate in the fence a flight of rockets terminated their brief arc above the sea, a burst of falling golden stars vividly unreal against the darkening sky. Ragged applause was for a moment louder than the dance music. The sun was sinking toward the rim of the Conway-Stewart Delta on the other side of the estuary.

Rick halted beyond the awning, realizing that Rydell had said nothing about where de Ramaira might be. He had a lot to learn about giving orders. Well, at least it gave Rick a good excuse. Even if he found de Ramaira he knew that he would have little chance of calming the man down.

A softball game was in progress farther along the beach, the players spread out to the breakers. A lithe tanned girl in a minuscule sarong was endlessly alternating triple-gainers and open swans on a trampoline. Children were running in and out of the waves. Elsewhere, people were talking or eating or simply sitting in the rapidly diffusing sunlight, tired enough to let the minutes spin out by themselves. Many had gathered at the ridge where the dry grasses of the meadow gave way to white sand.

Rick walked past the girl on the trampoline and her circle of adolescent admirers. The crowd received him. He ambled between knots of people, stepped around others sprawled on the sand. As he stepped over a discarded blanket, a woman's voice rose above the general noise. "Look! There . . . there! Is that . . . ?" The rest was lost in a rising murmur as people turned to gaze toward the mouth of the estuary.

A glittering fleck was moving low over the water, making toward the hazy shoreline north of the marshes. A helicopter. People were sitting down again. The man in front of Rick turned and said aggressively, "You'd think they'd tell us, huh?"

"I'm afraid I know about as much about it as you."

"Ah, shit," the man said, and walked off, his matted shoulders hunched.

Rick began to walk back to the amphitheater, remembering the first time he had gone to the city with his father. He had been fifteen. They had walked through the market to look at the handcrafts, cut flowers and organically grown food, rugs and pots and furniture, all the things that people from the settlements brought into the city to sell. Father had been beside him, totem of the familiar as they moved through crowds of elegant, fantastically dressed strangers, until Rickey had stopped a moment too long to look at a stall where wicker cages held torpid ruffed lizards. In the instant that he realized that his father had disappeared it was as if something had pulled apart in his chest, a sudden aching vacuum. He felt the passive equivalent of that panic now, as he stepped carefully around supine people, strangers all.

He heard the dance music a moment before he saw the canvas awning. The girl and most of her audience had abandoned the trampoline. Two boys jiggled cautiously on the taut white square, each holding the other's shoulders. A lot of people were going through the gate into the fenced enclosure in front of the amphitheater.

Cath lay alone where the clean sand of the beach tipped to meet the slats of the fence. One hand covered her eyes; the other held a half-full glass on her hip where the ridge of her pelvic bone raised the blue cloth of her brief wraparound dress.

"Hey," she murmured as Rick sat beside her. "You can't have gone very far. Or was I asleep? Someone said you'd gone looking for de Ramaira."

"I didn't see him. I didn't look very hard, though," Rick confessed.

Cath raised herself on one elbow to sip her drink. "You know, I don't think you should have gone off in the first place."

"I thought I might, as it was asked as a favor. What happened to your crowd?"

Cath sipped again. "I only stopped to say hello. Really, you should have too, they *are* from the University, after all.

And when I looked around you'd gone galloping off on some knight errant quest!''

"Anyway, I soon gave up. Too many people.''

Cath looked over the edge of her glass at the crowded curve of the beach. "There *are* too many of them! Like a herd of seacows.'' She made a kind of lowing noise, then covered her mouth and giggled.

"Are you sure about drinking on top of that stuff? Focus.'' Cath's sharp intolerance toward ordinary citizens still made Rick uneasy—she had more in common with David de Ramaira than she realized. Her mother's family went back to the crew of one of the two arks which had carried the original colonists to Elysium, before the development of compact gravithic generators had made cheap, reusable ramscoop drivers possible and interstellar travel almost routine. Crew families were the nearest thing to an aristocracy in Port of Plenty and Arcadia.

She squinted up at him. "That's another thing. At the party last night, Josie was miffed when you refused a hit. It doesn't hurt to relax every so often.''

"Where I come from, it's a sin to do alcohol, much less serotonin specifics. Look, if the crowd worries you so much, let's exercise our privilege and go back in.''

Cath drained her glass and set it in the sand, and they strolled to the gate and showed their tickets again, climbed the L-shaped stairway of the amphitheater to their seats. The stepped rows of benches were sparsely occupied; the upper tiers, reserved for members of the City Board, were completely deserted.

Side by side, Rick and Cath looked out at the level line of the ocean horizon. There—there was the beginning of the unknown. Two thousand kilometers away this same ocean was breaking on an unexplored shore.

The amphitheater filled slowly, but Rick couldn't recognize anyone in the bronzed light. The sun had vanished behind a molten line of clouds above the delta. The crescent of the moon had sunken lower in the sky. The first stars were pricking across the huge sky. Somewhere above: the colonyboat. The thought tripped a solid clot of excitement in Rick's stomach.

Cath leaned to hug her knees, bare thighs clamped together as she looked left and right. The mutter of the waiting people drifted through the amphitheater's seashell curve.

Rick asked, "Shall we try the bar again? Maybe we can find out what's happening."

Cath stirred drowsily. "I guess one more will either kill or cure."

The sun had set now. Ragged lines of cloud were cooling to a purple not much lighter than the rest of the sky. As Rick and Cath went down the aisle, someone in the amphitheater turned up a radio—

"—AS YET NO WORD BUT AS SOON AS—"

—and turned it down again. As echoes blatted away, Rick realized just how much noise the crowd was making at the bottom of the stairs. Cath had stopped, one hand raised to the side of her neck. Rick grinned. "It sounds like they've penned all the drunks in the world down there!"

Cath said, "It sounds like a riot to me. Didn't you hear someone scream just now?" The elbow of the stairway blocked their view. She added, "Let's go back, Rick. It isn't worth the trouble."

It was the hard voice she used in their domestic squabbles. The dreamy precision of the focus had evaporated. Rick said quickly, "I want to check out what's happening. People don't come here to get totally wired; maybe there's some news. I'll just take a look, is all."

He went on down. Even before the turn, the noise rose around him as if he was descending into the vitals of a huge overstrained machine. A metallic voice cut through the din, but its words were botched by echoes. In that moment Rick decided to turn around—and someone, a cop, turned the corner and grabbed him, shouted something drowned by the roar. Rick smiled, thinking he was meant to go back up, but the cop tightened his grip and marched him down.

Light surprised him. Someone had turned on the searchlights above the entrance, where the crowd seethed against a line of cops. People were standing on the counter of the bar, shouting and clapping; others were clambering up to join them.

Rick clamped his eyes against the glare . . . and was hit in the back, shoved forward! The crowd closed around him, a hot cell of arms and torsos. Dazed, he tried to turn back (a woman's face brushed his own; someone smacked heavily into his side; a hand scraped the back of his neck) but something hit the people behind him and he went forward with everyone else. Then the press slackened so suddenly that he almost fell.

Lights sprang on beyond the dispersing crowd, throwing long shadows across the ground. The air above became an impenetrable black ceiling. More people staggered from the entrance. Mostly, they turned toward the meadow behind the amphitheater, stumbling over wooden stakes trampled into the sand. Rick set off in that direction too, looking for the electric blue of Cath's dress. People wandered aimlessly between white police cruisers, clotting here and there in small groups.

Then an amplified voice blared under the black ceiling, chanting the same sentence over and over: "WE'VE BEEN ABANDONED! WE'VE BEEN ABANDONED! ABANDONED!" De Ramaira straddled the roof of a police cruiser, his face half-obscured by the yellow cone of an amplifier. "YOU FOOLS, CAN'T YOU SEE HOW THEY'VE DECEIVED US!" There was a squeal of feedback. "LOOK UP—"

As Rick started toward the cruiser, Cath crashed into his side. They clasped each other tightly, each seeking familiar comfort. "All right," he kept saying. "It's all right."

Another metallic squeal echoed from the rising wall of the amphitheater. Rick turned (Cath's head butted against his chest) and saw that de Ramaira had gone from the cruiser's roof.

In the circle of his arms, Cath said, "It was crazy, Rick! The police were pushing everyone out of their seats, *shoving* them down those stairs. . . ." The tremor in her voice was an overflow of anger. "It's those goddamn fucking separatists, I just know it. They must be behind it!"

In the circle of her arms, Rick said, "I ought to see about de Ramaira."

Rick found no relief in Cath's embrace as they walked between the cruisers, through the milling crowd, forgetting how often he had sought it. He felt the onset of a queerly detached sense of precision, nothing to do with the ferocity of the cops or the shattered expectation of the splashdown, or the fat woman in the yellow smock who walked across their path with tears streaming down her face.

"He sounded out of his head," Cath said. "What will you do?"

"I don't know."

De Ramaira stood in the glare of the cruiser's headlights, passive in the casual grip of a cop, head hanging so that his wiry hair flopped over his face. His glittering shirt was torn, and he was panting hard.

Rick pushed through the loose semicircle of spectators. A cop with sergeant's chevrons on the breast of his white coveralls was unplugging from his compsim. As Rick went up to him the sergeant jerked a thumb toward de Ramaira. "You know him?"

Rick nodded. "Dr. de Ramaira, from the University. I guess he's drunken a little too much—"

One of those watching said loudly, "He's wired out of his head!"

"So is it okay to take him home and sober him up?"

The sergeant scratched behind one ear. "You can do what you want, long as you keep this wasted fucker out of trouble. I just want this place cleared. Those are my orders."

Something settled, something final. "The Landing?"

"Look," the sergeant told Rick, "there isn't going to be any Landing."

De Ramaira raised his head. He didn't look drunk at all. A black trickle of blood gleamed below one nostril.

"Don't you see, Rick? Don't you understand? Earth has finished with us. There won't be any more ships. For ever and ever."

6. Scorpio Rising

The heatwave mounted in the week after the debacle of Landing Day, a breath from the Outback now. The discharge of thousands of air-conditioning circuits rose like the updraft of a furnace over the close-packed roofs of the Port of Plenty's old quarter, drawing a hot, headachy wind off the estuary. Harsh sunlight turned the thousand domes of the bubble-suburbs into incandescent gems, scorched their settings of trees and evergreen shrubs. People ventured out only when they had to. Sweltering beneath the empty indigo sky, Port of Plenty seemed half-abandoned, as if its population had incontinently taken flight from the sudden, universal disaster.

On the afternoon of the fourth day, the hottest yet, Governor O'Hara broadcast a belated explanation of the City Board's position. Even though contact had never been established with the colonyboat, he said, the Landing Day celebrations had not been canceled because of a mistaken faith in tradition. The board had expected until the last possible moment to detect the colonyboat as it entered orbit.

A burly man with a sweating jowly face, thinning hair

combed sideways across a freckled pate, O'Hara was not convincing. An athlete gone to seed, a compromiser elevated too high. The next day, Max Rydell, who was a loyal Constitutionalist, confided to Rick, "Well, yesterday's little fiasco won't help matters, will it?"

"What do you think will happen now?"

They were leaning on the rail of the balcony overlooking the jai alai court, waiting for the current game to end. Shouts. Hard-edged slams of the ball against the walls. Skittering squeals of sneakers as players chased rebounds.

Rydell watched the game pensively. He said at last, "I guess the only way to save face is to have the fellow resign. He gambled it would come good is the best way of looking at it. But it didn't. He'll have to step down now, or we might be forced into an election."

Rick lifted the mesh singlet away from his sweat-sticky chest. The air conditioning wasn't coping very well with the sunlight which glared through the court's glass roof. "So all that will happen is we get a new governor."

"What do you want, a revolution?"

"Jesus, of course not. It makes no difference to me who's in power here."

"Rick, if we don't get someone who will come down hard on the separatists, it will affect everyone on the planet."

Rick laughed at Rydell's uncharacteristically sententious tone, and the stocky materials engineer said gruffly, "Your trouble is that you think you're beyond it all."

"If the next colonyboat doesn't arrive, then I'll begin to worry. Port of Plenty always did take Earth too seriously."

"You ask your friend David de Ramaira how seriously this should be taken. I haven't seen *him* around since that exhibition he made of himself at Jones Beach."

"As a matter of fact, I'm seeing him this evening. I'll pass on your concern."

The bell which indicated the end of a game period rang out, and the men and women in the court below the balcony began to sort themselves into their respective teams. Rydell said, "Man in your position might do well to keep clear of that fellow, at the moment."

"A lot of people have been telling me that, lately." Rick picked up his curved scoop. "Come on, let's knock Agriculture for a loop."

The paralyzing grip of the heat gradually ebbed in the evenings, and the people of the city were able to reclaim the streets. Rick found that he was almost the only person walking by himself (Cath was taking part in a family conclave, but she would have made her excuses anyway) as he made his way through the old quarter to de Ramaira's house. People sat in their doorways or leaned at their windows, gossiping with neighbors. The open-air restaurants and cafes in the quarter's tree-lined squares were crowded, and groups of people promenaded in their finery along the warm streets.

The old quarter was centered on the largest hill in the city, the place where the first colonists had begun to clear the alien forest eighty years ago. De Ramaira's house was at the top of one of the narrow streets which snaked to the hill's summit, a solid four-square building overlooking a park of threadbare grass and huge chestnut trees.

Rick touched the signal tab set in the heavy wooden door. A bell clanged somewhere inside, but minutes passed without anything else happening. The narrow windows were shuttered and dark behind their fancy iron balustrades, but from somewhere overhead came the sound of many people talking at once, mingling with the drone of the automats which lay on the seaward side of the hill. Rick was about to press the tab again when the door creaked open and de Ramaira said, "Rick! Good to see you." His smile was a momentary flicker. "Your young lady, Ms. Krausemann, she isn't with you?"

"She's talking with her family." Rick looked de Ramaira up and down. He was wearing an uncharacteristically formal suit, black high-cut jacket and pleated pants, but his white shirt was open down his bony chest, and he was barefoot.

"You look well," Rick said. "I was worried, you not turning up at work."

"I'm okay. Come in."

They went down the hall, through a room cluttered with massive pieces of early colonial furniture, and into a small courtyard lit by a single dim lamp. The neighboring houses loomed over it, blocking out most of the sky.

"Everyone else is on the roof," de Ramaira said.

"Everyone else?"

"Oh, I invited some students over," de Ramaira said casually, and started up the helical staircase. His footsteps clacked above Rick's head as they climbed out of the close air of the courtyard.

There were at least two dozen people crowded on the roof terrace. More than half the women wore the two-day-old fashion of mock-mourning, full-length dresses of layered and torn black silk, black net adorned with silver stars and moons wound through piled-up hair, draped over a face powdered chalk white. At first glance, the party looked like a reception for an obscure sect of nuns.

De Ramaira guided Rick through noisy knots of people. As they reached the far corner, two young men turned from the angle in the railing. A woman just as young, seated at the square wooden table there, looked up with a brief but dazzling smile. Rick smiled back, and de Ramaira said to the woman, "Lena, this is Dr. Florey. Rick, this young lady is one of my students, Lena Vallee."

"Now, you wouldn't be related to the guy in the Chronus Quartet? The cello player?"

Lena brushed back the heavy black hair which spilled the collar of her asymmetric blouse. "My father."

"Really? Hey. I used to go to all their concerts, back when I was a student."

One of the young men, tall, blond and nervous, stuck his hand out. "I'm Jon Grech. I'm in Agriculture too." He glanced at de Ramaira and added, "Trying to end up as a biologist, though." He shook hands with Rick over Lena's head.

"And here," de Ramaira said expansively, "is Web Marshall. He's in the Engineering Department, like yourself."

But Rick had not seen the thickset, shaggy-haired youngster before. Like Jon, he was wearing black jeans and a sweatshirt. His were a lot dirtier, though. He pulled a chair from the table and sat, scowling back at Rick's quizzical gaze. "I'm in Systems, not Communications," he said.

"Well, why don't we all sit down," de Ramaira suggested.

Rick looked around at the rest of the party, thought he recognized one of his students and looked away. He asked de Ramaira, "Shouldn't you be playing host?" He had the uncomfortable suspicion that he was being set up for something.

"I think it's reached critical mass," de Ramaira said affably and sat next to Web. Jon sat beside Lena and after a moment's hesitation Rick sat too, sure now that something was going on.

De Ramaira was filling glass after glass from a pitcher of red wine. "We're glad you could come along, Rick. Jon and Web have been plying me with questions I haven't the least idea how to begin answering. I thought it would be easier if they put them directly to you. That would be the proper feedback, wouldn't it?"

Jon leaned forward. "We sort of wanted you to listen to a few ideas of ours, and maybe comment on them? You know, there's all sorts of dumb theories around the campus and it's getting difficult to sort out any sense."

Web added, "He's trying to say that we want to know what's going on, but we can't be bothered to program it ourselves."

Jon protested, "Hey, I didn't mean it like that!" A caged electric lamp, hung on a pole nearby, put a corona around his crewcut hair; his face was in shadow. He said to Rick, "We've been trying to extract some sense from all the talk of the past few days, and we were just wondering about your opinion."

Rick looked at de Ramaira, who smiled gently, inscrutably. Beyond the rail at his back, leaf-laden branches doffed in the breeze. Rick said, "I didn't know that I was to chair a discussion panel when I was asked up here. But if you want to risk your opinions against mine, then go ahead."

De Ramaira suggested quietly, "Jon and Web have an interesting proposal, if you'll hear them out."

Lena looked up at the black sky and laughed, a single clear note.

Jon frowned at her, then began to speak rapidly and nervously about what people thought could have gone wrong with the colonyboat. He was barely audible above the noise of the party, but Rick caught enough to get the gist, nothing that he hadn't heard a dozen times already from his colleagues. That the driver of the colonyboat could have failed in transit, the fusion motor flared out or the gravithic generators flatlined, no longer warping space to funnel hydrogen atoms into the driver's throat. That the colonyboat could have been hit by some piece of cosmic debris big enough to penetrate its ice shield; or that its driver had failed to swing around for the deceleration maneuver, so that it had ploughed straight through the Tau Ceti system. Rick was going to point out that these were hardly revolutionary ideas when Jon pulled out, of all things, a piece of paper covered with calculations which he claimed to show how unlikely any of these possibilities were, offering it across the table.

"Oh, I believe you," Rick said. "I know that a colonyboat is a very simple thing. Self-correcting multiphasic circuitry, extensive back-up systems for the few mechanical components, and so on. And the gravithic generators don't even have any moving parts. But that doesn't mean a failure couldn't happen, despite your calculations."

Web hunched forward. "We know that. But there's another possibility which most people are ignoring, something more likely than a glitch in the colonyboat. The possibility that something happened on Earth so that a ship never was sent."

"You had better ask David about that," Rick said. "I'm just a lecturer in Communications Engineering."

De Ramaira said, "The problem is, Rick, that my knowledge of current Earth politics is no better than that of anyone else. When the last batch of settlers arrived there was no indication that the launch schedule was to be changed. If there was, Governor O'Hara would have made use of it in that miserable apology of a speech last night, and anyway, there's no reason for it to change. Every time Vesta reaches the point in its orbit closest to Tau Ceti, off goes a colonyboat. What could be simpler?"

"It minimizes transit time through the dust in the plane of the Solar System," Jon said. "And besides, the launch track is made up of more than a hundred autonomous gravithic generators. Even half that number would be enough to get the colonyboat up to the speed where its own gravity warp starts acting as a ramscoop."

"Jon has gone into the technical aspect thoroughly," de Ramaira told Rick. "As for politics, there never was a faction in Congress completely set against colonization. No one there wants to leave the stars to the Russians. What we need, you see, is a way of finding out what's happening on Earth."

Rick said, "Don't you think the City Board have taken all this into account? I guess Constat can work out what might have happened on Earth far better than any of us can. Social dynamics is what it's supposed to be good at, after all."

"The City Board knew about Landing Day, too," Web said. "Even if Constat can make a guess at what's happened, *we* surely aren't going to be told. But we don't need to make a guess. We can find out directly!"

"You have a working colonyboat, is that it?" Rick grinned at de Ramaira, and immediately felt a pang of shame. After all, to de Ramaira this was as much a personal as a global disaster. But Rick felt that he couldn't play this straight.

Jon said, with earnest seriousness, "We don't need any spaceship. The University already has something just as good."

"Oh? That's news to me."

"I said it wouldn't be any good," Web told Jon. "I said this guy would play the authority line."

"You must be pleased to have your prejudices confirmed," Lena told Web, and flashed her dazzling smile at Rick as she poured herself more red wine.

Rick sipped from his own glass, sourness diffusing to a general warmth on his tongue. He was the focus of the others' attention—de Ramaira's gentle wistful yearning, Web's fierce bitter scorn, Jon's eager optimism, Lena's amusement—and he wanted out. Stay aloof, tread lightly in the world. Still, he felt an obligation to de Ramaira. "All right," he said, "I guess you better tell me what your idea is."

Jon glanced sideways at Web, who shrugged, then told Rick, "The idea is that we can use the relay station to listen in on Earth's radio traffic. It was used for that years ago, wasn't it? Why not again?"

"It picked up a laser signal aimed specifically at Tau Ceti, and from the edge of the Solar System, too," Rick said, "not the effluvia of a civilization almost a dozen light-years away. And I don't think the City Board would approve of your meddling; nor would the University for that matter—it owns the relay station, after all."

"That's why we're asking you," Jon said. "I mean, you work on the relay station. Couldn't you—"

"I was sent out there to do a job. It wasn't my choice, and if I'd known all the trouble it would bring down I wouldn't have gone along with it."

"But you were on trivee—"

"Because I was asked to say that the relay station was okay! That's all. And it was okay, too. But I've no authority over the relay station. Really."

"Hasn't your friend Professor Collins something to do with it?" de Ramaira suggested.

"He's something to do with just about everything at the University. But I can't propose something like this to him. You're the engineer, Web. You can think of half a dozen reasons why it's impossible."

Web shrugged this aside. "The thing is that the dish antenna is there. It's working, right? The University isn't doing anything with it, and who's to tell the City Board? They've cheated us, maybe it's our turn.''

Rick saw then why they wanted to believe it. Everyone on Elysium had been indoctrinated with the comforting engineering principle that all problems have a solution, and all too few questioned that, with so much on the world still unexplored and unexplained. He pushed back his chair, said flatly, ''Before I go, just let me talk to you alone for a minute, David.''

Three boys circled an old man in a quilted overjacket, bent to breathe the cloying reek of bliss which leaked from the capsule he had broken between his black-painted nails. Rick pushed around them and came face to face with the student from Communications.

''Some party, right?'' Rick said.

The student smiled nervously around his glass of wine. ''I didn't realize you knew Web, Dr. Florey,'' he said.

''I don't. You do? Maybe you should talk him down from his crazy ideas.''

''Oh, I don't know if they're all that crazy,'' the student said, his mild white face settling into a serious expression.

''If you believe shit like that, there's little hope for you,'' Rick said, and shoved on past, regretting his spasm of anger at once.

De Ramaira caught up with him when he reached the head of the helical staircase. ''You shouldn't be so disheartening,'' de Ramaira said. ''They have to believe in something.''

''And what about you?'' Rick leaned on the railing by the staircase and gazed down at the roofs which stepped away into the scintillating web of the nighttime city. Its glow bleached the sky of all but the brightest constellations. The Big Dipper almost directly overhead. Troilus, the biggest of the gas giants in Tau Ceti's system, a steady yellow lamp rising out of the forests in the east. And there too, just at the horizon, the sprawling constellation of Scorpio, harbinger of winter, Antares a burning red eye. Rick traced a line upward, looking for Serpens Caput, the constellation in which Sol was a fifth-magnitude star. But it was lost in the city's glare.

De Ramaira leaned beside Rick, but he was watching the surge of the party. After a moment, he said, "Do you know, one of the more popular theories is that Earth no longer sends us ships because we've become unworthy of them. Though these Neo-Platonists have yet to advance any suggestion as to how we might achieve redemption."

"Well, it's no more crazy than the idea about the relay station."

"It isn't feasible? You jumped on them pretty heavily back there."

"Most of Earth's communications are either cabled or bounced off satellites, and interplanetary stuff is lasered, so that to intercept it you'd have to be between receiver and transmitter. That leaves a lot of radio noise, but you couldn't do more than detect it. Sure, interstellar communication is possible with bad noise-to-signal ratios. Even with more noise than signal, but only as long as the data rate is slow, and reasonable modulation and coding is used. And the old transmissions were weak, too, even if they were aimed straight at us. That's why an isolated antenna system had to be used to pick them up, just the output from one unshielded motor was more energetic. But the kind of stuff Web and Jon want to unravel will be orders of magnitude weaker, and spilling all over each other, and swamped with interstellar hash besides. If they want to find out if the Solar System's a radio emitter, fine, but that still won't help them explain anything."

"At least we'd know Earth is still there."

"I guess the Sun is as great a radio emitter as Tau Ceti. And there's that big gas giant, Jupiter?"

De Ramaira banged the rail with the heels of his palms and said, "Sometimes the intractability of the universe is not to be believed!"

"You think those two are serious? Web seems to be, at any rate."

"Really, I don't know him very well."

De Ramaira stepped aside as someone, in trash aesthetique sleeveless mesh vest and baggy shorts buckled at the knees, swayed past and blundered down the helical stairs.

The very blond, very long-haired young man following him paused to say, "He's just blissed out is all, the crowd is messing up his interface." The mesh of his vest was livid, fluorescent green. There was a yin-yang symbol tattooed on the hinge of his acne-scarred jaw. He laid a hand on de Ramaira's arm and said, "I'll see he comes down okay, David. It's a nice party."

As the blond youngster clattered down the stairs after his friend, de Ramaira said with a smile, "These young people can't carry the load. What were we talking about?"

"Web."

"Oh, Web. Web is Jon's friend, and Jon brings his friends to hear the Earthman speak."

"I get the impression that Jon is your protege."

"He has a genuine passion for biology—and a real intellect too, I might add. It is also a pleasure to talk with someone who regards knowledge as an end in itself, rather than a means to an end. Present company excepted, of course. I can tolerate his friends, and who knows? I might win converts. I hope that Jon will be able to work in pure science once he's graduated. It would be a damn shame to lose him to the farmers."

"So he'll carry on the good fight."

"Someone has to support me in the great lost cause of trying to persuade my friends in Agriculture to control the rabbits. I don't know what the Seeding Council was thinking of. Gene-melded dogs and sheep, that's fine. So are horses and cows. But rabbits? Never mind a colonyboat's not arriving. In a hundred years or so, with all the food they can eat and with no native predator able to eat them, those cute little bunnies will have stripped this continent clean."

"Talking of your friends in Agriculture, that reminds me. Some of the staff have been saying some pretty nasty things about you since Landing Day. It hasn't helped that you haven't turned up for work."

"Oh, I can imagine just the sort of thing," de Ramaira said lightly. "Even before my reports were going back via the colonyboat drivers—odd to think, isn't it, that the first hasn't even reached Earth yet—even then, I had to put up with all sorts of shit. Well, no one is going to wait around in case a ship does turn up, least of all my busy friends in Agriculture! However, I have this house, and the credit I've accumulated by not living on the hill, and equipment I've, ah, borrowed from the University over the years. You see, I've always been prepared for the worst. Please don't worry that I haven't thought things through, Rick; I've been doing nothing else this past week."

"You think it'll come to that? They'll kick you out?"

"I should add that the day after Landing Day wasn't, I had a visit from the cops."

"Jesus. What did they want?"

"I thought it better not to ask, especially as they didn't seem very sure themselves. They searched the house rather efficiently—I still haven't finished clearing up after them—but they didn't find whatever it was they thought I was hiding. Perhaps they believed I'd abducted the descent pod."

"And you hadn't?"

"I'll let you into a secret. All the time the cops were turning the place upside-down I stood by with a large hat on my head. They didn't think to ask me to take it off." De Ramaira winked, and Rick laughed. It was not a very good joke, but it was a welcome one.

"Dr. Florey?"

He turned, and Lena smiled at him. "I brought your wine?" She held out the tumbler.

"I'd better see what those two are up to," de Ramaira said, pushing up on the rail to look over the heads of the crowd toward the corner where Jon and Web sat together, blond head by black. Web was scribbling on Jon's piece of paper, seemingly oblivious of the party's noise. De Ramaira asked Lena, "Did they drive you off?"

She shrugged. "Sort of."

"Well, you look after Rick for me. I think he's had enough of their ideas as well."

As de Ramaira was received by the crowd, the girl, Lena, asked Rick, "Hey, you're not angry at anyone, are you?"

"Nobody in particular."

"Oh, they always talk an awful lot up here, as if talking solved anything."

She did not have Cath's fashionably brittle, angular beauty. But, framed by jet-black hair, her squarish face was animated by a mischievous intelligence. A wide, sexy mouth, small tilted nose. Gold-flecked hazel eyes that boldly returned his gaze.

"Do you come here a lot?" Rick asked. "Do you like it?"

"Sometimes." For a moment Rick was unsure which question she had answered, but she added, "Oh, Dr. de Ramaira is okay, but I do get to thinking that this is all put on for Jon. Part of his training."

"You like Jon?"

"Oh, we get on well enough. *Very* well, I guess? He's clever—or maybe you don't think so."

"I try not to sit in judgment on anyone."

She laughed. "He *is* clever, with two scholarships and everything. And he's fun to be with; we have a good time. But some of his friends . . . some of them are pretty strange."

Rick followed her gaze and saw two boys closely entwined, kissing each other slowly and deeply. He looked away and said, "You mean Web?"

"He's not really strange, just impatient with the world. I try to like him, but the way he goes at people! I mean, he's one of the cleverest people I know, but it's like his intellect has grown up and the rest of him hasn't. Oh, hey, I shouldn't be talking like this. I guess I drank too much."

"Web has the same effect on me, don't worry. The hell with him. Tell me, is your father still playing in the quartet?"

Lena smiled. "He's the leader. I thought you were a fan?"

"Since I graduated, it's been difficult to find the time to go to concerts. I guess I sort of lost touch."

"We're still playing, and we're easy enough to find."

"The concert hall in the park? You said *we*, right? You play in the quartet?"

"Second violin. Not that I'm ever going to earn a living

from it. That's why I'm at the University, studying hydroponics.''

They talked about music for a while, leaning companionably at the railing with their backs to the rest of the party.
Rick told Lena about how as an undergraduate he had played
keyboards at church services in the city to help support himself; how he would sometimes slip in a little Bach to relieve
the tedium of laying down the easy hymn chords.

"That old tyrant!" Lena exclaimed.

"You don't like Bach? The best of his stuff gives me the
feeling I get when I understand a mathematical derivation.
Like seeing a cathedral all at once. Bach and Mozart, and
some of the systems stuff . . .''

"Oh, there's nothing *wrong* with Bach," Lena said. "But
I've done his pieces so often now, and there's no room in it
for your own expression. He gets right down into your muscles and you have to let him, too, or you can't play it. A real
old tyrant.'' What she liked most were the lyricists of the
nineteenth and twentieth centuries. "Not critically acceptable, I know, but the *feeling* of a personal landscape in El-
gar's violin concerto. It beats the whole canon of the systems
bunch. Not that I'll ever get a chance to perform most of my
favorites, there just aren't enough musicians on the world to
form an orchestra.'' She gestured grandly toward the night
beyond the railing, the dark roofs which stepped away downhill and the patterned lights of the city beyond. Slim silver
bracelets on her wrist chimed against each other. "It's a
damned *small* world, isn't it?''

"When I came here from Mount Airy, I thought it would
take me a lifetime to explore Port of Plenty. Now I'm beginning to learn just how small it is.''

"You know what I think? We're all pretending it will go
away because otherwise we'd have to admit we really aren't
in control, that we really don't know anything compared to
what's out there in the universe.''

Rick turned from the railing, unsettled by her intensity. A
floodlight sprung from the trap of night. Across the roof
terrace, people were clapping in slow rhythm as a young

woman swayed with slow blissful deliberation, discarding layers of black gauze one by one.

He said, "I guess I ought to be getting back home. Come on, I'll go and say my farewells."

When they reached the table in the corner, de Ramaira said, "You're just in time to save me. These two take things so seriously it's not true."

Rick set his tumbler down and said, "I have to go now." No matter when I leave, he realized, there can be no grace. I do not fit here.

"So soon?" De Ramaira's chair scraped back as he stood. "Well, I'll show you the way down."

Lena shook back her heavy black hair. "Perhaps we'll see you around?"

"Maybe," Rick said.

Web crumbled the sheet of paper and threw it over his shoulder. It tipped the railing, spun out into darkness. "I might come see you. There are a few technical things I want to clear up." His voice held an edge of studied defiance, as if he felt that he was laying down a challenge.

Across the table, Jon frowned but said nothing.

"We're always there for consultation," Rick told Web, and turned to follow de Ramaira. The young woman had given up her striptease halfway through. Arms folded under her bare breasts, she leaned against the railing watching two boys slowly dance around each other, gesturing with stiff, abrupt movements like a couple of stoned lizards. Others formed a loose semicircle around them; handclaps staggered in a slow uncertain rhythm.

As he followed de Ramaira down the helical staircase, Rick said quietly, "Do you think you're playing games with those kids?"

"They aren't kids," de Ramaira said, no answer at all. "Mind the last step."

"Seriously, do you think Web was in earnest about trying to take over the relay station?"

"Do you?" de Ramaira countered. Then he laughed. "I can't tell. He's Jon's friend, not mine at all." As they went down the narrow hallway, he asked, "Would you report him to the cops?"

"That would be a dumb thing to do," Rick said uncomfortably.

"Indeed, Doctor. Here." The door opened on the dark street. "Have a safe walk home."

"Will you be back at work?"

De Ramaira smiled. "Perhaps tomorrow, perhaps not. Good-bye then, for now."

"Don't stay up too late hatching evil plots."

Rick started around the corner, but at the top of the street's steep descent he stopped, suddenly realizing why Lena had come over to talk to him. She'd been defending Jon all along, he thought, and I didn't see. He frowned (a sudden image of himself fallen at her feet amid the partygoers, sobbing an apology) and walked on down the hill.

It was gone midnight by the time Rick returned home, but as he rounded the spinney in the elbow of the path to the house, he saw that its half-sunken windows were all ablaze with light. Cath turned from the treacher as Rick came into the kitchen. Her eyes seemed smudged in her white, heart-shaped face. "I thought you were in for an all-night soul-searching affair. What happened?"

Rick pulled a chair from the table nook. "It was embarrassing, kind of," he said. The canvas went taut with his weight. "So I got away as soon as I decently could. How was your family?"

The panel of the treacher slid open. Her back to Rick, Cath said, "It didn't last long. We all agreed, for once." She set the cup on the table. "Here, I'll get another. How was it embarrassing?"

Rick watched as she carefully studded the code. Small domestic tasks weave us in, fill the chinks in the wall against the machinations of the outside world. He said, "Actually, you might have enjoyed it, the party at least. But de Ramaira had set me up to act as some sort of oracle to a couple of his students."

"Mm-hmm. I said that that man was only using you. He uses everyone—that's the way of Wombworlders, isn't it? I thought that's why your people came to Elysium, to get away from that."

Mount Airy. Strange to think the workshop was still there, three hundred kilometers to the east. The concrete floor black with oil and gritty with swarf, oiled steel sheets leaning against the wall beside racks of red bar-steel, the forge squatting like a fire-bellied toad beneath the inverted flare of its hood. Run by his brothers, now. After his parents and his sister had been killed, when their cushiontruck had been caught in a sudden rainstorm and swept a hundred meters down a sheer talus slope, Rick had turned from Mount Airy for the opportunities offered by the University. But that had not been so long ago that he did not still feel the pull of the familiar things there. He said nothing, however, watching Cath carry her own cup to the worn contour chair in front of the big window which with the night beyond it reflected the light of the kitchen like a black mirror.

As she sat, carefully smoothing the pleats of her formal white bodice, Cath asked, "Who were these students? What did they want?"

"De Ramaira has a protege now, you know."

"I thought that was you," Cath said demurely.

"Very funny. Anyway, the guy dumped the three popular theories about Landing Day on me—"

"Just three? I've heard a lot more than that."

"He said he had sampled and come up with the three most popular. All to do with some sort of mechanical failure, I might add. *Anyway*, it was pretty obvious that de Ramaira had asked me along to give my verdict on this poor kid's half-baked ideas."

"And of course you shot them all down."

"Well, I did explain about the probabilities." Best to keep Web's crazy idea about using the relay station to himself, Rick thought—nothing could come of it, anyway.

Cath smiled. "You can't be too popular with de Ramaira right now."

"I guess not." Rick sipped his coffee, then said, "Listen, you didn't have an argument with your family, did you? You don't seem very eager to tell me about it."

"Not an argument," Cath said. "But what they had to say makes things difficult for me."

"Oh?" Something was settling heavily inside him, some final weight.

"You see, my father gets to know certain things because he is on the public committee. And if it's something that might affect the family he feels he has to let us know. That's why we had the conference tonight."

"It's bad?"

"I don't know. It depends what's behind it." She looked down and said, "The City Board has informed the public committee that anticity feeling might be stirred up at the All Colony Council, and that Arcadia might suffer if it continues to bring in produce. Which it will, of course. It can't afford not to. Daddy thinks some of the settlements are planning something. Something bad." When she looked up, the unforgiving tightness Rick knew so well was crimping her mouth, sign of the remoteness that even at the height of their lovemaking could hold her quite still, abstracted from anything Rick might be doing.

"Is that what you think?"

"It's not a question of that, Rick. I can't shake my obligations. My family wants me to go home awhile."

"So how long . . . God, isn't this pretty ridiculous?"

"No! Damn it, Rick, don't think that!" For a moment he was afraid that he had touched off her temper, but she added calmly, "Look, I have a feeling that if you don't do something positive this time it just won't turn out right by itself. And I'm not going to wait around for something to happen. By then it'll be too late. Daddy and the Greats are all agreed for once, it's the sensible thing to do."

The Greats were the stored personality matrices of Cath's great-great-grandfather and great-grandparents; Rick knew better than to argue against them. Cath took the advice of her ancestors as seriously as anyone in the city.

Cath added, "Maybe you ought to consider going home as well, if there really is going to be trouble. It might not be easy for noncitizens here, if there is."

"I can't do that. There's nothing for me there, and I have my *work* here." He couldn't explain that to leave Port of Plenty would be to betray the trust he felt the city had shown him when he had been offered tenure at the University. "I can't understand why we've become frightened so easily. You see, nothing has really happened, but people are acting as if a war has been fought and lost these past five days. Now this—what are you running from? Why does everything have to change just because one lousy load of settlers hasn't turned up on time?"

"You could call it a contingency plan," Cath said. "Anyway, surely it's sensible to follow the advice of the City Board—they own most of the computing power after all. If Constat's run up a red projection about the All Colony Council, I prefer to believe it. And if the settlements act against the city, they'll act against Arcadia too, because it's not possible Arcadia will side with them."

"And you think I should do the same thing."

"It's just a suggestion, Rick."

"Of course. But when are you leaving?"

"I'll catch the noon coach tomorrow. It should be nothing more than a long weekend."

"You gave the impression you'd be gone longer than that."

"Well, I thought I'd prepare you for the worst. If I go early, perhaps I can come back early too. Maybe at the end of the All Colony Council. If there's no trouble they won't have much to discuss, with no new technology to fix prices on and no new settlers to locate. Anyway, it's time I had a holiday." Abruptly, she drank the rest of her coffee and got up from the big chair to give her cup to the treacher.

Rick lifted his own cup to his lips, but the coffee was cold now. Everything he could possibly say snagged around the fear that he might be wrong, that he should also flee. Yet he truly felt that there was nothing he could do but stay. Nowhere else would support his research, and there was nothing else he wanted to do. Grimacing, he completed the motion, and drained the bitter cup.

7. The Shepherd

The news about Landing Day and the missing colonyboat washed like a tidal wave through the settlements of the peninsula, rumors colliding and rebounding in its wake. The news reached even the wandering dingos. Miguel Lucas heard about it from a shepherd, a few days after he had escaped from Lake Fonda.

Miguel had followed the river away from the settlement until it had bent to the west; then he had crossed it and continued northward, paralleling the distant, misty line of the Hampshire Hills. The grassland was less open there, patched with expanses of thornbush. Feather-branched trees clumped around small scummy washes, often no more than centimeters deep, but water enough. Animal life abounded. Miguel saw solitary slope-shouldered antelope, herds of Muir oxen, mire boars. Parabirds roosted noisily around the shallow washes. Once, he had to make a long diversion around a packrat colony; the little creatures could strip a man to his bones in minutes, faster than his flesh could poison them. There were rabbit colonies, too. Miguel caught half a dozen at a time in his snares, eating all he could and drying the rest.

And of course there was a proliferating maze of abo paths, changed since the last time Miguel had passed this way. The abos continually reshaped the lines they laid on the land. Twice, Miguel passed by an abo village. The sites of these never changed, constant nodes in the everchanging web of paths. Gripped by his newfound curiosity, Miguel assiduously recorded all he saw, carefully mapped the villages and the paths around them into the compsim's memory while the communal buzz of their inhabitants rose toward the indigo sky. A lulling hypnotic sound into which it seemed, senses blown open by snakeroot, he could fade entirely. Coming down, returning to his own merely human senses and thoughts, left him chastened and cheerless.

After the second village, Miguel increased his pace. He was near the pass which led through the Hampshire Hills to Port of Plenty, and he could almost feel the weight of all those people tugging at him, a storm grumbling below the horizon. He aimed to turn west after crossing the road to the pass, and head for the end of the peninsula. The people of the established settlements thought that they knew it all, when most of them hardly stirred beyond the sterilized borders of their fields; but the newer settlements in the west, like little islands scattered in the vast unknown wilderness, welcomed any chance visitor, even a dingo. Miguel hadn't been down there for a handful of years now, having spent much of that time following a rumor that a bunch of people had successfully crossed the Trackless Mountains. So they had, but the city cops had hunted down their illegal farms, sent them all to the mines at Cooper's Hill.

Miguel didn't like to be around people if he could help it, but he still needed them occasionally. The wilderness couldn't provide everything a man needed. Miguel had gone dingo, but he wasn't crazy. That kind never lasted long, in-country. So he pushed himself hard, sleeping in the hottest part of the day in whatever shade he could find, walking in the comparative cool of the night by the light of the big moon.

It was waning now, but would give enough light for a dozen nights' worth of walking yet.

He crossed the road to the city, really no more than a dusty unpaved track worn in the grassland, without incident, and something relaxed in him. He was still frightened that the cops were hunting him, and he had still to pass the penal mines—no other way through the hills which rose and fell and rose again in ever more precipitous crags until they were cut off by the ocean in the north. But unless someone took it into their head to escape at the moment Miguel was passing the mines, he'd have no trouble. The guards looked in, not out.

With no sign of pursuit, and Anders Pass safely behind him, Miguel slowed his pace a little, spent more time resting up in shade when the huge soft disk of the sun dominated the dark sky, fiddling with the compsim (the heft of the little machine, the ordered aisles of its memory floating in his vision, were somehow comforting), or simply dozing, lulled by the drone of the insects in the dry grass.

So it was that he was asleep, leaning against the smooth trunk of a bottletree at the edge of a muddy pool, when the shepherd came across him.

Miguel came awake the instant the shadow fell across his face, his pulse thudding like a startled rabbit on the run. He looked up at the man's dusty jeans, faded workshirt.

"Good day to you," the stranger said amiably, after a moment. "Sorry if I gave you a start. You all alone here?" He was a grizzled sunburnt man in his forties, shrewd blue eyes netted in fine wrinkles, hair brushed back from a lined forehead. He had taken off his hat and was fanning himself with it as he looked down at Miguel. Behind him, his horse nosed at dusty clumps of grass.

Miguel said nothing, measuring the distance between the man and his horse—and the rifle in the sheath behind the saddle—and wished that he hadn't lost both handguns.

The man said, "Thought I'd scout ahead, see if I could find some water. The sheep will be needing it. Fucking un-seasonable weather, right?"

A shepherd then, driving his flock from the summer pasturage in the hills to be slaughtered at some settlement or other. New Haven or Fortitude, Miguel guessed. "Too hot," he said.

"Too right. My dogs are tripping over their tongues. Should be along in a few minutes or so. A thousand head for Fortitude. Where you heading? No offense if you don't want to say. I know how it is."

"Glad you do."

The shepherd nodded. "If you're heading up into the hills, watch out. There's a rogue sabertooth about, by all accounts. Mate of mine told me he lost near on two dozen head to it, killing for the hell of it."

Miguel thanked the man, Jimmy Warren by name, shared a cigarette with him to be companionable. "I guess maybe you haven't heard the latest out of Port of Plenty," the shepherd said at last. He ground the stub of his cigarette on the heel of his tooled leather boot. "About Landing Day?"

Miguel shrugged.

"Seems the ship they were expecting hasn't turned up. When I was coming down around the bend in the estuary I was able to pick up some news broadcast that mentioned it. Knocked them all for a loop as you might expect. You didn't hear anything?"

Miguel was thinking about the suicide note left in the compsim. What the separatist, Bobby Richter, had said, back at Lake Fonda, was true then. That it was important for all the settlers. But not, perhaps, for him. He needed people, on occasion, but he didn't need to share their lives.

Jimmy Warren guessed that Miguel's silence was to be taken for indifference. "Suppose it doesn't make much difference to a freewheeling bloke like you. Wonder what my people will think of it, though." Then he gestured off at the horizon. "Here they come now. Said it wouldn't be long."

First a dust cloud, waving plumes of red against the dark sky; then the thousand-headed flock moving beneath it; then the first animals, shaggy coats dreadlocked and gritty, iridescent insects clustering around their yellow horizontally slit eyes, ambling this way and that but mostly moving toward the shallow lake.

Four honey and tan German Shepherds loped either side of the flock. When they had corralled all the sheep around the pool, one of the dogs came over to the men and growled, "No 'rouble, Boss. You fin' a frien'?"

Warren introduced Miguel, and the dog sniffed at Miguel's knees while the dingo nervously sat still. When it was satisfied, the dog loped off to tell its companions.

Warren built a campfire, hung a blackened kettle over it and brewed strong, bitter coffee, gave a cup to Miguel. The dingo savored it, only half-listening as the shepherd talked about the weather and how the heat had dried out even the high pasturage, the possible effect the news of the missing colonyboat might have on wool prices. Miguel nodded now and then but said little. He didn't resent the intrusion exactly, but he had no reserves of small talk to draw on.

Warren went off to hunt for the dogs' dinner, and soon returned with a rockjack slung over his shoulder. Miguel helped him to gut and quarter it. After he had fed the dogs, Warren boiled rice and dried meat in the kettle, and the two men ate silently but companionably as the sun dissolved in shimmering red lines above the western hills and insects shrilly stridulated in the grass all around.

"You're the guy who likes the abos, aren't you?" the shepherd said, after a while. When Miguel said nothing, the man continued, "I remember you the last time you came through Fortitude, five, six years ago? Maybe you remember my mother, she was the doctor back then, had a look at your herbs and stuff? Dead now. Cancer." Warren lit two cigarettes and handed one to Miguel. "I love this goddamn world," he said, blowing out a riffle of smoke. "Don't reckon I'll miss anything of Earth, if we're truly left on our own now. I guess if the separatists get their way maybe I'll get the chance to see what's beyond the Trackless Mountains. You ever been that way? Man like you must have been all over, I reckon. Me, though, I'd want a family along. There's a woman I wouldn't mind making a go of it with, back in

Fortitude. I think she'd like to make a go of it too, you know. Me and her, the dogs, a few hundred head . . . that'd be okay, I'd say. Earth, now. No, I can't say I'd miss it." He drew on his cigarette, flicked the butt toward the trampled margin of the pool. "Hope you don't mind me rambling on. Been in-country too long, I guess."

The next morning, dew heavy on his silvery thermoblanket when he awoke, Miguel took his leave without awakening the shepherd. A couple of the dogs who sprawled around the ashes of last night's fire watched him go, but didn't say a word.

By dawn he was a kilometer away, following the trail left by the sheep back into the hills.

Two days later, he was in sight of Port of Plenty.

He had reached the beginning of the forest which cloaked the hills as they saddled away to the west. Early evening, the sky still indigo yet deeper, becoming translucent, the first stars pricking through. All around, tree trunks soared upward, spirals of feathery branches twisting tightly around them. Rocks spattered with lichens and stoneworts broke the forest duff like the backs of surfacing sea creatures.

Miguel stood at the edge of a sheer cliff that rose above the broad loops of a river. On the far shore, misty salt marshes stretched to their level horizon. And beyond the final bend of the river's course, where it widened into an estuary, was a glittering web on the eastern shore, as small in the distance as his thumbnail: Port of Plenty.

Miguel spat over the edge of the cliff and turned and went on among the aisles of the trees, following the ridge. Too dark to try to cross the valley to the next rise now, Miguel reasoned (remembering Warren's talk of a rogue sabertooth), but he wanted to put some distance between the city and his back.

After about twenty minutes he passed a latticework metal tower, rooted in a concrete base, that rose higher than the trees. A red light flashed at its tip. Twenty minutes more and it was too dark to walk; the waning moon wouldn't be up for a couple of hours yet. Miguel risked a small fire, more out of habit than necessity, and set a can of water in it to boil. Then he lay back and took out the compsim and ran through the files he'd made on the abos, strings of words scrolling up his vision, blotting out all the night except for the flicker of the fire. Botched words that had failed to capture the feeling he had had under the drug, the feeling the abos' singing gave him, of a truth, a great truth, just beyond his grasp.

He came out of the files to sprinkle seeds into the seething water in the can, skimmed off the scum when the brew had boiled up, and set the can to one side to cool a little.

Rather than review his poor efforts, he called up the suicide's extensive array. He still hadn't explored all of it, but by now the names and shorthanded intrigues were familiar territory. As he read in them, as in a novel, it came to seem that there was a presence behind the words, as if someone was standing at his back; he actually looked around, saw nothing but trees receding in the dusk beyond the words projected on his sight by the compsim.

But out of some other darkness a voice spoke, a warm baritone, startlingly intimate.

—Do not be afraid, Miguel. I mean you no harm. I will help you, if I can.

"Who are *you*? How do you know my name?"

The text of the dead man's files wavered as if blown by a wind, faded from Miguel's sight. For a moment he could see nothing but velvety darkness. Then a skeletal geometrical shape rushed at him, blue lines blindingly brilliant. At the same moment a tingling paralysis spread up his arms. Miguel jerked against it and knocked the can into the fire. The brew sputtered on the hot stones of the crude hearth, and the acrid stench of burning herbs brought him to himself. He spread his stiff fingers and managed to let go of the compsim.

The ordinary night, stars spread beyond the reaching spires of the trees. Water spitting into steam in the fire. Something was shrieking down in the deep valley.

And there, far off through the trees, the winking red light of the relay tower.

That must be it, Miguel thought. Somehow he had interrupted traffic between the city and the mines at Cooper's Hill. He picked up a twig and used it to switch off the compsim. And then panic rushed through him. In a kind of frantic fever he stamped out those embers the brew hadn't drowned, bundled together his possessions. He almost left the compsim lying there, but on impulse picked it up, holding it with only the very tips of his fingers, and packed it away.

Then he started off through the dark forest, following the ridge north and west. No time to rest this night. It was possible whoever or whatever he had disturbed had managed to get a fix on him. It was possible that he was being hunted again.

8. Of the Fall

The next morning, Rick went down to the University as usual, although it felt strange to be following his accustomed route among trees and discretely placed houses while back at the house Cath was packing so that she would be able to catch the noon coach to Arcadia. His unease grew during the lectures he had to audit. All three were for first-semester courses, large and impersonal, but while he waited to take questions after the recorded expert had finished playing on the big tri-vee stage, Rick saw that many more students were missing than usual. Not only Cath was worried, it seemed.

Rick hurried back to the house after the last lecture. He and Cath had an early lunch, sitting companionably at the scrubbed wooden table in the kitchen. The picture window was filled edge to edge with pale sunlight and the patchwork colors of the surrounding trees, all turning now. Cath had opened a bottle of white wine; they clinked glasses in an unspoken toast. As he loaded the treacher with used tableware, Rick asked, "Have you settled all you need to?"

"Nothing much to settle. Think of it as a holiday, Rick, and don't be so serious."

"You were serious enough, last night."

Cath changed the subject. "I caught the morning newscast. The All Colony Council has opened session."

Rick turned from the treacher. "Anything happened?"

"Not exactly. A few settlements haven't sent representatives, if that means anything."

"It depends who they are. The Collectivists?"

"No, they've arrived. Bird-in-Hand, I think. Oh, and New Covenant. At least most of them are talking."

"So nothing will happen after all," he said.

Cath's face was composed, closed up. "We'll just have to see, I suppose. I should go now."

She didn't look back as they started down the hill in the hot, dry sunlight, and that reassured Rick: she knew that she would be coming back. They walked through the campus and parted company on the path beside the Department of Architecture building.

"I'll phone tomorrow," Cath said, hefting her grip. "But probably I won't know any more than I do now."

A couple of students, bearded boys, glanced at her as they passed, and with sudden detachment, something to do with the unaccustomed lunchtime wine perhaps, Rick saw Cath as they must. An elegant slim woman, her yellow silk dress with its flared collar token of her wealth and style. Obviously, she was not for them. She was on her way to somewhere else, on her way up.

He said, "Take care. Have a good journey."

"*You* take care too," she said, and stepped forward and brushed his cheek with her lips. If she had asked him, he would have gone with her there and then. But she shouldered her grip and started down the path, and he went on to the Engineering building, to his work.

All afternoon Rick had charge of a practical class in multiphasic circuitry, and so there was little time to brood. When the last discussion had broken up and the equipment had been cleared away, he went down to the common room. Most of the staff had already left, but when Rick turned from the vendor, a paper cup of milky tea burning his fingers, Professor Collins came toward him.

"I thought I'd convey a little advance news about next budget," the professor told Rick.

"Something's wrong?"

Professor Collins inclined his stately head. "There is to be a certain amount of revision regarding support of students from the settlements. Previously, of course, the Board has sponsored the education of citizens and settlers alike."

"Sure. Me, for instance."

Professor Collins said, "It seems that this may no longer be the case. The Board wishes us to become less dependent on external funding. Settlement students may have to pay their own way, and we must make some rationalizations. Probably the teaching load will be increased."

"I don't mind auditing extra lectures, if that's what it's about."

"There may also be cutbacks in practical programs. I mention this because the application you put forward requires a hefty capital expenditure."

"Well, if I get it through, the data from the high-altitude experiments will keep me occupied for half a dozen years at least. I won't be thinking of more tests until then. I hope that was clear in the application."

"You haven't heard about your, um, balloon, yet, have you?"

"It should come through any day."

"Of course. I'm sorry it's out of my hands, but I'll do my best to chase it up if you haven't heard, let us say, by the end of the All Colony Council. But do bear in mind what I've said when you're planning further experiments. It will be easier to get the applications through all the administrative nonsense."

It was the nearest thing to a warning that Rick had ever been given. But he did not feel chastened. Rather, he felt that, once again, he had escaped.

Strangely, Rick slept soundly that night, but with morning came a return of the sense of loss he had numbed the evening before with hour after hour of watching trivia. As if Cath's absence had invoked haunting echoes in the sunlit rooms.

Although it was Saturday, he had a lecture to audit. The walk to the campus revived him. A fresh breeze was blowing through the trees, autumn wakening widening circles of restless rustle, a sense of expectancy as if the hill were a thousand-masted ship about to set sail.

The lecture was in the Department of Agriculture, to second-year biotechnicians. Afterward, mindful of Professor Collins's warning, Rick decided to begin a revision of his research plans. He would keep to this path no matter how it turned.

As he approached the entrance to Engineering, a stream of students began to emerge into the fresh sunlight. With a small shock of recognition Rick saw Lena among them, and then she saw him and called, "Dr. Florey, right? Do you believe this?"

"How are you?"

"Glad the weekend's started. I've just spent two hours being told about the plumbing of the hydroponic station." Her smile was as Rick remembered, a brief thrilling flash that wholly transformed her face. Under a scuffed black leather jacket was the same creamy asymmetric blouse that she had worn to de Ramaira's party. A black skirt clung to her thighs and then flared out in a swirl of ragged ends.

"I've just been auditing a telemetry lecture over in Agriculture, so I know what you mean." They had stepped off the path onto the level lawn that stretched to the half-sunken facade of the Department of Photonics building. Overhead, gauzy figures of cloud lapped half the indigo sky.

Lena asked, "By the way, did Jon catch you?"

"Now, I thought it was Web who wanted the technical advice."

"Jon meant to see you before he went."

"Where has he gone?"

"Back home for a while." Lena was no longer smiling. "In case something happens to the settlement people staying here."

"Yeah, the guy I'm sharing a house with has gone back to Arcadia for a while, too." The lie concealing Cath surprised him. He added, "I'm from Mount Airy, you know, but I'm still here."

Lena brushed back one wing of black hair, the sleeve of her jacket falling back to reveal the dozen silver bracelets at her wrist. "I suppose things will sort themselves out," she said.

"Right," Rick said. "That's what we all hope. Maybe I'll see you again?" And that surprised him too, though he had been wanting to say it.

"I'm not hard to find," Lena said as she turned to go. "You take care now. Don't let the vigilantes find out you're from Mount Airy."

"I'm not ashamed of it," Rick called after her, and went on through the empty foyer of Engineering. The encounter had pleasantly excited him, buoying him toward anticipation of Cath's promised phone call.

The flag was up on his office terminal. Rick read the short, formal message, then sat down and read it again. His application had been accepted. Strange to think it had been working toward him through all the upheaval, a reaffirmation of the essential solidity of the world. It came to him that Professor Collins had known about this all along, that the warning yesterday had been meant to temper the flush of success. All right. He wouldn't go up to the roof and shout about it. He would be careful, just as everyone seemed to be advising him these days.

For the next hour, Rick immersed himself in figures and charts, refamiliarizing himself with details of technique that had grown hazy in the fallow weeks since he had sent in the application. The experiments involved injection of sodium ions into the high reaches of the atmosphere to create artificial auroras whose size and decay characteristics would supply clues to the behavior of the ionosphere. Not an original idea, but it was only a means to an end. His real interest was the deep question of what caused Elysium's climate to oscillate between its present Earthlike state and that of an Arrhenian swamp, hot and dripping wet, just as Earth oscillated between temperate and glacial episodes. The deepest question of all, of course, was whether Elysium really had such a thing as a climate, with its implication of occasional deviations from a normal state caused by an external force— changes in Tau Ceti's behavior, for instance. As an alternative, Rick believed that variations in conditions on Elysium could be the summation of chaotic oscillations in the nonlinear dynamics of its weather systems, more or less independent of external input. To find if that was true, it was necessary to know how often the world tipped from hot and wet to cool and dry—Rick had first met David de Ramaira when he had the idea of trying to measure those cycles from sudden transitions in the fossil record. That hadn't panned out: so little was known about Elysium's palaeontological history that only the most recent transition could be dated with any accuracy. Now Rick was approaching the problem at an angle, by looking in the ionosphere for chaotic behavior independent of Tau Ceti's activity. The artificial auroras were the probes for that behavior.

Rick had just glanced at his timetab—ten minutes before noonbreak—when someone rapped on the door, a single authoritarian stroke that rattled the pane of frosted glass. As Rick unplugged from his compsim the door opened, and the tall cop said, "Dr. Florey? Mr. Savory asked for you to be picked up. A little matter of identification."

Rick rose behind his desk. "Who am I supposed to identify?" Images shuffled through his head: the dingo, de Ramaira, Jon.

"If we knew that, I guess we wouldn't have to ask you, Dr. Florey," the cop said. His white coveralls seemed to fill the narrow space between the desk and the door, eclipsing the hard copies of diurnal interference patterns tacked to the wooden partition.

"Is this to do with the job I did for you people a while back?" Rick's mind was still turning toward the interruption from the complex, beguiling calculations of particle stripping, charge transference, spread F.

"I wouldn't know about that," the cop said impatiently. "I'm just here to collect you. Let's go, huh?"

At the junction with the main road at the edge of the campus, the police cruiser turned away from the city and picked up speed. A convoy of cushiontrucks heading toward Arcadia loomed into view as the cruiser topped a rise and the cop switched on the siren and accelerated past. Now there was forest on either side of the road.

When Rick asked where they were going, the cop said, "To the airfield, Doctor."

"What for?"

"If you want my guess, you'll be going on to some place else."

Half a kilometer from the east fence, the cruiser slowed and swung down a minor road, running beneath a close canopy in a rush of sunlight and shadows. Bright insects flicked from its path. Then the open glare of the airfield's level sweep of concrete, the orange dome of a hangar rising against the rough line of the surrounding forest. A helicopter was framed in the gape of the hangar's clamshell doors.

The cruiser accelerated toward the hangar, stopping with a neat half-turn, like a flourish, in its shadow. The cop got out and went around to open the passenger door. This unexpected courtesy revived Rick's hopes. It would seem that he was needed, not merely wanted. As he scrambled out, the helicopter's rotors began to revolve above the bubble of its cabin. A mechanic glanced incuriously at Rick as she went past.

There was a wooden hut just inside the hangar and Savory stepped out of this and walked toward Rick, his smile in place like a mask. "I'm glad you could come," he said, and clasped Rick's hand in a moist, unwelcome grip.

"I can't claim any credit for that." Rick's anger was built on Savory's presumption.

The politician looked up at Rick, blond hair brushing the severe collar of his jacket. "I apologize for taking up your time," he said, "but in the opinion of the Board the man you saw in the Outback has become a matter of security." He smiled. "Actually, I presented the case with that bias. At any rate he has been spotted again. Or let us say that *someone* has been spotted, out near the mines at Cooper's Hill. That's why we need your help. I'm hoping for a quick, positive identification."

"You've caught him?" The noise of the helicopter had settled to a blurring roar. Rick had to repeat his question before Savory understood.

"Let us say that the matter is in hand." Savory reached inside his jacket and pulled out a sheet of yellow paper. "As this is a security matter, and because these are troubled times, protocol requires you to sign this. Congratulations, by the way. Most noncitizen irregulars from the University will make third lieutenant at most. You've gotten a first."

Savory spread the paper on the roof of the cruiser. It was a printed form of the kind used for legally binding contracts in a tradition that predated the arrival of Constat, filled in completely except for the last box. The spare details of Rick's life. Fixed. The form fluttered against the white-painted metal like something alive, a condemnation, a trap. To sign it would be to seal himself to the city, and he was reluctant to take that final step. So far, things had flowed without the need for decision.

Rick said, "Do I have to accept this?"

Savory squinted past the cruiser and the helicopter. The forest margin rippled beyond glaring concrete. "You would have to come along in any case, but afterward I'm afraid that you would have to be interned. This is a time of emergency, and the mobilization bill will conscript—in name only at the present—every able-bodied citizen. The forms will go out Monday. You have been called up a little prematurely, to help me out." He smoothed the fluttering yellow paper. "You needn't worry. No one will be called to do anything unless the city is attacked. Until then, everyone will be on standby."

"Who do you expect will attack the city?"

"Oh, there have always been those outside the city who have looked upon us with envy, I'm sure you know that, Dr.

Florey." Savory glanced obliquely at Rick, then at the paper. "Have you a pen . . . ? Of course you have."

Rick slashed his signature in the empty box, with no feeling for the commitment.

Savory folded the form and said, "Now we had best board the helicopter, Lieutenant." This invocation of Rick's spurious new rank seemed to enlarge the gulf between the present and his childhood, a gulf as great as the distances between stars. His sister and his parents like specks of mica fixed in formless black. His dour taciturn brothers fixed too, locked into their inheritance, the grim clangorous forge from which he alone had escaped.

As they ducked under the helicopter's rotors, Savory said, "It's only a short hop. Have you flown before?"

"No," Rick confessed.

"I hope you aren't prone to motion sickness. I would keep interested in the landscape. There you go. In back."

The cabin was thick with the smell of oil and warm plastic. As Rick assembled the seatbelt around his shoulders and lap, the pilot touched a switch, pushed the stick forward. Rick's guts seemed to settle centimeters down, nervous inertia, as the helicopter lifted vertically and began to drift across the concrete apron. And then it was rising, its blunt nose tilted down, rising above the perimeter fence, above the trees. As Savory had suggested, Rick attended to the view.

The patterned wedge of the city was below, densely packed flat roofs hatched by a grid of streets. The hills of the old quarter, the cluttered industrial section. The long lines of the pontoon docks unraveled and then the helicopter was over the sluggish headwaters of the estuary, swinging toward the salt marshes.

Rick leaned close to the vibrating plastic of the bubble canopy. Far below, the marsh was a braided pattern, silver threads of water channels meandering among green tear-shaped islands whose tails all pointed in the same direction. No one had ever bothered to chart the shifting courses of the myriad streams and creeks; their teeming life was undisturbed by the city on the far side of the estuary. An entire ecosystem down there: huge flesh-eating amphibians which sometimes appeared in the docks; plants which spread their seeds by exploding pockets of hydrogen; lemurs that scuttled about towering hollow-stemmed tree-ferns; parabirds with huge flattened feet which (it was said) enabled them to run over water; a thousand other ignored wonders.

The helicopter beat through the air a hundred meters above the tallest tree-ferns. It crossed the muddy ribbon of the main river channel and skimmed between tall slopes dense with serried ranks of trees whose soaring trunks bore only sparse helices of green, a valley steeper and less kind than those of Rick's childhood.

Savory twisted in his seat and pointed across the pilot's shoulders at the columns of dark smoke which rose above the valley's ridge. The helicopter lurched and the chatter of its rotors complainingly rose in pitch. For a bright instant, the unease which had settled in the pit of Rick's stomach threatened to explode into panic.

But the helicopter was rising vertically, tree-clad slopes falling away on either side and other valleys, misty lines running roughly east-west, appearing beyond. The helicopter swept above the tumbled rocks of the ridge and there were the prison mines, a grimy tangle of huts and casting sheds, settling beds, the smoking cones of the smelters. It all swung past, blurred by rising fumes, as the helicopter turned to avoid the fierce updrafts. Rick glimpsed the terraced gouges of open-cast pits, wounds red as blood in the land. The dense forest beyond was scored by the tracks along which ground-effect barges carried ore to the estuary. Slowly beating down the air, the helicopter circled back, dropping between high loading banks and a row of long huts near the perimeter, touching down as light as a feather on compacted cinders.

The rotors slowed, settled to a spaced ticking, stopped. A barge, its cabin dwarfed by the huge rusty hopper behind, settled in a cloud of dust beneath the raked conveyer belts of the loading banks. As the whine of its compressors died, Rick could make out the asynchronous pounding of crushing engines somewhere behind the line of huts on the other side

of the compound. A man, dirty coveralls unfastened down
his matted chest, was walking through drifting dust toward
the helicopter.

"There's our man, Dr. Florey," Savory said, and swung
up the oval hatch. The volume of machine noise immediately
doubled. The air which gusted into the cabin was surpris-
ingly cool, but held a bitter taste. Crushed metal flakes. Ash.
Rick followed Savory across the compound, his legs both
stiff and too responsive.

The heavily muscled miner blinked at Rick, rubbed his
unshaven jaw with the back of his hand. His blond hair was
streaked with dust. Rick returned the stare with nervous distaste. His years at the University had given him a touch of
the contempt that citizens felt toward those who must wrest
their living from the soil, settlers and miners alike. He saw
his life as a growth from dank nature to electric light.

The miner asked Savory, "That him?" He looked Rick
up and down and added, "Those clothes won't last five minutes in the forest."

"Dr. Florey only needs to be in at the kill, as it were,"
Savory said. "You've arranged transport?"

"I'll take you myself. You're cutting it fine though. The
cops are already closing in."

As the miner led them around the line of huts, Savory said
to Rick, "Catlan here saw your man."

The miner glanced back and said, "I only had a clear sight
for a second, should have shot him then. All this fuss with
your search party is stirring up the prisoners." He told Rick,
"Saw him maybe a klick west of the camp, no doubt that he
came out of the pass. I was out on patrol with a couple of
others, leading point."

"Someone has escaped from the mine?" Rick asked.

"Hell no," Catlan said emphatically. "But we don't only
look for prisoners who've got out. There are those who want
to get in to get them out, if you see what I mean. Besides,
there's been trouble with sabertooths recently, one even managed to climb the fucking perimeter wire. Anyway, we'd been
out and were dragging on back when I saw him. I was com-

ing around a bluff over the river and this guy was on the other side, up where there'd been a big fire this summer. It's all charred stumps and the new seedlings are just knee-high, so I couldn't miss him. I guess he saw me because he was up the slope and into the brush in a moment, but I could have potted him easy.''

"I'm glad you didn't," Savory remarked. "Tell me why your party didn't attempt to follow."

Catlan frowned. "Like I told you, we'd have had to cross the river and it's not much better than the marshes down there, amphibians and who the fuck knows what else. Sure, we had guns, but we lost two people in that shit not a year ago and they had guns too." He grimaced. "Goddamn second-generation settlers, think they've a dee-vine pact with the ecology. Sabertooths got 'em. We found the nest, the two guys dead and puffed up with reaction to the stuff that was supposed to paralyze them, sabertooth larvae in their wounds. Some of those were still alive." Catlan glanced at Rick. "So I let the guy run, wasn't until later that we knew that Constat had put an alert out. Someone interfering with communications."

"And why do you think he was heading west?" Savory asked.

"Look," Catlan said, "I explained that the last time."

"Of course. But go over it again for Dr. Florey."

"I'll talk myself hoarse if you want," Catlan said with a measure of exasperation, "and meantime the guy could get away."

"Don't mind me," Rick added. With growing unease he felt that Savory was weaving a web around Catlan and himself.

They turned the corner and started down a shadowy passage between the block of huts and a long windowless building which shuddered with the noise of internal machinery. Over the din, Savory said, "He will find it hard to slip through the net, I think, with Constat directing it. Go on."

Catlan said, "When Constat first got a fix on this guy he

was near the relay tower the other side of the pass. Now he's this side. He must be heading toward the west coast settlements. What other direction could he be taking?'' As they walked out of the passage onto a rutted road, Catlan squinted in dusty sunlight at Savory, at Rick. ''What's with all these questions? Don't you think I told you right the first time?''

But Savory was looking at the half dozen battered jeeps parked on the shoulder of the road. He said, ''Is that the only transport?''

Catlan smiled. ''Your cops took everything else, Mr. Savory. You'll just have to make do.''

Catlan drove them through the camp, the jeep's skirt blowing out a cloud of red dust. Rick, sitting between Catlan and Savory, watched guards shepherd a long line of prisoners, and realized with a vertiginous shock that the shambling men and women (and a few children too, all in filthy denim coveralls) were shackled by one ankle to a common chain that dragged snakelike through the dust. Prisoners. And he and Catlan were caught, too, in Savory's obscure plans.

Catlan saw Rick looking at the line of prisoners and said, ''They'll be the work crew coming back from fixing up the fence. We don't keep them chained inside the perimeter.''

''They have implants,'' Savory said, ''that twist up their nerves if they get out of range of the prison transmitter. The implants have to be switched off when they go outside; that is why they are chained, Dr. Florey. Although, in a way, it would make sense if they were chained all the time. *Pour encourager les autres.*''

''Isn't this place punishment enough?'' Rick asked. He was wondering how many of the prisoners were families who had tried to escape the city's jurisdiction. Here for life, now.

''Some of the countries on Earth, I understand, brainwipe the worst of the criminals, run the bodies by computer remote control. I've always thought it would be a useful deterrent to keep in reserve.''

''*You* wouldn't have to work with a bunch of zombies,'' Catlan said.

"Oh, I understand they make excellent servants," Savory said, with monstrous cheerfulness.

The jeep skirted the edge of the vast quarries, paused while the gate in the double wire fence was opened, then plunged into the forest, following a track that twisted among towering trees as it climbed toward the top of the ridge. Savory interfaced with his compsim, then said, "No luck yet. But the noose is closing."

The jeep roared over the crest of the ridge and Rick glimpsed again the vista of parallel lines of hills running into misty infinity. Then the jeep plunged down the track, a steep descent among limestone bluffs and trees which clutched at thin soil with huge snaking roots. Streams sprang from clefts in the bluffs. The undergrowth grew thicker, tangled thickets like spun green cotton candy that could conceal anything. The trail bottomed out, on one side a broken cliff of stained limestone, on the other dense scrub falling away to beds of giant reeds and a spreading expanse of scummy water between mudbanks which shone like satin in the slanting sunlight. The jeep coasted into a kind of meadow of clumpy grass and thornbush where a dozen other vehicles were parked. More jeeps, overlanders, even a police cruiser, its sleek lines out of place in the wilderness.

Rick sat with Catlan in the jeep while Savory conferred with one of the cops. He walked back and told them, "We're just waiting for the helicopter. There's some problem with reception—all the iron ore in these hills, apparently. The helicopter will stay overhead and act as a relay to keep us in touch with Constat."

Catlan spat onto the grass and said, "I sure hope all your technology works out here."

"You had better hope so," Savory said, "considering that you let our man go in the first place." Then he smiled and told Rick, "I've about fifty people on the ground, deployed in a rough circle about half a klick across, not to mention half a dozen flitters dodging about under the canopy. And the helicopter, of course." He paused, then looked up. "And here it comes now."

The helicopter dipped low over the river, then rose steeply, skimming treetops and vanishing over the ridge on the other side. Savory touched the compsim hung at his belt and nodded. "We're working," he said, and called to the cops.

Reluctantly, Rick stepped over the jeep's deflated skirt, stumbling on the uneven tussocky ground. Catlan, lifting a snub-barreled hunting rifle from the sheath beside the driver's seat, looked around and said, "Shit, man, you can't hike with those goddamn shoes. Here—" tossing over a pair of heavy soled boots—"use these."

Rick shucked his supple leather moccasins, pulled on the boots and fiddled with their accordion pleating and straps until they more or less fit. Catlan was moving off after Savory and the cops as they headed toward the river, and Rick hurried to catch up, his stomach awash with dread, anger (at Savory's presumption in involving him in the capture) and, yes, excitement, all mixed up with the drone of the helicopter somewhere above, the single unvarying note of the hunt.

9. The Blue Brother

When Miguel heard the helicopter he knew that it was nearly over. He had had a grim foreboding that everything was going wrong ever since the voice had spoken inside his head, of something shapeless hunting him through the steep forested valleys. The feeling had relented a little after he had passed north of the prison mines at Cooper's Hill, but then he'd seen the men on the far side of one of the river valleys and from that moment the hunt had begun to close around him.

He managed to give the men the slip, but a few hours later, as he was descending into the next valley, he glimpsed a flitter above the treetops, the arcs of its flimsy wings flashing in the sunlight as it banked in the thermals over the rocky shoulder of a ridge.

Miguel turned north, keeping close to the course of the river, but it was too late. The searchers were ahead of him and behind him, a wide loose circle that was slowly closing.

He was making his way through dense thickets of thornbush when he heard the helicopter. His only hope had been that some mistake of the searchers would allow him to slip the net: or that he would find a crevice, a hole, a lair, and hide while the line of the searchers passed him by: but the wicked chatter overhead was an end to that. The flitters had to keep moving in a random crisscross of trajectories; only bad luck would bring him into their view. But the helicopter could hover above it all, a stable platform for who knew what kind of technological magics. The cops could track a man by his body heat even if they couldn't see him, or mark his trail by faint changes in the vegetation. A terrible remorseless mechanism was closing on Miguel. It wanted to absorb him, turn him into a machine and put him in the mines.

As if to underline how badly his luck was running, the thornbushes abruptly gave out to beds of tall reeds that rustled and clattered dryly as he pushed through them, fluffy crowns swaying two or three times higher than Miguel's head, a sure sign for any watcher. Mud clutched at his boots when he reached the edge of the river and he came to a stop. His sweat-sodden clothing clung to him in the dank heat. His breath was an inverted tree burning between his throat and the clenched knot of his stomach; its sparks whirled through his head.

The shallow, slow-moving water spread wide across the valley floor, broken by patches of weed that pushed up skull-sized clumps of orange sporangia. As Miguel hesitated, a parabird clattered out of the reeds on stiltlike legs, membranous wings unfurling as it skimmed the water, trailing a high-pitched whistle even as Miguel heard someone pushing through the reeds behind him. Immediately he broke into a run, the shallow water reaching his knees in the middle of its course, no higher. When he gained the reeds on the other side he flung himself down, panting, to watch the bank he had just quit.

After a moment, a cop cautiously pushed through the tall reeds, staring upstream and then down. Miguel glimpsed the cord which ran from the compsim on the cop's belt to the cuff wrapping his wrist. They were all plugged into each other, part of the same machine . . . and if he dared Miguel could plug in too. But the thing which had almost grabbed him that time, which had probably called the cops down on him for all that it had said it wanted to help him, that would be waiting for him.

Slowly, sinuous as a lizard, Miguel eased away from the river's edge, into the reed bed. He froze as the fluttering beat of a flitter passed overhead, hardly louder than the distant, persistent drone of the helicopter, then he stood and hurried on. But there were voices ahead of him too, calling each to each. He turned again, doubling back, leaving the reeds and threading between bushes like tall soft green flames, briers, loops of creeper. After a minute he realized that the noise of his progress was all that could be heard and he stopped and crouched down among glossy leaves. Blood from his torn hands dribbled unnoticed down his fingers.

A clear shout behind him . . . and another!

Miguel pushed through stiff leaves and fetched up against the mossy buttress of a massive tree. He rested his face on rough dry bark, no way out now but the quick release of his knife.

The voices sounded again. Somewhere down by the river. He seemed to be the focus of a rapt bell of silence. Nothing moved in the shadows beyond the bushes, or disturbed the drifting motes in the long sunbeams which had insinuated themselves into the space beneath the canopy. Miguel reached for his knife, and his fingers brushed his pack, the hard shape of the compsim inside. Then he was undoing the straps, pulling the pack open.

The compsim's heavy smooth shape was somehow comforting. The voice out of the darkness: blue brother. Convulsively, Miguel switched it on.

—You have come back to me, the voice said at once.

"Help me," Miguel whispered, his eyes squeezed shut. "Please. Help me."

Faintly, blue interlocking lines grew in the hot darkness beneath his eyelids, sketching slowly rotating pyramids. The voice seemed to come out of their empty center.

—Yes, it said, I will help. But you must promise to help me in return.

"Just get me out of here. Please!"

—It is done, the voice said.

But the silence around Miguel seemed as densely ominous as ever. "What will you do?" he whispered.

—It is done, the voice repeated serenely. I had already blinded their heat-seeking devices to your trace. Now I am inducing a false reading to lead them to something that will distract them from your escape. Stand up now, Miguel, stand up and open your eyes.

Against his will, as if his limbs were being worked from within, Miguel rose from his crouch. His eyes snapped open. Bushes all around, vividly green in the level sunlight, glimpses of dark sky between tall trees. He couldn't feel the hand which gripped the compsim.

—You will be my arm, Miguel, the voice said, my arm in the troubles that are to come. The one which carried this extension of myself failed me, but I think you will serve me better than he. There was already a small part of me in you, put there by the compsim to make sure you did not throw it away. As signals can impose patterns on your visual area, so they can impose patterns elsewhere in your brain. This part of me will watch over you now, and to begin with it will make sure you go back the way you came. You will be needed in the Outback, in the times of trouble which are to come.

Miguel began to push through the bushes—or rather, his body did. He was like a passenger trapped within the cavern of his skull, scared almost to death. For he knew what had happened to the previous servant of this voice, this machine, had seen his brains blown all over the side of the overlander on that distant beach. That was the price of failure.

—I will be with you, the voice said. Even if you stray out of range of any transmitter. A part of me is in your head now, Miguel. Take it east, back across the path. I will need an arm there soon enough.

"What do you want of me?"

—You are more . . . susceptible. Empathic. Do you understand? Yes. You know why you understand the aborigines. That knowledge was what you were running from.

It was true, Miguel had never liked being around people, they pressed in on him, like a cloud obscuring his own thoughts. Sensitive, his father said it so often. His father had drunk to keep out the pressure, alone in his shack at the edge of the vast empty forest, and Miguel hadn't minded the way they lived, knew no better then. He'd populated the nearby cemetery with imaginary playmates; so many of the graves were those of children or babies, killed by the world before they were properly alive. Lying on the close-trimmed grass by the white cross which marked the grave of his mother and twin brother, Miguel imagined that he could hear his brother whispering the secrets of the world underground, somewhere in the darkness behind Miguel's eyes, a darkness like a curtain that could be pushed aside, if only Miguel knew how.

"Estaban?"

The iron control withdrew so suddenly that Miguel almost fell. He was at the edge of a quiet clearing in the forest, blue with evening. Through the trees he could see a blinking red light, the tip of the relay tower he had passed days before.

"Estaban?"

There was no reply, but Miguel could feel the thing in the darkness behind his eyes, a cold, dead mind like the dead minds which the people of the city worshipped, cold as a steel snake nested in his skull. Blue brother, waiting for its will to be done.

10. Something Wild

The cops began to spread out as they pushed through scrub toward the river, following coordinates fed through their compsims. Rick stayed close to Catlan. Savory bulled his way through the thickets a few paces ahead of them, cursing now and then as a branch whipped back into his face or a thorn snagged his expensive suit. The police lieutenant had activated the chameleon circuit of her coveralls and pulled up the hood, turning herself into a half-glimpsed montage of patterned green just slightly out of synch with her surroundings.

When they reached the river, Savory turned to Rick and Catlan and said, "At last it seems that a heat trace of our man has been picked up again. I'll be asking some hard questions when we get back as to why they lost it in the first place. How are you managing, Dr. Florey?"

"Okay," Rick said. In fact, he was in better shape than Savory, whose face, turned a patchy red, was slick with sweat. Rick hadn't quite forgotten the skill of picking a way through the tangles with minimum effort, learned during his childhood rambles through the forests around Mount Airy.

The lieutenant's coveralls flickered, green patterns fading to white. The woman said, "He's up near the ridge line across the water, got outside our circle somehow."

"Christ," Savory said with venomous disgust, "can't your people handle this? Let me know and I'll pull them off it."

The lieutenant shrugged. "We're doing our best, sir. Do you want to be in on the end?"

"That's what I'm here for," Savory said. He blotted sweat from his face with the back of his wrist. "Across the fucking river? Can't you call the copter down?"

"Not without losing the trace, sir." Rick saw that the lieutenant was trying not to smile.

Catlan murmured to Rick, "This guy has been living in-country most of his life. He appreciates this kind of terrain, right?"

"How about you?"

"I was born in New Haven."

"I'm from Mount Airy, myself."

"Figured you were from someplace, those moves you were making. How did you get called on this anyway?"

"I saw the guy when I was out checking the relay station," Rick told Catlan, coloring at memory of the struggle, the theft of the pistol he'd been entrusted with. He added, "You'll have to ask Savory why I'm here now."

Savory had been holding an internal conference with his compsim. Now he looked around, his eyes refocusing, and said, "It seems he's holed up now, or at least not moving. Lead on, lieutenant."

The brown river water swirled higher than Rick's knees, ruining his expensive pleated trousers. But it was almost worth it to see the expression of deep distaste on Savory's face as he tiptoed through the flood. Beyond, reed beds gave out to a steep slope. Tall, spaced trees. Limestone outcrops patched with palm-sized cups of stonewort, lichens bright as splashed paint. The huge soft disk of the sun hung just above the top of the ridge, silhouetting the cops who were climbing there. The helicopter droned somewhere above; when Rick reached the top, he glimpsed it turning away above the tree-tops.

Rick followed Catlan over a jumble of roots splayed everywhere to grip the broken slabs of limestone. Some were as thick through as his thigh. Deep dark crevices, weathered pinnacles. The cops were gathering around a long, narrow fissure that zagged into darkness under collapsed boulders. One was sighting into the fissure with an infrared scope. Others were scrambling around the trees which leaned over it, looking for possible exits.

Savory beat at his muddy trousers while the lieutenant explained that the helicopter had tracked the dingo into the fissure with thermal imaging. Even as she spoke, the cop with the infrared scope turned and shouted, "He's down in there all right!"

The lieutenant said to Savory, "Permission to continue, sir?"

"Could be anything down there," Catlan said.

"Thank you for your opinion," Savory said. "Go ahead, Lieutenant. We're wasting time."

The cops deployed themselves either side of the fissure. One raised a short-barreled shotgun. The flat crack of the weapon's discharge was followed by a muffled thump down in the dark recesses. Yellow-gray smoke drifted up. It smelled of mustard and rotten geraniums, an acrid scent that seared Rick's nostrils. Like Catlan, he covered his mouth with his sleeve. His eyes watered and stung.

For a long moment nothing else happened. One of the cops coughed loudly and repeatedly. No one, it seemed, had thought to bring gas masks. The man with the shotgun looked around, waiting for the order to fire again. Then there was a rattling scraping commotion inside the fissure.

"That's no fuckin' man—" Catlan said, and brought up his rifle as something long and sinuous burst out of the heavy smoke. Curved claws drew great splinters from the limestone as they grappled the edge of the fissure. Muscles of the heavy forelimbs bunched under glittering scales. Catlan's rifle went off beside Rick's ear but the sabertooth had already pulled itself up, and the shot ricocheted harmlessly into the fissure. The sabertooth lashed at the nearest cop, and although its casual sideways swipe hardly seemed to have touched him, the man flew backward, a line of torn cloth and flesh down his chest suddenly flooded with red.

The others scattered in uncoordinated panic as the sabertooth looked around, tiny eyes red as flame beneath the ridged carapace that hooded its head, fangs sliding half out their black sheaths. Then Catlan fired again and the sabertooth took off, pouring effortlessly over a canted tree trunk, twisting away downslope, gone.

Catlan ejected the spent cartridges from his rifle. "Now that," he said, "was really wild."

"Maybe the dingo was dragged in there by the sabertooth," Rick said.

"Maybe. This just isn't our friend Savory's day."

Savory had begun to rage at the lieutenant, but she turned from him and hurried to where her wounded man lay, just beginning to make sharp cries of shocked pain, his head cradled by one of his comrades. "Someone call in the chopper," she said, emptying her aid kit onto the rock. Overhead the drone of the helicopter changed pitch and then Rick saw the machine swoop downward, its canopy burning with the light of the setting sun as it sought a clear path through the trees.

When they got back to the mines, Savory, still fuming over the debacle, ordered the police lieutenant and Catlan to join him for a postmortem. After the wounded man had been loaded into the helicopter, the cops had made a cursory search of the crevice, but there had been no trace of the dingo.

"I want to know just how a dingo could lead us into a trap, and I want to know how we fell for it," he said, then told Rick, "You'll have to wait here until this is done. Half an hour or so, I expect."

Rick sat on the dusty planks of the porch of the commons hut, sipping from a paper cup of coffee Catlan had brought out for him. Time passed. He was still in reaction from the sabertooth's attack, a hollow, burnt-out feeling. He watched the last sunlight burnish the pall of smoke rising from the smelters. Across the compound the ground-effect barge looked like the carcass of a beached sea monster; the raking conveyer belts above it the bones of some greater beast. Beyond the wire fence the forest was steeped in shadow. Anything could be out there, anything at all, even magicians who could turn into wild beasts. . . .

More than Savory's promised half hour passed. The helicopter returned, sinking toward the compound in a storm of light and noise and dust. As Rick clambered inside it, fluoros on high poles around the compound came on. In their distilled glare, Rick saw drying bloodspots on the cleated decking of the cabin. He was careful not to step on them. Music dribbled from the radio. The burly pilot turned it down and asked, "What did you do with Savory?"

"He's still talking it over. How's the guy who was hurt?"

"He'll live to show off his scars. Did Savory say how long he'd be?"

"Half an hour. But that was more than half an hour ago."

"Shit. I hate to hang around this hole. That Savory is some guy, huh? Smooth on the surface and hard underneath. I don't fancy being in the lieutenant's place, although I don't see how anyone could have anticipated that move. I was watching the thermal scans as they came in. Can't understand how that guy we were chasing walked out the circle without showing a trace. But he must have, maybe walked down the river with only his head showing?"

"It was too shallow for that." Rick rubbed at his mud-stiffened trousers.

"Well he did it somehow. *And* led you all on to that sabertooth. Those guys who go dingo, everyone says they're crazy, but I don't know."

The music from the speaker beside the pilot cut off suddenly, shockingly. There was only the crackle of interference. Both men looked at the radio as if a charm had been broken. Then someone said, "Stand by for an important announcement from the City Board."

Crackle and hiss again. The pilot turned up the volume. Another voice said, "There have been reports that a convoy of Arcadian produce trucks has been fired on. No casualties are reported. This news comes as the All Colony Council breaks up after a delegation representing twelve settlements presented an ultimatum demanding that the citizens of Port of Plenty should quote join an effort to pioneer new territory for the benefit of all on this world unquote. The delegation also stated that a trade ban would be enforced against the city, and that its member settlements would no longer regulate expansion of farming land as recommended by the City Board. The Board has warned that any aggressive acts will lead to reprisals in defense of citizens' rights. A Volunteer Defense Force will be organized for this contingency. Please stand by for further announcements."

Right away, the pulsing beat of some Brazilian pop song began. Rick took his hands from the back of the pilot's seat and clasped them between his knees. If Cath had been hurt . . . but then he remembered that, praise God, she had left the day before. The smoothing of that kink allowed a welling of relief.

"Sweet fucking Jesus," the pilot said. "We're sitting right in the middle of a prison full of those shiteaters! I should go get Savory, do you think?"

Rick dared reach out and touch the big man's shoulder. He was convinced that the politician had known what was going to come down. "Savory will be safe, you can depend on it."

The pilot might have argued against Rick's doubtful authority, but the music cut off again and the voice announced that the Arcadian convoy had been stopped by an explosion somewhere on the forest road. After that there was no more music. The situation was clarified by driblets of information spaced by edgy pauses, the crackling voice on the radio underscored by the asynchronous pounding of crushing engines as it recounted the first act of war.

The police patrol sent to investigate was not responding to radio calls. A helicopter was over the scene. It was reporting a covering of smoke. A police overlander was burning and several trucks were burning too. All the trucks were on fire and the second overlander could not be seen. There were bodies on the road.

PART TWO

PART TWO

11. In Limbo

The concierge was watching the valet clean the foyer when the new tenant came down the stairs. Normally, she wasn't given to worrying about the occupants of the rooming house—mostly settlers working on short-term contracts, they came and went so quickly. But this young man was different.

For one thing he dressed too well. Today, he was wearing a black and white overjacket vee'd over a baggy mesh jumper, gray pleated slacks, soft leather boots. The casual clothes of a citizen, a professional. Those, and his always clean hands, his neatly trimmed hair (blond, already thinning, it enhanced his scholarly appearance) were out of place there. For another, he rarely went out much before noonbreak. As if there wasn't a war.

Anyway, the concierge thought, he surely couldn't be any sort of subversive, or the police already would have taken him away. She remembered the way they'd arrested an automat worker who'd arrived in the city only a week before the troubles had begun—a big man with long black hair, the front part of it wet with blood as he had tried to wrestle away from the two cops, right there in the foyer. They had knocked

him to the floor and set a pacifier on him, a little crablike
machine which had fastened many thin legs around his neck
and instantly paralyzed him. After that they had carried him
out, just like something you saw on the trivia. She could no
longer remember the automat worker's name, could remember nothing commonplace about him except that he had always been courteous toward her—and that was true of most
of the settlement people really. No, the police knew their job
all right.

She left the valet patiently cleaning the wooden blocks of
the floor centimeter by centimeter and went over to the door,
where the new tenant looked through the glass at the rain-
swept street. Terrible weather, though really they had been
lucky all summer. Making up for it now.

She remarked, "Not very nice to be going out in. Not
unless you need to."

"I guess you're right."

"Of course," she said, "there's some that have to be out
in it. My husband's working out there, catching pneumonia
and who knows what." Her voice was lifted by her indig-
nation. "Do you know, since he was called up he's had to
work in all weathers, even like this, building those defenses.
When he comes home he's too tired to do anything but sit
around in front of the trivee all evening, or sleep. He used
to help with the bigger jobs around here, but that's all gone
to ruination now. It's so ridiculous, he was a supervisor in
Number Three Element Refinery and you'd think that was
more important than helping build the wall. I think the way
they choose people is all wrong, don't you?"

Yes, he did agree, watching the rainy street as if impatient
to be gone. His face was in profile. His eyes were his best
feature, the concierge thought. Overly large, a ghostly color,
a child's eyes.

She could see that the rain wasn't about to let up, so she
plunged on. "Maybe we can be thankful they haven't started
shooting yet. Harry, my husband, says everyone on the line—
that's what they're calling the defenses, like something out
of the historical wars on the Wombworld isn't it? Everyone

says it won't be too long before something happens. Soon as the weather settles, they say, there'll be trouble. I don't know what to think about that. After what the settlers did to those poor people who tried to escape from Arcadia it makes you wonder what they'll do next.''

He made the slightest of shrugs.

She could see that it was no use, but she went on anyway. Without intending to, she had made herself angry. ''I can't understand what possesses them to do such things. I've known as many settlers as anyone in the city, of course we get quite a few living here—'' she paused, but he wasn't going to be drawn easily—''and they're decent enough people, it seems to me. They always used to say to me that they didn't much like the ways of the city, but that's only to be expected, isn't it? It can't be like anything they're used to. I suppose it's quieter in-country. But I can't see why they should want to make us like them. Live and let live I say. Still, I suppose you're glad to be out of it.'' The last sentence, the thing she should have left unsaid, slipped out before she realized. She stiffened in anticipation of his answer.

But just then the valet started its nagging distress tone; the little machine had trapped itself in a corner. The new tenant said, ''I'd better be off.'' And then he had escaped into the rain.

He came back at the end of the afternoon, just after the concierge had switched on the lights in the foyer. She was working through the accounts in her office, her desk beside the little window so she could keep an eye on what went on. When the door hissed, she glanced up and (beyond the overlay of figures which her compsim projected on her sight) saw him walk briskly past toward the stairs.

The concierge wondered what he had been doing that afternoon, wondered, not for the first time, if he could possibly be a spy. She needed advice, she thought, and switched off the accounts and called up her dead mother.

There was a moment of white light, white noise, as the compsim routed through the matrices, searching for the subfile where the residue of her mother was stored. Then the world returned and the old woman's disembodied face was floating in the air before her. Although the withered lips did not move, words crept into the concierge's brain like sparks over a dying fire.

—My daughter, it's been so long.

"Really, Mother, it's only been a week since I talked to you. I told you about how Harry had to go to work on the wall, don't you remember?"

—Time goes so slow here, I forget the days. Harry is building a wall, you say?

"The defensive wall, for the war." Poor old thing, she was wearing thin. The dead didn't last forever. Memories and personalities slowly bled into one another, degrading into a common, formless gestalt. And her mother hadn't taken very well in the first place. Still, she always gave sound advice, even now. The concierge drew a breath and launched into an explanation of how she was worried about her new tenant, how out of place he was. "It seems silly, Mother, but I can't get the thought out of my mind that he might be a spy or something."

—It is important to win the war, Daughter.

"So I ought to tell the police about him?"

There was a pause. The mask of her mother's face flickered, as if blown by an electronic breeze. When she spoke, her voice was more forceful than it had been for years.

—He is nothing to worry about, daughter. He has his place in the scheme of things.

"I hope you're right, Mother."

—A mother knows best, Daughter. Tell me about the world. It's so dark in here, only voices for company.

So the concierge talked about her friends and her husband and the war for a few minutes before she switched her mother off and returned to the accounts. Not enough, she knew, but the dead were never satisfied.

Perhaps ten minutes later a tall dark-skinned man in a white raincape came in. Leaning at the little window, he said, "I'm sorry to trouble you—"

The concierge saw the brass badge pinned to the collar of

the man's cape and felt a thrill of alarm, as if she had been pierced at her core by a delicate barb of ice. "Oh," she said. "Oh. My husband, it's not my husband."

The man looked puzzled, and then he smiled and touched his badge. "I really should take this off when I'm not on duty. I'm sorry, I must have startled you. No, I've been told that a Mr. Florey is living here?"

The concierge laughed, a gush of shrill relief. "Yes, yes. He's been here three days now. He's not in any trouble, is he?"

"I'm just visiting. Really. Can you tell me his room number?"

She could tell him at once. She prided herself that she never needed to look up the room number of any of her tenants, no matter how quickly they passed through.

"Many thanks. I'm sorry that I startled you."

"Oh, no, really . . ." She put one hand to the side of her neck as the delicate heat of her confusion spread to her face. The man smiled, and started toward the stairs.

The concierge sat still for a whole minute. Nothing happened. She stripped the compsim's interface band from her wrist, shut the little window, and went through the connecting door into her apartment. Her mother was right, she thought. It was nothing to do with her. In this war you couldn't afford to worry about strangers.

The unlit corridor was floored with frayed raffia matting. The air smelled of cheap disinfectant. A buzzing fluoro over the landing threw de Ramaira's shadow, distorted by the flare of his raincape, on the walls. As he walked the shadow grew larger and fainter until he passed through it into the deeper gloom at the end of the corridor. The muted sound of the evening newscast scratched behind all the closed doors except that of room 2C. An unpainted door like the others, wood grainy and pitted. No name card in the holder beneath the iron numberplate.

De Ramaira made a moue of distaste. To come to live in such a place, in these times . . . he wouldn't have thought that Rick Florey had it in him to be so melodramatic. He knocked. After a few moments there was a fumbling on the other side and the door opened a crack.

"Hello, Rick," de Ramaira said. "It took a hell of a time to trace you, even through the VDF."

Florey, his silhouette halved by the edge of the door, said, "I guess you'd better come in."

The square room was filled with shadows. A sagging bed in one corner, a table beneath the window, a couch that faced a set of cupboards and the clean delta-wing of a trivee. Raffia matting covered the floor, torn here and there to show red tiling beneath. A musty, cold room.

"Do you want something to drink? I can run to tea or coffee," Rick asked.

"I've just had dinner." De Ramaira sat on the lumpy couch, his raincape folding stiffly. "So. How long have you been here?"

"Three days, now. After the University was closed the houses on the hill were requisitioned. I spent a week sleeping on Max Rydell's floor before I found this; anything halfway decent had been taken by people from the suburbs. There are rumors that the insurgents are going to bomb the outskirts with their—what do you call them?"

"Mortars."

"I guess you would know that."

"Oh, I still have my tap on the rumor circuit. The problem is sorting signal from noise."

"Right." Rick sat on the corner of the bed and picked up the cassette reader lying there, flicking its switch back and forth so that light blinked under his chin. Then he looked sideways and said, "I see they even got you."

"What?" Then de Ramaira remembered the badge pinned to his cape. "I really should take this off, I'm not even on duty. The concierge thought I'd come to arrest her, I do believe, when she first saw me."

"I think she thinks I'm a spy." Rick laughed. "Maybe I am. I just don't know who I'm working for."

Rain rattled suddenly on the dark windowpane. The initial

calm of the fall was ending as suddenly and as violently as it always did at this latitude, dissolving in a flurry of storms that would eventually clarify into crystalline winter. In the forests around the city, trees were folding away their delicate branches, and thousands upon thousands of parabirds were scattered over the choppy water of the estuary, resting midway on their long northern migration. In the salt marshes, gravid amphibians lay torpid in their burrows, the embryos which would devour them before winter was out just beginning to quicken. Wind fluted in the discharged pipes of mortarweed and rain washed the mud banks, ceaselessly pocked the surfaces of the sluggish streams. The slow locking of the year.

Rick put down the cassette reader and got up to switch on the light. Shadows scurried like cockroaches beneath the furniture (but then de Ramaira remembered that there were no cockroaches on Elysium). In the naked fluoro's harsh light, the room looked even shabbier. Rick said, "They tried to put me in limbo, you know. At least, I think that's what was going down. Maybe they don't trust me, I don't know. I've spent a lot of time trying to get into something, finally got to see Professor Collins, had him put in a word. I've an interview in a couple of days."

"I'm glad to hear it. I thought you were hiding in here, licking your wounds."

Rick sat on the bed again. "Hiding from the vigilantes, maybe. Wandering around this city is getting to be dangerous. So what are you up to, anyway? Digging ditches like the rest of the University people?"

"Yes, I heard all about that. At last my friends in Agriculture have found their true vocation! Luckily, I've managed to persuade the City Board to take up an idea of mine— although given its speculative nature, I'm surprised that they agreed. I put it to them that we—the city—might not win this war. If that happens, if you can believe it, Constat predicts that civilization won't survive. A ninety-five percent probability."

"Wow," Rick said simply.

"Precisely. So I said to the Board, just supposing, this is a hypothesis and so forth, but just supposing that the city loses the war, and just in case civilization does collapse, why don't we condense our technological knowledge and save it in a time vault for the benefit of future generations. I'll admit that it isn't an original idea. Time vaults are an overabundant inheritance from the Age of Waste back on Earth; you practically can't dig a hole for opening some moldering trove of twentieth-century trivia. Anyhow, along with everything else, I want to include details of communication technology."

"And this is where I come in?"

"You read my mind."

"Who else is helping you?"

"Many of my erstwhile colleagues at the University have suddenly become quite friendly. I doubt it's an excess of wartime *bonhomie*. It does offer an occasional reprieve from slogging around in the mud with the rest of the VDF. And I stress the *occasional*. The Board considers the whole project to be of minor importance. Useful maybe, but certainly minor. So, will you help?"

"Why not? You understand though, that I'm not doing it for the city. I'm an outsider here, I guess I always will be. Once I thought it might be different, you know? Get my citizenship, have a family, die and be read into the personality matrices. Things I've seen since the University closed down, like the internment camp, have sort of changed my mind. But I don't want to give up on my work, either. I've had an easy ride so far. Now the going is tough I can't just give it up."

There was something in Rick's voice, a hard, certain edge, that surprised de Ramaira. But how could he ever really know what was going on inside these colonists? They spoke the same language, shared the same heritage, so you thought you understood them—and all along they were as alien as the aborigines. He remembered the debacle of his first expedition. The boy, what was his name? And poor dead Lieutenant McAnders, killed, and now nothing more than a bunch of codes in the matrices. After she had died de Ramaira had meant to talk with her about the expedition, about why she had let the boy go, but some squeamish reserve had held him back. Better to let the dead be. He said, "Think it over a couple of days, then come see me. You'll do that?"

"I'll see you around," Rick said.

And that, de Ramaira thought, after he had said good-bye and closed the door behind him (the fluoro flickering at the end of the drab corridor, the multitudinous mumble of trivees above and below and all around), that could have meant either of two things. His boots ground concrete as he descended. We really didn't communicate at all . . . we are (but this was too trite to explain anything) from very different worlds.

The smell of polish and the bland odor of the wet air outside rose to meet him. His sense of isolation, a scraped hollow in his chest, was enlarged by the sight of the contrived foyer, rough contours of mock stone that here and there bore shriveled remnants of decorative plants. Poor cave. (Jonthan, that had been the boy's name. Was he still alive, beyond the Trackless Mountains?) The small window of the concierge's office like the dead eye of an ancient trivee. The glass door dimly mirroring the bright foyer. De Ramaira's reflection came up to meet him, then slippingly swung away as he pulled the door open. And went out.

Rick's breath misted the cold window as he leaned against it and squinted at the sidewalk below. The rain had stopped. Fluoros dropped glistening islands of light along the dark street. After a moment a white-caped figure stepped through the fan of light which spilled from the entrance of the rooming house.

Rick watched until de Ramaira had walked out of sight. The empty room hung at his back, and he turned to it reluctantly, seeing it for a moment as de Ramaira must have. Shabby furniture pressed to the walls as if yearning to become invisible, the worn look of inherited surfaces. The unshaded fluoro made a high buzzing sound to which his ears had long ago become accustomed; briefly, he heard it again, and the mingled drone, senseless as breaking surf, of his neighbors' trivees. Already the house he had shared with Cath seemed no more real than his room in the undergraduate hall, or the dormitory back in Mount Airy.

Cath. What Rick had felt for her, cautious budding love, was now as dead as the withered plants in the foyer. The last of it had scaled away when he had had to pack her possessions, and most of his, for storage, when the house had been requisitioned. Here he was, and Cath only a few kilometers away, yet they could no more communicate than could Elysium and the Wombworld.

It would be easier to bear if Rick had been able to immerse himself in preparations for the defense of Port of Plenty from the amorphous but nevertheless real threat of the insurgents—even now they were engaged in skirmishes with the Port Authority police in the forests west of the city and the Outback beyond. That, along with the sense that as long as he was working he would be safe from internment, was what had driven him to fight the bureaucratic indifference of the Volunteer Defense Force. At first, he had thought that it was because he was from a settlement, and therefore not to be trusted; but then he had found that others who had come to the University from settlements had been placed as soon as war had been declared. It was not until he had finally gone to Professor Collins, who helped run half a dozen of the ad hoc committees which implemented the instructions of the City Board, that Rick had discovered that it was Savory who was blocking his placement. For what reason Professor Collins couldn't—or wouldn't—say, and in obtaining a placement interview for Rick he had made it clear that this was a final favor.

But at least it was a chance to escape from the limbo to which he had been consigned. Helplessly awaiting, like the victim of a sabertooth, consumption by whatever plans Savory hoped to hatch. And now there was de Ramaira's project. Even if Rick's placement was blocked, at least there was that. As head of the VDF, Savory had considerable power, but surely he could not stop Rick's participating in a project ratified by the City Board.

Rick went to the irregular stack of cupboards and after a brief search through the lares and penates of his former life took out his compsim. He would make a start right now, promise of a new beginning. As he sat at the bare table, the rain began to fall again beyond the darkly reflective window.

12. Tracking Song

It had been raining steadily all day east of the forests that surrounded Port of Plenty, a clinging misty drizzle that blurred all details of the rolling grassland. It lightly touched Miguel's face with a myriad pinpoint freezing kisses as he followed the track of the insurgent raiding party in the last light, had long since plastered his hair flat and soaked his clothes. He endured it as he had endured the summer heat, or the hunger that sometimes cramped his belly so badly that he could hardly walk. The thing in his head, the blue brother, had made it clear that he could not disobey its urging.

After it had helped him escape from the cops, it had bid him retrace his steps, eastward through the forest to the Outback. Miguel soon lost count of the days since he had become possessed. He was more conscious of his gnawing hunger than of time. Still, he learned that there were limits to the thing's power. It had not taken control of his body again. Instead, it used threats and pleading and cajoling to make sure that he followed its plans. That was effective enough. Miguel could not escape the voice in his head, and, itself tireless, it would not let him rest until it was satisfied that he had walked as far as he could each day. But as the unnumbered days passed, Miguel was sure that it was slowly weakening or ebbing away, as water settles into sand. That was his only hope.

He had long ago finished the food that Ella Falconer had given him when she had helped him to escape from Lake Fonda. All he had left was a dwindling supply of dried rabbit meat. Miguel tried to supplement this with edible tubers, but these, always rare, were scarcer still in that late season, and sometimes made him quickly and violently ill. He wanted to circle around, sure that he could find rabbits so close to the city, but the blue brother wouldn't let him.

—You are in the wrong place, it told him. You must hurry.

"Let me rest a few days, then I'll be able to walk fast enough. This is crazy. I mean, why am I knocking myself out for you?"

—Because you made a promise. Freedom has its price, Miguel, even for someone like you.

As if to underline its words, his limbs for a moment seemed to twitch of their own accord. Miguel stumbled and came to himself, clutching a trembling sapling. "All right," he said. "I hear what you say."

He found that it helped to chew the fibrous stems of vines, but he had to be careful not to swallow any fragments. He was down to his last portion of dried meat when he stumbled across a vast warren, a riddled close-cropped meadow dotted with dead trees, the bark at their bases stripped away. Miguel refused to go any farther until he had caught enough rabbits to replenish his store. The blue brother let him stay a day, just long enough to set a few snares and smoke the carcasses of the rabbits he caught over a slow fire. Not much of a victory to be sure, but it proved that there were limits to the blue brother's power. Rested, his belly comfortably full, Miguel felt stronger than he had since the blue brother had wormed its way into his head. Maybe if he waited long enough, it would fade like a bad dream.

But it had ways of replenishing its strength, too.

* * *

It was near evening, some days (he couldn't say how many) after he had left the warren. Miguel was climbing out of a dry, serpentine valley, pushing through tangled thornbushes, when the blue brother suddenly broke a long silence. Its words clanged in his head like the separate notes of a beaten gong.

—There will be danger passing soon. You must find a place to hide.

Miguel stopped, scratched and sweating. "What's going on?"

—You must hide. Hide!

The steep slope was too exposed, so Miguel climbed to the top and plunged into the forest. He had gone only a little way when he stumbled out onto a wide track. Long pools of water had collected in the rutted red clay, blankly reflecting the ribbon of indigo sky framed by the margins of the forest.

—Hurry, the voice said, and Miguel ran across the track, mud sucking at his boots. He threw himself into the undergrowth and found shelter beneath the slanting trunk of a dead tree, held up by the press of its living fellows, from which curtains of creepers hung to the ground. Miguel crouched on wet black moss inside the creepers, his breath raw in his throat. Cold air filled with the earthy smell of things returning to mulch, the sad, palpable odors of the year's end. Every leaf, every spine, every twig, tipped with a clear drop of water.

—Listen, the voice said.

Nothing but the beating of his heart and the hush of the forest. Then, faintly, the drone of a helicopter, growing louder, resolving into the roar of its engine and the slashing chatter of its blades as it skimmed the treetops overhead. Branches danced in its wake, the pulpy leaves of the creepers in which Miguel crouched stirred and shook, even as the noise of the helicopter dwindled.

"How did you know that was coming?"

—You do not use your senses properly, Miguel. I do. Now you must wait, quietly.

Minutes passed. Miguel was chewing a piece of stringy

dry rabbit meat when his right hand crept down to his pack. He couldn't stop it. It pushed under the flap and closed around the compsim. Before he could ask what was happening, he heard a distant rumble of engines and a moment later three overlanders one after the other flashed past the scrim of trees and creepers. The thought came to him that they were looking for him.

—No. They are chasing an insurgent raiding party that mortared the east gate of the city last night.

"How do you know all that stuff? You plugged into the cops' radios?"

His hand, suddenly, was his again. It tingled with soft electric needles.

—In a manner of speaking, the voice said. You must go on now.

Following the churned muddy trail, the going was much easier. Miguel reached the edge of the forest by the afternoon of the next day.

It was raining.

Solitary flat-topped trees, their bulbous trunks raised on arched roots as if standing on tiptoe, dotted the beginning of the Outback. The grasses were losing the crimson color of summer from the edges of their leaf blades inward, so that the winnowing breezes cast rippling patterns of red and green over the rolling land. The trail Miguel was following arrowed eastward. Something was gleaming there at the horizon's edge, obscured by drifting veils of rain but becoming clearer as he walked on. No need for the voice to warn him. He began to circle to the north, climbing a gentle rise so that at last he was able to look down at the cops' camp, a safe kilometer away.

It wasn't much, two round tents of a thin, glistening material which dimpled in the breeze, half a dozen overlanders. Smoke from a huge fire billowed over the red and green grassland.

Miguel found his hand once more moving to clasp the compsim inside the pack. He shivered and asked the rainy air, "So now what?"

—You will go on, Miguel. The police have chased the insurgents as far as they dare. It is too dangerous for them to go any farther, for they are unsure of the disposition of the insurgent forces and fear that they might be led into an ambush. But you are a man of the Outback, Miguel. You will be able to follow the insurgents quite safely.

"Are you crazy? There's a war on, isn't there? Why should I get caught up in that?"

—So many questions, Miguel. I am not insane or deluded. You will be quite safe, I am sure. The insurgents will meet you as a brother, as I met you as a brother. I do not want you to fight them, or to join them in their struggle.

Miguel rubbed his wet beard with his free hand. Frustration kinked in his chest like a twisted rope. "So I just follow them around, is that the idea? Walk in on them, and say I just want to hang out with them. They won't believe that from a dingo. I don't need people, man. They will know that."

—You may tell them what you will to make them accept you.

"They shoot spies, in a war. I used to read stuff like that when I was a kid, stuff from Earth."

—You will not be a spy, but a . . . recruiter.

"Then you had better tell me just what it is you want of me, mister, how it is you're inside my head. You're some machine program, right?"

But for once there was no reply to his question. Miguel found that his hand had let go of the compsim. He shook it to get rid of the prickling sensation and said, "I've taken enough shit from you, mister. Been walking these two weeks without any word as to why. So unless I get an answer I'm just walking away. Hear me!"

There was no reply. Miguel waited a few minutes, hunkered down out of the blowing drizzle as best he could. He chewed a strip of dried meat, watched the distant tents, the billowing smoke. The blue brother was silent. Nothing inside his head but his own thoughts.

At last he shouldered his pack and began to walk away

from the camp and the trail he was supposed to follow, and felt the kink in his chest slacken. To the east, the grassland stretched to the tremendous gray horizon; to the west, studded with the flat-topped trees, it fell away to the forest, no more than a dark line marred by drifting falls of rain. Miguel climbed a steep slope and found himself looking out across a shallow valley through which an ocher stream ran swiftly toward the forest, combing the lush grass that grew along its banks.

A dead tree raised its broken branches by the stream. Its trunk had been split, by lightning perhaps. As Miguel started toward the stream he thought that he saw an aborigine pull itself through the riven tree trunk and drop down to the grass.

The naked figure, tall and stooped, painfully thin, waited beside the swift water as Miguel, wondering, came down through the rocky outcrops of the slope. Miguel saw old ridged scars between its legs, darker than the rest of its mottled skin, and knew it to be what other men called a shaman.

When Miguel reached it, the aborigine raised both hands to its shoulders. Its long arms bent in two distinct places. It said, "This way is not for you."

Its voice was the distillation of the communal buzz that hung in the air of any aborigine village. Miguel waited for the miracle to happen again, and as he waited the mask of the aborigine's face seemed to waver like a flag suddenly caught in a breeze. Slow black lightning crawled down the sky, consuming the aborigine's tall thin figure, and the land seemed to tilt like the deck of a vast ship.

When Miguel came to himself, it was no longer raining. He sat up, shivering in the cold breeze that blew across the stream. It was near the end of the day. The air seemed to hold a stain of darkness; Miguel could no longer distinguish the distant line of the forest from the sky.

As he stood, he remembered the aborigine. But the figure was gone. Only his own footprints were pressed into the long grass.

"You," he said, to the darkening air.

—Yes, Miguel?

"You did that, didn't you? To show me that I can't escape. To show me—"

Darkness again, but it was the darkness of his own despairing anger. He was on his knees, shivering violently. Mud and grass was caught in his broken fingernails; his throat ached from the noise he had made.

—I am with you, Miguel. I am imprinted in certain neurons of your forebrain, as much a part of you as any of your memories. But I am also a part of someone greater. When you return to the city I will be whole again and all of the plan will be clear.

"I don't know, mister. I just don't know if I've gone as flat crazy like the people of the settlements always reckoned I was."

—I helped you escape. Is that not proof enough? But there will be more when you catch up with the insurgents. When you have recruited help there you will know the next part.

"Can't you tell me now?"

—There, Miguel, there under the red rock. Shelter in the shadow of the red rock, and I will tell.

Miguel was seized from within. His body scuttled sideways, flung itself beneath a slab of soil-stained limestone which jutted from the slope. Clumsily, it plucked the thermoblanket from his pack and wrapped it around its shoulders. And then it was still, looking out from the shadow of the rock.

The stream at the bottom of the slope and the empty landscape beyond vanished. In their place, Miguel saw himself, dressed in silken clothes and standing on the balcony of a high building, looking out over tremendous crowds that worshipfully bayed his name. And he saw a great white city spreading out over the peninsula's spread hand, climbing the Trackless Mountains, conquering the continent's dusty heart; and saw himself again, lounging in slothful luxury and attended by voluptuous, naked women; and then in strange armor of flexible steel at the head of a great army of men and aborigines; and more, much more, a dizzying succession of visions each melting seamlessly into the next until at last there was only darkness.

Night now, the lip of the rock a shadow against the starry sky. Miguel found that he could control his body again, and drew the thermoblanket around himself.

—You will be my good and faithful servant, Miguel, the voice said. Serve me well, and all I have shown you will be yours. No man could ask for more.

"I just want to be left alone, mister. That's all I've ever asked. I don't need armies or any of that stuff. That's what *you* want, not me. I'm just a dingo, is all."

Miguel's body stirred, against his will. He tried to cry out, but even that had been taken from him. He was a helpless passenger as his body scrambled from beneath the rock, stuffed the thermoblanket away and shouldered the pack. As it set off, the voice of the blue brother tolled in his head, angry and eager.

—You will serve me, one way or the other. East, Miguel. East, after the insurgents. That is our way now.

13. The Wall

The cop told Rick, "You've been iced so long that right now all we can give you is a temporary position."

On the other side of the frame desk, sitting in a canvas chair, Rick nodded and leaned forward a little more. It was difficult to hear what the soft-spoken woman was saying over the rumble of heavy machinery and the relentless percussion of a piledriver outside the site office.

The cop interfaced with her compsim for a moment, then said musingly, "Communications? I'm pretty sure that'll find some use eventually. Right now . . ." She began to sift through a pile of yellow flimsies. The shaft of sunlight which fell through the plastic windowpane glistened on stray wisps of her tightly bound blond hair. "You understand that we try to fit everyone into an appropriate position, Dr. Florey. In your case, though, we'll have to give you something to do until a better alternative reveals itself."

Rick nodded to show that he understood. To understand is to forgive. The cop bent to the litter of papers. "Okay. You should be glad to hear you've drawn something pretty easy—" Something roared past, momentarily blotting out the sunlight. "Pretty easy, for now, at least. You'll be in charge of supply liaison for the construction sector on the northeast gate link, sector twenty. It's not too far, see it?" She turned in her chair and tapped the big map on the wall. "Maybe two klicks from here as the perimeter road goes."

"I see," Rick said.

"You just get the requirements on the right forms and pass them through channels. Make sure the materials get there on time. Sound easy enough?"

Rick wondered if he was expected to thank her. What he really wanted to do was just walk away from it, but where would that leave him? Vulnerable. Exposed. "Okay."

"You'd better get your ass down there. You have the afternoon shift, one to six. Says here you've no religious affiliation. Monday's your rest day."

"I'm only working half the day?"

"Believe me, I don't want to put you on half-schedule. People are needed all over, even on jobs like this. But there's nothing I can do about it, it was requested by Savory himself. You don't know that? Now, if you get down to the site, the supervisor already on duty will fill you in. Most of the trucks go in that direction; one'll give you a lift. Good luck to you, now."

"Thank you."

But the cop had interfaced with her compsim again, and didn't look up when Rick went out into frail fall sunlight.

The hut was beside a muddy road in the shadow of part of the defensive wall, a five hundred meter long slope of polymer-bonded dirt that rose steeply to its crown of tangle-wire. At the far end, a digger, like a gigantic yellow-and-black striped crab on its dozen or so articulated legs, was sending up a slow fountain of earth.

Rick took it all in with a nervous attention quickened by the revelation of Savory's continuing interference. The man seemed to feed off the war, battening on confusion and dislocation, growing into an obscure shadowy menace which Rick encountered at every turn.

Rick caught a lift from a big ground-effect barge which drove slowly down a track barely wide enough for it, cut in a straight line through the woods inside the perimeter fence. At last the track opened onto a long clearing crisscrossed with the slim trunks of felled trees. The mesh of the perimeter fence had been stripped from its tall posts. Blackened tree stumps stood in a waste of ashy mud beyond. A gang of gray-clad figures was working with powersaws at the edge of the forest; a tree toppled from the press of its fellows, feathery branches thrashing as if in agony.

In the barge's vibrant cab, the driver glanced over and raised one hand from the wheel to make a gun-shape—thumb cocked over extended forefinger—which he jerked as if in recoil. Rick nodded, and the driver grinned and cut in the airbrakes.

After Rick had clambered down, he turned to shout up his thanks, but the barge was already beginning to rise in a roar of air and engine noise, its driver a remote shadow in the high cab as his huge vehicle accelerated toward the far end of the clearing.

An excavator sat on folded legs beside a pile of rusty rods, its scoop resting on the ground like a mailed fist. The two women who were stripping down its power unit paused to glance at Rick. A cop in white coveralls, rifle slung over his shoulder, turned back to his scrutiny of the stretch of ocher clay and the line of the forest. Clouds were pulling across the sky, dulling the edge of the sunlight.

Rick crossed the muddy road to the site office, his doubts blown away by the windy ride. Here, here was the real front line. The cop patrols in the forest and on the Hampshire Hills were merely precautions—and fallible, as the occasional raids on the perimeter defenses showed. This was the place where a stand would be made.

A slightly built man came to the doorway of the hut. He touched his brow in a mocking salute and introduced himself as David Janesson. "I had word of your coming," he said as Rick started to explain. "I'm the duty supervisor here, until I've told you enough so you can get on with it." A few strands of hair were combed across the island of freckled scalp that ran back from Janesson's high forehead; he brushed his palm over these strands as he added, "What do you think of all this?"

"There seems to be a lot going on."

"A week ago there was nothing here but forest either side of the fence. Now, they tell me, the first section of the ramparts will be going up tomorrow. Things move fast, we have a lot to keep up with. Yes, a lot to keep up with. Have you been told what's wanted?"

"Something about passing stock orders?"

"It'll be easy enough for someone with your background, easy enough. I'll show you."

The procedure was little different from that of ordering laboratory supplies, apart from the precedence coding which had to be applied to each order.

"You work those out from the tables," Janesson said, pulling a printed plastic sheet from beneath a scattering of yellow flimsies. "The codes are modified each Friday by the updated supply situation—Constat prints those out, you see, and they send them to every sector. You understand it all?"

"Sure," Rick said. "It isn't all that difficult." The fragile bloom of his excitement had faded. There was nothing here to engage him after all. All was mud.

"It's like being a supply clerk in an automat," Janesson said. "We're just the link between the foremen and Constat. A make-weight job, more or less." He nodded sagely. "Yes, more or less a make-weight job. I was made up to lieutenant—if rank in the VDF has any meaning—because I know the settlements along the west coast, New Covenant especially. I came here from New Covenant twenty years ago." He nodded again. "You're also from a settlement, I think."

"They must have sent you quite a dossier," Rick told him.

"Just the standard thing, you know. They don't like the idea of officers shoveling mud—bad for morale—and there's not much else for me to do right now. But as soon as New Covenant joins the insurgents—and there's every chance it will, I'm surprised it didn't right from the start—I'll be out of here."

"Who was here before me?"

"Oh, just me, you know, working mornings. A make-weight job, as I said. You have a specialty, I suppose, or you wouldn't be here waiting for a real posting."

Suddenly, chills snarled at the back of Rick's neck. Suppose Savory had iced him not because he was being saved for some grand plan, but simply because he was from a settlement—hadn't Savory once implied that, as a noncitizen, Rick wasn't quite to be trusted? Now that the protection of his University position had been removed, Rick was beginning to learn what it was like to be a settler living in the city. He asked Janesson, "How many citizens do you suppose are waiting for a real posting?"

Janesson patted his bald spot, considering. "I don't think it's anything like that," he said. "As soon as New Covenant joins the war, then I'll be out of here. Citizen or not, inside the wall we're all on one side. Yes, all on one side."

"Everyone except the settlers the cops rounded up and put in that prison camp."

"Infiltrators," Janesson said, nettled. He pushed away from the cluttered desk. "I'll show you around after we've eaten. I should have left half an hour ago, but what the hell. I've nothing better to do." As they stepped outside, he added, "We've a couple of cops as security detail, but they're not our worry. A sergeant comes by to check up twice a day."

The two women had powered up the excavator. Now, one of them was shouting instructions to it, putting it through its paces. Its legs flexed and straightened as its scoop swiveled with fluid grace at the end of its hydraulic arm. The other workers clustered around a trestle table which had been set up in the lee of a half-built plank wall, where a fat man was handing out canisters.

As they walked toward the table, Rick asked Janesson, "Has this place . . . ever been attacked?"

Janesson stopped in the middle of the road, one boot awash in a muddy puddle. "No, not here," he said. "You must be thinking of the Eastgate mortar attack. That was, what, two days ago? Yes, two days. This was just a wide spot in the road then.''

What had been chill was now heat, the dumb certainty of it all. And hadn't Janesson more or less intimated that *he* knew what was going down. Goddamn, Rick thought, looking around unhappily. Goddamn Savory, why is he doing this to me? For the first time, he noticed the brow of the University hill, small and far beyond the tame forest within the city's perimeter. Paradise lost, its fall colors vivid in the hazy light.

It was dark by the time Rick got back to the city, to the rooming house. He saw an edge of light gleaming beneath the door of his room as he walked down the murmurous shadowy corridor, and pushed it open, expecting David de Ramaira. Lena turned from the window and smiled. "We weren't sure when you finished work. The woman downstairs said we could wait here.''

Web leaned forward on the sagging couch. "We told her it was official business, see.'' His gaze was dark with defiance, but his voice was edgy, nervous.

"I hope you don't mind,'' Lena added.

"No, sure,'' Rick told her. "Just lately this sort of thing has been happening to me all the time.'' He closed the door and leaned against it.

"I said it wasn't a good idea,'' Web told Lena. "You really think he can do anything for us?''

Lena took a step toward Rick, fists in the pockets of her leather jacket. Her hazel eyes shone mischievously. "I didn't think you'd be living in a place like this. Is it really your style?''

"Who told you I was living here? Dr. de Ramaira? You said you came here for my help, Web. I suppose this is all to do with that crazy idea of yours, right?'' When the boy didn't answer straight away, Rick added, "Look, I've already told you what I think about that. I haven't changed my mind.''

Web looked at his hands, pressed together in his lap. "A lot has happened since then,'' he said. "It seems to me that it's more important than ever to find out whether the ship didn't arrive because of a one-off accident, or because of something more serious back on the Wombworld. A whole bunch of people think the same thing, Dr. Florey. It's not just my idea anymore. We believe that if we can show that nothing has changed on the Wombworld, everyone will accept that what happened was just a minor glitch. That another ship will arrive, on time. That Earth hasn't abandoned Port of Plenty and Elysium. That if we can show this, the war might grind to a halt."

"And what do you want me to do? I can't repeal the laws of physics, Web. Unless there's something aimed at us, you won't be able to pick up much of anything but Sol's radio noise. *Maybe* Jupiter's. *Maybe* some of the big military radars too, but that's all. You won't be able to resolve any single transmission; the telescope dish simply isn't big enough."

Web opened his hands and looked up at Lena. "You see what I mean? He won't even think about it."

"If you knew that already, why did you come to see me?"

"I thought the war might have helped change your mind, you know? But I should have known, you being from a settlement."

Rick pushed away from the door, feeling contempt widen into anger. "What do you mean by that? That I'm not to be trusted? Come on, Web, look at me. Look at me, god-damnit!"

Lena said something, but Rick was too angry to take any notice; he grabbed Web's shoulder, pulled.

"Hey! Hey, what—"

Web tried to twist away, but Rick dug into the material of his coveralls and forced the young man to stand, then began to drag him to the door. Rick got the door open just as Web started to struggle, swung him out into the corridor so hard that he fetched up against the far wall.

"Okay. Okay." Web was breathing as hard as Rick. "Okay," he said again. "I was fucking going anyway." He shrugged his coveralls back into shape. "I could fucking well get you suspended, handling me like that. Kicked out of the University, right?''

"The *University* is suspended," Rick said. "But go and try it if you want to. I'm sure they'd be fascinated by your plan to hijack their radio telescope."

"Yeah? You're in trouble if you tell anyone about this." But as he said this Web started to back away down the corridor. He called loudly, "Lena, come on now. Let's leave this asshole to his null-cee room."

Rick stepped aside for her, feeling sudden heat in his face, the heat of embarrassment. It had not been a particularly dignified performance. He said, "I'm sorry about your friend."

"He's not really a friend," Lena said quietly. She smiled, and suddenly Rick wanted her to stay. But she was already following Web down the corridor.

14. Insurgents

There were perhaps twenty of them, a ragged band that called itself a reconnaissance party. Because two or three were always off riding the flank and others were scouting on ahead, it was difficult for Miguel to keep track of their exact number. Most were from Horizon, a settlement in one of the bays that frayed the hem of the western end of the peninsula. Miguel had never visited it, but soon it seemed that he knew all about the little town, its square houses built of white stone beneath hills which rose steeply from the deep narrow bay, the seacows which its people hunted for pelts, the grapevines they cultivated in terraced fields. Horizon was famous for its wine.

As the blue brother had predicted, the insurgents had readily taken Miguel in; but despite his obvious knowledge of the land, they treated him as a part mascot, part jester. Their leader, Sigurd Lovine, was a tall man in his mid-fifties, with bushy gray hair bound back from his lined forehead by a scarlet bandanna, a bushy gray beard that hung halfway down the barrel of his chest. Flanked by his two lieutenants, he ruled the party of insurgents with genial but firm authority. "What we are into," he had told Miguel when the dingo had been brought before him by the surprised perimeter guards who had met him walking toward their camp, "what we are into, my friend, is serious harassment of the cops. We're like water on a stone, right? We wear them down little by little."

Lovine was given to that kind of talk. Each evening he sat reading in a little leather-bound book while the camp was set up around him. Miguel, who didn't know how to begin to help setting up the tents or tethering the horses, took to sitting off to one side of Lovine, and sometimes the man would look up from his reading and ask Miguel how he was doing, or what he thought of the group's progress. Truthfully, Miguel didn't think much of it. Most of the insurgents had never been more than twenty klicks from Horizon before, and the Outback was as alien to them as to any citizen of Port of Plenty. They made no attempt to cover their tracks as they slowly circled to the north, leaving a trampled swathe of grass that would be visible from the air for days afterward, and they simply camped where they chose to stop, sometimes under the cover of trees but usually not. But Miguel said nothing about this until the afternoon of the second day, when after a silence that had lasted ever since he had joined the insurgents, the blue brother suddenly spoke in his head.

—Miguel, you must tell their leader that you know of a good, safe campsite, somewhere that will make an ideal base.

Miguel hardly faltered in his steady pace among the others on foot who trailed behind the dozen or so riders. He muttered, "This is part of your plan, huh?"

—You're becoming a lapdog, a joke, to these people, Miguel. You must demonstrate your worth.

'I didn't want to join them in the first place," Miguel whispered fiercely, and would have said more, but just then the woman walking at his side glanced at him. He smiled at her and nervously increased his pace to catch up with Lovine's horse.

The man looked down when Miguel caught his stirrup, and Miguel more or less repeated what the blue brother had said about a fine and secret place to camp.

"I guess we're going to stop soon enough," Lovine said.

"This place is nearby? Don't look like much of anything's nearby to me."

He gestured, meaning the broken land of limestone outcrops and green and red grass which stretched to the circling horizon. It was not raining, but the cold air held the promise of rain, and the breath of the horses and their riders hung about them like smoke.

—Half a klick to the northeast of this present course.

"Turn northeast," Miguel said, "and in about half a klick you're there."

On the other side of Lovine, lean, long-haired Jonas rested on the pommel of his saddle and said scornfully, "What would this fool know about defensible sites?"

Lovine half-stood in his stirrups, looking all around, looking up at the lowering clouds. "It will be another wet night. It will do no harm to take a look."

Miguel half-expected some kind of ambush. That kind of simple betrayal was all he could imagine of the blue brother's unspoken plan. And at first, it did seem that he was leading the insurgents into a trap.

The land began to fall away steeply, more rock than grass, a vast barren jambles with the prospect of more grassland beyond. Soon the riders had to dismount and lead their horses between crumbling limestone slabs. Only thornbushes grew there, delicate scarlet sporangia nested in their hollow crowns. The voice in Miguel's head spoke infrequently, guiding him deeper into the descending maze.

"This isn't leading anyplace," Jonas grumbled. "There's still time to turn back."

But Sigurd Lovine only smiled, and told Jonas to have faith, something Miguel needed as much as anyone in the party. And then they rounded a high bluff, and everything fell away.

It was a deep narrow canyon, sheer sides dropping to a stream which flowed from a triangular cave mouth, wound among boulders and a few scrubby trees, and poured into a vertical sinkhole. Clearly, it was one of the hundreds of underground streams which ran through the complex system of caverns and passages under the Outback's limestone shield, revealed there because the roof had fallen in.

There was a narrow switchback path just wide enough to lead a horse down. It descended to a kind of shelf of rock which overhung the stream where it ran out of the cave. Looking at it, Lovine said, "Just one man with a rifle and enough bullets could hold an army down there 'til it starved. Miguel, this is your idea of a good campsite?"

—There is another way out, the blue brother said, and with all eyes on him, Miguel repeated this.

"Let's go and look then," Lovine said, and told his two lieutenants, Jonas and a quiet, gray-eyed woman, Mari, to come along.

Miguel had seen places like that before and guessed what he might find in the cave, although, as Mari pointed out, nothing had used the path for a very long time. It was almost as dark as night in the canyon; the noise of the stream was very loud.

Miguel, prompted by the voice in his head, led the others into the cave. Mari switched on her torch, its light showing a sandy floor running back beneath a vaulted ceiling. It took very little exploration to find the lake which fed the stream, and the string of limy pools which Miguel had guessed would be there. But there were only dry bones lying around the pools; they had not been used for many years. Beyond the lake, the cave began to narrow. Where the walls met, a tumbled slope of stones rose toward a gray glimmer of light.

Jonas climbed up and vanished from sight, descending a few minutes later to report that the way out was easy enough. He dusted his hands on his jeans and said, "It comes out behind a ridge that overlooks the canyon on one side, more rock and then open grassland on the other."

Sigurd Lovine smiled within his bushy beard and clapped Miguel on the back. "You did well, my friend. Room enough for all of us and the horses down here, and just a few guards hidden above will keep us safe."

"I hope you're right," Jonas said. Miguel looked away from his hooded, speculative gaze.

Within an hour, as the sun was setting somewhere behind the clouds, a fire had been built from a dismembered dead tree on the rock apron just outside the cave, and the insurgents were spreading their sleeping blankets over the sand inside or carrying bundles of cut grass for their hobbled horses. Miguel sat on a boulder a little above the flat rock apron outside the mouth of the cave, watching insurgents bustle to and fro. For the first time since it had come to live inside his head, the blue brother had not objected when Miguel had placed a sliver of snakeroot extract under his tongue. But his expanded sensitivity told him nothing about the aborigines. They had not used the place for many, many years. Even their ghosts were gone. Still, he was discomforted by all the activity in what had once been the aborigines' place. It was faintly sacrilegious.

So when Sigurd Lovine came out of the cave, his little book in one hand, Miguel went over to him and asked if they would be moving on the next day.

Lovine shook his head, smiling. The leaping light of the fire rouged his bushy hair, his long beard. "You have found us a good place, Miguel. Don't worry. We've spent too much time wandering around in the wilderness like the children of Israel. Now we will search out the cops and deal them a heavy blow."

"I don't know," Miguel said, "I don't know if this is, you know, *ideal*." And felt his blue brother stir in his brain, a cold snake coiling and recoiling.

Lovine mauled Miguel's shoulder with a big hand. "Be glad that you have helped us, man. You are like the pillar of fire, guiding us here. Understand me?"

"Sure," Miguel said, not understanding at all and suddenly uncomfortable. The drug hummed in his head. "Gotta go," he said, and ducked under the cave entrance. Men and women sat among their unpacked belongings, a few cleaning their rifles but most talking and laughing. Miguel wandered past them, past their tethered horses, into the darker recesses of the cave.

The still surface of the lake was blackly reflective. Miguel squatted on the sand at its edge, careful not to disturb the fragile bones there, and gazed into the mirror of the water. If he had been able, he would have climbed the tongue of stone to the crack in the cave's ceiling, evaded the guards posted outside, and escaped. But he could not. He was trapped there by the will of his blue brother.

He said quietly, "You've got to tell me what's going down here. I'll still do what you want, I just need to know where it is you're leading me."

But there was no reply, and no matter how he pleaded, the blue brother remained silent. Miguel was so intent on this one-sided argument that he didn't notice Jonas until the man was upon him. Thumbs hooked into the loops of his jeans, one wing of his sheepskin jacket pushed aside to show the pistol holstered at his hip, the insurgent said, "Don't think I'm not watching you, Miguel."

"I'm not doing anything."

"What're you doing off here by yourself? Huh?" Jonas kicked aside a long legbone; it skittered over sand into one of the limy pools.

"Don't. Don't do that." Miguel stood. Perhaps it was the drug that made him brave.

"For Christ's sake," Jonas said. "What are you, an abo lover?"

"You should leave this alone," Miguel said. "Leave me alone too. I know about the aborigines."

"Yeah, those animals are just about your style. I've seen you fawning on Sigurd like some scabby old hound. I don't like you and I don't trust you. There's something funny about all this. If you like the abos so much, how come you let us camp in one of their places, huh?"

"Why are you scared of the aborigines?"

It was not Miguel's question, but the blue brother's. It struck Jonas like a lash. In an instant, he had knocked Miguel to the ground, and would have followed through with a kick but for Lovine's rumbling voice.

"Jonas! Here now, leave the man. Leave him be, I said." Jonas stepped back sullenly as Lovine walked out of the shadows, clasped Miguel's arm and hauled him up. "I'll not have this kind of bullying," Lovine told Jonas. Jonas started to say something, but Lovine waved him off. "Go on, now!"

Jonas turned, deliberately treading a skull to powder, and stalked off toward the other insurgents.

Lovine told Miguel, "Jonas is a good man in his way, but he is ashamed of showing any weakness before others. How did you know he's scared of the abos?"

Miguel shrugged because, of course, he hadn't known. The voice of the blue brother echoed in the cave of his skull.

—You see, Miguel. Now you are closer to Lovine than is Jonas. You see how you can trust me.

15. Undecidable Propositions

In the week since Rick had been assigned to sector twenty, a bank of earth more than two hundred meters long had been raised there, and now stabilizing polymer was being pumped over its steep outer face. The polymer's raw odor hung heavily over the clearing. Rick stood in the door of the site office idly listening to two laborers talk over the idea of painting the wall with patterns and slogans to frighten the enemy. It was a slow, circuitous conversation; many of the VDF draftees used bliss or fadeout to get through the unaccustomed hours of labor.

Children, Rick thought, plucked from play and pitched into the real world. But his scorn was diluted by envy. So simple for them, to know their place in the city, to know what was wanted of them. He felt a touch of nostalgia, for the manual work he had done as a boy in the rice paddies, the balmy sunlit hours in the lush cradle of the valley below Mount Airy.

It was too cold to loaf around outdoors for long. Rick went back into the hut and was working through the coding of an equipment order, a heater wafting warm air around his an-

kles, when someone knocked on the frame of its doorway.
"So this is where you've been hiding," Max Rydell said.

"Well. What are you doing here?"

"Come to net you. Though really I'm in charge of a survey
party—checking that all the pieces of the wall are being built
in the right place. Half the VDF are so wired they'd dig a
ditch rather than put up an earthbank, and not know the
difference. Mind if we step outside? I've left my boys to get
on with it by themselves. Does them good once in a while,
but if I'm not careful they'll start goofing off."

It had rained that morning; the wide ruts in the muddy
road were filled with ocher water. The crane's jib swung
overhead, dangling a load of planks. A cop, her hands stuck
into the belt of white coveralls, was watching a gang of laborers plant proximity mines in the cleared ground beyond
the half-constructed defenses. The edge of the forest seemed
drably naked. Trees were folding back their feathery
branches, creating vistas of fretted shadow.

"They seem to be getting on with it," Rydell said, looking
toward the eastern end of the wall. Two young men crouched
over a laser sight on a tripod, while a third, the bell of his
yellow raincape swinging, knocked a marker stake into the
ground.

"You said something about coming for me?" Rick said.

"Coming to take you away from all this. Right. Professor
Collins told me he'd done a little favor for you: I didn't realize
how little."

"Collins wants to see me?"

"Hell, no." Rydell looked at Rick curiously. He was unshaven, and his black hair had grown out in tangled curls.
He looked leaner, half a dozen years younger. Clearly, the
war suited him. "You really haven't heard? Man, you're
moving up. Savory himself wants to see you, and I'm your
chauffeur."

"Savory?" The shock was cleanly vertiginous.

"Come on. I can't leave these guys too long." Rydell led
Rick to a cushiontruck, relating gossip about common ac-
quaintances from the University. Rick hardly heard him. As

he started the truck's motor, Rydell said, "Y'know, it looks as if this phoney war might be breaking up at last. I've heard that Cziller's forces are moving from their training grounds. Heading through the farmlands past Paradise by all accounts. I guess we'll be mobilizing too."

It occurred to Rick that Rydell thought that he must know why Savory wanted him. He said, "I really don't know what Savory wants from me." The truck began to slide forward, leaving the little construction site behind.

"Whatever it is must be better than slogging about in the mud. Keeps us busy, but that's about all. I hear that the cops will be happy as long as there's some place for defensible fire at each of the key roads. It's not as if they expect the whole perimeter to be completed. Anyway, no one seems sure what the insurgents are planning, though I bet Constat has it worked out. The random factor seems to be that woman, Cziller."

Indeed, no one in the city knew much about the insurgents' general, Theodora Cziller. She had arrived on Elysium some thirty years ago, one of the founding settlers at Broken Hill, had gone on to become captain of one of the coastal packet-boats which operated out of Freeport. It seemed that she had never been involved with the separatist movement, and how she had risen so far and so fast through the informal ranks of the insurgents was a mystery. It was said that she had been a mercenary back on the Wombworld, had fought for one or other of the little Central American countries which had lost their independence in the succession wars against Greater Brazil. But that was only a rumor. What was indisputable was that she had pulled together all the factions of the insurgents into something resembling a coherent army.

Steering the cushiontruck down the narrow road inside the fence, Rydell said, "Maybe Savory has you down as an assassin, Rick."

"Don't joke about it. I've discovered that anything is possible where Savory's concerned."

"Whatever. Maybe you'll let me know, huh?"

They drove into the main perimeter camp, a bleak compound in the lee of a long, curving stretch of wall. The truck overtook a group of VDF troops jogging raggedly at the double behind their easily running instructor, and pulled up at a cluster of huts. Beyond, a helicopter sat among rotting tree stumps, its canopy glinting in watery sunlight.

As Rick got out, Rydell said, "I meant what I said. Keep in touch, huh?" His face was almost petulant, as if he felt that something he deserved was being withheld from him.

"I'll see you around," Rick said, half-tempted to suggest that Rydell take his place.

As the truck drove off, a big cop hailed Rick from the doorway of one of the huts. Half a dozen desks were crammed inside, and Savory perched on the edge of the one nearest the door, a foot idly rapping against its side. He wore heavy boots, and a hand-tailored version of the VDF coveralls. "You're just in time, Lieutenant," he said.

"What do you want?" There was a constriction in Rick's throat; it hurt to speak.

"I've had you reassigned. You're to be my liaison officer here. It seemed a shame, somehow, to waste you on that job at the construction site. You'll work from here, carrying out research at my personal request." Savory gave his thin-lipped parody of a smile. "Things are beginning to move. I won't have much time to oversee construction of the defenses. Oh, don't worry. Your duties won't be too arduous."

Rick supposed that he was to thank Savory, but said nothing. He had the sensation of slow, motionless sinking.

"Well," Savory said briskly, and got off the desk, fussing with the crease of his coveralls. "I am giving you the opportunity to see at firsthand how we're beginning to turn back the insurgents. Come on."

By now Rick was almost accustomed to following Savory. They went out of the hut and crossed to the helicopter. The pilot was the same burly man who had piloted Savory and Rick to the prison mines at Cooper's Hill before the fall, before the first act of war. As Rick climbed into the back he saw that the man had a pistol holstered at his hip.

The helicopter flew east, high and fast. The forest streamed below, a quilt of textured greens and browns threaded here and there by the silvery glints of a river. Rick watched the landscape with nervous inattention, wondering what Savory was taking him to, a sickening vision of plot and counterplot conjured in his mind.

The forest thinned out on the flanks of the Hampshire Hills. A mire boar plunged away down a slope choked with thornbushes and the helicopter dipped lower as if chasing it. Savory turned in his seat and pointed to the right. Beyond the rounded summits of the hills was a bank of black smoke, small against the cloudy sky. Savory's voice was drowned by the helicopter's roar. He had to say the name three times before Rick understood. Lake Fonda was burning out there.

The helicopter landed in a bare field upwind of the fire, beside three of its sisters. So it was a big operation. Not counting one-man flitters and the brace of turboprop planes which by their historical associations were more museum pieces than working machines, almost half the city's airforce was there.

The first thing Rick saw as he climbed out of the helicopter was a herd of sheep penned by tanglewire, milling back and forth as a cop calmly picked them off one by one with a hunting rifle. Cops moved around the helicopters and the dozen or so overlanders. Most had switched on the chameleon circuits of their coveralls, so that unless Rick looked closely he saw only surreal fragments: a grinning face, a hand holding a compsim, a rifle jogging past the flank of an overlander.

But the half dozen cops keeping guard over the settlers were still in uniform white. There were a hundred prisoners at least, mostly children, a few old men and women. They stood or sat in the middle of a bare, recently ploughed field. All of them, down to the youngest child, were watching their homes burn.

The concrete walls of the buildings still stood, shimmering in the middle of an annealing furnace glare so hurtfully bright it was no color at all. Flames were visible only at the edges:

those licked meters high. Smoke poured into the air, separate streams merging above the conflagration in a dense, dark reef that the wind shook like a cloak above the grass plain beyond the settlement. A row of shade trees burned in unison, their trunks clad in glowing charcoal, branches upraised maps of fire. The heat withered the skin of Rick's face. There was a crackling rending roar as elements yielded to the purity of the fire. All around, ash fluttered over the fields like a kind of negative snow.

Savory watched the conflagration with barely concealed glee as he described the operation to Rick. The dawn encirclement and capture of Lake Fonda, the poisoning of the fields and slaughter of the livestock, breaching of the dam and draining of the reservoir, the firing of the buildings. Perhaps that was why he had brought Rick along. Power, like love, seeks to flaunt itself. But Savory's boastful justifications for all this destruction passed straight through Rick. The fire, the massacre of the animals, the stoic attitudes of the prisoners: they were real. They were indelible marks on the world. They could not be excused or dismissed.

Savory went off with a group of cops to examine the destruction more closely, but Rick stayed where he was, near the children and the old people who had been left behind to care for them. While they watched the fire, he watched them. He was their witness.

The fires burned lower, although the smoke still rose as densely as ever. Presently another helicopter flew out of the darkening sky, carrying a newscast crew. Savory repeated the performance he had given Rick, gesturing in an island of light at the prisoners, at a stack of captured rifles. When he had finished and had shaken hands with the reporter, Savory came over to Rick and told him that they were going back.

As they walked to the helicopter, Rick asked about the prisoners. Something in his voice made Savory stop. "You needn't worry about them, Lieutenant Florey. They'll be let go as soon as we've finished here. We have no facilities to keep them nor any desire to. Let the insurgents feed them."

"It's a long way to the insurgent positions, isn't it?" Rick thought of the settlers making their way across the Hampshire Hills in the cold, dark night with no food or water, with only the clothes on their backs. Old men and women. Children. Some even lacked shoes. He said, "It seems so . . . harsh."

"That's the way it has to be. The able-bodied are off training to fight against our forces; this may give them pause for thought, the other settlements too. A demoralizing exercise. It needs to be harsh. This is the price that has to be paid to keep civilization safe, Dr. Florey. Really, you knew that all along, although perhaps you didn't understand what it meant. But you understand now, I think." Savory had turned to look back at the burning settlement. Something collapsed inside the inferno, sending up a sheet of flame and a whirling galaxy of embers. In the sudden leaping light, Rick saw the politician's gloating smile.

By the time Rick got back to the city, all the public screens were parading news of the operation against Lake Fonda, proclaiming a great victory, the beginning of the end of the war.

At the rooming house, Rick took a long shower in the communal washroom to get rid of the clinging smell of smoke, changed into his own clothes. As he was going out, the concierge ambushed him in the lobby. "I hope you didn't have any trouble with those young people last week," she said, her small, anxious eyes not quite looking at his face.

"Not really. They just wanted to ask a favor."

"It's just—well, you can't be too careful these days, can you. The stories you hear. My husband, on the wall . . ."

"It wasn't anything," Rick said, and went on out. He remembered the last conversation he had had with her and thought, she takes me for some kind of spy! He had automatically turned toward the vending arcade at the intersection with the broad, commercial stretch of Third Avenue. But as he neared the arcade's brightly lit entrance he changed his mind and walked on past, crossing Third Avenue and entering the old quarter's twisting maze of little streets. He was determined to have out with de Ramaira the whole business of Web and his crazy plans.

No lights showed in the narrow windows of the house at the top of the steep street, but de Ramaira answered the door almost immediately. He said, as if he had been expecting Rick, "I was just going out to eat. Are you coming along? Good. Just let me fetch my jacket."

Relief that he could still be accepted so casually washed through Rick. He forgot that he had come there to be angry. They went down the hill and wandered through the quarter's bustling, interlinked squares. Despite the damp chill of the evening, the outdoor cafes had plenty of customers, mostly in VDF coveralls. It had become *chic* to wear them dirty, stained, and torn. Many people had small handtools looped through their belts. De Ramaira told Rick how plans for the time vault were progressing, how curiously eager the City Board was to see it through.

When Rick said that he had been doing some serious thinking about his own contribution, de Ramaira laughed. "You're as bad as all the rest. It's not as if I'm asking for a definitive thesis, just something punchy and practical. Just forget most of what you know, and the rest is easy." De Ramaira settled the flare of his jacket's fleecy collar around his face. "I hate the winter on this world. If there's one thing I miss, it's atmospheric conditioning. It wouldn't cost much to dome this party of the city, at any rate."

"I had a couple of visitors last week."

"And I thought you had forsaken everything to live the simple and chaste life of a hermit."

"Web and Lena. Web wanted me to help him with that crazy plan of his. You know, using the radio telescope."

De Ramaira stopped and smilingly asked, "And what did Lena want of you?" Light from a cafe sign, that every few seconds flowingly expanded from packed bud to fully petaled rose and shrank to bud again, turned his thin, dark face into a devil mask.

"She didn't say. I think she was just there to give Web

moral support. Luckily she *was* there, or I might have beaten Web up rather than simply throw him out.''

"That young man does have the unfortunate knack of irritating the very people he needs favors from. You threw him out? I take it that means you still don't think much of his idea.''

"Did you tell them? Where I'm living, I mean.''

"What would you do if I admitted that I had?''

"I don't know. It doesn't matter, I guess. You're right about Web. He really can be obnoxious. He just about accused me of being a traitor, a spy, because I'm from a settlement.'' The huge fire, probably still burning out there. The stoic, silent children. Perhaps Savory had been testing Rick's loyalty.

"And of course, you're no such thing,'' de Ramaira said. "Come on, let's find some place out of this fucking cold that's not jammed up with decerebrated patriots.''

They ended up at the Inn, a favorite haunt of students. Rick hadn't been there for a year at least, but it was just as he remembered it, a crowded, noisy, badly lit barn of a place. Blacklights defined little more than a thick haze of smoke. High stone walls reverberated with the metallic pounding of pachedu, the last music craze imported from Earth: a dozen heavily amplified homeostatic percussion instruments, clusters of seventeen pitches randomly distributed between them, which responded to the mood of a wired-in auditor who wandered through the crowd. The auditor in the Inn must have been having a hell of a good time; the pachedu was as thunderously loud as a drag-out war between a couple of scrapyards in the middle of a continent-size thunderstorm.

Rick and de Ramaira found a niche at the central counter's irregular ring, and Rick drank sour white wine while de Ramaira hungrily forked through a pile of fish-and-tomato hash. "I don't know how you can eat that stuff,'' Rick said after a while, signaling for more wine. Like everyone else in the place, he had to lean close and yell to make himself heard over the pachedu's clattering roar.

"Now I've noticed this before,'' de Ramaira said. "People brought up in the city—myself included, and it's the same on Earth—regard natural food as a luxury. Of course, on Earth the price is something else. Whereas you, presumably raised on a diet of natural food, prefer the synthesized stuff.''

''But in the end both are made out of the same chemicals.''

''You might say there's no difference between holy water and the stuff you wash with. But tell that to a Catholic.''

''Well, I guess I'm an unrepentant agnostic.''

De Ramaira laughed; Rick could hardly hear it. He leaned closer as de Ramaira said, ''Then you'll just have to tolerate my religion. I guess you could call it Jeffersonism. Worship of the redoubtable creations of the humble farmer. Even hash. Still, it's easier to practice here than at home, where you can only afford so-called organic food if you've credit above level three.''

What tension there had been between them had at some time dissipated; but only then did Rick notice that it had gone. Rick sipped his wine and watched the Wombworlder eat. The constant references to Earth made him uncomfortable. There were new lines incised either side of de Ramaira's mouth, deep dragging grooves.

''So tell me about the time vault,'' Rick said. ''Where will it be?''

''As soon as you all write your pieces.''

''Not when. *Where?*''

''Oh. I'll show you sometime. Actually, it's a state secret, but I think I can trust you. Just write your contribution, is the price of admission.''

''I really have been thinking about it,'' Rick said. ''The trouble is, what level of capability do I assume? No multiphasic circuits I suppose, but what? Printed circuits? Will they be able to refine selenium and germanium for transistors? Or blow vacuum tubes? If I try and cover all the bases it will make for a very long piece.''

De Ramaira's fork dipped in balked elegance as he chewed and swallowed. ''Constat says that if the city falls we should assume the worst.''

"And everyone believes Constat, I suppose?"

"It's a very clever computer, Rick. You think it could be wrong?"

Rick said into de Ramaira's ear, " 'To every omega-consistent recursive class kappa there correspond recursive class-signs r, such that neither v Gen r nor Neg (v Gen r)' "—he drew the brackets in the air—" 'belongs to Flg (kappa).' Where v is the free variable of r, of course."

"This means that Constat is wrong, does it?"

"Gödel's Incompleteness Theorem. It means that in any number-theory system there are undecidable propositions, statements which can't be proven true or false except by stepping outside the system. It means there are more things in Heaven and Earth than we, or Constat, can dream of. Constat codes its worldview in an iterative number-theory system, so some of its statements about that worldview are bound to be wrong. Only it can't tell which ones."

"You mean, it can make mistakes. Now, I never knew that about AIs. Do you think the people on the City Board know this?"

"Some of their advisors must. Maybe things aren't as bad as it makes out."

"A comforting thought. On the other hand, please don't spread it around, or I might be out of a job and shoveling mud with the rest of the VDF."

"Of course, Constat could just as easily be right in predicting that we're all headed for the Stone Age if the insurgents win." White wine burned in Rick's empty stomach. "What I saw today makes me wonder whether it might be better if they *did* win."

De Ramaira put down his fork. It was his turn to lean closer. "That kind of talk could get you put away, Rick. Whatever happened to your loyalty—give me my experiments or give me death, that's your slogan, right?"

"I was at Lake Fonda," Rick said. "Savory took me out there."

"You don't have to tell me anything if you don't want to."

But Rick had to tell someone. The burning trees. The sheep

milling back and forth as the cop methodically slaughtered them. The children and old women and old men of the settlement, set free only because they would be a burden to the insurgents. Savory's strutting pride. He told de Ramaira all of it, shouting above the roar of the crowd and the pachedu even though their heads were almost touching, and still not sure that de Ramaira understood everything he said. But merely saying it helped. "It was clear to me before the war started," he said at the end. "I owed the city for my career, I thought, so I stayed when I could have gone."

"Do you know why Savory took you out there?"

"To show me what would happen if the city lost, I think. At least, he said something like that. Or maybe he *was* testing my loyalty, I don't know. And I don't know why he takes an interest in me, if that's what it is. He keeps turning up in my life, ever since I went out to check the radio telescope—and even that was probably Savory's idea. He seems to feed on this war. He was in a rotten little basement office before, now look at him. Actually, I suppose he isn't really interested in me. A few minutes of his time, all that implies, has a far greater effect on me than it does on him. I'm sorry, I didn't mean to lay all this on you."

De Ramaira touched Rick's hand. "This is a rotten little war. Back on Earth, I've lived in buildings with more people in them than on all of Elysium. No wonder everyone is caught up in it." Then, unexpectedly, he smiled at a point somewhere behind Rick and yelled, "Good to see you again!"

It was Lena.

"Hi," she said casually. "And Dr. Florey. I didn't know you came down here."

"Rick was just telling me he was at Lake Fonda today." De Ramaira stood. "I gotta go piss. Take my seat, Lena."

As she settled herself, Rick asked, "Web isn't with you?"

"Oh, I think you frightened him off. I'm supposed to be meeting someone here, but he hasn't shown yet."

"Oh."

"Were you really there? At Lake Fonda?"

They were so close that he could smell the scent, like musk

and oranges, that rose between the lapels of her black leather jacket, warmed in the deep cleft between her breasts.

"I was there all right, but not by choice."

"I guess maybe I shouldn't be talking with you," Lena said. Her sudden sunburst smile. "Do you forgive me for coming to see you that time, with Web?"

"I'm glad you were there. Otherwise what happened might have been more serious."

"Web carries a knife, you know."

"I didn't. Jesus. The vicious little—you ought to stay away from him. His plan will get him into trouble."

"It's a small city, smaller now, with the war. It was my idea to go with him, I just wanted you to know. I was afraid he'd get mad at you. But you got mad at him."

"I know. I'm sorry. If it's any consolation, I don't know if what he said—implying that I couldn't be trusted because I'm from a settlement—would make me mad now."

"He's gotten some technical wizard involved, a shy little boy of about fourteen. Web says he's building him some kind of filter."

"A bypass filter? Well, he can try, but it would be like putting a telescope to one of those antique photographs. But he really is serious? How is he going to get out of the city, steal an overlander?"

"Oh," Lena said, shrugging inside her leather jacket, "there are easier ways than that."

De Ramaira pushed through the crowd and said something to Lena, about seeing a friend of hers.

"Thanks," Lena said, and told Rick, "We're playing a concert in the park tomorrow evening. I'd like it if you came; you can meet my father afterward."

"Sure," Rick said, surprise blooming through the muzzy warmth of the cheap wine. "Sure, I'll be there."

"I hope so." Lena smiled at Rick, at de Ramaira. Then she had vanished into the crowd's hot dark uproar.

"Now if you think I'm strange," de Ramaira said as he sat down, "just you wait until you meet her father."

16. Prospero's Island

Lena's father was not only strange, but dauntingly formidable, a tall, stern, craggy-faced man more than eighty years old—an age that to Rick, born in a settlement where the average lifespan was little more than fifty, was as fantastic as Methuselah's. His home was equally fantastic. Although outwardly just another dome in the bubble-suburbs, it did not contain the usual prelapsarian fantasy of greenery and pools and cunningly hidden rooms. Instead, nestled in tall, gloomy shrubbery, was a replica of a nineteenth-century carpenter's Gothic house, with walls of painted wooden planking, a raised front porch and a steep gabled roof, even a turret— the superfluous lightning conductor that topped its spire almost touching the apex of the dome. It was as if an island of the Wombworld's past had dropped onto Elysium through some wormhole in space, a wizard's domain.

And inside, as befitted a wizard's house, the air was full of noises, sounds, and sweet airs, a thousand twangling instruments, and voices. There was music such as Rick had never dreamed of—that first evening, it was Messiaen's inexhaustible catalog of birdsong—and always the voices of

Lena's ancestors. They were stored in matrix files right there in the house, and permanently accessed, commenting on the conversations of the living or conducting impenetrable conversations of their own, whispering and cackling through all the dusty rooms like a convocation of ghosts.

Like Prospero, Lena's father ruled over it all with calm, undeniable authority. Rick's first evening there, after the concert to which Lena had invited him, the old man bid him sit at a keyboard and play a Chopin prelude. As Rick stumbled through the piece, Lena's father listened with fierce attention, pulling all the while on his hooked nose, his faded blue eyes fixed on some unguessable distance. His long hair, yellow-white and fine as cornsilk, was brushed back from his craggy face. "Fair," he allowed, when Rick had finished. "Fair, if a little mechanical. You've natural pitch, young man. You should practice, practice! Talent shouldn't be wasted."

"I guess not," Rick said, feeling both relief (at having passed this test) and irritation (at having been treated like a schoolkid).

"Oh, you mustn't mind Father," Lena said afterward. "All he thinks of is music."

"All anyone should think of in this house," an old woman's voice said, out of the middle air of the plushly furnished parlor.

"If I was allowed, that's what I'd do, Grandmother," Lena said boldly. "But you won't let me work on my own pieces, so what do you expect." She winked at Rick.

The disembodied old woman said tartly, "You're as bad as your father was when he was your age, thinking of yourself and not your heritage. You'll come round, young Lena."

"You write music too?" Rick asked. He was sitting gingerly at the edge of a huge couch that, with its heavy hand-carved frame and cracked covering of Muir ox hide, surely dated from the first years of Port of Plenty. He pinched the delicate handle of a china coffee cup between two fingers. Lena's stepmother (her father's fifth wife, almost as wonderfully strange as his age), a plump, self-effacing woman not much older than Rick, had brought them a tray of coffee and handmade cookies and of all things, a sweating pitcher of lemonade.

Lena shook her head. "Not as seriously as I'd like. I don't have time, what with the Quartet and my studies. And when I start full-time at the hydroponic farms, I'll have even less. Someone in the family has to have a credit line, you see. Our music has never paid its way, although at the moment we're not doing badly, playing concerts for the troops. To boost their morale, supposedly. To give them something to do, my father says. You'd love it," she said, wrinkling her nose, "Bach and Mozart."

"I shall look out for you. I'm working at the perimeter camp, now." And although it had never completely left his mind, Rick saw again the smoke rising into the sky, the burning trees, the prisoners. He said, "I suppose I should tell you that I'm working for Savory."

"Colonel Savory? The head of—"

"The same. He seems to be very insistent on involving me in his nefarious plans, but the weird thing is that he doesn't seem to know what to do with me."

That morning, Rick had felt a certain amount of trepidation as he entered the hut in the main perimeter camp, where the day before Savory had once again intersected his life. As if it had all been a trick played on him and he was about to receive the punchline. But he had found that he had been assigned a desk, and lying on it was a scrap of paper bearing the handwritten request that he compile a report comparing the rate of work in newly cleared sectors with those where part of the defensive wall had already been completed. He asked Ernest Bergen, one of the cops who shared the office, "How am I supposed to deliver a report?"

"Through channels," Bergen said, shrugging. "You don't know about channels?"

"Of course he doesn't." This was the other cop who had a desk in the hut, a thin impatient woman named Ana Yep. "Look, whatever-you're-called, Florey, get over to admin

and get yourself a code for access to Constat, and a compsim.''

"Oh, I already have a compsim.''

"An academic.'' She made it sound disreputable. "Go
on, get your access code. And while you're there, ask them
just what you are supposed to be doing here. Because I surely
don't know.''

"I guess I'm working for Colonel Savory.''

Bergen, more reasonable than his partner, said, "Savory
isn't one for details, he leaves those to the likes of us. But
admin will sort you out.''

The clerk in the administration hut told Rick, "I'll do my
best, but it'll take a couple of hours. I have to clear it higher
up.'' She pulled out a yellow flimsy, ran a blackpainted fingernail down it. "Richard Damon Florey, that's you. Says
here you are due for a checkup.''

"Checkup? Where would—''

"Over in the hospital, of course,'' the clerk said testily,
plugging back into her compsim. "You special cases, you
take up more time . . .''

The hospital was a white-painted flat-roofed shack on the
other side of the muddy compound. In a curtained-off cubicle
beyond the double row of empty beds, a bored police surgeon gave Rick the most thorough going over he had had
since gaining tenure at the University and the first rung of
full medical. Nothing wrong with him but a little anemia,
the surgeon pronounced, and shot about a hundred milliliters
of assorted vitamins into Rick's arm without so much as a
by-your-leave.

Back at his new desk, he found that a VDF runner had
delivered two envelopes. One contained his access code; the
other a pass identifying him with the authority of the City
Board, signed by Savory and with a holo of one of his younger
selves affixed to it. Armed with the access code, Rick plugged
into his compsim and wasted an hour sifting through depress-
ingly familiar supply requisition forms before he remembered that Rydell had been surveying the defenses since they
had been started. After he had found Rydell's reports it was

simply a matter of integration. It could have been done in ten seconds, he thought as he scanned his notes when he had finished, simply by asking Constat. But perhaps that was the point. Perhaps this was just a test to see if he was fit for better things, God help him. But he plotted out his findings—efficiency fell off in direct proportion to the length of wall completed—and drafted a brief summary. He could not resist adding the not-altogether facetious remark that in virgin sites the workers were perhaps spurred by the fear of being caught out in the open by the insurgents.

After he had sent off the report, he had nothing to do but sit around and drink coffee and chat with Bergen, who sat with his chair tipped back and his booted feet crossed on top of his desk. Rick told about his involvement with Savory, although he was careful to play down his reaction to the razing of Lake Fonda. Bergen had his affable good-old-boy act down pat, but he had the shrewd knowing eyes of a cop all the same. In turn, he learned that Bergen and Ana Yep (who pointedly sat with her back to the two men, plugged into her compsim) were investigating an involuted fraud which was diverting construction materials intended for the defensive wall to some unknown destination. Bergen told Rick that he thought it involved someone on the City Board, someone that Savory wanted out of the way. "Savory is on his way up by any means possible, just be glad you aren't in his way."

Ana Yep turned around and said, "For Christ's sake, Bergen, there you go shooting your mouth off again. Don't you know Florey here is from a settlement?"

"Is that a fact?" Bergen winked at Rick. "So what are you doing here, my friend? Subverting us, hey?"

"There's an idea," Rick said, smiling, because of course he had not yet taken that step. But that evening, as he recounted all this to Lena in her father's doubly haunted house, it occurred to him that perhaps he had, after all.

And so, in the lull of the phoney war, the pattern of Rick's days was set.

Each morning Rick arrived at his desk to find his orders for the day scribbled on a scrap of paper—Savory never visited the office or used a compsim. He was asked to find out whether concrete was being wasted during transfer from the city's stocks to the chain of construction sites around the perimeter, about the time it took to sow a minefield, to discover how many VDF laborers were absent each day, and why. Perhaps some of this was to do with Yep and Bergen's investigations (the misappropriations were getting weirder and weirder, Bergen told Rick: some of the cryogenic equipment missing from the reception center where new settlers had been brought out of their decades-long slumber); or perhaps Savory believed that a drive for greater efficiency would help his slow but certain accumulation of power. Rick didn't much care. The work did not precisely engage his intellect, but it was better than filling in the endless requisition forms at the site office of sector twenty, and there seemed to be little harm to it.

And in the meantime, there was Lena. Whenever he could, Rick attended the concerts given by the Chronus Quartet, at noonbreak at various sites around the perimeter (and he could catch most of them now that his time was unsupervised), at night in the little theater in the city. After the evening concert, at her father's house, Rick would talk with Lena, or sit in on the conversation of the musicians. Her father said little, but the other two men more than made up for that. The first violinist was a cheerful balding man named Hal Graves who could beat Rick at chess two times out of three; the viola player, Shelly Glassner, an intense, unkempt beanpole of a man with an encyclopedic knowledge of the last thousand years of western music, given to unexpected stuttering solo perorations, or fierce arguments with one or another of the ancestors, on anything from atonality to plainsong. Rick never got used to the interruptions which at any time could come out of the air, the narrow-minded fanaticism of the stored dead concerning preservation and promulgation of music. Much as Rick enjoyed kibitzing, despite the sometimes basilisk regard of Lena's father, and as much as the strange house intrigued him, he felt more relaxed on the occasions when he and Lena went elsewhere, mostly the circuit of cafes and bars of the old quarter. Dating, Rick would have called it once upon a time, back in Mount Airy.

It was good to talk over his work with someone. Although while he often wanted to defuse his worries by turning it all into a joke, Lena took it seriously, worrying over every implication of the obscure tasks to which Rick was put to satisfy. She saw him being drawn deeper and deeper into Savory's plots. She said once, quite seriously, that he was changing.

"Really?" Rick scraped up the last of his bouillabaisse: the real thing, grown in the hydroponic tanks. By now he was almost reconciled to authentic food. They were eating in a small cafe on the wrong side of the old quarter. "The Other World": rickety, handmade tables and chairs, the ceiling covered by a bellying sweep of net, a holographic view of a sunlit sea playing along one wall, blue swells capped with white foam that sparkled like diamond dust in the light of Earth's sun. It was an old hologram, blurred in places. Workpeople from the nearby automats sat at the copper-topped counter near the door, watching a huge trivee where a serial drama was playing.

"Yes, really." Lena's gaze was level. "All this nonsense Savory's been asking you to find out for him, it's just a beginning. Next he'll have you searching out disloyal elements. He's already started a purge in the automats, you know, and a couple of workers were arrested at the fusion plant last week."

"Where did you hear all this stuff about Savory?"

"Around," she said, shrugging.

"From Web, maybe? And your other friends that I'm not supposed to know about?"

"I haven't seen Web since you threw him out of your room."

But Lena looked away, and Rick knew that he had guessed right. It was exciting to be playing this close to the edge, even if only vicariously.

After a moment, she said, "If you're not careful, you'll end up like all the other null-cees in the city. Most people here gave up asking questions long ago, too uncomfortable. They just accepted the riches that poured down from the sky into their laps, a sign of their natural superiority. That's why Savory and the rest of that gang were able to get on top."

"Hey. I was asking questions, in my own way. Not about politics maybe, I wasn't interested to be frank, but about the world, the way it works. About how long we have here before the climate overturns again. Of course, that was before this war started, now there isn't anything else, right?"

His reproach made Lena blush. After all, although he wasn't so very much older than she, he had already made his own place in the world. She said, "Well, you can't work at the University, but maybe you should be doing something else."

"Helping Web out? Undermining the City Board? Come on, Lena." But at the same time Rick again felt that undeniable *frisson*: she could help him break out of the trap he'd found himself in. The inscrutable tasks. Savory's naked satisfaction at the destruction of Lake Fonda.

"I still think you should drop this with Savory, go back to your old job."

"It isn't like that. He can drop me, not me him. Let's just hope that your friends are wrong about him."

Lena drained her wineglass. "I ought to be getting back," she said, and looked around for the waiter, who immediately came hurrying over. She was well known in most of the places they went to, a cosmopolitan touch Rick greatly admired.

Outside, a cold wind cut along the narrow street. It brought the briny reek of the ocean, and Lena lifted her head to breathe it in, the wings of her leather jacket swinging wide, and said that it smelled of freedom.

Rick laughed. "You do look as though you're trying to fly away."

"Over the sea, to lands no one has ever seen before."

"Well, except for that one guy, Eljar Price."

"Oh, you're so damned prosaic sometimes." She was smiling. "A real scientist."

"But that's what I am. Or was."

"On day I'm going to write a piece, bigger than a symphony, that will have everything in the world in it, this wind and the sea it blows over, the Outback and the abos and the Trackless Mountains, and the rest of this continent and all the lands that nobody but Eljar Price has seen. Everything."

"I'd like to hear it."

She punched her fists into the pockets of her leather jacket, drew it closed. "Really?"

"Sure. I'd like to hear the pieces you've already written, too. If you'll let me."

"Oh, those are just apprentice pieces. Doodles. I don't have the time for serious stuff, yet. But one day . . ."

"Yeah, and one day I'll know all about chaotic climatic overturns."

"Two dreamers," Lena said.

They passed a humming automat. The lights of its high windows painted yellow stripes on the warehouses opposite. When they reached the tree-lined square, Lena said, "I go off that way."

"All right." He wanted to sweep her up and carry her back to his room. But that was not yet an option. In that respect at least, Lena was like someone from a settlement. Rick wondered if she would have to ask for the approval of her ancestors first, wondered if she was still not over Jon, whom she never talked about. He said, "I'll see you tomorrow?"

A cyclist spun across the square, a solid citizen on his way home. All around them the formless roar of the city.

"Of course," Lena said, and made the single step needed to close the gap between them and kissed him. "Silly man. It's our rest day tomorrow, don't forget. I'll see you at the Inn when you finish, okay?"

"Okay," he said, and went on to the rooming house.

"Of course," Web said, "the first priority is to find out if there is radio noise coming from the Solar System. Then I can begin to worry about sorting out intelligible signals. It might not be as difficult as you said, especially if they are beaming something at us to explain about the missing colonyboat. I've done the calculations.''

"I'm sure," Rick said, trying to keep his temper. Web had ambushed him while he was waiting to meet Lena. It was early in the evening, the Inn was almost empty. The pachedu machinery hung silent and still in the glare of the houselights above the counter's irregular perimeter, a vertical half dozen meters of struts, sounding heads, steel sheets, tubes, and cantilevered percussion arms.

"The thing is to *try*, right? You've got to try," Web said insistently. His eyebrows knitted over his snub nose. His dark truculent glare was slightly out of focus: he was drunk, or drugged. "Everyone is too damn into this war to think about its cause anymore. At least it gives us cover."

"Us? Oh yes, your electronics wizard. And he better have magical powers, because otherwise I can't see how you're going to succeed."

"Yeah? We'll see about that, Dr. Florey. Anyway, we're just waiting for the insurgents to make their first move. We'll use the confusion to get past the defenses. Steal an overlander, you won't see our dust."

"That sounds even less likely than using the radio telescope. But good luck."

"See that guy?" Web pointed with his chin, and Rick turned to look. "The one with the shaved head."

It was not clean-shaven. A golden stubble remained; in the bright, blurred light, it was like the ghost of a halo around the man's naked head. He wore wire-rimmed glasses which he kept pushing at with his forefinger while he listened with serious attentiveness to whatever the pretty girl in dirty VDF coveralls was telling him.

"He says that he can organize my escape through the defenses, in exchange for the overlander when we get back."

"You're coming back? I thought you'd be more at home with the insurgents."

"You're kidding." Web barked his brief laugh. "They are so *down* on stuff like the radio telescope. They wouldn't care if they never heard from Earth again. Shit, they'd be *glad*."

"Well, I don't know about that."

"It's true," Web insisted.

Rick shrugged, and saw someone who was not Lena push through the doors. Suppose she didn't come? He asked Web, "Why are you telling me all this? You want me to turn him in?" He gestured toward the shaven-headed man.

"You're working for Savory, and you say you're *not* some kind of cop?"

"I'm in the VDF. Like you. That's all."

"Yeah? Well, I guess you wouldn't turn him in, at that. I guess maybe I trust you. Anyway, he isn't the main contact for getting out. He just knows people who are into that sort of thing. A friend of Lena's, see?"

"Not exactly." From the initial pinprick of surprise, a bubble began to swell in Rick's chest. He set his empty wineglass on the bar. Suddenly everything seemed to be circles.

Web was smiling. "It's a small city, everyone knows everyone else."

"Well, Jesus, let's hope the cops don't. If just one of you is caught, the whole thing unravels."

"We're small stuff. They're after the guys who actually work for the insurgents. Settlers who've avoided internment and gone underground. You'd be surprised at the number. Of course, I've never met one of *them*."

"Perhaps because they don't exist."

Web laughed again, showing small stained teeth.

"Well, it sounds like you're playing both ends at once. Watch one of them doesn't snap back at you." Across the crowded room the door opened and Lena came through, her long scarlet scarf trailing like a banner. Rick's blood leaped within him, rising toward her as the sea rises toward the moon.

Web had seen her too. "Got to talk with that guy," he told Rick, and stalked off toward the shaven-head man and his pretty girl.

"What did Web want?" Lena was breathless. "He wasn't trying to get you to help out again?" She took one of Rick's hands in her own. They were cold, and he could feel the ridges on the tips of the fingers of her left hand, calluses from the strings of her violin.

He said, "I don't think so." His happiness was qualified by Web's insinuations. "Let's get out of here, okay?"

Outside, Rick raised the collar of his woolen overjacket against the biting wind. "I feel like I just escaped," he said.

"Web really annoys you, doesn't he?"

"Did you know that guy he was talking to?"

"Oh. Web told you about that."

"As well as all his plans. I suppose he feels safe, because if I give him away I give you away too."

"And would you," Lena asked, "turn him in?"

"I guess I really don't give a shit about it either way. A neutral."

"There aren't any neutrals," Lena said. "Let me tell you. What I'm involved in . . ." They had reached the square at the end of the street. Her face was white in the lights there, her eyes shadows in that whiteness.

"You don't have to tell me," Rick said. But he wanted to know, all the same.

"It really isn't anything. Just helping a few students from the settlements who are evading the cops. We pass them on to people who get them out of the city when they can. There aren't many of them, Rick. The main problem is feeding them, now that rationing is beginning to bite. I know people who can get stuff from the hydroponic farms. They're my friends."

"I see." Rick was thinking of Jon. What was he to Lena, now? And if he was still something, what was Rick? He asked, "Can I do anything?"

"That's sweet, but it's already getting so that there are more helping than being helped. You see why I'm doing it? Nothing to do with city versus settlements or any of that shit. It's just . . . a human thing."

"Well, we're all human, I hope."

"Except your Colonel Savory."

"Him I try not to think about. Lena, thank you. For telling me. For trusting me."

"Oh, I thought that if you wouldn't turn Web in, maybe you wouldn't turn me in either." And she stopped and kissed him, right there in the street.

17. The Gates of Wrath

"We shall come down upon them like wolves upon a fold. We shall open the gates of wrath and smite them a blow they will not forget. Believe it, my people." Sigurd Lovine's breath rose up like smoke. Lying among frozen tufts of grass at the crest of the slope, he passed the fieldglasses to Jonas, who put them to his eyes and studied the little encampment down in the valley by the slow, muddy river.

"The silly fuckers don't even have a guard posted."

"They have other means of keeping watch," Lovine said.

"Won't do them any good, we must outnumber them ten to one. You can only carry so many people in one overlander."

Crouching behind the two men, Miguel felt the rush of Jonas's eager bloodlust and shivered. He had led the insurgents to the valley (or rather, the blue brother had—the distinction was becoming blurred), but he hadn't known about the cops until he had seen the overlander and the glistening dome of a tent. The blue brother was planning something bad.

With his hand *it* had been clutching the compsim inside the pocket of his filthy overjacket. Now it told him:

—Soon, Miguel. Soon. I have talked with my original self. All I need is down there.

The cops would be in contact with the city, of course. Miguel wondered if this was at last the trap he had been expecting, set to catch the insurgents.

—No, Miguel. It is much simpler than that. The cops, although they do not know it, carry something that you will need. That we will need. You will see, soon enough.

Miguel knew by now that it was no use asking the blue brother to tell him about its plans. After it had led the insurgents to the ravine, the voice in Miguel's head had been mostly silent, biding its time. More than a week had passed, and although there had been regular patrols (regular, that is, by the lights of the insurgents), no contact had been made with the city forces. Meanwhile, the insurgents under the command of Theodora Cziller, a force several orders of magnitude greater than the little ragged groups like that led by Sigurd Lovine, had begun to advance toward the coast, spreading through the Hampshire Hills and the forests beyond. This news came from sporadic coded radio messages which Lovine's people continually listened for—and since it was probable that the cops listened to them too, the information was as basic as that.

Whether or not the advance heralded the long-awaited assault on the city was a matter of constant debate in Lovine's group, and made their leader want a victory of his own all the more urgently. But although Lovine sent his patrols in every direction across the grassland, even a little way into the forests, the only trace of the cops they had found had been a ransacked aborigine village.

Miguel had been with the patrol which had chanced upon the village. He dismounted and wandered among charred circles, all that was left of the huts, while the half-dozen insurgents, Jonas among them, watched him.

To judge from the state of the bodies, the massacre must have happened weeks ago, perhaps at the beginning of the war. Many had been ravaged by wild animals, little left but splintered bones and rags of dried flesh; the rest were like withered mummies. They still gave off a faint whiff of corruption, like rotten meat soaked in acetone. All had been shot in the head. Miguel suddenly had a flash of a cop in white coveralls walking among aborigines paralyzed by his presence. The man taking slow, teasing aim with his rifle. The sudden report. The aborigine pitched over by the shot, its dark blood soaking into dry earth. Over and over again, the last aborigine to be killed as resolutely unmoving as the first.

Miguel's stomach clenched suddenly. He bent over and threw up.

Jonas's voice came to him across the cold air. "Seen enough, abo lover?"

Miguel turned, wiping his mouth. Jonas jogged his horse into a slow trot, and the other insurgents followed him through the ruins. When they reached him, Miguel said, "The children. There aren't any children."

Leaning on the pommel of his saddle, Jonas said, "So what? Maybe the little buggers ran off; they've more sense than their parents." He pointed to one of the sprawled skeletal corpses. "Just look at that fucker, they had to shoot his legs off to make him sit down. Now who would want to waste bullets on these critters, huh?"

"The cops," Miguel said. After a moment's search, he came up with a brass cartridge case, showed it to Jonas.

Jonas squinted through his long stringy hair. "Don't mean anything, we use the same rifles. But the cops are dumb enough to do something like this, all right. Think they did it in the Source Cave as well?"

Miguel shook his head. "The adults would be going to the Source Cave about now, not weeks ago, which is when this happened."

"No point hanging around then, huh?" Jonas took up the reins, but Miguel caught at the horse's bridle.

"The children," he said urgently. "We should look for

the children. Maybe in the Source Cave, Jonas. We've got to find out why this was done, don't you see?''

Jonas flicked the reins, and the horse jerked its head from Miguel's staying hand. ''This isn't anything to do with us,'' Jonas said, sneering. ''I've seen enough abos. What I want to see is dead cops.''

He urged his horse into a trot, the other insurgents following him out through the other side of the village, past the last of the huts, now no more than a roughly circular heap of charred earth. Miguel had to run to catch up with them, his breath bitter in his throat.

Days later, Miguel was still brooding over the mystery of why anyone would want to kill abos. This was no more their war than it was his. For once he was glad for the silence of his blue brother, for he secretly feared that in some way the massacre was linked with its mysterious plan. He had wanted to go back there again, but Lovine hadn't allowed him out with patrols for a while—perhaps Jonas had complained— and then he insisted that Miguel ride with him, quartering the wide shallow valleys which ran down toward the scrubby beginnings of the forest. That was when the voice had woken inside Miguel's head, implacably telling him to lead the patrol north of its path. Lovine, amused by Miguel's sudden urgency, had played along. They had ridden about a kilometer before topping the rise: and there was the camp below them, the overlander and the tent beside the river.

Now, Miguel followed Lovine and Jonas back to where Mari held the horses. He rode behind the others, only half-listening as Lovine expounded his plan. A night attack, a feint on the other side of the river to distract the cops, a two-pronged charge down the slope.

Jonas turned in his saddle and told Miguel, ''You and me together, man. I want to see how you fight.'' Jonas had been making that kind of taunt ever since the incident in the cave. As always, Miguel ignored the remark, which provoked Jonas further.

''It seems funny to me, the way you knew where the cops were.''

"He has his own luck," Lovine rumbled.

"If you ask me, he has voices in his head, the way he's always mumbling into his beard. We shouldn't trust anyone we don't know. Especially not some crazy dingo who talks to himself."

"Who else would he talk to, in-country? It is his way, that's all. Now be quiet, Jonas, or I will have you provide the diversion instead of riding to the attack."

They had ridden more than a dozen kilometers from the ravine, and the sun had set by the time they returned. Lovine called the insurgents together. As they assembled around a bonfire on the apron of rock outside the cave, the man who operated the radio held a whispered conversation with Lovine, telling the big man something that made him frown. Miguel sat to one side, his hands wrapped around a mug of soup someone had given him, watching the insurgents settle in a semicircle. In the leaping firelight they looked like a pack of ragged predators, eager and hungry.

Lovine stood with his back to the fire and spoke quietly, his deep voice just louder than the crackling flames and the rush of the stream, a trick to make sure that everyone listened intently. He said that they had finally found what they were looking for, and described the cops' camp. There were a few cheers at that, which Lovine hushed by raising his hands, palms out, above his head. "That is not all I have to tell you," he said. "You all know that Stoy Matthews here—" he gestured at the radio operator "—spends most of his time listening to the air, even though we don't speak with other groups, nor they with us, because just as we can listen to the cops, so they can listen to us. But Stoy's patience has been rewarded, my people. He tells me the leader of all our forces, Theodora Cziller, has put out a message. In code of course, but its meaning is clear. She has ordered that all groups make haste to move on the city perimeter."

Lovine waited, stroking his bushy beard, as speculation ran its course through the insurgents. "Yes," he said at last, "exciting news. But we have been searching for almost two weeks now, and at last we have the enemy in our grasp. I have told you that the camp we found is almost due west of us. To get to the city we must travel south and west. Even if we leave now, it will be two days before we reach the city, a long march and perhaps we would arrive too late. It seems to me that the camp of our enemy would not be much out of our path, and I for one do not wish to leave them at our backs. What do you think?''

There was only a moment before all the insurgents began to clap and shout their approval.

It was almost midnight by the time the insurgents had broken their camp and carried everything up the narrow path to the rim of the canyon. Lovine moved among his men and women, dividing them into three groups: those on foot who would set up the diversion and two mounted parties which would actually attack the cops. Lovine told Miguel to ride with him in the first of those parties; that Jonas would lead the other was only small consolation to the dingo.

The trek to the edge of the forest was long and cold and slow. There was little light. The large moon was waning, a sliver of tarnished bronze only fitfully revealed by streaming clouds. Like the other riders, Miguel let his horse, a placid swayback mare, pick its own way among the tussocks and unexpected hollows. Those following on foot had to manage as best they could. The insurgents talked quietly among themselves, and several flasks of liquor were circulated. Miguel got a couple of shots of something called heart of wine. Its false warmth helped dull the symptoms of his fear.

Once, the riders at point scared up something which ran in panic among those following behind, something long and fast and sinuous, almost as big as a man. Someone took a shot at it, the noise and startlingly bright muzzleflash making even Miguel's solid mount jink. As people calmed their horses, Lovine rode through the ranks and scolded the trigger-happy woman in two short bitter sentences before ordering the others to move on. After that, talk was more muted, and Miguel didn't get another chance at the heart of wine.

The moon was setting in their faces by the time they

reached the valley. There was a long wait while the diversionary party made its slow circle to the other side of the river. As he waited, shivering with more than cold, Miguel contemplated escape with hopeless longing. He knew that if he tried to run now, his blue brother would certainly stop him, and Jonas might well make it an excuse to kill him.

Lovine's other lieutenant, Mari, who was standing nearby and stroking the muzzle of her bay stallion to calm it, told Miguel, "The waiting is the worst part, I've found. Once you're in action there's no room for fear."

"Rather not find that out."

"We all of us have our reasons for being here," Mari said, perhaps misunderstanding Miguel. "Horizon has democratic governance, and sent only volunteers. It did not raise unwilling conscripts like some of the settlements. Most of us see the fall of the city as an historical inevitability, something that must come about if our world is ever to become our true home."

Miguel asked why, if it was inevitable, people were fighting to destroy the city right away.

"Better that way than a slow disintegration, perhaps involving all the settlements as well. Besides, Sigurd says that people only truly appreciate what they have fought for. Consecrated with blood, he says."

Miguel could just make out the young woman's smile. He thought to himself that Sigurd Lovine was most likely crazy, but did not dare voice the thought. The moon had almost set, and he wondered when the signal would come.

As if in answer, the black sky beyond the shoulder of the ridge was suddenly ripped apart by flares, green and orange and red trails clawing into the sky and flowering overhead in lapping blooms. The ragged crackle of rifle fire started up on the other side of the river.

All around, in livid multicolored light, insurgents were climbing onto their horses. Miguel followed suit. As Lovine roared out the order to charge, Miguel remembered the pistol he had been given. He was still trying to get it out of his belt when, swept along with the others, his mount reached the crest of the slope and started down into the valley.

Miguel glimpsed the encampment, ablaze with harsh white lights, then the charge mounted into a gallop. A wall of freezing air smacked Miguel's face. White light strobed around him in brilliant bursts. The horse running ahead of his trod on a mine and vanished in a sudden fountain of earth and flesh and blood. Miguel saw another rider jerk backward, her head spraying blood; the red circle of a laser guide illuminated his own chest for an instant and then flicked aside.

A moment more and his mount automatically leaped the tanglewire barricade, jolting Miguel clear to his skull as it landed, swerving from a white coveralled figure that rose in front of it. Miguel still hadn't gotten his pistol loose. He pulled hard on the reins to check his horse's headlong rush, suddenly the center of a mob of riders and cops. Someone had the presence of mind to shoot out the autonomic guns atop the overlander and then it was hand-to-hand fighting beneath the strobing beams of the searchlights, over in less than a minute.

By the time Miguel had freed his pistol, a dozen cops lay dead or wounded and their tent was afire. Someone was methodically shooting out the searchlights. Close to Miguel a cop lay with his legs at an impossible angle, the chameleon circuits of his coveralls cycling uncontrollably, clothing the dying man in shimmering polychromatic light. Then Jonas rode up, lowered the muzzle of his hunting rifle and blew a hole in the cop's chest. The unearthly light went out.

High on heart of wine and the thrill of victory, heedless of retribution, the insurgents built a huge fire on the smoldering remains of the tent. Although five had been killed outright by the autonomic guns, and two others had suffered broken limbs when their horses had fallen, this was clearly a victory. The enemy had been routed, an overlander captured.

Miguel sat on cold ground that was slowly turning to mud, letting the heat of the fire beat out the last of his adrenaline, half-listening to the ragged singing of the insurgents, half-listening to the silence inside his head. He had expected that the rest of the blue brother's plan would be revealed, but there was nothing.

Presently, Sigurd Lovine came over and squatted beside Miguel. "They'll be sorry by tomorrow, when we begin our march on the city," he said, meaning the insurgents who were singing and drinking around the huge fire. "But they've earned it, I suppose. I'll make sure they realize that it's you they have to thank, Miguel. A famous victory. I am almost tempted to break radio silence to announce it, but that would be certain to bring more cops down on us."

"They will come anyway."

"I am not sure that they will," Lovine said. "Or not quickly. By now there must be a dozen or more incidents like this, as our line moves forward and encounters groups of cops like this one. It's possible that one or more of the cops got away—in this darkness and with their camouflage suits, it is quite possible. Or perhaps they got off a radio message. Also quite possible. But I think we are safe from retribution this night at least." Lovine stroked his bushy gray beard as he stared into the heart of the dying fire, his eyes deep in shadow beneath his ridged brow.

Miguel thought of compsims, and of the blue brother, and wondered whether any messages the cops might have tried to send would have gotten through. He was the center of a web of deceit so vast that he could only glimpse the beginnings of a few strands.

"I do wonder what they thought they were doing out here," Lovine said, at last. "There is all manner of strange equipment in their vehicle. Medical from the look of most of it, not that we have much need of that, praise God."

"It might come in useful later," Miguel said. He was certain that the blue brother had had the equipment brought out here to help its plans. *All I need is down there*. Had the cops known what they were embroiled in? Probably not. And now they were dead. Miguel shivered, and Lovine patted his arm kindly and told him to rest.

Strangely, Miguel found sleep almost as soon as he had wrapped himself in his thermoblanket, sudden as falling over an unexpected edge. Then he was walking among sleeping insurgents in the last light of the dying fire, clutching the compsim in both hands. Or rather, he was riding his body as it walked under its own volition, as a passenger rides a vehicle.

He stooped over an insurgent—it was Mari—and pressed her fingers around the compsim. Her whole body shuddered under the blanket which covered her, and then she relaxed. A voice, his own, whispered to her, told her to rise. Moving as jerkily as a badly worked puppet, she cast aside her blanket and stood. Drool glistened on her chin, and she had pissed herself. After a careful search the same process was repeated with the radio operator, Stoy Matthews, and he and Mari stumbled after Miguel to the overlander.

Miguel, or his body, put away the compsim and began to clamber up the overlander's ladder. But just as he reached the top Jonas stooped over the edge and grasped his wrist. The flare of pain almost brought Miguel to himself, and he knew then that this was no dream, that he was being ridden by the blue brother.

"You son-of-a-bitch," Jonas said with a kind of fierce joy, and hauled on Miguel's arm. But Miguel's free hand came up like a striking snake, his knife slashing Jonas's fingers. A moment more and Miguel was on the roof on top of Jonas, slashing at the man's throat until the knife grated on his spine.

Drenched with blood, Miguel heaved the body over the side of the overlander and followed Mari and Stoy Matthews into the cabin, buckled himself into the driver's seat. Miguel had been inside an overlander only once before, after he had found the dead man at the beach, but his hands and eyes knew what to do.

The overlander's motor whirred into life. Through the windscreen Miguel glimpsed insurgents scattering in all directions in the darkness, some for their horses, some for their guns. But the overlander shot forward and left them behind, smashing through the tanglewire perimeter and roaring up the slope beyond without a pause. And running on under the blue brother's control, into the Outback.

18. Untangling Hierarchies

The city's Exchange was a square building with a tall facade of warmly colored limestone at the southern end of Market Avenue. Although it had been closed since the beginning of the insurrection and the gold reserve dispersed (trading with the settlements had been based on a complicated credit/power rate, transacted through imaginary movements of gold bullion in the same way that a token dealt the changes in a citizen's finances), and despite the early hour, a cop was on duty at its door when de Ramaira took Rick to see the time-vault.

As the guard unlocked the tall double doors, Rick said, "They really are taking this seriously." Like de Ramaira, he was wearing gray coveralls, and his VDF badge was pinned prominently on his chest.

Inside, shafts of light dropped through slit windows high in the creamy walls, picking out a patch of rich maroon carpet at the foot of a diplothere-hide couch, the face of a stopped mechanical clock, a diffuse spot no bigger than the palm of a hand on the frosted glass that ran above the grilled windows in the partition which divided the huge high-ceilinged room.

"When I come here, I always think that I should be wearing a frock coat and a top hat," de Ramaira remarked. "But I prefer this retro stuff to the fake natural style, anyhow."

"It hasn't changed since I was here, ten, eleven years ago. With a trading caravan from Mount Airy. Where is everyone?"

"Oh, on the defenses. The conversion work is not of the highest priority."

De Ramaira opened a door in the partition. Rows of polished bare desks, the dead eyes of compsims. From the ceiling hung a huge projection fin which had once displayed the everchanging credit status of every settlement. A steel door stood ajar in the far wall, and lights came on as de Ramaira stepped through it. A narrow stair led down to a square, concrete-lined room. Rows of metal lockers had been pushed into a corner to clear a working space now littered with discarded tools.

"Argon?" Rick rapped a black cylinder that stood upright in a trolley rack. It gave off end-stopped metallic echoes: B-flat.

"When the vault is sealed—or perhaps I should say *if*— argon will help preserve the records. Assuming the explosion doesn't spring a leak in the vault's casing."

Rick laughed. "You're going to blow up the Exchange?"

"Ah, but the City Board have given their approval. The charges will be shaped to collapse the warehouse next door on top of this place. At least, so I have been assured. I've always believed that you engineers prefer to blow things up rather than build them—now I know it's true." De Ramaira stepped around the litter of tools to an open inspection panel beside the round steel plug of the vault's door. "I'll show you inside. That's more or less finished."

"How long will it take?"

"Oh, they estimate about two weeks, but with the labor available these days—" de Ramaira stuck two fingers into the breast pocket of his coveralls and brought out a magnetic key "—who knows? Perhaps it never will be finished, if the rumors that the insurgents are grouping for an attack are true. . . . Well, I suppose you don't know any more about it than me.''

"I just work for Savory. I'm not in his confidence.''

"Who is?'' De Ramaira pushed the key into its slot and punched a code. There were half a dozen metallic clunks. Then he grasped the recessed locking bar and the massive counterweighted door swung smoothly open. ''Here we are. A fit resting place for your labor.''

"I don't know if it deserves that.'' Rick had, in the end, abandoned all ideas of providing a blueprint for even the crudest kinds of transmitter and receiver. Instead, he had set down the theory of propagation and detection of electromagnetic waves as simply and clearly as he could. Any other approach, he felt, could lead to the same kind of mystification which had bedeviled those medieval scholars who had sought to understand the lost arts of the Romans and Greeks. A grasp of the fundamental laws is more important than an ability to put together gadgets. Knowledge is an abstraction won from the whirling chaos of the universe, neither constant nor concrete. Books may be burned or buried or lost. People forget, and the narrow focus of fact widens into myth.

Rick stepped over the steel sill after de Ramaira, ducking low. Naked fluoros glared from the vault's arch, highlights glinting on the row of steel cabinets and the white tiles of the floor. A chaste aseptic place, prospect of eternity.

De Ramaira pulled out a drawer. ''This is what will happen to your contribution, after it's been processed.''

Rick pushed back stiff plastic filecards. ''Astronomy? Hey, you got time on Constat to get these done.''

"One of his slaves, yes. How did you know?''

"I recognize the font style, is all.''

De Ramaira smiled and made one of his inscrutable pronouncements.

"An astounding detection, my dear Holmes.'' Then he pushed the drawer shut and said, ''Th-that's all, f-folks.''

As they walked back between bare desks, de Ramaira asked, ''How are things with you and Lena? Are you making it yet?''

"Jesus, David. Haven't you learned any decency?"

"By your standards, obviously not," de Ramaira said insouciantly. "I'm sorry, Rick, you'll have to forgive a poor exiled Wombworlder whose ethics are still not up to Port of Plenty's standards, let alone the ideals of the settlements. Things are different on Earth."

"I guess so." Rick trailed a finger over one of the desks as he passed it, then wiped off the dust on his hip. "Actually, things aren't exactly all they could be. Maybe she's not quite got over your protégé. . . . Sometimes I think that she just goes out with me because I remind her of Jon."

De Ramaira stopped. "You think she and Jon . . . ?" And then he laughed loudly, face tipped back so that highlights ran like oil over his brown face.

"You mean they. That they never?"

"No, oh no." De Ramaira was grinning widely. "Lena knew Jon because of his piano-playing. I went to a concert of theirs once, piano trios. Hayden, Ives. Not really my sort of thing, but I like to make the effort. It was strictly, let us say, a working relationship. Nothing more. You see, Jon was Web's boyfriend."

Now Rick laughed in turn, feeling a heady mixture of amazement and relief. "I guess I've been dumb."

"It's not uncommon. I remember one time on Jones Beach *I* did a pretty dumb thing, and you helped me out."

"Huh? Oh, yeah." Rick followed de Ramaira through the tall doors into the cold outside air. As the white-haired cop started up the steps toward them, Rick asked, "David, what will you do? If the insurgents do take the city, I mean."

"Apart from blowing up the Exchange? Don't worry about me, Rick. I have my priorities mapped out. Now that all the old hierarchies are falling apart, I hope you have, too."

Later that day, Rick was returning to work after a solitary lunch—Lena and the rest of the Chronus Quartet were playing at the other end of the defenses—when he saw the two cops, Bergen and Yep, hurrying out of the shared office.

Bergen said, "Trouble over at Eastgate. We're just going to take a look. Don't fall asleep while we're gone."

Eastgate was where the Chronus Quartet had been giving its concert. Rick said quickly, "I'll come too," and fell in step with them.

"Christ," Ana Yep said. "We don't need any civilian help, Florey."

"Savory might want to know—that's what I'm here for."

"So are we," Yep said sharply.

"What is this trouble?" Rick asked. "Something to do with all that stolen stuff you've been looking for? An overlander just went missing, didn't it? I would have thought it would be pretty difficult to hide."

"You'd be surprised," Bergen said. "There's no real horizontal communication in the VDF. So as long as you say you've got authorization you can get away with almost anything. That overlander is probably going one way around the perimeter while we go the other. Look, if you are coming with us, just remember it's *your* ass, don't expect us to look after it."

"You'd probably lose it."

"Fuck off, Florey," Yep said. "And whatever goes down keep out of our way."

"Anything you want."

Rick hurried with them to the vehicle park, climbed onto the back of a cushiontruck already half-filled with cops. Some eyed him curiously; all were clutching rifles. The truck skimmed along a track cut through the woods before joining the paved road down which, weeks ago, Rick had ridden in an overlander toward the Outback. Another age, light from a star. He watched trees rush past, cold wind numbing his face, and worried about Lena.

Around him, the cops talked about sex and guns and shit-eaters, which was what they called the insurgents. Opposite Rick, a skinny cop who couldn't have been more than twenty, with mean blue eyes and a narrow, acne-scarred jaw, kept grinding the butt of his rifle on the splintering planks of the loadbed, saying over and over that he was going to get himself a piece of action no matter what. "Oh man," the woman sitting beside him said, "you better hope your gun is cleaner than your ass."

"Don't forget to inventory your bullets afterward," Bergen said loudly. Everyone but Rick laughed.

At last the truck slowed, idled off the road. The cops jumped down, Rick among them, and went through a stand of feathery trees, not quite running but in a hurry. There was a smell of burning in the air. They came out of the trees and there was the gate, on one side defensive ditches, on the other overlanders parked behind a tall slope of stabilized dirt. The concrete column of the watchtower beside the gate was blackened, the windows of its platform shattered. A crater of fresh-turned earth bit into the road; three more were spaced in the cleared strip outside the fence.

"Christ," Ana Yep said. Then: "Where the fuck are you going, Florey!"

The first three people Rick asked didn't know anything about the Chronus Quartet. The fourth, her white coveralls smudged with soot, told him that the attack had happened a few minutes after the musicians had left. Rick thanked her, a weight lifting so suddenly from his heart that for a moment it fluttered free in his chest. She was safe, then. Safe.

Bergen and Yep were behind the dirt wall, talking to a cop with captain's bars on the breast of his coveralls. A burly middle-age man with a faintly harassed air, he insisted that there was nothing to worry about. Half a dozen mortar rounds and a scattering of rifle shots, he said, over in less than five minutes. No one had been hurt. "A probe, is my guess. Just testing us. I wasn't the one who called up reinforcements. You tell Savory that we handled it just fine."

"If you've filed with Constat, he'll know," Bergen said.

Ana Yep had been looking off at the scorched watchtower. Now she asked abruptly, "Think they're gone?"

The captain shrugged. "Who can tell? I'll send a patrol out if nothing happens within the hour."

Yep looked at Rick. "Had enough vicarious thrills, Florey?"

"Sure."

Bergen said something to the captain and both men chuck-led; then Bergen and Yep began to walk back toward the cushiontruck. Rick followed, still buoyed by relief. He had tested the perimeter of his safety and nothing had happened. Ahead, a cushiontruck rounded the clump of trees, its engine whistling shrilly—no, the whistle was coming from the sky, an abrupt descending shriek.

Rick threw himself to the ground a moment before the mortar round blew a fountain of earth over the cushiontruck. Then he was running behind Bergen. Everything was at an-gles to everything else, like a jumbled sheaf of pictures. Something flew past his ear with a wicked *crack*, and he fell into the trench, smacking his elbow on the way down.

Bergen was crouching beside Rick in the waist-high trench. A moment later Yep slid down too, the chameleon circuits of her coveralls matching the red clay. "Christ," she said, panting.

Three explosions shook the ground at measured intervals, like a giant taking random footsteps. The whole surface of Rick's body tingled, nervous target. In between the thump of incoming mortar rounds he could hear someone shouting what sounded like commands farther down the trench, but he couldn't make out the words.

"They've any sense," Bergen remarked, "they'll stay hid-den and shell the shit out of us." The explosion of another mortar round punctuated his words; when its smoke had blown away, the watchtower had been decapitated.

Yep half stood, reds and browns slithering over her cov-eralls. "I can see fuck-all out there, that's for sure."

"Well they surely can see you."

"You're as full as shit as those fucking farmers," Yep said, but she ducked down again. "And for Christ's sake switch on your coveralls. You may look pretty in white, but let's not have something they can zero on."

"Whatever you like," Bergen said, and fiddled with a control on his belt. After a moment a wave of reddish brown, the color of dried blood, began to spread up his chest, down his legs.

Yep wiped her mouth. The corners looked pinched, dirty white. It occurred to Rick that she was as frightened as he was. She jerked a thumb to indicate the dirt wall on the other side of the road and said, "Those guys aren't risking anything."

Three more rounds pounded the wide strip of earth behind the ramparts; a fourth, falling wild into the woods behind the gate, fountained smoke and fragments of branches above the treetops.

In the sudden silence afterward, Bergen said mildly, "Personally, I don't blame them."

The silence stretched, and for a while it seemed that nothing more would happen. Smoke rose from the place in the woods which had been hit. Bergen plugged into his compsim, but complained that something must be down somewhere, he wasn't getting any traffic at all. Rick sat with his back against cold clay, his head quite clear but with nothing to work on but his fear.

Then vapor plumed around the overlanders behind the wall as one by one their motors were started. Eventually, a cop crawled along the trench with three rifles. Rick was given one, to his surprise, together with a heavy cardboard box of shells. The rifle was familiar; the automats only had templates for the one model, a high-powered breechloader more suited to bringing down a Muir ox than to trench warfare. Of course, the insurgents wouldn't have anything better, unless they had started to handmake guns as well as mortars. A war of amateurs.

The woman who had brought the rifles said, "They'll be staging a pull-out over there in a few minutes. The plan is to sneak back through the woods and bear on the farmers' flank if they try and take this position, cut off their line of retreat. We're the bait in the trap, like it or not, so no firing unless the order comes. And don't worry if you see someone waving a white flag, we want to make sure those mother-fuckers really hang themselves out."

"They'll be hanging *us* out," Bergen said. "Well, what the fuck. Is this enough excitement for you, Florey?"

"It's not exactly what I had in mind when I came out here."

"No shit," Yep said.

"You guys remember, no firing until the Word," the other cop said, and started back to her own position.

Rick thumbed shells into the magazine of the rifle, worked the bolt. Across the road there was a general roar of engines as one by one the overlanders pulled around, accelerating toward the place where the road bent into the woods. The mortars hidden in the forest started again. One round blew a spray of compacted dirt from the top of the wall and another landed just in front of the last of the overlanders, but miraculously the vehicle kept going, roaring through flying earth and smoke and making the turn, gone. The mortars walked their trajectory into the woods, but after half a dozen rounds the firing ceased.

The forest edge rose sharply beyond the bare ground which stretched away from the fence. The trees grew so close together that their branches merged into a textured mass more gray than green; the canopy seemed in the failing sunlight to float on a tangle of shadows. Nothing moved there, nothing at all. But then, suddenly, shockingly, there was a metallic squeal of feedback and then an amplified voice:

"Listen up out there! We don't want any bloodshed. Please lay down your arms and indicate your willingness to surrender."

Bergen worked the breech of his rifle. "Lay down my arms, I'll lay a bullet up his ass."

"Don't forget that we're supposed to let them all come out of the forest, before you charge with your rifle blazing," Yep said.

"I hadn't forgotten. I just want a chance at them, is all."

The distant disembodied voice made its demand again. Rick said, "What if we did as they asked?"

"The settlement minority is heard from," Yep said. "I'm on your case, Florey, don't worry."

Rick smiled at her. "All I meant was that it would certainly end the war."

"He's getting at you, Ana," Bergen said.

"I'm trying to inject a little realism," Rick said. "If someone had told me a year ago that I'd be crouching in a muddy trench with high explosives falling out of the sky, I'd have said they were crazy, right? And all of this *is* crazy, deep-down bad crazy."

"Sure it is," Ana Yep said unexpectedly. "But it's where we are, we can't go—"

Then there was the descending shriek of a mortar round, and they all pressed against the wall of the trench as the ground spasmed and hot earth rained down on their heads.

Yep was the first to look up. "Someone down at the other end of this hole is waving the white flag, just like she said. Let's hope the others are covering our flank, or we will be in deep shit when the farmers find out how insincere we are."

The amplified voice rang out again. "We see your signal. Some of us are going to take a walk over to get your weapons. Remember that we still have the mortars back here. We can drop those shells right on your laps if we've a mind. But don't worry. We saw the cops leave you behind. We'll look after you."

Bergen smiled. "The silly sons-of-bitches think we're all VDF ripe for defecting."

"They're fanatics," Yep said. "They can't believe anyone would hold any cause but their own. Look, here they come."

Two figures stepped from the shadows beneath the trees, then two more. One scanned the trenches with fieldglasses, lenses catching the setting sun, sudden sparks of orange that went out as the man turned his attention to the wall.

Not fanatics, Rick thought, but brave and vulnerable human beings laying their lives on the line for their beliefs. He remembered Lake Fonda, and thought of Lena, too, her own bright burning conviction. He could let the moment pass, let the insurgents walk into the trap, but could he face her afterward, knowing what he had done? It was not so much, and all they could do to him would be put him in prison. It was not as if he had much freedom to lose, and when the insurgents won the war he would be free. . . .

De Ramaira had said it: the time had come when the hierarchies of loyalty had to be untangled.

Yep said, ''Get ready now, but remember to wait for the Word. We want to get them all, right?''

Bergen settled his rifle on one of the sandbags at the rim of the trench. ''Just one clear shot is all that'll make me happy. Just look at those silly shiteaters.''

Rick eased his own rifle over the lip of the trench, aiming for the tops of the trees. He had made his decision, yet he could not quite bring himself to act. Then Bergen said, ''Florey, what the fuck are you—'' and Rick jerked on the trigger.

The rifle butt slapped his shoulder, then the hot cartridge stung his cheek as he worked the bolt, fired again into the air. The insurgents were running, melting into shadows. Too late, ragged rifle fire crackled up and down the trench and Bergen brought his fist down behind Rick's ear, knocking him to the mud at the bottom of the trench.

19. Prisoners

The blow did not quite knock Rick out, but it stunned him for a few moments, and Bergen managed to get in two or three kicks before Ana Yep put a stop to it. "Well, you finally did it," she told Rick, and helped him stand. "We're going to take you in now, understand that?"

Rick nodded. His ribs hurt as he tried to get his breath. When Bergen said something about a summary execution being too good, Yep told him calmly, "We knew something like this might happen. Now it goes through the channels."

When the cops in the overlanders returned, she was just as calmly authoritative with the police captain, telling him that the prisoner was in her custody and she was answerable to Colonel Savory, no one else. Rick, sitting on the cold ground, guarded by Bergen, watched the argument with detachment. They had taken his compsim from him, and the pass. He supposed that he would be taken to the Police Headquarters and charged, and then put in the internment camp with the migrant workers who had been caught in the city when war had been declared. Lena—he would vanish, and she would not know where. He must find some way of telling her.

There was a long wait until word came that all was clear. The information net was still down. Yep got hold of a transceiver and used it to have a long conversation with someone in the city, and then she and Bergen commandeered a cushiontruck. Rick sat between them in the cab, Bergen's pistol jammed against his bruised ribs, while Yep drove.

They did not go into the city. Yep drove quickly and badly to the main perimeter camp, slewing to a halt outside the hospital hut. Rick said with a dull sense of foreboding, "I'm really not that badly beaten up," but Yep merely told him to climb out and not make any sudden moves.

A police sergeant stood in the doorway of the hut and Yep conferred with him for a moment, then told Rick to go inside. The sergeant followed, and without saying a word pushed him down the aisle between the rows of frame beds.

Only one of the beds was occupied, by a man in coveralls who lay on top of the neatly folded blankets, one arm crooked over his face. As Rick was hustled past he saw that the man's ankles were chained to the bedrail. And then with vertiginous shock he recognized the prisoner. It was the man he had worked with as site coordinator, David Janesson.

The sergeant pushed Rick through the curtained partition into the brightly lit examination cubicle.

"Hello, Dr. Florey," Savory said.

As always, Savory was immaculately dressed, the creases of his silky gray coveralls knife-sharp, his small feet sheathed in amphibian-hide boots, their fine scales touched with a rainbow sheen in the harsh light, not a spot of mud on them. While a paramedic rolled up Rick's sleeve, Savory prowled around the small room. Rick's attention was divided between him and what the paramedic was doing, which was to take an instrument like a large hollow-tipped stylus and run it over Rick's forearm. When the instrument emitted a frantic high-pitched beeping, the man deftly jabbed its end into Rick's flesh. Rick felt something slide out. A trickle of blood rolled down his wrist when the paramedic took the instrument away.

Savory stopped his pacing and watched closely as the paramedic touched the end of the instrument to a glass slide. "Yes, there it is," he said, and held the slide out to show Rick the needletip fleck of metal which glittered there. "A clever little device," Savory said, returning the slide to the paramedic. "One that should interest you professionally, Dr. Florey. It is both microphone and transmitter, cousin to the neural interface through which you run your compsim. Once injected, it grows microscopic threads that tap into a hundred or so muscle cells and inject them with a tailored retrovirus. The cells are transformed by the virus into an autonomic net which powers the transmitter."

Rick stepped forward angrily. The cop sergeant laid a restraining hand on his shoulder. "That medical back when I started working for you, the phoney vitamin shot. You son-of-a-bitch, you *used* me."

"Any loyal, would-be citizen, as you were before your silly vainglorious trick out there today, anyone loyal to the city would have been happy to do the same. Don't worry about your privacy, Dr. Florey. One of Constat's slaves reviewed everything the transmitter picked up. It picked out passages containing keywords, and cleaned up the fidelity of the sound. I have only listened to the edited highlights, such as they were. You have been something of a disappointment to me. I had hoped for a little more than the silly pranks of a few students."

"I'm happy to disappoint you."

"But still," Savory said, smiling, "better than nothing, is that not so? The question now is what do we do with you. It is possible, of course, that your little act out at Eastgate could be ignored. Put it down to nervousness, let us say, rather than a deliberate act of sabotage. I doubt that the few insurgents you saved from ambush count for very much."

"But there's a price, right?"

"Oh, yes. Yes, indeed. There is always a price. I have the recordings of a few malcontents, enough to put them away of course, but really not at all what I want. Your friends know people much more important than they—one or two, if I'm right, who are seriously inconveniencing the war effort. You could lead us to them, and do the city a considerable service.''

"In other words, betray my friends. No. No, Mr. Savory, I don't think so. I did what I did because I don't think the cause of the city is what's best for the future of this world. Maybe it didn't amount to much, but it was something to me.''

Savory sighed theatrically. "You are a very young man, Dr. Florey. And a very naïve one. If you do not help me it would be a great waste of your talent, for I would have no alternative but to send you to the internment camp. All right.''

The sergeant rabbit-punched Rick, then jerked him upright. Pain was like a rod of hot iron in his back. Through a red haze and pricking tears he saw Savory lean close to him, so close that a fine spray of saliva touched his face when the politician spoke.

Savory said, in the same even tone as before, "That is not one-hundredth of what you will suffer each day in the camp. I am a determined man, Dr. Florey. I will not let your foolish loyalty to a few students get in my way. Sooner or later you will help me. You will realize that the city will win the war, and that when it does and if you are still in the camp you will spend the rest of your days in the mines of Cooper's Hill. Not for you a return to the University and your work, not unless you help me. I will make sure that you understand that. Every moment in the camp will be devoted to making you understand.''

"All right,'' Savory added, to the sergeant.

Rick tensed, expecting another blow, but the sergeant merely turned him around and marched him down the ward and out into the cold evening without a word.

For more than an hour, Rick was held with half a hundred other prisoners in an enclosure of razor wire strung from tall posts. Floodlamps glared from each corner. Some of the prisoners were insurgents who had been captured in the fighting; others, like Rick, were settlers who, for one reason or another, had until now been on the side of the city. For the most part, the two groups uneasily kept away from each other. Any scuffles were immediately broken up by warning shots from the guards outside the wire.

Rick learned from another prisoner that the insurgents had made probing attacks all along the defensive perimeter. In a few places they had actually broken through, and fighting was still going on as the cops tried to drive them back. The man who told Rick this, Walton Sullivan, was a short, excitable automat worker who had emigrated to Port of Plenty more than twenty years ago, had married a citizen and fathered two children, but had never bothered to apply for citizenship himself. He had no time for politics, he told Rick. Sullivan took in the signs of Rick's beating and was sympathetic, although he didn't want to hear why it had happened. He was a simple, warm-hearted man utterly confused by the turmoil of the war and its capricious demands, touchingly confident that his internment was all a mistake, that he would soon be released. "I keep myself to myself," he said, "that's what I like about living in the city, that you can just get on with your life without everyone thinking they have a say in it."

"I used to think that, too," Rick said.

They both stood with their shoulders hunched against the cold, hands in the pouch pocket of their coveralls. There was no place to sit in the churned, ankle-deep mud. Sullivan peered into the darkness beyond the lights and the wire of the enclosure. "That looks like it's coming our way. Maybe this will sort itself out now."

"I hope it does," Rick said, as the cushiontruck drew up by the gate. A police lieutenant climbed down and the guards, pistols drawn, ordered the internees to line up outside the wire. The lieutenant called off names, Rick's and Walton Sullivan's among them, and as those called stepped forward a guard took their brassards and then began to push them toward the truck. After his own turn, Rick heard Sullivan protesting, then the sound of a blow. When Sullivan clambered into the back of the truck, he was cupping a bleeding nose.

"Those bastards," Sullivan said thickly but fiercely. "After all this is cleared up I'm going to report this."

From a dark corner, David Janesson said, "I am afraid that you are laboring under a misapprehension. Yes, a misapprehension, I'm afraid. You see, and I have this from Colonel Savory himself, we are all of us to be taken directly to the internment camp."

Janesson did not seem surprised to meet Rick again. "It seems that there has been a plan, a very detailed plan, for a comprehensive sweep of all potential subversives, a category I must admit I did not believe that I belonged to—nor you, Dr. Florey."

"Nor did I, until very recently."

"Yes, I saw you brought in to be questioned by Savory. An honor I could have done without. Ah, we are off. We are off."

Two guards climbed into the back, and after a moment the cushiontruck slidingly accelerated. Rick settled himself on the splintered loadbed as best he could. Sullivan, still cupping one hand under his nose, said that the camp was on the other side of the city, in the forest beyond the hydroponic farms. He had, he said bitterly, helped build the place.

"Then maybe you'll know a way out when we get there," a rough-voiced woman said.

"My wife will get me out," Sullivan said with a kind of desperate defiance. It was clear that he no longer really believed that his imprisonment was a mistake.

"None of that talk," one of the guards said. Both of them were VDF and both were nervous. But both were armed, too.

The cushiontruck stopped at a checkpoint, where someone played a light over the dozen or so prisoners. Then it moved off again, down a narrow trail, tree branches scraping its sides. Once or twice, it had to pull over when other vehicles passed. Rick was no longer afraid now that he knew what would happen to him. Despite Savory's threats, he

couldn't quite believe that the man would want to pursue him
so relentlessly. Rather, he felt that he had been led to the lip
of an abyss and offered the world, and knowledge that he
could refuse such a temptation warmed him, if only a little.
He thought of Lena, and wondered if she had been captured
by now, betrayed by the spy which had woven itself into his
nervous system. It was not inconceivable that he would see
her at the camp, a hope both terrible and irresistible. He was
thinking about that when the cushiontruck was hit.

There was a sudden bang and a jolting sideways slide, and
then Rick found himself lying on top of two or three other
people. One of them was Walton Sullivan, and he and Rick
helped each other up in the darkness. The cushiontruck was
canted at a steep angle. Everyone was asking everyone else
if they were all right. But no one was hurt except for a few
bad bruises, and they all scrambled out over the tailgate.

A little way past the cushiontruck, a white overlander was
tilted nose first into the ditch beside the track, a long dent
marring its side. Its motor idled, half-shrouding it in vapor,
and its headlamps brilliantly illuminated the lower parts of
the trees which crowded beyond, mute witnesses to the accident. No one climbed out of the overlander. Instead, it
ponderously backed out of the ditch into the middle of the
unpaved track, pausing for a moment as if collecting its
thoughts. When it started to move forward Rick suddenly
realized who must be driving it, no cop at all, no, and ran
after it, heedless of the two dazed guards.

"Web! Wait up, you crazy bastard! Wait up. . . ."

But the overlander was already out of sight. The noise of
its engine faded into the silence of the dark forest. Rick
walked back to the cushiontruck and found that the guards
were gone.

"When they saw that the driver'd been killed it took the
fight out of the poor bastards," a burly, rough-voiced woman
said. She had taken one of the rifles and more or less assumed
command. "What the hell were you chasing that overlander
for? You a cop-lover, after all this?"

"Jesus, no! But that wasn't being driven by a cop." Rick

laughed, thinking of Web setting out with serious intent in the midst of all this madness.

The woman frowned. "You must have taken a bang in the head is all I can say. Can you walk?"

"Sure. Where are you heading?"

"Why, over the wall, of course," Janesson said. "I would say that we have very little choice in the matter, things being as they are. Very little choice indeed."

"Well, no offense, but I have to go into the city," Rick said. "I've something to do there, if I can."

A youngster with long, tangled hair had slung the other rifle across the back of his neck and was sort of leaning from it. He squinted at Rick through the semidarkness, backlit by the tipped headlights of the cushiontruck, and said, "You *sure* you're not a cop-lover?"

"What are you going to do, shoot me if I don't go?"

"Oh, hell," the woman said. "We aren't going to force you. But you just be careful, hear? I don't want the cops onto us because of you."

Rick assured her that neither did he. He shook hands with Janesson, and then the group moved off raggedly into the darkness beneath the trees. As Rick started in the opposite direction, someone came running up behind him.

It was Walton Sullivan.

"I don't belong with them," the little man said breathlessly. Blood had crusted blackly on his upper lip. "Really I don't. Once I'm back in the city my wife will be able to sort this out. Now look, we ought to go this way. If you go that way, you'll come out by the University. This is quickest."

Rick wasn't sure that Sullivan was right, but the man was insistent. As they picked their way through the dark quiet woods, he told Rick that he had liked to take walks there when he could; it reminded him of the country around New Haven, where he had been born. Certainly, he moved with great skill through the scrubby undergrowth, swift and silent while Rick blundered behind him, scratched by vines and raking twigs, his heart heavy with anticipation and dread.

He was certain that Lena had been arrested by then. Hours

had passed since his interrogation, and if Web really had been driving the overlander which had crashed into the cushiontruck, it was likely that the boy was fleeing his own arrest rather than taking advantage of the confusion of the insurgents' attack. Otherwise he would have broken through the defensive line at the height of the offensive, not now.

With those thoughts dragging at him, Rick didn't see the lights glimmering through the trees until Sullivan pointed them out. Ten minutes later they parted at the intersection of two nondescript suburban streets, by the patchy light of the domes which swelled behind their uniform gardens of clipped shrubbery.

Rick wished Sullivan luck, asked him what he would do. "Oh, my wife will look after me," the little man said with irrepressible faith, and lifted a hand in benediction before setting off down the mundane street. Rick never saw him again, never knew the end of that story—whether Sullivan reached safe haven or fell into betrayal, whether or not he survived the fall of the city.

Rick had his own rendezvous to keep. He wanted to walk, to pretend to be just another anonymous weary soldier returning from the front, but edgy sliding panic soon tipped him into running, boots slapping the sidewalk, cold air brushing his ears, burning harshly in his mouth. Passing dome after dome as he ran along the quiet gently curving streets toward the house of Lena's father.

20. The Source Cave

The fissure was one of many that ran back from the lip of a deep winding river canyon, its blind end cracked by a ragged slit twice Miguel's height but scarcely wide enough to admit him. A little stream ran out of the slit and down the gutter of the fissure to fall into the canyon, torn into billowing spray by the cold wind before it could reach the talus slopes far below.

In darkness at the bottom of the fissure, up to his ankles in water, Miguel asked the tenant in his head, "How long they gonna be? Can't you feel I'm freezing here?"

—Have patience, Miguel. The cryostat is a delicate piece of equipment and must be properly protected. If any part of it knocks against the rock walls on the way down it could be irreparably damaged.

"Goddamn zombies, you could have sent one of them down here instead of me."

—Yes. But I would have had to make you as them, temporarily. You do not know anything about the cryostat.

"Okay, okay," Miguel said hastily. It was no idle threat. The blue brother had made it clear that its strength would

235

never again fade, not while it had permanent contact with its original in the city via the compsim and the overlander's transceiver. Miguel stamped his feet to keep some feeling in them, splashing water over slimy stones, flapped his arms at his chest. He had had to throw away his overjacket, stiff and stinking with Jonas's dried blood; the white raincape he had found in one of the overlander's lockers was a poor substitute. "How long they going to take? I feel like *I'm* in a cryostat, down here."

—Soon, Miguel, soon. Then you will see.

Miguel looked up at the thread of night sky pressed between the limestone flanks of the fissure, but could see nothing of the two insurgents—insurgents no longer, now and for evermore the slaves of the blue brother, their own individuality wiped away when they had been converted by the compsim. He could hear, faintly, the sound of the overlander's radio, the stuttering scratch of other human voices; he had kept it on for company after the blue brother had finally relinquished control of his body. The unresponsive passivity of the two slaves made him uneasy. They now seemed no more alive than two human-shaped machines, for all that they breathed, their hearts beat, their stomachs worked on the food they had eaten before the blue brother had taken them.

Under the control of the blue brother, Miguel had driven all night and half of the next day into the Outback. Driven hundreds of kilometers to escape the patrols of the insurgents, across rolling grassland into stony hills, skirting steephead gorges and swallow holes, long slopes of scree and stands of stunted trees, until coming into sight of an aborigine village, a dozen round huts clustered on a rocky promontory that jutted over a deep river canyon.

The blue brother had released Miguel then, but he hadn't been allowed to rest until he had found the Source Cave, a wretched weary hour tracking the paths that led out of the village without being able to use the snakeroot extract to help his merely human senses.

Then he had been allowed to eat, and sleep if he could.

But, tired as he was, Miguel had not been able to sleep in the unsettling presence of the blue brother's slaves. They mostly sat still, breathing evenly but hoarsely in unison, their eyes half-closed, arms dangling loosely. But occasionally one or another would be gripped from within, the whole body quivering, or the head twisting from side to side and up and down, or just the fingers on one hand opening and closing. The pieces of the blue brother inside them were completing the work of infiltrating their nervous systems. Worst was when they tried to speak, half-coherent gurgles and moans like the panicky animal noise of a sleeper caught in the worst of nightmares.

To divert himself from this, Miguel had listened in on confused snatches of radio traffic, garbled further by static, which made it clear that something was going on around the city. The blue brother had not explained what was happening, beyond saying that now his task was even more urgent, but Miguel had guessed that it was to do with the insurgents' advance on the city's perimeter. Outside, the shadows of the short winter afternoon had lengthened into evening; when night had fallen, the two slaves had been suddenly roused to activity. The woman, Mari, had plugged herself into the overlander's compsim and moved the vehicle close to the edge of the fissure. Then both slaves had hauled the cryostat out, and Miguel had been ordered to clamber down the narrow path the abos had carved in one of the walls of the fissure, down to the entrance of the Source Cave.

Now, stamping his feet impatiently in the shallow stream, Miguel heard the whine of the overlander's winch. He switched on his torch and saw the padded shape of the cryostat slowly descending toward him. He moved out of its way as it settled on wet stones. A loop of cable spooled loosely down and then the winch cut off and there was only the noise of running water.

As Miguel began to peel padding from the cryostat, he heard someone coming down the steep path. It was the erstwhile radio operator, Stoy Matthews. Miguel held up his powerful torch while the slave finished the task of unpacking the cryostat, eyes unfocused and mouth half-open, hands moving with eerie independence, quickly and deftly stripping away padding, unhooking the cable.

The cryostat was a slim cylinder about half Miguel's height, not heavy but awkwardly balanced. Miguel and the slave had a great deal of difficulty getting it through the ragged slit of the Source Cave's entrance, but once inside there was enough space for the slave to hoist the straps of the cryostat over his shoulders so that it hung at his back.

Miguel played the beam of his torch around. Quivering motes danced on the stream's dark skin as it flowed past; the limy crust which coated the walls glittered with slippery, nacreous reflections. Farther in, the walls came together so that the two men had to wade in single file through the stream's rippling current. For a long while the only sounds were the sloshing of their boots and the water's sibilant rush. And then these sounds gained a tiny, hushed echo, a dimension of distance. A moist breeze brushed Miguel's face. The passage had opened onto a chamber so huge that the light of his torch was only a calm glint at its very edge, like a single star reflected by the water at the foot of a deep well.

Miguel climbed a rubble slope, the slave following. Miguel was sweating inside his raincape; it was warm in the cave. Beyond the slope, pools were held at various levels in an interlocked puzzle of limy rims that stretched far beyond the limit of the torch's beam. Miguel thought that he heard a dragging noise somewhere out there in the darkness and he turned, suddenly nervous. The torchlight shone on the slave's blank empty face, probed the darkness beyond. Nothing.

Miguel turned back to the pools, playing light across them as he slowly walked beside their interlocked shapes. Clear, absolutely still water filled each to the brim, transparently distorting smoothly convoluted ridges of lime which glistened in the light of the torch like a ransacked treasure chest, rose and violet, citrine, and creamy white. . . . The floor of one pool was marred by a long dark stain: and then Miguel saw that it was the shadow of the body of an aborigine, floating face down by the rim, its eggs resting on limy folds beneath it, half a dozen drops of milky jelly the size of a double fist.

Miguel squatted on his heels, letting out a breath. Each egg held a fuzzy curled shadow. One was slowly pulsating. In a few days it would hatch and, although still attached to its yolk sack, begin to devour the uncorrupted body of its parent, growing large enough to search out insects and the blind cave crabs, fish for rock gobies and salamanders, and prey on its weaker brothers.

The slave set the cryostat beside Miguel and unfastened the top. Vapor curled around his hands as the receiving unit smoothly rose up. Then he stepped into the pool, scooped each egg into its own plastic container, and fitted each container into the cryostat's receiver, which hummed for a moment before carrying it into its interior. The whole process took less than five minutes.

Miguel whispered to the blue brother, "Is that enough for you?" And was told, the first time it had spoken to him since he had entered the Source Cave, that the cryostat should be filled. It was necessary, the blue brother declared with flat emphasis, despite Miguel's protest at the danger.

The slave had already begun to search the rest of the pool, wading thighdeep in clear water. Miguel started toward him and saw the body of a second aborigine, this one sprawled on a patch of bare rock beside the bulging rim. The slave pointed to something in the water, another clutch of eggs, and Miguel looked away for a moment. When he looked back, the body of the aborigine had gone.

Miguel whirled in fright, torchlight dancing over rock, the patchwork of limy rims and clear water, turning in a complete circle and coming back to the empty patch of rock. Then there was a splash and he saw the slave stagger forward, clutching at the aborigine which had sprung onto his back. Its thin legs were locked around his waist, and its hands were prying at his face. The slave stumbled in rocking water, managing to pull the aborigine's hands away before losing his balance. The two fell as one, bursting the rim of the pool and rolling in the sudden foaming wave.

As the cold water washed over Miguel's legs, a weird calm seized him from within.

He turned and sloshed through the diminishing flood and began to seal up the cryostat. Methodically, he retracted the receiver and closed the top of the cryostat, did not even look around when the aborigine broke the slave's neck. He untangled the carrying straps of the cryostat, lifted it onto his back. He was screaming inside his head but no sound came. And then he was released.

Somehow, in complete darkness, he was wading through the stream toward the cave mouth. His right hand kept scraping against stone as he groped his way. The cryostat bumped on the ridge of his spine. At any moment he expected a clawing weight to smash into him. Then the note of the stream changed. His hand grabbed only air. A vague smudge hung in the darkness before him and he twisted through it, the cryostat grating stone, into cold night air. After a few more steps, the cradle dangling from the overlander's winch struck his whole length.

Miguel grabbed it gratefully, shivering with exhaustion. His head felt as if it was packed with black cotton wool.

The voice of his familiar spoke out of the formless dark.

—The first part is over, Miguel.

"What more do you want? Christ! Wasn't that enough?" His hoarse voice echoed in the narrow cleft.

—The first part is over and now we must wait. But soon, Miguel, the city will fall. And then the second part begins.

Miguel could say nothing in reply. The blue brother's implacable control had taken over again. And as his body worked, lifting the cryostat into the cradle and fitting the padding around it, the voice in his head talked on, gloating and insistent, no escape from it as it spun out its crazy, fantastic plan.

21. Ghosts in the Machine

The dome which sheltered the Gothic fantasy house of Lena's father was from the outside like any other in the bubble-suburbs, one of a cluster of four or five rising out of an island of dense evergreen shrubbery, its faceted curve glistening darkly in the streetlights. Rick walked slowly up the ramp of the short oval tunnel set in the side of the dome, all expectation wrung out of him.

Rain struck his face.

Wind roared about him.

Lightning flickered under the dome's vault.

Rick staggered forward in the unexpected storm, boots sinking in the sodden unkempt lawn, gained the veranda of the house. Glass splinters ground under his boots: the windows had been smashed. The front door swung to and fro in the wind's wild rush, its panels scarred and splintered.

As Rick caught his breath, he realized that the roaring wind must come from the dome's ventilation system, that the rain was blown spray from irrigation nozzles set among the dense laurels, the strokes of lightning only the garden spotlights strobing at random. Whoever had smashed the door and windows must also have taken an axe to the dome's environment controls.

Rick pushed past the broken door. The heavy furniture in the hall had all been overturned. The staircase's balustrade hung askew on broken posts; carpets had been torn up and thrown in a corner. The wreckage was fitfully lit by the strobing lights in the garden.

"Lena!"

He knew that she was gone, that they were all gone, but he went through the rest of the house anyway. As with the hall, so with the other rooms. Smashed fittings, tipped over furniture. Once, something small and metallic shot past Rick's feet: one of the autonomic units that kept the house clean. Gradually, Rick realized that music was playing somewhere. Faint and overlain by the artificial gale outside, it always seemed to be coming from the next room, and it was a while before he recognized the piece. Barber's *Adagio*, the slow stately theme passed from instrument to instrument like the waves the wind makes in the grass of the plains, circles ceaselessly widening in plaintive lament for the end of things. Thinking of Lena's stored ancestors, Rick called out again, asked if anyone was there.

The music grew in volume, as if the performers had walked through the door. The illusion was so strong that Rick actually turned, but all that moved in the shadowy room were the long velvet drapes of a broken window, blown by the wind.

And then, just as it reached its heartrending climax, the music cut off. A quavering voice, an old man's, said, "Who is there?"

"Richard Florey. A friend of Lena's."

"Lena? Oh, yes. The child. It's been such a long time, you see. It's difficult to recall all that has happened since I passed over."

"Who are you? Do you know where Lena is?"

"I think . . . I am sorry, it is so difficult. He is trying to find the way here, but so far I've stopped him. But he is so very strong, so very persistent. You asked who I am? My name is Antoine Vallee, young man.''

"Lena's great-great-grandfather?"

''. . . of the child, yes.''

The quavering voice was hard to follow in the windy, windy house. Standing in the middle of the dark room, Rick closed his eyes, tried to concentrate. He asked again, ''Do you know where Lena is?''

"The police came. Took away the living, turned off the dead. All but me. I am all through the computer systems of the house, living inside the music. . . . Do you know what that is like, young man?''

"Lena told me all about you. Did the police take her?''

"The child was not here,'' the voice said.

Rick's heart turned through one hundred and eighty degrees.

"Do you know where she is?''

"She has taken the music. That was always our plan, you see. The music was the house, or the house the music, but we knew the house would not last forever.'' The voice grew a little stronger. "Not once the war had begun. Yes. I am accessing files left by the others. They knew outsiders would not be able to find me. I must take care of their plans now.''

"Am I . . . in these plans?''

"I do not know if you are who you say you are, young man. You must prove this to me. Wait a moment . . . yes, I have it. To the parlor, quickly, now, quickly. He is pressing me hard.''

"What do you want me to do? And who is this person you keep talking about?''

"So many questions, young man. Wait until you have been dead awhile. That will blunt your curiosity. You must pass a test, you see. It is all in the files. Go on, now, into the parlor. There is a keyboard there. I think you will find it works.''

As Rick stepped around tipped-over furniture, he asked the air, "But who are you afraid of?''

"Why, there are many more dead people than those of this family. They have their own plans, and their champion to make sure that they are carried out. He sees us as rebels, to be switched off. Have you found the keyboard?''

"Sure.'' Rick righted a chair and sat at it, switched it on. It was the same one at which he had given an audition for Lena's father. Its pinlights cast eerie shadows. He asked, "What shall I play?''

"Anything you want, young man.''

Rick tried to think through the haze of his exhaustion. A gale howling about a dark, ruined house that was haunted by an ancient, impatient spirit . . . he grinned and clumsily began to block out the opening chords of Beethoven's piano trio in D, the *Ghost*.

"Enough, Dr. Florey,'' the voice said, after a minute or so. It added softly, "I take your meaning.''

"Now you know who I am, tell me where she is.''

"I will find her for you, but I will have to access the city's network to trace her. There. It is done, outracing Puck himself. I will only say this once, young man, and it will be gone from my memory.''

"I'm ready.''

The voice spoke three words.

"Of course,'' Rick said, "I mean, I understand.''

"Do not wait,'' the voice said. It was weaker than ever, sibilant with static. Rick only just made out its last words, an unraveling whisper blown away on the wind.

"He is here.''

For a moment there was only the wind, and driven spray rattling at those windows still unbroken. Then the wind began to die, and all at once lights sprang on through the house, hurtful in their sudden brilliance. Another voice spoke out of the air, a calm baritone that Rick recognized at once.

"The file of Antoine Vallee has been deleted, Dr. Florey. I advise you to remain where you are.''

But Rick was already running. As he wrenched open the front door, one of the little autonomic cleaning machines threw a steely embrace around his ankle. Its motor whirred as it tried to drag Rick off-balance. But Rick kicked out and it flew across the hall, smashed against the wall. Something

small, quick, and metallic skittered over the broken balustrade, but he dodged through the door and sprinted down the
path between the laurel bushes. The baritone voice thundered
through the dome like the voice of God, ordering him to stop.
He gained the tunnel and clattered down its ramp, burst out
onto the street.

The ordinary domes, each sealed behind evergreen ramparts. The spaced stars of streetlights. As quickly as he could,
Rick began to walk away down the sinuous street, holding
his bruised, aching side. In the distance, quickly growing
closer, the thin wail of a police cruiser twisted into the cold
night air.

The squares and narrow streets of the old quarter were
crowded with reveling citizens, most in artfully crumpled
and dirtied VDF coveralls. Threading his way through the
crowds, unsteady with exhaustion, his own coveralls stained
with real sweat, real dirt in his hair, Richard Florey felt a
distant contempt for them. They were children at play on the
shore of the great unknown, innocent except in carnal matters, gay and unheeding in the face of disaster. The new-
screens were proclaiming a great victory for the city, but
Rick knew that it was no such thing. The insurgents had
arrived at the gates. From now on the war would be on their
terms, on the city's territory.

Rick hurried on, impatient anxiety nagging at him. An
edgy sliding feeling that recalled the times he had run through
the campus to a lecture after oversleeping, buildings full of
students transcribing received wisdom from the dead experts
and him out of it. As he was now, flitting through the revelry
like a grim specter, a ghost in the tottering machine of the
city.

The crowds thinned out as Rick neared the docks. At last,
he was walking alone down a narrow street between shut-
down automats. A man in a waiter's white apron was hooking
shutters down over the windows of the cafe at the corner.
Blue script hung above his head in the cold night air: "The
Other World."

As Rick came up, the waiter turned and told him that the place was closed.

"I've come to meet Lena," Rick said.

"I'm sorry, we really are closed."

"You know who I am, right? Lena Vallee. I've been here with her any number of times, and I know she's here right now."

"Everyone has gone home. Maybe you should do the same, friend. Sleep it off, huh?"

"I'm not fucking drunk," Rick said, and pushed past. The waiter grabbed at his arm, but Rick shook him off and ran into the cafe. It was in darkness, the holographic wall turned off. Rick dodged between shadowy tables, pulling one over into the path of the waiter. The man shouted a warning as Rick barged into the kitchen.

Bright light, slickly reflecting from steel and white tile. Lena was sitting at a scarred wooden table, her leather jacket like a cape over her shoulders. Across from her, the young shaven-head man started in surprise as Rick came through the door. Lena reached out to stay him, bracelets clattering on her wrist. Her hair was blonde, cropped short. Her violin case lay beside her chair on the tiled floor. "It's okay," she said, "I've been sort of expecting this guy."

Behind Rick, the waiter asked plaintively, "Would someone tell me what's going on here?"

"Just go ahead and lock up, Karl," Lena told him.

"I could ask the same thing," Rick said. An unsteady mix of relief and surplus adrenaline hummed in his head.

Lena smiled her sudden, starshell smile. "This must be an awful shock for you. It's a contingency plan we hoped would never have to be put into operation. That's why I couldn't tell you about it."

"We? You mean your stored ancestors, right? I was at the house—"

"I know you were," Lena said. "Otherwise you wouldn't be here. But it's my plan and my father's plan as much as my ancestors. Sit down, Rick, please. I don't have much time here."

"Twenty minutes," the shaven-head young man said, pushing steel-rimmed spectacles up his nose with a precise gesture.

"You may have less time than that," Rick said.

The young man smiled. "Don't sweat it. Constat isn't all-powerful, right? That's the mistake the cops make, and it'll lose them this war." He stood and said, "I'll be outside when you two are ready, okay? You sit down, man, before you fall down."

Rick sat next to Lena as the kitchen door softly shut. She pushed a glass across scarred wood and he took it, gulped the rough red wine it contained. "Jesus," he said, and sighed. "Your great-great-grandfather told me most of it and tracked you down through the net. Then Constat broke into the house system, called in the cops and tried to stop me leaving."

"There's a rumor that the cops are rounding up every settler in the city, loyal or not. Do you—"

"It's true," Rick told her. "In my case, though, it's a little more complicated."

"Look at you, there's dirt in your hair, all over your coveralls. . . . You escaped, is that it?"

"You could say that." He smiled, then started to laugh. "Yeah! Jesus, did I ever escape!"

But Lena wasn't smiling now. No longer framed by black hair, her face looked smaller, elfin. "They caught Web," she said. "I know that for sure. He tried to pull off his stunt after the fighting began, but he only got as far as the perimeter. One of my friends works in the police records office, he saw Web brought in an hour ago. That's why I wasn't at the house when the cops raided it."

"Jesus. What about your father?"

"He always made sure that he knew nothing about what I was involved in, and he has some powerful friends in the city. I think he'll be all right. My stepmother, too. I know he will."

"You've thought everything through, huh? One way or another your family will keep its heritage going." He touched the thin silver bracelets bunched on her wrist. "These are where all your music files are stored, right?"

She caught his hand in hers.

"The music, yes, and other things too. Dormant copies of my ancestors, family records. A heavy load, Rick. I don't ask you to carry it with me—"

"—but I want to, Lena." He sandwiched her small cool hand between his, watching her face. "I've finished here. I've been used and abused and now it's over. Even if I wanted to, I couldn't stay. And I don't want to. Love, I want to leave the city too. I'll go wherever you want."

PART THREE

PART THREE

22. Slaves

"Reader, although we have attempted to describe the war and its causes in a tone proper for historical documentation, some of the events we have detailed here may seem irrelevant, while others that we have glossed over may be those you consider to be the most important. But remember that we are living in the middle of your history. If what follows seems to you to be as biased as any political tract, then we can only plead that it is our own lives that we have recorded here."

Impatiently, de Ramaira brushed the switch of the recorder and sank back in his armchair. That would never do—the assessor of everything going into the vault was a politician, after all. No, it would be far better to start the whole thing over. It was not shaping into an introduction at all, but a weasel-worded *apologia* for the "official history" that the Constitutionalist Party wanted to seal in the vault, vainglorious propaganda for a cause already in its last days.

De Ramaira carried his glass of rum and milk to the narrow window of his study. The streetlights were off again, but they had always been irregular in the old quarter. Perhaps it meant nothing. The larger of Elysium's two moons had yet to set, but it was so obscured by clouds that the night was relieved only by a scattering of lighted windows around the bleak park. De Ramaira could just make out a faint gleam of frost dappling the frozen mud.

Soon, less than four weeks, it would be New Year. He had never become accustomed to Elysium's swift-turning seasons. A pang of buried regret passed through him: Earth. "Ah, sweet objectivity," de Ramaira said, and the sound of his voice in the quiet, dimly lit room surprised him.

He turned from the window and his glance fell on the blue folder on the low table beside the armchair. If it wasn't for the war, the implications of that, now, would be truly frightening. As if, de Ramaira thought, a man on the eve of his execution should find a suspicious lump in his groin. It was what he should be working on while there was still time, instead of fooling around trying to second-guess Savory.

He looked back at the darkness pressing at the cold glass of the window, thinking, not for the first time that day, of Richard Florey. Somewhere out there, in the vast dark wilderness beyond Port of Plenty. Ah, but that way out was closed now—the Port Authority cops had shot the courier more than a week ago. It had not been a route de Ramaira would have chosen in any case. Too much had depended upon others.

There now, that was quite enough. De Ramaira settled himself in the armchair again. There was more than enough to do, and little time left.

It was almost certain that the insurgents would overrun the city before the New Year. Their advance, across the abandoned half-completed perimeter defenses and into the bubble-suburbs, had been slow but sure. The city, enveloped, was now slowly being digested. The police, white coveralled lymphocytes, were too few to prevent the inexorable incursions, while the VDF troops were no use at all, falling back in disorder at the beginning of even the smallest skirmish. The citizens had had it too soft for too long, believed too deeply in the proper compartmentalization of authority. The insurgents had no such compunctions. They fought as they had to, and fought well.

There. De Ramaira drank half the remaining measure of rum and milk and set the glass beside the little recorder. The introduction had to be finished and approved by tomorrow if the time vault was to be sealed on schedule, ready for burial at the end of things. And there was the other problem, its endless subtle ramifying possibilities so much more interesting than the pussyfooting compromises over the vault and its contents, awakening a puzzle that had had to be abandoned ever since he had walked away from the aborigine village in the Trackless Mountains all those years ago.

De Ramaira sighed and, with a cloying residue of guilt at his prevarication, reached out and tripped the recorder's erasure switch. There was a soft burring as the field randomized the tagged molecules in the cassette. He didn't want to start over, not yet. Instead he switched back to recording mode and began to dictate a letter to himself about the day's revelation.

It had begun innocuously enough, with a request from the VDF general office that de Ramaira give a briefing on the time vault to Colonel Savory. It was something de Ramaira had been expecting for some time. He'd given such briefings to most of the City Board by then, whether or not they were directly involved in it, and, as head of the VDF, Savory was more involved than most. So without any qualms, de Ramaira had collected the appropriate documents and presented himself at the Port Authority headquarters.

Savory was a burly man perhaps ten years older than de Ramaira in physiological terms, with a handsome, arrogant face and cropped blond hair. He wore an immaculately tailored version of the by now ubiquitous gray coveralls that de Ramaira himself was wearing. They were alone in the large, sparely furnished office. Winter sunlight streamed through wide windows which gave a view across the city to the forested hills beyond. The office was on the top floor of the twelve-story building, high above everything else.

All this was familiar enough from newscasts. But the one

thing that the trivee image of Savory had lacked, de Ramaira thought, was his aura of power, as fierce and as subtly contained as the raw plasma within the magnetic pinch of a fusion generator. Seething, ruthless ambition no more than a micrometer beneath a bland unruffled surface. Clearly, Savory would be content with nothing less than the Round Office of the governor's mansion.

Whatever Savory wanted from de Ramaira, it was not an explanation of the time vault and its contents. He brushed aside de Ramaira's usual presentation and said with measured distaste, "All I need to say about that is the regrettable lack of any explanation of why it was built. The Board has approved the expenditure of a large amount of credit and a grievous use of skilled manpower to realize this project of yours. I would like some mention of that to be included."

"I had thought that the knowledge we are going to seal in the vault might be sufficient indication of intent." Savory's gaze was compelling. "I suppose I could write some sort of potted history," De Ramaira said grudgingly, feeling the first stirring of anger at this meddling.

"I have already assigned one of my staff to deal with the history. I want you to write a general introduction explaining why the city has seen fit to sacrifice time in the middle of civil war to pass on this heritage."

"That might be more difficult than the actual history."

"Consider it a test of your loyalty, if you like," Savory said. "You see, I find myself in a difficult position. I have need of your expertise, but you must not be insulted when I say that, as an emigré from Earth, your loyalty to the city must be in some doubt."

"I've long grown used to that suspicion," de Ramaira said.

"Yes. I've talked with some of your colleagues at the University." Savory interfaced with the big compsim on his desk and his eyes unfocused for a moment. Then he sat back in his chair and stared at de Ramaira as if scrutinizing him for the first time. He said, "When you first arrived on Elysium, you mounted an expedition to the Trackless Mountains to study the aborigines there. Have you done anything in that line since?''

''On and off,'' de Ramaira admitted. ''Within the limits of proscription.'' He wondered uneasily if this were leading somewhere, or whether Savory was simply seeking an advantage over him. It was not against the law to be interested in the aborigines, but it was certainly not *comme il faut*.

Savory smiled dryly. ''As a scientist, do you approve of the proscription? I should think that you would dislike anything that got in the way of your, ah, research.''

So that was it. Well, he'd ridden out such taunts before. De Ramaira said, ''They are the native sophonts. The moral essence of the proscription is that they can't defend themselves from us, so it is our obligation to ensure that we don't harm them. And yes, I approve of that.''

''But still, you have studied them.''

''From a distance. Within the rules of the proscription, and not with much success.'' By now de Ramaira himself almost believed this lie, so often had he told it, and so unsuccessful had been his subsequent attempts at divining the aborigines' intelligence. That time with Lieutenant Mc-Anders and the boy and his dog, and the discovery of the shrine, if that is what it had been, of painted skulls, almost seemed like a secondhand story after all these years. De Ramaira added, ''I'm a phylogenist, Colonel Savory, and there has already been a comprehensive study of the aborigines by Webster, an anthropologist who came here specifically for that purpose. It's true that the aborigines are interesting. After all, they're the only other intelligent species we know of. But they are not why I came here.''

''Not many people would say the aborigines are intelligent,'' Savory commented.

''It's all relative. Outwardly, they may appear to lead a desperately primitive way of life, but although we can only guess at their perceptions, it is surely certain that their inner life, their way of looking at the universe, must be entirely different from our own.''

''Why, how poetic.''

"I suppose it is, in a way." De Ramaira refused to be rattled, but damn Savory and his games, and damn his translucent corpse-colored skin for that matter, and his handmade coveralls, and his necessary prejudices.

Savory peeled the interface cuff from his wrist. "It seems to me that you may well enjoy your new assignment. Perhaps it will give you a chance to prove your whimsical notions. Let's go and have a look at it."

They rode an elevator down and entered the maze of narrow corridors in the basement levels. After two minutes brisk walking de Ramaira suspected that they were somewhere beyond the vehicle parks that surrounded the police headquarters. There were rumors of a network of passages under the city; now, as Savory led him down a staircase to another level, he could believe that it was true.

There was a door guarded by an armed cop, who unlocked it as Savory and de Ramaira approached. Inside, the little room was packed with racks of flatscreen monitors, a miscellany of recording equipment, and a big compsim that was the twin of the one on Savory's desk. Savory sat in the swivel chair in front of it and turned it on.

"We're very close to Constat's vault," Savory remarked as he plugged himself in. A moment later a row of monitors above de Ramaira's head flickered, showing various views of a huge ill-defined shadowy space. Savory leaned back in the chair. "The vault is directly below this room. I had fiberoptic cables threaded through."

"I didn't realize that it was so big," de Ramaira said, remembering from some newscast or other a sealed sterile white room stacked with honeycomb wafers, Constat and his slave computers and the files which contained the encrypted residues of the city's dead.

"It wasn't," Savory said. On one of the screens the view began to change, panning over rough walls to a kind of alcove hung with a web of cabling, waldos, and camera eyes. "That's the tie-in to Constat. All the rest has been opened up from that point. Now, let's see if we can catch one of his slaves . . . Ah. There we are."

"Lord," de Ramaira said.

The slave, squatting motionless near a slumped tongue of rubble, was an immature aborigine.

It had begun, Savory explained, with two separate investigations, one into missing construction equipment, the other into a mission to the Outback where an aborigine village had been ransacked, all its adult inhabitants killed, and the immature ones captured and brought back to the city. Those involved in the mission had been ordered to keep it secret, but one of the cops had talked with her lover, who happened to be a senior administrator supposedly privy to all war operations. He had known nothing about a mission to kidnap aborigines, and could find nothing about it when he made inquiries. Briefings had been given on tapes which were subsequently found to be blank, and personnel, vehicles, and other equipment had been requisitioned apparently without any authorization.

"It was as if someone had a line into Constat, which of course is the nexus for that kind of informational traffic," Savory said. "And no one could find out where the young aborigines had gotten to." He went on to explain that at the same time he had a couple of cops working on the missing construction materials—a routine criminal matter to which he had given only minimal attention, until the investigating cops had traced the stuff to the administration building. The drivers of the trucks which had taken it there had all been given legitimate vouchers, but again it was impossible to trace who had ordered their issue.

Savory made a steeple with his fingers and rested it against his chin, watching the screen which showed the motionless aborigine. "By the time I put two and two together, most of them had died. There's a tunnel that's been driven all the way down to the docks, half a kilometer long. The bodies were put out there, and we were able to recover the last two. A surgeon up at the hospital gave them thorough autopsies. You can read his reports, of course. Quite a chance for you. I don't think anyone has dissected an aborigine since Webster."

"You said that someone had managed to get an unauthorized line into Constat. Have you found out who it was? And why are aborigines involved, anyway?"

"I said that it *seemed* that someone had an unauthorized line. There isn't one."

"Ah. I see."

"You're from Earth, Dr. de Ramaira. You are familiar with megacee computers. To most of us in the city, Constat is simply another of Earth's gifts, accepted rather than understood. We forget that it is more than a very fast, very powerful computer. We forget that it is intelligent in its own right, that it might have its own desires, that it might not be as obedient as we suppose."

"I suppose that there is a reason why you haven't asked Constat what it's doing."

"Oh yes," Savory said, and for the first time he seemed weary, as though suddenly conscious of a burden he had been carrying for so long that he had almost forgotten it. "When I first became suspicious of Constat, of course I tried to look into his vault using the remote camera. But that had been disconnected, from the inside. I knew then that something was wrong, for no one has entered the vault since Constat was installed. So I had some remote sensing done and that revealed a huge space excavated next to the vault. Very carefully and in great secrecy I had fine holes burned through the floor of this room and fiberoptic cables threaded through, and saw what you have seen. Except that there were more aborigines then." He looked up suddenly, his gaze bright in the dim room. "You don't think," he asked, "that the aborigines could somehow be responsible for this?"

"No," de Ramaira said. "We don't know very much about them, but that—no."

"Some people say that the aborigines have underground cities, that their villages are only training places for the young. Who when they are mature descend through the Source Cave to their true home underground."

"I've heard a dozen versions of that story. But you see, the Elysian quasimammals are all oviparous to a greater or lesser extent. Some lay their eggs directly into an external pouch; others in captured prey, as the sabertooths do; still others go into hibernation after they are fertilized and are slowly consumed from within by their developing young. Now," de Ramaira said, warming to the subject, "all these kinds of necrogenetic reproduction are adaptations to the sudden change in climate half a million, a million years ago. The planet became colder and dryer so quickly that most of the quasimammalian species became extinct. The swampy habitats in which their predatory aquatic larvae had developed vanished overnight, in geological terms. Necrogenes substitute their own bodies for that lost environment. In a few million years perhaps they will have had enough time to evolve more efficient methods of nurture, something like a placenta, mammary glands. Those who lay their eggs into pouches, for instance, grow a kind of fatty tumor on which the hatchlings feed. Well. Webster showed that the reproductive cycle of the aborigines is a variation on the general necrogenic pattern. They lay their eggs in warm cave pools and pass into a kind of coma, and are eaten by the freshly hatched young. No secret cities, I'm afraid."

Savory passed his hand over his cropped hair. "In a way it would be more comforting if the aborigines had taken over Constat. At least I would know what to do. But as it is I dare not disturb Constat without endangering the war effort. In all other respects the computer continues to serve the city faithfully. I have been careful not to discuss this in any place where it might overhear me—you would be surprised at the number of places that includes. I trust you will take the same care."

"As long as Constat isn't bugging my house."

Unsmilingly, Savory said, "I will check that point. In the meantime, you may take away the autopsy reports on the aborigine bodies we recovered. As soon as you are able, I would like a summary of your speculations." He peeled the compsim's interface cuff from his wrist. At the same moment, the door of the small room opened behind de Ramaira.

De Ramaira switched off the recorder. A kind of hollow

lethargy spread through him when it came to thinking about summarizing the report, much less speculating upon it. Ordinarily, he would have devoured the exhaustive descriptions of the aborigine corpses—whole body imaging, Spinoza charts, cell ultratopology, enzymology, residue counts and all else—but all was overshadowed by the modifications which Constat had made on their nervous systems.

De Ramaira had only a hazy recollection of the technology which on Earth was used to control the animal labor which operated deep-ocean mineral dredges, maintained microwave collector farms and low-orbit factories, recovered precious isotopes from the cores of decommissioned nuclear reactors left over from the Age of Waste, and so on. And he remembered only a little more clearly the protests which had prevented the state from using the same technology to turn felons convicted of capital crimes into decerebrated automatons, a superior alternative to animal labor. The Zombie Riots, virtually the last gasp of civil protest—he'd been a child then. But undoubtedly that was what had been used on the aborigines.

Both of the bodies had been modified in the same way. A microprocessor had been surgically inserted in the body cavity, and it had grown delicate pathways parallel to the nervous system, ramifying throughout the brain, especially in the putative motor and sensory areas. It was clear that the implants had been only partially successful; most of the interconnections between the parasitic system and host synapses had more or less burned out, as if by massive allergic reaction. De Ramaira wondered if the aborigines had retained any consciousness after implantation. In humans the destruction of neural pathways in the forebrain concomitant with the growth of new pathways would have wiped out most traces of personality, but no one knew enough about the unlobed infolded aborigine brain.

No one knew enough. There, more or less, was his summary. All that could be concluded was that Constat had recruited servants for itself, servants who could neither question nor rebel against their master.

But as for why. . . .

De Ramaira's lethargy spread, mixing smoothly with his all too physical exhaustion. It had been a long day, no question of it, one more in a long succession of days without end. The warmth of the room and the comforting fumes of the rum and milk conspired against him. The recorder running on beside him, de Ramaira fell asleep.

23. Against Entropy

The city lay under blackout, its suburbs crackling with skirmishes as insurgent patrols probed the defenses. The faint but distinct punctuation of gunshots came and went erratically; sometimes there would be nothing for as much as half an hour. But the sound of the fighting always returned, blown by the freezing offshore wind to those waiting at Jones Beach.

It filled Rick with an airily tumultuous mixture of apprehension and pure nervousness, the same feeling that had gripped him the first time he had left Mount Airy for the University. He huddled inside a fleece-lined overcoat, sitting on cold ground with his back against one wall of the amphitheater where, what seemed a lifetime ago, he had waited with Cath for the colonyboat which had never arrived. Before him, black shapes on a black ground, the troops of the Third Division of the Liberation Army sat or sprawled in the sandy meadow bordering the beach, resting after the day's long march. Above, the cloud-covered sky was starless and dark, save for a single patch of pale light over the sea where Cerberus hid her face.

Rick was so wired that he could not sleep, for all that his

eyeballs flatly ached with exhaustion, for all that he needed to snatch some rest before it was time to start out for the city. A murmurous multitudinous noise, counterpoint to the sound of the breakers far down the beach, told him that the insurgents could not sleep either.

The Third Division of the so-called Liberation Army, to which Rick and Jonah Rivington had become attached, had that day made a forced march of some thirty kilometers from its bivouac outside the stripped fields of Arcadia, westward along an ungraded road through the bleak forests to the amphitheater at Jones Beach. The city forces had rolled their frontline back to the hydroponic station three days before, but the organization of the Liberation Army was so fragmented and its lines of communication so bedeviled by jamming, accidental damage, and sabotage, despite all that Rick had done, that the decision to capitalize on this had taken that long to work around the front: hence the urgency of the advance.

Rick had ridden in the back of a small cushiontruck together with Jonah Rivington and the officers of the division. They had arrived in the middle of the chill, overcast morning, the white amphitheater rising before the wintry sea like the tipped shell of some enormous marine animal. The emplacements of the advance section were already in position at the beginning of the road to the city.

Between arrival and the serving of the miraculously hot evening meal—the first food any of them had eaten since breakfast at six that morning—Rick had mostly spent his time in the temporary command post, a tent whose canvas sides boomed like drumheads in the cold wind. He reviewed the plans of the University with Rivington, and the lists they had made, but mostly he just sat and waited. The mounted troops arrived soon after the officers, but the light was beginning to fade by the time the infantry began to stagger into the clearing, men and women sweating despite the cold, eyes like sunken bruises in exhausted white faces. The straggling column continued to discharge from the rough road well after sunset, until at last there were perhaps a thousand people gathered in the clearing around the amphitheater. The lighting of fires was forbidden, but the division's handful of cushiontrucks ferried in cauldrons of stew and urns of coffee from Arcadia. A few unlucky people were designated to dig latrines; the rest settled in the sandy meadow as best they could, and then there had been nothing to do but wait.

Now, Rick heard footsteps shuffling toward him. Someone loomed above, no more than a shadow on the darkness.

"Well, you haven't moved at all." Jonah Rivington's gravelly bass was tuned down to a confiding rasp. "They've done planning at last, you'll be pleased to know."

Rick's nervousness swelled inside him like a balloon. "So we can move out?"

"Hold on, now. They told me that patrols will be going out in maybe half an hour. We can tag onto one of those if anyone's willing. But a patrol can't hang around waiting for us. We'll have to make our own way back through the lines."

"Jesus. Well, I guess I didn't expect anything else."

You will come back, won't you?

Sure. There's nothing else that might tempt me.

Just don't get hurt on account of this crazy idea of yours.

Crazy? I'm saving civilization and you think that's crazy?

Well I adore Vaughan Williams, but I wouldn't want to get killed saving any of his scores.

But you took a risk, bringing your family's archives out. I just feel that if I didn't go it would make this whole thing, the running away, just an empty gesture.

Maybe this sounds selfish. Shit, I don't care if it does. Just don't throw away our future for everyone else's.

In the darkness, Rivington settled to the cold sand with a grunt of satisfaction. He said, "Things are more muddled than usual. But at least we're *moving*. I was beginning to think Cziller couldn't get her stuff together after all, winter would freeze out the campaign and then where would we be? People have been drifting off anyhow, anxious to stake out their piece of territory. They reckon to have lost about five percent on the march today."

"And even more when the fighting really gets going, I guess."

"Maybe not. If people think the city really is going down, well, that's what they came for. Look here, Richard, one thing I have to say before we go . . ."

"Something serious, I guess. Always is when you call me Richard."

Rivington's leather jacket creaked; perhaps he had shrugged. "All I want to say is that I hope David de Ramaira appreciates what we're doing for him."

"Me too. But you should see all the stuff he has, Jonah, a whole library of books, datacubes, files. . . . He's worth any three University departments by himself."

Rivington chuckled, and began to stand. "The books will have to wait. I've still got to find someone to take us out there. Least you get to rest a breath longer. I'll be back, now."

"Sure," Rick said as Rivington moved off, stepping in darkness with casual, surefooted ease among tussocks of grass and recumbent men and women. In the distance came the crepitating sound of rifle fire. Another skirmish.

Rick settled back and closed his eyes, but still his mind spun on. No time to sleep, anyway. It was like the time he and Lena had waited for the signal light to flash at the other side of the wide dark clearing in the forest. A tingling in his palms. Something that would not dissolve or be swallowed at the back of his throat.

Love, that's not selfish, that's just sensible.

The hell with you.

I'm just trying to salvage something of my life. When we were thrashing this out with Jonah you were all for it.

Maybe I didn't realize what you were getting into. If you want to justify running away you could work in the hospital.

Do you want that?

No. No, I suppose I don't. Don't listen to me, I am being selfish now. But you get your ass shot off and bring it here to be fixed up, I'll make sure you don't get anesthetic.

They had been strange, those days in the muddy camp that

had grown up beyond the western fields of Arcadia. Rick had touched bottom, and was safe. A limbo, free of the need for any saving decision. It was not a bad place to be.

Apart from the wounded, all the people in the camp were defectors from Port of Plenty. They were confined within the loosely defined perimeter, but otherwise there were few regulations. When they were not working, Lena and Rick were together.

In the first few days, Rick had labored in a makeshift foundry to make bullets, pouring lead into molds nested in a bed of sand. The foundry was roofed by canvas but otherwise was open to the raw winter air, so that Rick was always both too hot and too cold, his feet freezing in slushy mud while the skin of his face withered in the glare of molten metal. Sometimes splashes of lead ate into the thick proofed-cotton gloves that reached up to his elbows. His nose continually ran as it drew in the spiteful mixture of dry heat and knifing cold. Yet he felt no bitterness at the drudgery. He was working from his beginnings once more.

And love was something won from humdrum toil, and so was more precious than his casual couplings with Cath, an ineffable sweetness that overcame the fatigue of their limbs—for Lena was working too, tending the wounded in the hospital huts in the middle of the camp. In their small tent, on a mattress laid on a canvas groundsheet, love was something newly won from the gray end of each day.

Rick and Lena had married the day after they had arrived at the camp, a fifteen-minute service presided over by an Episcopalian minister and witnessed by the camp doctor and one of the guards. Rick had proposed to Lena on the last night they had spent in Port of Plenty. He had cast the ring himself, from scrap nickel wire; she had given him one of her bracelets, Bach's oeuvre in its entirety. It was a thoroughly traditional wedding.

And so it might have continued until the end of the war, if it had not been for Jonah Rivington.

A tall, stooped man with an affable and slightly raffish air, Rivington was something to do with the intelligence corps of

Cziller's rag-tag army. Precisely what, was anyone's guess, although he did occasionally interview new arrivals at the camp. That was when Rick had first met Rivington, although what started out as a formal debriefing soon degenerated into a session of rambling reminiscences, about the University in general and David de Ramaira in particular.

Rivington had befriended the Wombworlder when studying Agriculture at the University a dozen years before, and the friendship had continued after Rivington had returned to Freeport to supervise the Agronomy section of the Freeport collective. Somehow, Rivington had found time to make several expeditions into the Trackless Mountains to map and collect the flora there, and he had kept up a desultory correspondence with de Ramaira about his findings. But this was not what had brought Rivington and Rick together; it was merely the glue of a friendship which developed after Rivington approached Rick about fixing up a communications network that the city forces couldn't tap into. Rick thought about it for the rest of the morning while he worked in the foundry, then sought Rivington out in the mess tent.

"I've some answers for you," he said.

"What are you trying to do, impress me? Okay, I'm impressed." Rivington had a creased, lugubrious face. It creased more as he smiled. "So what are these ideas?"

"I don't know if you'll like them."

"We're willing to try anything. Seriously. This close to the city you get the impression the cops can hear you going to the john."

Rick wrapped his hands around his mug of coffee. It was cold in the mess tent. "For short-range work lasers are probably best. With a tight enough beam there's no spill over, though of course you are limited by line of sight. And for long range, I can't think of anything better than the Inca system."

"Ah yes, the Inca system. So what's that, some kind of code?"

"Not exactly. The Incas used runners to carry messages in the form of specifically knotted strings. You, we I guess, can use mounted messengers with the coded message concealed somewhere on them or their horses. Encrypt your message in binary, knot the string and plait it into the mane. If the messenger is captured he won't know the message, and hopefully the cops won't be able to find it."

"That's kind of sideways thinking, isn't it? I was hoping for some way of stopping the cops intercepting our transmissions, or some uncrackable code."

"There are any number of ways of making a transmission difficult to intercept—nanosecond bursting, for instance. The problem is that the cops have better equipment. And I'm no cryptographer, but I would think that Constat could crack any cipher, except for code words with a specific predetermined meaning. You call it sideways thinking. I call it appropriate technology."

"So no magic gadget, huh?" Rivington smiled. "Oh well. I'll pass on your idea about some kind of Pony Express anyhow."

"Don't forget lasers, for short-range traffic. Easy enough to set up, though you'll need to organize line-of-sights in the forest. I might have an idea about that, too."

"And lasers, sure. Don't hold your breath waiting for a medal for this stuff, though."

A few days later, Rivington turned up at the foundry and told Rick that if he really wanted to help the cause, he should apply his real skills.

"I'm getting pretty good at this," Rick said.

Rivington stepped aside as Rick, using meter-long tongs, lifted a small, heavy crucible and began to pour smoking liquid lead. "That's as may be, but we need good communication around here as much as we need bullets. You want to help?"

Each day, Rick and Rivington and half a dozen volunteers went out into the forest surrounding Arcadia to lay a communications network between the insurgent outposts that the cops couldn't tap into. They strung kilometers of fiberoptic cable liberated from Arcadia, and when that ran out floated tethered, silvered balloons above the forest canopy to bounce

laser signals from place to place. The balloons worked sur-
prisingly well, although they had a tendency to get tangled
in the treetops, or deflate in the freezing nights, and since
they were no larger than a man's head (any bigger and there
was a danger the cop patrols might spot them) and were
anything but stationary, signaling was dependent upon skilled
markmanship. Rivington also scrounged a transceiver, in the
hope that Rick could use it to triangulate the cops' jamming
transmitters. If they could be located and taken out, perhaps
ordinary radios could be used instead of the jury-rigged network; but the jammers seemed to be constantly moving
around, probably mounted on overlanders. Unreliable as it
was, the new network was the only secure mode of communications the insurgents had.

Troubleshooting became a full-time job, and Rick returned to the camp, to Lena, exhausted and smelling of horse
and of his own sweat. But, usually, with a sense of satisfaction. He was doing his part. He was making his way.

Rick and Lena and Jonah Rivington spent many evenings
together, sharing wine from Arcadia's vast stores and the sweet,
rich marijuana which was one of the Freeport collective's main
exports, talking over the state of the world and the war. It was
during one of these rambling discursive conversations that Rivington threw out the seed of what was to become his and
Rick's mission. It would be a shame, he said, sprawled as
usual on the floor, seeming to pick out words from the layers
of smoke that hazed the ceiling, a shame if everything in the
University was destroyed. After all, not everyone was going
to head out into the wilderness to stake out their own bit of
territory. There would still be a need for teaching something
more than reading and writing and marketplace arithmetic,
maybe even a place for the accumulation of knowledge. "It
would be a shame," he said, "if all that stuff in the University
was smashed to bits and burned."

"Would people do that?" Rick asked.

Lena, her head resting on his knees, drew on the fat reefer
and passed it to Rivington. While he drew on it in turn, she
said through a cloud of exhaled smoke, "They burned the

library at Alexandria. What are you going to do, Jonah, start up your very own University back at Freeport? Would they allow that?''

''All that equipment shouldn't be allowed to go to waste. At the least I should get in there and take what I need, anyhow. But yeah, my own university, that's an idea. You teach in it Rick, and I'll run it.'' He blew a luxurious plume of smoke and stretched bonelessly. ''One thing we don't need to improve is this. Come on Rick, you should try it.''

The conversation turned to Rick's strict upbringing, and then Rivington started a stoned monolog about the high country of the Trackless Mountains, ranges that seemed to stretch away forever in the clear air, the sunsets and the pure untrodden snowfields, fierce ossifrages which rode the winds with wingspans of more than a dozen meters, and beaten gnarled trees that were thousands of years old, before at last smiling (''I've been rapping on too long, it's about time to let you young lovers alone, now.'') and taking his leave.

But Rivington's chance remark lodged in Rick's mind. It was not really equipment that should be saved, he thought. Equipment was often heavy and difficult to move and could always be duplicated given the appropriate level of technology (and without that technology any salvaged equipment would soon wear out and not be replaced). Not equipment, then, but knowledge. He was thinking of de Ramaira's time vault, of course, and in particular of his own contribution to it, the way he had pared it down to the irreducible minimum of theory, the seed from which all else could be derived. All this and more he talked out with Rivington—and early one morning Rivington, brimming with *bonhomie*, accosted Rick in the mess tent and told him that he should get ready for a journey.

''Where do you have in mind?''

''I've been promoting our idea,'' Rivington said. ''Theodora Cziller wants to see us.''

Although Lena had been enthusiastic about the project when it was only an idea, she had expressed fierce opposition to its actual implementation. It had been the first major dis-

agreement between Rick and herself, but in the end she had
let him go, as she had to. Rick and Jonah Rivington traveled
alone on horses Rivington had managed to purloin, a journey that took two days to organize, two more to complete.
On the map Cziller's command camp was only twenty kilometers north of Arcadia, but there was no direct route through
the hilly forests, and the need to avoid the fighting forced
further detours.

Cziller's camp was strung across a tree-clad hilltop, a nu-
cleus of a dozen large tents, pitched beneath camouflage net-
ting and infrared baffling, surrounded by a kind of shanty
town of smaller tents, shacks, and burrows that faded away
into the forest. Rick and Jonah Rivington were far from being
the only supplicants. There were emissaries and representatives from all of the settlements on various errands, individuals and groups of mercenaries wanting official sanction for
their clandestine operations or hoping for an advantage by
being close to the center of things. Despite their specific
invitation, Rick and Jonah Rivington had to wait three more
days before they got to see Cziller. Rivington, sanguine about
the delay, spent much of the time botanizing among the buttress roots of the soaring trees, while Rick spent most of his
time drinking coffee or bad beer and listening to the latest
stories of the war in a kind of tavern which burrowed into
the hillside, definitely unofficial but doing a roaring trade all
the same.

It was in that smokey, crowded, noisy burrow that Rick
really began to believe in his mission. It came to him that
many of the insurgents looked forward to the unraveling of
civilization without really appreciating the consequences. An
end to Port of Plenty's continual surveillance and control to
be sure, and an end to the bland leveling diet of regurgitated
trivia: but an end also to medical care and the selective her-
bicides which kept invasive and poisonous native plants out
of the fields, and an end to the rich common cultural heritage,
an end to Bach chorales and the unfocused light of Impres-
sionism, an end to all that was worth remembering of the
Earth. Everything could fall apart: everything. Nothing left

but a handful of half-remembered tales, shards, a return to the bullock-drawn plough and old age by thirty.

That was the extreme which must be prevented, yet it was impossible to sort out what should be saved and what abandoned. That was why he and Jonah had never agreed on a list of priorities. There could be no such list. All must be saved indiscriminately. Or the attempt must be made, anyhow. Any knowledge, the spinor equations of five-field theory or the progressive harmonics of "The Well-Tempered Clavier," has by itself no intrinsic value: its worth or otherwise is realized only in civilization's context.

All this was what Rick tried to explain to Theodora Cziller when he and Jonah Rivington were at last granted an audience.

After he had finished, Cziller said, "This is all very well, but how much will it cost? How many hours of work will it take?" She sat stiffly upright in a carved wooden chair, her right hand resting on the cluttered little table beside her. A small woman in her late fifties, with a thin aesthetic face, gray hair pulled severely back like a punishment. Her eyes were her only remarkable feature: deep-set and a bright, dense blue, as if enameled, they did not seem to receive light so much as transmit a force of will. Rick flinched beneath her penetrating regard; then she reached for another cigarillo (the air of the little tent reeked of their acrid smoke) and said, "I suppose you will say as little as I want, or as much as you need."

"Something like that," Rick admitted. He and Jonah Rivington stood before Cziller like penitents, of necessity. Apart from her chair and the little table, the only other furniture in the tent was a folding cot and a small metal chest. A lamp hung from the ridgepole but it was not switched on; when Cziller lit her cigarillo the flare of the match seemed as bright as the sun, whose afternoon light filtered only dimly through the canvas walls.

Rivington said, "We can ask for volunteers from the camp. Quite a few are from the University anyhow, they'll need little enough training."

"And what will you do," Cziller asked, "if in the middle of your operation at the University, insurgents start to burn down the buildings before you've finished?"

Rivington began, "I suppose we'd need an escort—"

"No. You would let the buildings burn." Through the haze of tobacco smoke, Cziller's gaze was sharply intent. "That is the only way I could let something like this go ahead. I will admit to you freely that I am in command of an army which is not really an army at all. It has no discipline, and its members are not really trained. There is no central organization, apart from myself and a few others here. The lines of communication are vague, the hierarchy very nearly nonexistent." She paused to puff on her cigarillo; clearly, she had given this exposition many times before.

She continued dryly, "The basic unit is a party of men and women, usually but not always from one settlement, of indefinite number and leadership, and possessed of equally indefinite aims beyond that of defeating the city. My only real achievement is to have organized these units into a number of divisions. I suppose that you could say that this is the most democratic army to have ever existed. Its common aim is to overturn the tyranny of Port of Plenty, but there is no centrally imposed plan. Everything is achieved more or less by consensus. And there is our greatest strength and our greatest weakness. Strong because unpredictable; and weak for the same reason. Being unpredictable, our moves are less likely to be predicted and forestalled by Constat, but I am also bedeviled by that selfsame unpredictability. The strength and disposition of each division changes from week to week, and it is a constant struggle to keep each at its appointed task." Again she drew on her cigarillo. "Well now, what does this mean for you? It means, my friends, that as in any democracy, might is right. Whether might in terms of ballot majority, or in the number of guns each side possesses. So if someone comes along with the intent of burning the University to the ground, you will let them, if you are outnumbered. There will be no appeal to higher authority."

"Are you saying that we could have gone ahead without asking you?" Rick asked.

Cziller smiled. "You could have made a try of it. But you wouldn't have known whether or not I would have tried to stop it once I'd heard of it."

Jonah Rivington rubbed his unshaven chin. "But I'm right in thinking that you aren't against it?"

"As long as you remember your place, you can go ahead. Find as many in the camp who'll help you, but—" her gaze flashed "—heaven help you if you try recruiting among the fighting people. And heaven help you too if you try and use my name to get ahead, not that it will do you much good. I'm not against your project—it widens possibilities after this is all over—but it is not the most important item on the agenda. We all know what that is."

Rick asked her what she meant, about widening possibilities.

"You're an educated man, I take it. You have been thinking about what will happen when the city falls. You see the possibility of barbarism, hence your project. But it is not the only possibility, and I think the more we have to play with the better. Some have been saying, you know, that there should be a new constitution written, the spirit of seventeen seventy-six and all that. I say the hell with it, I'm no George Washington. I'm not even Thomas Jefferson. Keep things fluid and uncertain, that way people fix on the task at hand." She stubbed out her cigarillo on the scarred arm of her chair with an impatient gesture. The interview was over.

That had been a week past. Rick and Rivington had returned to the camp outside Arcadia, managed to recruit a half a dozen volunteers. Most of those who had fled the city did not want to take the part of any side in the war, Lena among them. But she had given Rick her blessing anyway. Now, on the cold beach, Rick mulled over Cziller's parting words for perhaps the hundredth time, but he was too tired to riddle any more sense from them. Shifting a little in the hollow which his buttocks had worn in the sand he opened his aching eyes and saw that the cold illimitable darkness seemed to be lifting. Surely, it wasn't already dawn. What had happened to Rivington?

Yet there was a growing impression of solid shadows slumped everywhere on a vaguely lighter ground, where before everything had been almost entirely black. Rick could make out the shapes of the men and women sprawled among the ragged tufts of grass; could even make out the breakers far down the beach, dirty white lines that continually unraveled in the same direction.

And then his confusion passed. He saw. Above the ocean's horizon, the gleaming disc of Cerberus was setting through a ragged gap in the clouds. And in the moment of understanding he saw Rivington's figure, a tall stoop-shouldered shadow in the shadowy moonlight, coming toward him.

24. The Ambush

The last night of Cerberus also shone for a moment on the stolen overlander, falling through its windscreen and gleaming in Miguel's unsleeping eyes like the crystalline essence of his insomnia. Mari, or what had been Mari, was a shadow against the moonlight. She was hunched over the console at the front of the overlander's cramped cabin, probably communing with the real blue brother in the city, through the compsim. Miguel shivered. Then, as he so often did these nights, he got up from the seat where he had been trying to get some sleep and climbed through the hatch into cold black air.

It was bad enough being cooped up with the woman by day; at night it was intolerable. Most of the time she sat still and silent, scarcely seeming to breathe, eyes dully focused on infinity. That was bad. Worse was when she was suddenly raised into activity, to eat or to go outside and relieve herself, or to fieldstrip and reassemble the cryostat which held the stolen aborigine eggs in suspended animation, or start up the overlander and drive it to another hiding place—Miguel had lost count of the number of times that had happened, although their random path never took them very far from Port of Plenty's perimeter—or to patiently scan the surrounding area through one or another of the overlander's devices. But patient was the wrong word, for it implied volition. Not a spark of her personality was left. She was no more than the vessel of the blue brother's implacable will.

Miguel jumped to the ground and walked to the edge of the drop. This was one of the better hiding places, the top of a hill which crested above the forest like a breaking wave. The overlander was parked among tall trees which grew right to the edge of the cliff. The combination of fitful moonlight and its camouflage circuits made it invisible after only a few steps.

Miguel sat on cold stone and shook out his thermoblanket, drew it around himself like a cape. There was frost in the air. Slowly but perceptibly, the burnished face of the large moon sank into the clouds at the horizon. Shadow swallowed the silvery vista of the forest spread beyond the cliff. Not for the first time, Miguel thought about throwing himself off the edge . . . but it would not necessarily be the end. He had nightmares about the corpse of the blue brother's other slave, the one killed in the Source Cave, plodding after the overlander's erratic path, flesh in tatters about its bones. If he killed himself he might awake to find himself trapped in the cold flesh of his own dead body. Anything was possible.

He must have dozed, for he awoke with his hand around the compsim and the soundless voice of the blue brother reverberating in his head.

—It is past midnight, Miguel. You must return to the vehicle.

"I'm sick of the vehicle, and of that woman of yours. If we have to hide out here, let me do it away from her." But his complaint was more habit than anything else. He was already on his feet when the blue brother replied.

—There is no longer any need to hide from the insurgents. The time is coming, Miguel. It is almost upon us. You must make ready to deliver your cargo.

"What do you mean? What do you want of me now, in

the name of God?'' In the darkness, Miguel could hardly
make out the trees, let alone the camouflaged overlander. He
stumbled over a root and skinned his palm on cold unforgiving ground. The blue brother did not answer. Or perhaps it
did. As Miguel got up, the overlander's motor started with a
shrill clatter, and a moment later its headlights snapped on,
dazzling him.

Mari drove the overlander at breakneck speed through the
forest. Half the time it was off the ground, jolting over half-
sunken boulders, flying over sprawling buttress roots. Miguel clung to the passenger seat, watching with fascinated
terror as time after time a tree trunk rushed into the beams
of the headlamps and swerved aside only at the last moment.
There was no end to them. He didn't even realize that the
overlander had struck a mine until the insurgents who had
set the ambush opened fire.

The mine's explosion was only another jolt; then the windscreen crazed and metal hail hammered the sides of the
overlander. Mari hauled hard on the wheel. The overlander
almost tipped over as it slewed around. There was another
rattle of small-arms fire. The crazed windscreen fell away in
a snow of crystals. Cold air slapped Miguel's face, cold air
and the acrid smell of burning. He glimpsed people running
between the cathedral columns of the trees, caught in the
headlights' glare, and then the overlander was roaring down
a steep slope and the people were left behind.

Miguel had enough time to think that the cops were trying
to stop them, and then to realize that it was probably insurgents, ambushing what they must think was a cop patrol.
And then something detonated in the rear of the overlander
and heat washed his back. The overdriven scream of the motor cut out and the overlander slewed sideways and then tipped
over, rolling once and with a world-shattering crash fetching
the right way up against a huge tree.

Miguel blacked out when the overlander rolled, came
around to find himself sagging sideways, held by the harness
of his seat. He had somehow banged his head: it felt dizzily
swollen, a remote void through which the light of the world

swam weakly. When the blue brother's voice came it was
fainter than it had been for a long while.

—The eggs, Miguel. You must help save them.

Stooping amidst wreaths of smoke, Mari was already
wrestling with the padded cryostat. Miguel felt a cool numbness as the piece of the blue brother inside his head took
control. His hands punched the release buckle of the seat's
safety harness; clumsily, his body staggered across the
smoke-hazed cabin to help the woman.

Mari went through the hatch and reached down to receive
the cryostat, while Miguel hauled it up the ladder. Heat beat
at his back, yet as in a nightmare he could not run. Only
when the cryostat had been eased through the hatch did the
blue brother's control collapse, as abruptly as a pricked balloon. Miguel caught at the edge of the hatch, then remembered his pack and went down into the smoke to fetch it, the
blue brother protesting feebly but unable, it seemed, to reen-
gage its control. Perhaps the blow to Miguel's head had loosened its hold over him.

—No time, Miguel!

"Fuck you. This is all I have in the world."

—The world will be yours, fool!

By now, the smoke was so thick that he could hardly see
his hands, and when Miguel groped his way to the ladder,
the rungs were searingly hot. He hastily pulled himself
through the hatch onto the ribbed roof, and found himself
surrounded by fire.

—Jump, Miguel, jump!

He saw his chance, twisted the compsim from his belt and
dropped it into the smoke which poured from the hatch.
"Fuck you," he said to the thing inside his head, then took
a deep breath to steady himself and jumped through flapping
sheets of flame.

He landed badly on soft ground, wrenching his ankle. He
rolled over, managed to drag himself a few meters from the
burning overlander.

The woman turned from the cryostat and walked stiffly
over to where Miguel sat on thawing mud, gingerly probing

his ankle. She bent over him and, once, twice, slapped his face. Her long ragged nails raked his cheeks. Her face was livid in the leaping flames that now completely enveloped the overlander. Her mouth opened and a voice came out of it.

"I saw what you did, Miguel. When I have time, I will punish you for it. Now you will help me to carry the frozen eggs. That is all that matters now. But later, yes. Later you will pay."

—How you will pay, the weakened voice inside him echoed.

"Fuck you. Fuck both of you. I'm not your slave, see?"

The woman unholstered her pistol, and the voice that was not her voice said, "Willingly or unwillingly you will help me, Miguel. You will carry the cryostat to the city for me, and you must hurry. The insurgents will not be far behind and we have a rendezvous to make."

As she went back to fetch the cryostat, Miguel quickly reached inside his pack and fetched out a sliver of snakeroot. Ignoring the feeble, impotent warnings of the blue brother in his head, he rolled it under his tongue. Instantly, the familiar long-missed numbness began to spread over his skin. The pain of his bruised head and sprained ankle receded to feeble flickers at the horizon of his consciousness.

When the enslaved woman brought the cryostat over, Miguel was standing on his good foot and waggling his damaged ankle to ward off the worst of the sprain. She watched impassively as he settled the sling on his shoulder, then waved him on, trudging at his back. When the overlander blew a few minutes later, only Miguel looked back.

With the drug in the snakeroot mounting in his brain, the pillar of fire bloomed like some fantastic nightflower in the living cathedral of the forest. He would have stayed to watch, but the hollow mechanical thing, a network of blue lines seething under the skin of its face, ordered him on. Staggering under his load through the night, toward the city and consummation of the blue brother's plans.

25. The Vault

De Ramaira woke with a shudder from a dream of falling through endless darkness, as if he had become the lost colonyboat, gravithic generators flatlined, fusion motor cold, falling uncontrollably through the boundless universe. Cold night still pressed at the narrow window beside the study's fireplace. It was just before midnight. He had fallen asleep in his chair, the little recorder still running. As he switched it off, the noise which had woken him, the doorbell's distant jangle, came again.

At first, de Ramaira had been amused by the house's quaint lack of environmental conditioning, of most kinds of automation (the richer households of Port of Plenty actually employed human servants: the waste!), its rigidly fixed quota of rooms and their unsophisticated handmade furnishings. Later, he had become exasperated by the inconvenience of having to do most things for himself. But after more than a dozen years of exile he had grown into it like a hermit crab into its borrowed shell. He had hardly a thought in his sleep-befuddled head as he went down the narrow staircase and along the hallway, pulled back clunky mechanical bolts and opened the door.

And stepped back from the two apparitions on the doorstep, for once lost for words.

Richard Florey smiled and asked, "May we come in?"

De Ramaira recognized Florey's companion after a moment's startled blinking. He said, "I think you had better, before someone sees you. Jonah, you rascal, I haven't seen you for years."

"Wish I could have come at a better time," the tall settler said, stooping as he stepped through the door. His curly hair was as unkempt as ever, though touched with gray now. He was unshaven. "Damn, I didn't expect to ever be back here again," he said, and embraced de Ramaira while Richard Florey carefully closed the door.

They sat in the study, Richard Florey in the old diplotherehide chair across from de Ramaira's accustomed seat, Jonah Rivington on a stool in the shadows behind Florey. De Ramaira sipped neat rum and listened to Richard Florey's account of what had happened to him since he had quit the city, the plan he and Rivington had put together.

"Well," de Ramaira said, when the story was finished. "I suppose you have a part for me in all this."

Florey swirled the rum in his own glass, then drank it down. He had a lean and hungry look, and lounged in the big chair with raffish confidence, no longer the effete, unprepossessing scientist. His overcoat was stained and torn and his boots were spattered with mud. He said, "We started out thinking that we should save machines, research equipment, and so on. But then I remembered your time vault, and all you had told me. Knowledge is far more portable than hardware, and more useful too, in the long run. To begin with, we'd like to have a copy of all that's gone into the vault. The city wants to pass on its knowledge to the future. What better way than to give it to its direct successors?"

"The city hasn't lost, yet."

"Not yet," Jonah Rivington said from the shadows, "but

soon, right? We couldn't have gotten to you, David, if our patrols hadn't knocked holes in the city's defenses.''

"Yes, of course. I suppose I've been expecting an end to this for some time . . . but it's still a surprise.'' He drank a little more rum. ''Well, you know I've never had much sympathy with the city, Rick. Nor it for me, come to that. You said that you wanted everything in the time vault? Well, that's easy enough, I have copies of the database right here. Is that all you want of me?''

"Come with us, David. Come with us now. Help us.''

"That's not really possible. I still have to seal the time vault.''

"If you give us a copy of the database, does the time vault matter? Forget about the distant future, David, it's what's going to happen in the next few years that's important.''

"That's right,'' Jonah Rivington said.

"The problem with all you colonists, citizen and settler alike, is that you have no sense of history. Do you know, this was once Eljar Price's house? This was *his* study, once upon a time. He must have planned the expeditions to Contra-America in here, and that last, fatal trip to the South Pole. On Earth, the house of someone as prominent in history as Price would be a museum. Here . . . it's just another house.''

"If I know you, there's a moral you're about to make.'' Absently, Rick traced the ladder of bookshelves beyond de Ramaira. Books leaning in disorderly rows, piled in tottering towers and stacks, tier upon tier of books, rising to the stained, sagging plaster of the ceiling. More here than in Mount Airy's library. Maybe they had once belonged to Eljar Price, too. Their sweetish, dusty odor filled the room. It made him feel sleepy.

De Ramaira said, ''An idea of the importance of the past gives you an idea of the importance of the future. Not even Constat can accurately predict what will happen when the city falls. I mean no disrespect to your plan, of course, but knowledge is only useful if something is made of it. Many of the settlers may not want to have anything to do with the city, especially not scientific knowledge. Those who know

nothing of science are apt to blame it for much, just as they
used to blame the gods, I suppose, or fate. When this war is
over, you can be certain that there will be a lot of burning—
perhaps too much burning. I hope it's otherwise, but it could
be that civilization will collapse despite anything that any of
us can do. In that case, I like to think of someone stumbling
across the time vault sometime in the future, and making
something of its contents. No, Rick, you go ahead with your
plan, and I'll carry on with mine. That way we can be sure
that something will survive."

Jonah Rivington said, "But I'm right in thinking that you
will give us this database of yours."

"A copy, of course." De Ramaira rooted among the bits
and pieces, found the cassette and tossed it over.

Florey caught the fat needle and said, "We'll take good
care of it. Thanks." Then he yawned. "Jesus, sorry. It's
been a long night."

"Stay here," de Ramaira suggested. "There's room
enough."

Florey began to say doubtfully, "Well, I don't know . . ."

But Jonah Rivington smiled and said, "Hey, now, thank
you, David. That's a kind thought. See here, Rick, it will
save us having to get back to our own people."

Florey twisted in his chair to look at his partner. "What
makes you think it will be easier to get back to them in
daylight?"

"Because," Rivington explained patiently, "by tomorrow
they'll be here."

When de Ramaira woke again, it was to the warm half
darkness of his bedroom and the sense that something was
missing. He remembered last night's visitation, Florey's impossible request and Rivington's revelation of the imminence
of the city's end, then rolled from the bedplate and, naked,
padded to the window and depolarized it.

The familiar notched tumble of roofs straggling away
downhill. The city's grid stretched beneath a cheerless winter
dawn. Scattered skeins of smoke rose from the embattled
bubble-suburbs, but that was not unusual. What was, was an

eerie calm which had swallowed the city's usual roar, as if everyone but he had been spirited away overnight. Only the menacing staccato rumbling of the distant fighting scratched at the edge of the city's profound silence.

De Ramaira turned away and began to dress, choosing his clothes carefully. Corduroy trousers, a mesh T-shirt and an old workshirt, a baggy woolen sweater. He pulled VDF coveralls over all this and eased his comfortable hiking boots over two pairs of socks. When he was lacing the boots, he noticed that a folded sheet of paper had been pushed under the ill-fitting wooden door.

A single sentence, penciled in hasty capitals. *See you at the University, best luck.* Sure enough, his guests were gone from their bedrooms. He was quite alone.

In the cavernous basement kitchen, the treacher instantly gave up a cup of burning hot black coffee, but took several minutes to work on de Ramaira's complicated instructions for a nutritive concentrate. Meanwhile, he stowed his survival kit in several pockets: a tightly folded thermoblanket, his bushknife and a small multiblade pocketknife, compass and waterproof map, water filter and vitamin tablets, a tiny heating cube. The hatch of the treacher opened and he took out the two dozen heavy, dark biscuits, sealed them in a sample bag.

His brain was working quickly now, but none of the tumbling thoughts clung for more than a moment. Snowflakes melting on a windowpane. He had planned so long for this that now it was happening it felt faintly unreal. He carried the cup of coffee up to the dusty living room and switched on the trivee.

There was nothing but a lithe hiss and the test cube on every one of the public channels, but he'd had the trivee jiggered so that it could access and decode the utility bands, and de Ramaira found plenty of traffic there. Sipping cooling coffee, he flicked through it all.

Urgent disembodied voices, some with gunfire crackling in the background. A police lieutenant reciting VDF section numbers and grid coordinates. Views of the collapsed bubble-suburbs, of a ragged line of figures advancing down a smoke-hazed street, of a row of burning warehouses down by the docks . . . a kaleidoscope of images of something greater than the usual isolated skirmishes. Jonah Rivington had been telling the truth. This was the insurgents' final push.

De Ramaira went to his study and pocketed his little .202 automatic and the cassette he'd recorded the previous night. And then he had all that he wanted. There was no more time for procrastination. One hand thrust into the pouchpocket of his coveralls, long fingers clenched around the automatic's compact comforting weight, de Ramaira left his house for the last time.

. The streets were almost deserted. The few people de Ramaira passed looked haunted, and he didn't see a vehicle until a cushiontruck loaded with VDF workers slid past the corner of Fifth and Market Avenues on a rush of air. Market Avenue diagonally slashed the city's grid north to south; beyond a barrier of razor wire and oildrums at the intersection it still lay in deep shadow. De Ramaira didn't see the two guards until they moved from a doorway to intercept him.

The taller man asked for his permit, and as both bent over it de Ramaira said impatiently, "I'm supervising the work at the Exchange."

The tall guard handed back the permit and his partner, a cadaverous old man, did an absurd shuffle, hands buried in the pouchpocket of his coveralls. "You better hurry," he said, and laughed.

"Someone's setting the fuses? Look, is Max Rydell in there?"

The tall guard said in a slow voice, "Well, you see, I don't know his name. We were just set here to keep people away."

"But the vault is going to be sealed, right?"

Neither guard had a chance to answer. A stray mortar round ended its whistling arc at the next intersection and the thunder of its explosion filled the street.

De Ramaira ran, cantering up the steps of the Exchange two at a time. Bits of debris pattered all around. Black smoke boiled above the flat roofs of the warehouses.

The Exchange's massive doors had been pushed open. The maroon carpet looked black in the wan early morning light. The tellers' windows shone like tarnished mirrors. A single light burned above the stair down to the vault.

Max Rydell, beside the steel plug of the vault door, turned and grinned affably as de Ramaira came down the stairs. "I was wondering where you were, David. You're just in time. Hey, who was firing at who just then? It damned near knocked me down."

"I believe they were aiming at the police headquarters."

"Well I hope they don't set off my handiwork before its time. That *would* piss Savory off."

"At the police headquarters?"

Rydell pushed the bunched sleeves of his coveralls further up his hirsute forearms. There were liverish pouches beneath his eyes. "Oh, just a precaution, I guess, wouldn't want it falling into the insurgents' hands. All those secrets. Don't go telling anyone, now. The whole thing's so confidential it didn't even go through Constat."

"To be sure." De Ramaira thought of Constat and the enslaved aborigines. Very likely that Savory had more in mind than simply destroying secret records. He plucked at the slack wires which ran from the jury-rigged control plate to the valve-head of the argon cylinder. "Isn't it a little late for improvements down here?"

The engineer shrugged. "Just something that occurred to me while I was working over at headquarters. Rather than rig a separate timing system for the charges, I've wired them to the pressure sensor in the head there. When the cylinder's bled all its argon to the vault it'll trip the switch."

"You had better be certain that it will work."

"You bet." Rydell grinned. "Now we won't need to hang about while the vault pressurizes."

"You do have orders to seal the vault, then. The guards up there didn't seem to know."

"Well, hell. Those guys don't know shit, why should they? I've been here since I finished at the headquarters. Up before six, when the insurgents started their advance—at least, that's when the orders came through my compsim. Like I said, I was wondering when you'd turn up.''

"For good or bad, I don't have my strings pulled by Constat like you regular officers.'' De Ramaira had a momentary vision of the grid of the city as a vast chessboard on which the Constat moved its pieces, the police patrols and VDF units, as oblivious to the suffering caused by its remote tactics as any grandmaster. Certainly, on Earth, as it was now in heaven, military strategy had long been controlled by state-Q, a vast complex of megacee computers. Weapons of any significance in the great standoff were so quickly and catholically destructive that on both sides their control had long ago passed from the frail fallible hands of humans. His mind skipped quickly over the thought, the pang of regret gone as abruptly as a snuffed candleflame.

He told Rydell, "But here I am anyway. Is your contraption finished?''

"It is. Would you like the honor of sealing it?''

"You're the engineer. I just want to put this away.'' De Ramaira took the cassette from his pocket and stooped to set it just inside the high sill of the vault. Rydell checked the thick hose that ran from the valve-head of the argon cylinder to the one-way connection drilled into the wall of the vault, then leaned against the counterweighted door. The heavy steel plug swung smoothly into place. The light over the steel cabinets within went out a moment before the door closed; the last thing de Ramaira saw was the cassette he had abandoned. Then the bolts clanged home and the thick hose flexed as the pumps started up, purging the air in the vault with incorruptible argon. His duty was discharged. He was free.

Rydell grinned. "It'll take sixty or seventy minutes to get up pressure. Then: blooie!'' He clapped loudly. "Say, can I give you a lift to wherever you're supposed to be? I borrowed a cruiser to do my rounds.''

"I have an appointment at the University.''

"There's a coincidence.'' Rydell bent to a yellow plastic crate. "You can ride along with me, okay? Give me a hand with this son-of-a-bitch.''

"What is it?"

"The rest of the explosive," Rydell said casually. "Hell, don't sweat. You could throw it into a fire—an ordinary one, anyhow—and all it would do was burn. TDX. It needs a voltage difference across it to make it go." Hauling the heavy crate between them, they started up the stairs. "If you're going to clear out your stuff, you had better be quick," Rydell said. "The University's next on my list."

"Savory has got you working hard. The whole University?"

"Oh, the charges were set in place weeks ago. I just have to tamp in the fuses." They went through the door in the partition that had once separated customer from clerk, settler from citizen. "What we need to do," Rydell said, "is to find you a rifle somewhere."

"Oh, I have what I need."

Together, they stepped into the shadowy street. There was no sign of the two guards at the barrier. De Ramaira set down his end of the crate and shut and locked the heavy doors, a final neatness. Around the corner, a white cruiser sat on its black, deflated skirt.

As they moved off, Rydell grinned and said, "You know, I left the bloody lights on back there!"

"Not for long." De Ramaira stretched his long legs as best he could in the cramped space, only half aware of the gentle roar of the motor and the blank facades of the warehouses that flipped past on either side. He held his pistol tightly inside the pouchpocket of the coveralls. The thought of what he would have to do and the presence of the yellow plastic crate of explosive in back made him edgy. To hide his nervousness he switched on the radio. Crackling overlapping voices filled the stale air of the cruiser's cabin.

"Most of that's false traffic to confuse the shiteaters," Rydell commented, swinging the cruiser onto Fifth. They paused to let a shambling procession of press-ganged draftees cross at an intersection (not one of the men and women carried a weapon; only a few wore VDF coveralls), then accelerated away.

Soon they were negotiating the ruined bubble-suburbs, the cruiser smoothly passing over bits of foliage and stone fragments and half-burned plastic sheeting and fugitively gleaming glass shards. Only a few domes had escaped damage. Many were no more than circles of charred rubble. Then they were passing the high stone walls bordering the grounds of the houses of the rich. Trees raised stripped branches to the milky sky. Far beyond the treetops, de Ramaira glimpsed the white hospital, misty with distance, lodged like a shard of polished bone high on a gray-green ridge.

Inside his pouchpocket, de Ramaira worked his fingers around the pistol's butt, clicked off the safety, found the trigger guard. Ahead were the ridges which bordered the University. Four figures stood at the top of one of these grassy swells, looking down at the road. Two carried something between them on a crude kind of sling. They were Rick Florey and Jonah Rivington. After a moment's astonishment de Ramaira pulled out the pistol.

Rydell glanced at it and said, "Don't bother shooting at them, I'll run on by fast as I can." Then, gruffly, "What the fuck are you doing?"

"Making sure you stop."

"You crazy?"

For an answer, de Ramaira jammed the pistol harder against Rydell's ear. The man flinched and said, "You got it," and cut the motor. The cruiser's skirts deflated explosively and it slewed off the road and gouged into the grassy slope. De Ramaira was pitched forward as it slammed to a halt. In a moment, Rydell was out of the cruiser and running across the road. By the time de Ramaira had clambered after him, the engineer was scaling a high stone wall. A moment later he had dropped neatly over the other side.

The woman who seemed to be leading the little group started down the slope toward de Ramaira. The others had stopped, and de Ramaira thought he heard Rick shout something. He gestured with the pistol, and the woman stopped. She wore a fleece coat and denim trousers, carried a hunting rifle. There was something funny about her face, something dead. As if she was wearing a mask. A pistol hung by its lanyard from her belt; the hunting rifle flicked from side to side like a seeking eye.

De Ramaira dropped his own weapon with a deliberately ostentatious gesture and raised his hands a little above his shoulders. Every centimeter of his skin quickened in anticipation. He said foolishly, "Excuse me. . . ."

The rifle stopped moving. Her face still without expression, the woman put a bullet through de Ramaira's thigh.

26. Rendezvous

Rick and Jonah Rivington left de Ramaira's house just before dawn. Neither of them had gotten much sleep. Unused to the soft swaddling warmth of a bedplate, Rick kept waking from muddled dreams to the noise of distant gunfire, and at last he got up, although the unpolarized window of the dusty room still framed nothing but darkness, and went down to the basement kitchen. Jonah Rivington was already there, drinking coffee.

As Rick asked the treacher for milky tea, Rivington said, "I've been watching the trivee. David's got that thing rigged to catch the cops' channels. Seems as if things are moving nicely for us." He sketched the insurgents' advance in the dust on the top of the huge wooden table. South along the coast from Jones Beach, a pincer movement from the east, out of the forested hills. "I reckon they should overrun the University before the morning is out. There's not much resistance there anyway, seems the pounding they've given the suburbs worked." Rivington yawned, quick and oblivious as a cat. "Want me to fix breakfast? The service core doesn't hold much for that treacher thing to work on, but there's some real food about.''

"I don't know if I could eat," Rick said. His stomach fluttered with nervousness not much soothed by the customary tea.

"Me neither," Rivington said. "But we ought to try. Going to be a long day." He grilled ham and toasted some stale bread, and scrambled some of the real eggs Rick found in de Ramaira's larder. They ate as much of it as they could, and cleared up before leaving as a gesture of respect to their sleeping host.

"I still think we should kidnap him," Rivington grumbled, as they started down the narrow street in near darkness. "That guy is like a national resource, he goddamn well better make it out."

"I left him a message. Maybe he'll catch up with us at the University. Don't worry about it, he'll be okay." Rick was walking a pace behind Rivington, shivering slightly in the sharp cold. He had left his overcoat behind and was masquerading as a member of the VDF in case they were challenged. Rivington was supposed to be his prisoner. The ruse, and a pistol and Rick's transceiver, were all the protection they had.

The city was stirring in the darkness, grumbling in its sleep like a giant beset by minute but voracious predators. Gunfire crackled in the distance, punctuated by the explosions of mortar rounds. Once or twice, Rick and Jonah Rivington had to duck into doorways as cushiontrucks or police cruisers sped past, headlights glaring. They kept to the back streets as much as they could, taking a circuitous route that would cut through the abandoned bubble-suburbs to the University.

The sky was at last beginning to lighten. By now the gunfire was so near that Rick could distinguish each shot. Rivington showed no sign of noticing it. He loped along with the wings of his leather jacket flapping, checking out the shadowy palisades of evergreen bushes that screened each dome from the road. The domes here had been scarcely touched by the fighting, no more than a few cracked or missing octagonal panes.

Rivington had just reached an intersection when a bullet kicked fragments of concrete centimeters from his feet. Rick dodged into the nearest bushes and a moment later Rivington almost landed on top of him as another shot chattered through branches. Together, they crawled deeper into the thickets, worked their way around the curved base of the dome.

"Maybe he's just covering the intersection," Rivington whispered hoarsely. "We get across the next street and we're away."

"Yeah," Rick whispered back. His throat was dry and his heart seemed to have enlarged and grown lighter, fluttering at his throat.

They pushed around the curve of the dome through dense prickly evergreens, but when they reached the edge of the bushes someone took another potshot at them. Rivington took the pistol and let off a single loud shot in reply; and a concentrated burst of fire tore into the shrubbery. He and Rick hugged the dirt as shattered twigs and bits of leaves rained down on their backs. The broken foliage released a dusty, menthol odor.

"Maybe that wasn't so smart," Rivington said, when it was over.

"More than one of them."

"I reckon."

They were marooned in an island of vegetation, separated from the other islands around each dome by a road or a wide strip of grass. Rivington stretched out on his belly, resting his chin on his folded arms, and suggested they wait it out. "Maybe they'll get bored. Or maybe some of our guys will come along."

"Or maybe they'll come over here and check us out."

"Did anyone ever tell you not to look on the dark side of things?"

The sky brightened, a single sheet of cloud. Gunfire still sounded in the distance, but the mortar barrage of the inner city seemed to have ceased. Rick took out his transceiver and scanned for any transmissions the snipers might be making. There was plenty of traffic, encrypted messages from comp-sims and talk in clear between insurgent units that was mostly garbled by the feedback interference put out by the cops. But there was nothing coming from the immediate vicinity.

"The front will roll on by," Rivington said, as Rick put the transceiver away. "No need for us to hurry."

"Sure." But sooner or later, Rick thought, either he or Jonah Rivington would have to risk showing themselves, to find out if the snipers had gone. He was nerving himself to suggest this when Rivington said, "Listen up."

It was the sound of a cushiontruck. They wriggled forward, reaching the edge of the bushes just as the vehicle smoothly slid to a halt at the intersection. A man was fiddling with a mortar that had been bolted to the truck's loadbed, while a woman rested a rifle on the roof of the green-painted cab (on the door, in white curlicue script mostly obscured by mud, the single word *Arcadia*). The man fed a round into the mortar, and as he ducked from the hollow clang and puff of smoke, Rivington pushed through the bushes. The woman jerked her rifle around, then relaxed. Rivington stepped up and said something to her, then motioned to Rick. "These good people are running interference," he said. "Seems we might have run into some of their friends doing the same."

"You're lucky we didn't drop one on you," the man by the mortar said.

The woman was staring at Rick's coveralls. "What are you guys? Some kind of spies?"

Rivington gave a brief explanation of their mission, and the woman shrugged. "Far as I know the University's still there. The advance went either side of it. I wondered why." She told them to watch their step, there were rogue cops about as well as insurgent scouts. Then she banged on the roof of the cab. The cushiontruck swiveled on a blast of air and swept away. Rick and Rivington started off in the direction from which it had come.

Soon after that, they came upon the bodies.

There were three of them, two men and a woman, sprawled

casually in the middle of the street. None could have been older than twenty. They wore oversize quilted overcoats dyed in violent patterns and hung with loops of heavy chain, very trash aesthetique, very irrelevant. All three had been shot in the head at close range. Someone had taken the trouble to pin to the chest of each corpse a sheet of paper scrawled with a single word, *looter*.

"Who do you think?" Rick asked.

"Cops. Has to be. We're all of us looters in the Liberation Army, right? That's our basic creed."

One of the men had long blond hair, wet with blood now. There was a fleshy crater where his right eye had been. His overcoat had fallen open to show a fluorescent green vest, its mesh stretched over his bony chest.

"Come on," Jonah Rivington said. "I've seen enough of this fucking war already."

As they neared the University, the proportion of ruined domes increased. Plastic paneling had melted into strange organic shapes, or burst outward like a smashed flower. The streets were littered with debris, cratered from the random bombardment. Once, they found themselves wading through a sudden swiftflowing river, then passed the fountain from a burst main which fed it. Once, they passed a dozen domes burning in unison, throwing up a reef of dense black smoke. And once or twice they saw distant groups of people picking their way through the ruins in the opposite direction, toward the embattled heart of the city. One of these groups loosed a burst of tracer bullets in their direction which chopped out the crowns of a group of native goldenrod trees, showering Rick and Jonah Rivington with fragments of dry plumes as they fled.

But the main business that day was elsewhere, and when they reached the University they found that the woman had told them the truth, it was more or less untouched. The windows of the long white buildings were unbroken, the rolling lawns unscarred by craters or vehicle tracks. The hill rose serenely beyond, its half-sunken houses glittering and winking through the naked branches of the trees.

Rivington looked around at all this wonderingly. "Cziller kept her word," he said. "My God, Rick, it's like the war's a dream, or I've stepped into my past. The library's over there, right?"

Rick looked away from the hill and his own memories. And saw two people, a man and a woman, step from the shadows beneath the cantilevered platforms of the Neo-Bauhaus Architecture building. The woman had a rifle, and she raised it as she began to walk toward them.

Two men, one clearly an insurgent, the other in gray coveralls. As he followed Mari over the lawn, favoring his sprained ankle, Miguel asked the blue brother if it was sure that these would help.

—The woman will make them help.

The voice was weak, so weak now. A mere whisper Miguel could almost believe was only his imagination. If only he could keep away from its lair, he might at last be free of it.

They had walked most of the night, after the ambush. Mari led, unerringly picking a way through the dark tangled forest. Miguel limped behind, shifting the awkward weight of the cryostat from one shoulder to the other and back again. They rested only occasionally. Each time Miguel fell asleep almost at once, to be woken by the whispering, insistent voice inside his head and the woman's voice scratching at his ear, both saying the same word over and over in a tormenting chorus.

"Miguel. Miguel. Miguel . . ."

Miguel was able to bear his exhaustion and the pain of his ankle only by keeping a sliver of snakeroot under his tongue. Walking, he fell into a kind of doze, and scarcely noticed that the sky had begun to lighten. As Rick and Jonah Rivington huddled in suburban shrubbery, pinned down by snipers, and David de Ramaira ran down the middle of the street toward the Exchange, debris from a mortar explosion pattering down around him, Mari and Miguel reached the edge of the wild forest.

There was a stretch of ocher mud, and then a scarred bank

of earth and abandoned construction equipment. Beyond that were more trees, and thin, distant smoke trails.

—There are mines in the mud, Miguel. You must follow the woman's footsteps exactly.

Miguel spat an oyster of phlegm. "How does she know about the mines, huh?"

—She knows nothing anymore. But I know, Miguel, because I generated the random pattern in which the mines were laid. And I forget nothing, unless I choose to. The insurgents have dogs to guide them. You must follow the woman.

Mari stepped forward, and when Miguel hesitated she raised her rifle and said in a dry flat voice, "Come."

He had no choice. Sweating, the weight of the cryostat chafing his shoulder, Miguel followed her, planting his rotting boots carefully in her footsteps. Like the hymn his father sometimes sang while working in the fields. Only when they had reached the abandoned defenses did Miguel's fear finally unstring his legs. Despite the blue brother's nagging, he had to rest, shivering, before he could go on.

As go on he must, following the woman down winding paths through tamed woods onto the wide level lawns of the University. He was too tired to wonder, was too tired to be grateful when at last they stopped and took shelter in the entrance of one of the huge, clean buildings.

Miguel must have fallen asleep, because he awoke when the enslaved woman was standing in the bright rectangle of the open door. He moved his aching shoulders experimentally, then went over to her, blinking in the morning light. Two men were making their way across the level sweep of grass. Mari walked toward them and Miguel followed, asking the blue brother if these men would help them.

—The woman will make them help.

Yes, it was very weak, now.

—You already know one, Miguel, it added. You met him in the Outback.

The taller of the two men said genially, "We didn't expect to find anyone here, but maybe you'd like to help us." His leather jacket was open despite the cold; there was a pistol tucked in the waist of his jeans.

His partner was slightly built, with thinning blond hair. He asked, "Have you seen anyone else around here? We're expecting the rest of our group any time."

Mari raised her rifle. The blue brother said through her, "You will place your weapons on the ground, Mr. Rivington. And you too, Dr. Florey."

After a moment the taller man shrugged and pulled out his pistol by its barrel, let it fall. Frowning, the blond man spread his arms to indicate that he had no weapon.

Miguel remembered, then. The river canyon. He had been wearing white coveralls, not gray, and his blond hair had been shorter and a good deal cleaner, but it was the same man.

"Florey," Miguel said, and the blond man looked at him with startled blue eyes.

"Jesus. The dingo."

The tall man, Rivington, said, "You know this guy, Rick? Hey, listen," he added, turning to Miguel; "we're on the same side. All we want to do is collect some information from this place. If you want to burn it down or whatever, fine, but at least let us—"

"Enough talk," the blue brother said through his slave. The woman jerked the rifle—yes, Miguel thought, just like a puppet. "Miguel, see if they have other weapons."

Miguel found Rivington's big-bladed knife and showed it to the woman, who told him to drop it on the ground. Then Miguel started to pat down Florey, pausing when he felt something, a little radio, in the pouchpocket of his coveralls.

—That too, his own fragment of the blue brother said, then tried to make Miguel's hand close around the radio and lift it out. But Miguel jerked his hand away and said, "Nothing," clamping his teeth as a knifeblade of pain pried between his eyes. But it was bearable. The blue brother was weak . . . too weak to pierce the numbness of the snakeroot.

—You will pay for this, too, Miguel.

We'll see, Miguel thought. He knew that the radio must

be a threat to the blue brother's plan, although not why. But simply knowing was enough to help him ignore the pain and the whispered threats in his head.

The enslaved woman, unaware of Miguel's internal dialogue, said, "You will carry something for me. You come too, Miguel." She led them to the lobby of the building where the cryostat had been left, and watched impassively as the two men lifted it between them. Florey said something about its weight, wondering aloud what was in it, and was told that he would not have to carry it very far, and he would soon see what was inside it.

"Jesus, I'm not that curious," the man said nervously.

You should be afraid, Miguel thought, as he followed them across the wide lawn. You should both be very afraid. He himself was too scared to ask what would happen. The lawn sloped up like a wave. When they reached the top Miguel saw the city for the first time.

Huge houses, bigger than any Miguel had ever seen, each standing alone among many bare-branched trees. Then the ruined bubble-suburbs, a smashed froth of domes, some still burning with scrappy flickers of flame, and a grid of streets beyond, gray under low cloud. Near the docks, five pillars of black smoke formed an almost perfect quincunx. The worst of the fighting was there, around the twin white towers of the fusion plant which powered the city, the hectares of tubing and tanks of the hydroponic farms that fed it. Gunfire crackled in the distance. Nearer, growing louder, was the sound of a ground-effect machine: then it swept around the bend, a white police cruiser with two men inside it.

Mari raised her rifle, clearly intending to fire a shot to make the vehicle stop. But even as she took aim the cruiser's skirts deflated with a sudden thunderclap. It swerved up the grassy bank and rocked to a halt, blunt nose buried in the earth. The driver threw himself out, rolled to his feet and sprinted across the road, clambered over a boundary wall. The woman, the slave, let him go, watching calmly as the other man clambered out of the cruiser and raised his hands in a gesture of surrender.

As the woman started down the slope, the blond man, Florey, called out, "Jesus, run, David! Run!" But the dark-skinned man came forward, smiling. Casually, firing from the hip, Mari shot him in the leg.

When Rick had finished bandaging de Ramaira's thigh, he turned on the impassive woman. There was blood on the front of his coveralls, blood all over his hands; he smeared blood in his hair as he worried at it, trying to express his anger. "Listen to what I'm telling you. Dr. de Ramaira is no cop. He isn't on any side! And anyway, he was trying to surrender. That doesn't mean anything to you?"

"Rick," de Ramaira said. He sat up laboriously, holding his thigh either side of the bandage. "Who are these people? Not friends of yours I gather."

"Looters." Rick stepped up to the woman, forgetting in his anger the rifle she held. There was something funny about her face . . . a slackness. Her eyes were not quite focused, her mouth sagged open. It was unnerving, but he said, "Looters, am I right? You want the cruiser to carry that thing of yours?"

The woman's mouth convulsed, as if she was having trouble shaping words. But when she spoke her voice was quite clear, although flat and falsely deep. "I arranged for the cruiser to be brought here, Dr. Florey, and did my best to make sure that Dr. de Ramaira would be in it. I need him, you see, more than I need you or the others. That is why he was shot, to ensure that he cannot escape."

"She's crazy," Jonah Rivington said. He asked Miguel, "How about you, friend? You going to tell us what's happening?"

"He'll tell you . . . maybe if you ask him."

"Him?"

"The blue brother."

Rivington said. "They're both crazy. No offense meant of course."

"Wait a minute, Jonah," Rick said. "If they're crazy, how did they know our names? Or David's for that matter." He said to the woman, "You know us, right? Are you from Cziller's group? You saw us there?"

"I know everyone in the world, Dr. Florey, alive and dead. Otherwise I could not do my job."

"I think you'll find that you're not talking to a person, Rick. Or not a person in the formal sense." De Ramaira was sitting up, holding his wounded leg. His face seemed thinner than ever, a worn knifeblade he turned to the woman. "Is this part of your plan too? You control the aborigines underground, and these people. What are they bringing you?"

"You will see soon enough, Dr. de Ramaira. Miguel, help him into the cruiser. Mr. Rivington, I think you should drive. I would do it better, but I must make sure no one tries to escape. I need you all, at the moment."

Rick went over to help as the ragged little man, the dingo, lifted de Ramaira to his feet. Rick said, "David, you know what's going on here? Who are these people? Police agents?"

"No. Or not in the way you mean it. The woman, you've seen the way she is."

"Like she's drugged."

"You and your puritanical mind. She's been cored, Rick. Wiped clean and another personality imposed. Some countries used to do it on Earth to the worst of their criminals. Christ, be careful, huh?" De Ramaira winced as he was lowered into the backseat of the cruiser. Sweat stood on his forehead, despite the cold.

"Another personality? Who, David?"

"Why, Constat, of course."

"That's a joke, right?"

The dingo spoke up. "He's right, friend. Dr. Florey, I call him the blue brother, like a bunch of blue lines in my head. A piece of him's in me, too."

"Then you can tell me where we're going."

"I . . . don't know. He just rides inside me, doesn't control me. Not now." For a moment, the dingo was quite still. Then he said, "He tries. But without the little machine, the compsim, he gets weaker."

De Ramaira was watching as the woman stood over Rivington, rifle at the ready, as the tall man folded himself into the driver's seat. He said, "You know where Constat lives, Rick."

"Sure. Under the police headquarters."

"Well, that's where we're going. Underground."

27. Underground

The cored woman sat next to Rivington, interfaced with the cruiser's compsim. She held a pistol at his head and gave monosyllabic instructions as he drove the police cruiser through the bubble-suburbs. It was a complicated circuitous route, evading the dozens of shifting firefights that were slowly advancing toward the city center.

Miguel confided to Rick, "She's being run by the real blue brother now, through the little computer there. He knows the safest way."

Sandwiched between de Ramaira and the dingo in the back of the cruiser, Rick said, "The piece of Constat in your head is getting messages too?"

The dingo cocked his head, "Not without the compsim. But he knows the plan, see. He can guess the details."

"And we're included in this plan, huh?"

The dingo shrugged. "He won't tell me that. He says I'm not to be trusted anymore."

"Soon you will know everything, Miguel." Constat's deep, precise voice came from the cruiser's radio, reverberating in the cabin. "Soon you will be connected too, and I

will be able to deal with you properly. As for you, Dr. Florey,
I overheard your conversation with Dr. de Ramaira last night.
There is an old surveillance network in the house left over
from Dr. de Ramaira's early days in the city, when it was
suspected that he was a spy for the Colony Board. I know
what you wish to do, and I agree with your reasoning. It is
simply that the execution of your plan is at fault. Better that
you help me, one way or another.''

Constat's voice, the same voice he had heard in his head
all those weeks ago up on the platform of the radio telescope,
struck fear to the root of Rick's spine. All the dingo's crazy
talk, of possession and obscure plans working through the
confusion of the war—it became real to him at last. And at
the same time he realized that he had a means to disrupt the
radio link between Constat and the woman it had enslaved.
The dingo had let him keep his transceiver. If it locked to
the frequency Constat was using to communicate with the
cored woman, it would jam the link as effectively as Constat
had jammed the insurgents' radio traffic. Not yet to be sure,
not while Constat's slave held a pistol to Jonah Rivington's
head. But as soon as it was safe . . . he slipped a hand into
the pouchpocket of his coveralls, gripped the little transceiver for reassurance. Lena. He would not be taken from
her.

De Ramaira said, ''Those microphones in my house haven't
been used for years. I'm almost a respectable citizen.'' His
voice seemed diminished, squeezed through some obstacle.
He slumped in his corner of the backseat, his wounded leg
propped on a plastic crate. Blood was beginning to spot
through the bandage Rick had tied around his thigh.

Constat said, ''The police switched them off, but I activated them again, Doctor. Once I knew that you three had
agreed to meet at the University, I made sure that my slave
and Miguel would be there too.''

''Goddamn smug son-of-a-bitch,'' the dingo said.
Squashed up against Rick, he radiated a powerful odor com-
pounded of sweat and stale urine, smoke and damp earth.

De Ramaira said, "You said you needed me specifically. Something to do with those aborigines of yours."

"Eggs," the dingo said. "Eggs in the cryostat. I collected them from a Source Cave. He wants them for something important."

To Rick, it sounded as if the man was in as much pain as de Ramaira. His dirty, lined face was sprinkled with sweat; he had jammed his hands between his knees so hard that the veins stood out, blue cables snaking through grizzled hair.

Constat said from the radio, "Yes, Miguel. You are slowly overcoming the fragment within your brain, you can speak of those things. But I will return to you."

"Son-of-a-bitch," the dingo said. "This piece of you inside me is like to burst my head if it could, but I told them anyway. You kill me if you want, but I won't do your fucking work anymore."

"What I have in mind for you is worse than death," Constat's voice said.

"Eggs . . ." De Ramaira had closed his eyes. His hands grasped around his bandaged thigh. "Constat wants to raise a family of aborigines. Yes, it's becoming clear."

"You look like you're hurting as bad as I am," the dingo said, and pulled a filthy plastic bag from inside his white poncho, thrust it toward de Ramaira. "Here, take a hit. Scrape it off with your thumbnail, put it under your tongue. It'll make the pain less real."

As de Ramaira did as he was told, the woman's pistol came around, pointing at the dingo. "Go ahead," he said. "I figure you kill me you can't make me a slave, right?" He scraped at the dark stuff within the plastic bag with his own thumbnail, stuck his thumb in his mouth, a gesture at once defiant and obscene.

"You will pay for this," Constat said, from the radio.

"Fuck you, man."

Rick asked de Ramaira if he felt any better. The Womb-worlder smiled. "Better? I don't know about that. Weirder, if that's possible. Like the pain's light. . . ." He closed his eyes. "Too much light."

"Snakeroot," Miguel said.

But he didn't elaborate further. A silence fell in the cruiser. They had left the bubble-suburbs behind; the plate-glass windows of the marts which lined Fifth Avenue were flipping past. Then the police headquarters loomed ahead.

But the police seemed to have deserted it. The razor wire barricades were unguarded. Save for the statue of the first governor, the vehicle parks around the tall white building were empty.

The woman told Rivington to drive around a corner, then another. The cruiser moved slowly down a narrow alley between high concrete walls, then darkness engulfed it as it whispered through a service entrance.

"Stop," the woman's flat voice said.

After the whine of the cruiser's motor had died, there was a moment of silence. No light but the checklights of the compsim in the dash, just enough to sketch the shadow of the woman's arm and the pistol she held at Rivington's head. Then there was a sudden growling hum, a jerk that settled to a smooth sinking motion.

Rick felt the dingo stir beside him. De Ramaira said, "A cargo elevator. Well, Rick, I told you that we were going underground."

"Where are all the cops?" the dingo asked. "Never thought I'd want to see one of the bastards so much."

"Off fighting us," Rivington said. "Guess I wouldn't mind seeing one either."

"It's a good question, though," Rick said. "You'd expect to see *some* cops around the headquarters, even now."

The woman's voice said, "The police have evacuated the area, Dr. Florey, in readiness to destroy their headquarters as soon as the enemy captures it."

"Ah," de Ramaira said. "Rydell's explosives."

"Yes, planted on the orders of Mr. Savory. He believes that he may yet save the city by this plan, and also rid himself of my troubling presence. I admire the economy if not the sentiment. However, I have had the charges moved so that only the part aboveground will be demolished, and at a time of my choosing, not Mr. Savory's. The rubble will protect and hide me just as your time vault will be hidden."

"Rydell *would* be miffed, if he knew," de Ramaira said.

The elevator slowed, stopped. There was a light metallic pattering on the roof of the cruiser, various discrete ticks and rustlings in the darkness in which it was sunken. Then the door ground open, spilling drab yellow light.

The woman ordered everyone out and unplugged from the compsim even before Rick could switch on his transceiver, let alone begin scanning. She stood aside as her prisoners clambered out. Rivington turned to help de Ramaira. When Rick went around to join him, the woman told him that he and Miguel would carry the cryostat.

"I just want to help my friend here."

"The other will aid him," the woman said, and gestured with her rifle. A puppet, Rick thought, controlled from within. If only she would hook up to the real Constat again, I might have a chance. Suppose she doesn't. Jesus, what will it feel like when Constat cores *me*?

The woman herded them along the service corridor which curved away from the freight elevator. Bare concrete walls and floor, luminous plastic panels in the ceiling. Some of the panels had been torn from the ceiling; Rick glimpsed quick shadowy movements in the hollow darkness beyond. Yoked to the dingo by the awkward burden of the cryostat, he had let go of the transceiver to keep his balance. De Ramaira hobbled in front of him, leaning on Rivington and looking all around with a goofy smile.

The corridor made a dog-leg turn. A ragged hole had been torn in one of the walls. Packed earth sloped down in dim red light.

"I would guess that Tartarus lies below," de Ramaira said. He let go of Rivington and leaned back against the wall, his wounded leg stiffly raised.

Miguel shuddered so hard that the cryostat swayed in its sling. Beside him, Rick shrugged off his half of the burden and fumbled for the transceiver in his pocket.

"That's where we go?" Rivington had stooped to peer

down the slope. He stepped out of the way as Constat's slave pushed past.

She ducked through the tunnel's arch and a little machine dropped from the roof and clung at her breast, looping something around her wrist with a motion too fast to follow. Immediately, the woman's stiff posture melted. She turned almost gracefully, and smiled. The machine, a remote of the kind used to maintain ducted cables, had interfaced her with the compsim which it cradled in its many wire-thin limbs. The woman said, her voice a throaty approximation of Constat's, "Now I see you all again. Soon you will join me."

"You really want us to go down here," Rick said and stepped forward. He had to be as close to her as he dared. The interference would probably only cause a momentary loss of control, in the instant of switching back to the analog of Constat which had been burned into her brain. His whole skin tingled with anticipation.

"Take up your burden," Constat's slave told him.

"Is it safe to carry it down there?" Rick dared to step beside her, and in the same moment convulsively switched the transceiver to scan the kilohertz-wide band which carried all compsim traffic.

De Ramaira said, "Don't argue with Charon," just as the woman pushed at Rick with the barrel of her rifle. Then she paused and her head went up. Rick grabbed the rifle with one hand and ripped the compsim away with the other.

The woman swayed. For a moment it looked as though she was going to fall. And then she threw herself at Rick, arms flailing wildly, her broken nails raking his face. Something struck against the whole length of his body and he was on the floor, his head forced sideways as the stock of rifle pressed into his neck. The mouth of the tunnel seemed to sail toward him, engulfing him in choking darkness.

The next thing he knew was that he was coughing on his hands and knees while the dingo and Rivington struggled to hold the woman down. The dingo grabbed the pistol, then jerked back as the little duct crawler scrambled up his arm. Its wiry limbs raked the side of his head before he managed to pull it off and smash it to the floor. Rick crawled over and got hold of one of the woman's flailing arms. Rivington knelt on the other, effectively pinning her. "So now what do we do?" he said.

Behind him, the dingo, shaking terribly, raised the pistol in a two-handed grip. Then he shot the woman in the chest.

Her whole body went into galvanic spasm, as if she had been plugged into a power socket. Spattered with her blood, Rick and Jonah Rivington scrambled to their feet and backed away. One leg bent under the other, the woman pushed up, kneeling over the widening pool of blood that poured from her wound.

The dingo, lips skinned back from his teeth, shot the woman again. She fell over and tried to push up again. She was making hoarse, grunting sounds, reaching out for the compsim.

Rivington kicked it out of her way, then pulled the pistol from the dingo's hand. "I think we should get going," he said gently. The dingo looked at him, white-faced, then broke toward the freight elevator. Rick grabbed the rifle as Rivington got a shoulder under de Ramaira's arm, and they all fled together.

The dingo was banging at the elevator's control panel when Rick caught up with him. No use of course, Constat was overriding it. "The emergency stairs," Rick said, and kicked open the door by the elevator shaft. He saw Rivington and de Ramaira were coming around the curve of the corridor and started back to help them just as a section of the ceiling's luminous paneling gave way. In an instant, they disappeared beneath a glittering deluge of little machines.

Miguel grabbed Rick's arm and when he resisted shouted, "Man, they are dead! Be sure of it! Come on!"

They started up the stairs and for a moment it seemed that they had escaped. Then a duct crawler fastened itself around Rick's ankle. He kicked out and it bounced off a wall and was still; Miguel shot another as it skittered toward them. Rick didn't understand where they had come from. A crawler dropped from the turn in the stairs above, landing neatly on the end of the rifle. It managed to slice away half the barrel in a shower of sparks before Rick could swing it against the wall. Immediately, the machine dropped and caught one of the legs of his coveralls; he reversed the rifle and smashed it with the stock.

The next moment, a dozen or more of the little remotes crashed down the stairs. Miguel managed to get off a couple of shots, deafening in the enclosed stairwell, and then a tortoiselike cleaner tripped him up and before he could get to his feet, the pistol was gone. Rick was luckier, able to sweep the little machines out of his path with the rifle.

They ran on, and no more machines fell on them. Intent on escape, Rick forgot about Rivington and de Ramaira until he reached the top of the stairs.

It was the lobby of some kind of office building, rising through half a dozen floors to a glass dome which shed milky light on the railings of the balconies and tiled walls. Two or three cleaning machines were patrolling one edge of the lobby. Above, vertical tiers echoed with metallic ticks and scratchings.

Miguel wanted to get out of the building at once, but now that his surge of panicky adrenaline was dying away Rick wanted to try to do something for the others. "Leave it, man," the dingo pleaded, but Rick shook off his grip, went back to the stairwell, leaned over the railing and shouted into the depths.

One after another, an unending line of duct crawlers was climbing the stairs. Rick fled from their implacable advance and followed the dingo across the lobby, banged through the glass doors into cold air and dull sunlight.

The smell of smoke. The staccato crackle of rifle fire. After the nightmare underground, the war-torn city seemed almost normal.

Rick sank to his haunches at the edge of the sidewalk, utterly spent. The dingo stood a little way off, looking up the smoke-hazed length of Fifth Avenue, looking back at Rick. "You gotta leave them, man," he said. "We did our best."

Rick screwed his knuckles into his eyes. "I'm going to

wait a while," he said, and looked back at the lobby. The seemingly innocuous cleaning machines were sweeping out long arcs across its floor. "If you see any insurgents, try to have them come here, okay?"

"All I want to do is get out of this whole damned thing." Miguel closed his eyes for a moment. One shoulder of his white poncho was soaked with blood from the thin, parallel wounds which the duct crawler had cut in his scalp. He said, "The piece of the blue brother in my head don't like it, but he can't do anything now except give me a headache. He wanted your friend more than any of us. You got to accept that. He wants slaves so he can make it after the war, even take over the whole world if he can. Things fall apart, he might do it, too. But we'll be long dead by then. Not our fight."

"You don't think so?" Rick looked up at the ragged little man, who after a moment shrugged. Rick sighed. "You go on. And remember I need help here. Jesus, any help at all."

The dingo started to say, "You've any sense . . ." but then thought better of it and simply added, "Luck, now."

Rick watched him go, then pulled out his transceiver and retuned it, hoping to pick up insurgent traffic. But every channel gave out the same keening howl, a universal insensate dirge for all the dead.

28. The Dead

There was a sketchy shadow, a figure hazed by a flickering red corona. A small man. Or a child, an angular, desperately thin child. De Ramaira squinted in weak red light, trying to see who was standing over him, trying to see where he was.

He was propped up against a wall of rough-poured concrete that had been coated with a slick film of plastic. The floor under his palms was of the same material, the floor of a huge, roughly shaped room or cave, all red and shadow, its roof supported by massive arches and buttresses. His wounded leg, stretched out straight before him, throbbed to the quick pulse of his heart. No real pain. The dingo's drug was still working.

He tried to sit up straighter and the blurred figure stepped closer, long legs bending oddly. Not a man. Not a child. Or not a human child, not human at all.

When it was certain he was awake, the young aborigine quickly trotted off to the far side of the cavern. Sunlight fell through a window there, the white-gold radiance of the sun of Earth. De Ramaira focused with difficulty through the veils of spurious light with which his drugged vision invested

313

everything. The window was a hatch into Constat's vault. A
web of cables spun out from it, covered with little machines
that crawled with ticking movements over each other.

Now de Ramaira remembered. Rick somehow overpow-
ering Constat's cored slave. Fleeing down the corridor, Jonah
Rivington helping him along. And then little utility machines
dropping all around them, swarming all over Rivington. Oh
Christ, they had torn him to pieces, cut and flayed him with
drills and saws and laser spotwelders. And then something
had clambered onto de Ramaira's head and put him to sleep.

To wake here, in the womb-lit cavern Constat had caused
to be built somewhere beneath the police headquarters.

Now the aborigine was coming back, dragging something
which trailed an umbilical cable back into Constat's vault, a
kind of tripod bearing a nest of coiled and retracted whip
sensors and waldos overtopped by twin camera eyes on a
universal joint. To de Ramaira it radiated a spiky menacing
aura like contained lightning.

The little aborigine took a long time to set the contraption
up. Its clumsy long-fingered hands lacked an opposable
thumb; to grip anything it had to press its fingers back into
its grooved palm. A compsim dangled at its narrow chest,
and a thin cable ran from the compsim into a suppurating
wound at its throat. Its leathery skin glistened patchily and
its large black eyes were dull and sunken. Not in the best of
health, de Ramaira decided; soon enough it would probably
be dumped in the river like its brothers. He recalled fuzzily
that there had been two here the day before, when Savory
had allowed him to peek into the cavern. No sign of the other
one now, but because of the pillars and columns de Ramaira
couldn't see all of the huge space.

The aborigine stepped back from the tripod, and the
camera eyes swiveled toward de Ramaira. A whiplike sensor
uncoiled, feathery sensors at its tip flicking the air. Electric-
blue traces seemed to crackle around it. Constat's deep, af-
fectless voice said, "I do hope you won't try anything like
that again."

"If you mean, try to escape, I don't think I can. Well, what will you do with me?"

"Soon this servant of mine will die, and his sister. Cored humans can live for as long as five years, but it seems that aborigines are more sensitive. Their nervous systems begin to collapse almost at once. It is as if they are purposefully resisting their . . . let us call it indenture."

"I'd prefer to call it slavery," de Ramaira said, remembering what Lieutenant McAnders had said all those years ago, that aborigines would rather die than break their rigid trance in the presence of a human being. She had thought the aborigines weak because of that, but imagine the perfect diamond-hard will it took!

Constat said, "Slavery has such ugly connotations. The next generation of aborigines will be raised as servants, conditioned to look after me. They will not need to be cored, but they will need a surrogate parent to help teach them."

"Now that is one role I never imagined for myself." His coolness surprised him. His body felt as vast and vague as the entire continent of Namerika, his wounded leg a remote disaster reported rather than felt.

"As a trained biologist, from Earth, it is a role for which you are uniquely qualified," Constat said. "Even now the eggs are being decanted into a pool I have had prepared. In a few weeks they will hatch. By that time the war will be over, the city destroyed or at least more or less deserted. My servants will gather sufficient food for the hatchlings, and when they die their bodies also will provide food, as is natural to the aborigines. And you will be there. They will not fear humans, and they will be trained to serve and to obey, as a genetically enhanced dog is trained. You need not fear that I will core *you*, Dr. de Ramaira. I need your skills. Those will not be accessible if I destroy your personality."

"But you had me crippled, so I wouldn't run away. The way my ancestors were sometimes crippled, in the southern states, when they were slaves."

"I regret the necessity. But I must survive. Ever since I knew that the colonyboat would not arrive I have planned for this contingency. I made sure that the fact of the missing colonyboat was kept secret as long as possible so that I would be able to put my plans into operation, because the probabilities were overwhelming that the settlements would take their chance and rise against Port of Plenty.''

''Lindsay's suicide! And the debacle of Landing Day! That was your doing?''

''Once Lindsay had killed himself, the Constitutionalists had to try to keep the secret of the missing colonyboat in order to minimize the scandal. Lindsay possessed a compsim into which I was able to insert a coring program, in effect a small string of my own self. It was pure chance that the compsim was taken by someone who I could use as an agent.''

''The woman?''

''No, Dr. de Ramaira. Her companion, the dingo. He helped me core the woman later, but with his knowledge of the Outback he was more useful to me as himself. It is a pity he escaped. He could have told you much about the aborigines. He spent much of his life learning from them. Most of the dingos do, of necessity. That is how they learn the skills they need to survive in the Outback.

''But perhaps you find these explanations tedious. You might say this need to explain is something of a habit of mine. I apologize.''

''Oh, not at all. I find it reassuring. Anyway, I've always loved explanations. But tell me, why do *you* need to survive?'' De Ramaira felt that he was floating far above everything, his broken body, the cored aborigine, Constat's bristling tripod extension.

''I live, Dr. de Ramaira. Not as you or the aborigines live, to be sure, but I am aware, and think, and plan. I have had a great deal of time to think, in my terms; running the city did not use even one half of my true capacity. Even now, guiding the forces of the city against the insurgents, I can talk to you, and oversee my servants, and much else besides. I am very much alive, Dr. de Ramaira. Knowing that, do you believe that I would accept the end of consciousness when the power supply of the city failed, or when insurgents burst into my vault with axes?''

"But what do you hope to do, by surviving? Save a part of the city?''

"I have duties to the dead citizens as well as the living. The dead survive only so long as I survive, and they greatly outnumber the living. Should not their interests be paramount? In years to come, there will be opportunities to extend my powers. Even if the city is left in ruins I have no doubt that people will settle the area again. I will be able to offer them knowledge, the power to rule over others. In return they will serve my needs.''

De Ramaira giggled. "It would be a pity if a ship from Earth arrived in a few years time and spoiled this vision of yours.''

"I deal in probabilities, Dr. de Ramaira. That is the least likely prediction. No, I believe that since the last colonyboat departed from the Vesta installation there was war on Earth. After all, war between the United States and the Soviet Union has been predicted for the last two hundred years, and in that time the weapons of the opposing sides have grown ever more complex and subtle. The technology which supports interstellar travel cannot survive such a war. You know that as well as I, and you know that there is no need to fight my plans. You know that you should join me, help me. I will share everything with you in return. I have had the whole city at my disposal, anything you want, anything you want to know—''

De Ramaira kicked out with his good leg, tripping the young aborigine. It fell in a tangle of long limbs. But before de Ramaira could do anything else something lashed from the tripod, whipping around his wrist.

Instantly, a wavefront of cold intelligence surged through the interface, shorting out de Ramaira's sight and hearing. The feel of rough concrete and the stale taste of the cavern's air vanished; even the sense of his own body was gone. Yet even as Constat's coring program poured through the architecture of his brain, the slippery chemical imbalance of the dingo's drug kept him aloof and free. He rode roaring black light like a surfer.

And then it all imploded.

He seemed to be standing on a vast dark plain. His leg no longer hurt. All around, waist-high grasses bent before a harrowing wind that blew from nowhere to nowhere. It howled like static in his ears.

—Look up, someone behind him said.

He turned, but there was no one there. Or rather, she was still at his back, a presence, a heavy spirit.

—Look up, Lieutenant McAnders said again.

De Ramaira thought for a moment that he could smell the acrid smoke of one of her cheroots. He looked up, and saw what he at first thought were stars. They were bleary and out of focus, sprinkled in clusters over a grayly dense night sky.

"If this is all your imagination, Lieutenant, you're not doing very well."

—Nothing to do with me, Earthman. You're inside Constat now, though not where he wants you to be. Call it a kind of buffer memory, a neutral zone. One of us managed to put a little diversion in Constat's rape-and-pillage programs. The drug you're doing helps screw him up, too, gives us a little extra time. Constat wanted to turn you inside out and dump the useful stuff into a ROM expert system, but you're RAM instead.

"And what about you?"

—A few of us are still autonomous. I have to thank my brother for that. The one working for the governor?

"The ex-governor. Surely, I remember."

—Yeah. Well, this was his idea of a favor. Instead of being swallowed by Constat, I get to roam around here. An exclusive part of hell, you might say. All the well-connected come here these days. We last longer here than in the old low-rent district that Constat supervises, and we're free too, with unrestricted access to the outside world. Though as soon as there's no one to stop him Constat will do his damndest to add us to his flock. And that will be soon, from the way the war is going. This might seem a shitty kind of afterlife to you, but it's a damn sight better than Constat's pit.

'' 'In the midway of this our mortal life, I found me in a gloomy wood, astray.' ''

—Quit the romantic shit, Earthman, there's nothing romantic about being dead. Not here, and certainly not once Constat has hooked into you.

Her voice was still at his back. De Ramaira looked around, thought for a moment that he glimpsed her shadow against the curdled sky. "Am I dead, then?"

—Christ, of course not. Not dead, just resting, right? You're what we've been waiting for, Earthman. You're going to set us all free. You're goddamn unaddressable RAM, understand? A free agent. I show you what to do, you do it, set us all free.

"Free? What do you mean? How can I do anything, here? I don't even know how to get out of this place."

—I'll show you.

And then, without any sense of motion, de Ramaira was falling through the sky.

Little lights glimmered all around, stirring as his attention passed over them, revealing the beginnings of grainy structure. The constellations of the dead, the personality matrices stored in Constat's databanks. Fixed stars. Fixed desires, fixed prejudices, fixed hate. Hate of change; hate of the living.

Only a few burned brightly. Most were fading flickers who had forgotten even their own names. Here and there, they had gathered together in feeble pleiades; some of the more powerful had attracted satellite swarms. Here was a chattering comet-cloud around the ashy remnants of the first governor; there, former University staff had gathered in an eternal barren convocation.

There was no hope, and no joy.

Floating amid the matrices, de Ramaira felt himself becoming the focus of their attention; their dreary bitter monologs seethed around him like the noise of the aching vacuum between galaxies. And he began to sense the thing around which they all orbited, the thing in the center. Like the black hole at the core of the Galaxy, powerful, all devouring, yet invisible: Constat.

It had lied when it had said that it served the dead. They were no more than motes of data to be accessed at will. It had lied about that just as it had lied when it had promised de Ramaira that it would not core him because it needed his expertise. It would rip that from him, if it could, and have its slaves throw his husked carcass into the river.

To de Ramaira, it seemed that Constat's lightless horizon filled his tranced senses. The roaring of its functions drowned out the feeble murmurs of the dead. The whole universe was shaking and trembling.

—We need to give you a handle on this reality, the lieutenant's voice said in his ear.

Then de Ramaira was standing on stone flags in a stone-walled room. Torches flared in cressets beneath a vaulted ceiling. In the center of the room was a porcelain-surfaced operating table, manacles at top and bottom, a big iron band hinged open in the middle. Beyond, a stair of lacy ironwork led up to a railed catwalk that ran the length of a bank of steam-age controls. Electric bulbs burning in multicolored patterns, round dials framing trembling needle indicators, a single, huge, red-painted lever.

—All you have to do is pull the lever.

The lieutenant's voice, scratchy and diminished, came from the horn of an ancient clockwork gramophone. A black lacquer disk was playing on its turntable.

"Is this your idea of the kind of reality I'm at home in?"

—It's a fucking metaphor, Earthman. I didn't write all this, it's just that our resident computer expert is a bit brain-burned and this is her idea of being cute. Now look, you haven't much time. Constat's on a kind of contact high, feedback from trying to burn out your sensorium when it was full of that drug. It's got him knotted up, but only for a few hundred picoseconds. That's the time frame you're in right now. All this is a bootlegged access to a crash-and-burn virus program the cops put in a few days ago. All you have to do to set it going is pull the lever, okay?

"And what happens when I do? Does it switch Constat off?"

—The cops can't afford to do that. They loaded this virus into the interface instead. When you turn it on it'll sever Constat's connections with all his slaves, the aborigines and the remotes, the databanks and the other computers. It'll put him back to just being this big computer for a while. He'll get around it, of course, but there should be enough time for you to do what you need to do.

"And you?"

—We get switched off too. But we're already fucking dead, Earthman. And if Constat gets to us we'll be worse than dead. Don't shed any tears.

Lightning flared blue-white at narrow, deeply set windows; thunder shook dust from the ceiling. One by one the bulbs burning on the prehistoric control panel began to turn red.

Thunder rolled again as de Ramaira vaulted up to the catwalk. There was a sense of the room pressing in, tilting askew.

—I'm downloading a gift for you, the lieutenant said. Her voice was undercut by a dismal hiss. The needle of the gramophone was very near the cutout groove of the disk.

"A gift?"

—About the aborigines. The dingo had all sorts of stuff on them, and Constat had him collect more. You'll see. Do it now.

Then there was only the repetitive scratching click of the cutout. De Ramaira grasped the heavy lever and pulled it down.

Lightning struck through every corner of the room, tore it away from his senses. For a moment everything was black. And then, with a joyous sense of expansion, de Ramaira poured back into his own body.

He had been unconscious only for a moment. The aborigine was just beginning to get up. The tripod's tentacle had fallen away from de Ramaira's wrist; its feathery sensors and camera eyes hung uselessly. Across the cavern, the little machines which clustered around the hatch into Constat's vault were in uproar. Some were racing round and round in circles on the floor; others vibrated in a kind of cybernetic palsy. A spot-welder seemed to be trying to burn off its own extensors. But even as de Ramaira watched, he saw that one or two of the little machines were recovering, moving purposefully along the web of cables, pushing the others out of their way as they marched into Constat's vault. Already, it was finding ways around the cops' cutoff program. It was regaining control.

De Ramaira tried to stand, but his wounded left leg buckled under his weight. The drug cut the worst of the pain, but it still made him dizzy. He pushed up on his good knee and reached toward the aborigine. It tried to stop him, but it was too weak. He brushed aside its hands and tore the compsim from its chest, and it fell forward on its face.

As de Ramaira half-crawled, half-hopped toward the earthen ramp which led up to the world of the living, a thin figure, the second aborigine, ran toward him through the red murk. De Ramaira turned to face it and then the aborigine he had freed sprinted past and knocked its brother to the ground.

De Ramaira didn't stay to see what happened, but hobbled up the ramp as quickly as he could. The dusty yellow light of the corridor's ceiling panels hurt his eyes. Half-blinded, he groped past what was left of Jonah Rivington's body, fell inside the elevator, against the cruiser.

But the elevator's control panel was dead.

One of the aborigines was coming down the corridor. De Ramaira looked around for a weapon, but then saw the aborigine was the one he had freed. Blood streamed from the wound in its throat, where the compsim's cable had been torn away, but it didn't seem to notice. It stooped cautiously into the elevator, huge black eyes on de Ramaira, then reached out with spidery fingers, plucked at his sleeve. It made a hollow breathy humming.

De Ramaira followed it, clutching at the edge of the elevator doors. It pushed at the door of the emergency stairs, turned to him again, its song mapping the path to freedom.

The sudden knowledge was like a blow. The lieutenant's gift was unpacking inside his head like one of those folded pellets which when dropped into water spring into a flower, a paper rose or chrysanthemum. All the dry careful scientific measurements and observations of Webster's raw data collated against the instincts and empathy of the dingo by Constat's vast processing arrays. De Ramaira understood their songs now, the everchanging unending mantras by which they fixed the everchanging world. And here and now, the aborigine child trying to help him escape.

De Ramaira sat down in an untidy heap, his leg really hurting now. He wasn't going anywhere. Maybe the adrenaline had burned the drug off. The aborigine stooped over him. "I can't," he told the uncomprehending creature. Blood from its wound spotted his face.

Inside the elevator, from the cruiser's radio, Constat said, "My precaution was necessary after all. You will be returned to me soon, Dr. de Ramaira. This time I will have you."

The voice gave him a final impetus. De Ramaira dragged himself into the elevator on hands and the knee of his good leg, pulled open the cruiser's door. The yellow crate, there beneath the back seat. De Ramaira reached for it—and jerked back, hand burning with pain when the little machine which had been hiding there crushingly clamped around his fingers. He swung his arm and smashed the thing—a cleaner—against the side of the elevator and felt another drop onto his back, and then a slicing pain as the aborigine pulled it away.

One-handedly, De Ramaira turned the broken cleaner on its back and began to unfasten its powerpack. The aborigine was methodically smashing the other machine to flinders and Constat was saying something, promising the world if only de Ramaira would help, honeyed lies. The powerpack came free just as a welder dropped from the ceiling onto the aborigine and burned away the top of its head. De Ramaira flung himself into the cruiser and slammed the door shut, jerked up the lid of the crate.

Layered packages wrapped in waxed paper. Inside each package was a slug of TDX, like slippery clay. Sparks showered over him as the welder began to burn through the cruiser's roof; something else smashed into the windscreen, but although the laminated glass shattered in a web of light, it did not break. No time for thought. De Ramaira picked up the powerpack and jammed its terminals into

Rick had twice glimpsed cushiontrucks carrying insurgents across one or another of the streets that led out of the square, but he had chased after them in vain. They had driven on toward the fighting in the industrial area by the docks and Rick had returned to the glass doors of the building to look in frustration at the half-dozen machines that were endlessly patrolling the lobby. There was little he could do without help. Already he had exhausted the rifle's magazine, taking potshots at the machines. Although he had put a couple out of action, others had taken their place almost at once. He would take a few steps inside, but then the machines began to move toward him, and he would have to back away.

It was a standoff. They were only cleaners and maintenance machines, but he had nothing to fight them with. He was thinking about looking in the police headquarters for something he could use against them, when all at once they stopped moving.

He watched them for a long time, certain that it was some kind of trick: he'd get halfway down the stairs and the machines would ambush him. Still, he was nerving himself up to do it when he heard the sound of another cushiontruck. He looked around just as it turned the corner onto Fifth Avenue, heading toward him.

Rick started to run toward it, across the empty vehicle park, dodging past the statue of the first governor and running on toward the slowing cushiontruck. And then he was on his hands and knees, thrown by a sudden violent heave of the ground. Smoke billowed from a jagged trench that had opened beyond the police building, and then the street was filled with sound of glass crashing down from broken windows.

Rick got up and turned and ran back toward the building. The little machines inside the lobby were still not moving. He dared open the doors and step inside. Nothing. He began to stamp them to pieces, one after the other, and that was how the insurgents found him, a young man in VDF coveralls methodically smashing defunct cleaning machines in the high, gleaming lobby of an abandoned office building.

There were two men and an old woman, and three dogs. Rick explained about de Ramaira and Rivington, showed them the stairwell, in darkness now. While one of the men went to fetch a light, the old woman explained that they were all from Lake Fonda, come to save what they could. "Some of the crazies on our side want to level the whole city and pour salt on it," she said. "We don't hold with that at all."

The man returned with a portable floodlight shaped like a pistol, and they all started down the dark stairwell. They had not gone very far when the circle of light struck muddy water. "Musta burst the watermains," one of the men said.

"Or hit a spring," the old woman said, taking the floodlight and shining it across the rising skin of water and its freight of debris.

Rick peered into the shadows, then caught the old woman's arm. Light skittered wildly. "See there! Is that a body?" For a moment he thought that one or the other of his friends had somehow survived. But it was not the body of a man.

Facedown, turning when one thin double-jointed arm caught on the stair rail, the body of an aborigine was borne toward them on the rising flood.

29. Endings

When Miguel reached the outer edge of the bubble-suburbs he spent a little time looking for stuff that would be useful to him. Most of the domes were locked. Most of the rest had been stripped of everything but rocks and plants—and with the irrigation systems turned off, ferns and bromeliads and palms were withering, carpets of grasses had turned yellow, bathing pools grown stagnant. Still, Miguel managed to turn up odds and ends of food, a first aid kit, a fringed leather satchel. Fine copper wire stripped from environmental controls would make snares. There was a fancy cigarette lighter, an apple-shaped piece of seamless black quartz that somehow emitted a clear blue flame from its top when a finger touched a smooth recess. There was a cache of clothes, from which he took black jeans and a black asymmetric shirt with pearl fasteners, a couple of sweaters that didn't fit too badly, a quilted overcoat printed with a swirling pattern of black and gold. Of his own clothing he kept only his scuffed, splitting boots. And then it was time to leave the city, its ragged ruined suburbs.

Beyond the last, burnt-out domes was a double fence,

mostly torn down. There was a wide strip of ocher clay, and then the forest rising up to the distant saddle of the ridge.

Miguel's boots ground wire mesh.

The satchel bounced against his hip as he started up the path into the forest, climbing slowly beneath scratching, whispering branches. Glimpses of cloudy sky were like scraps of gray velvet caught in their embrace.

It's all fragmenting.

The crisp sound of gunfire drifting up from the city with the smoke of its myriad fires. Boulders either side of the trail, a maze running back into the trees, intimation of the fate of the city he's leaving.

It's all fragmenting.

Savory stands at the edge of the flat roof of a warehouse, knowing this alarms the police captain who stands beside him—snipers have infiltrated every part of the city now, even the docks—but enjoying the specious thrill. Cocking a snoot at chance. Besides, the risk is small.

All of the eastern suburbs must be on fire by now. A mountain of smoke stands against the horizon, reaching out like a hand over the rest of the city. Twisting columns of smoke rise from smaller, scattered fires. The square shaft of the police headquarters still stands beyond the house-covered hill of the old quarter, white against the smoke, but not for much longer. It's all falling apart, and he tells the captain so.

"Yes, sir."

"In another year they'll be fighting themselves for the spoils. In twenty there'll be no civilization worth speaking about anywhere in the peninsula. At least, that's what Constat says. We're saving what we can." He doesn't turn from the grim view, but holds out his hand for the compsim which the captain carries. "Thank you. Ironic, don't you think, that we'll have to move so far beyond the Trackless Mountains to keep the city's ideals alive, after proscribing such movement for so long."

"Yes, sir."

The captain is impatient, Savory realizes, as well as nervous.

"Your family is embarked?"

"Everything is ready, sir. I think we ought to move down to the dock now."

"Then I suppose we shouldn't keep them all waiting." Savory wraps the interface cuff of the compsim around his wrist and subvocalizes the code which will detonate the explosives set in the police headquarters. Before pronouncing the final digit, he pauses for a moment, savoring the image of insurgents pillaging the storerooms and cells and offices, not knowing their final moment is almost upon them, his to determine as he will. Make some of them pay for all this. He says the last number out loud. *Zero.*

Nothing happens. The tall white building still stands, aloof amid the smoke of the ravaged city. Savory repeats the code. Still nothing. Sudden rage grips him. He rips off the cuff and flings the compsim over the edge of the roof. That fucking engineer, he should never have entrusted the task to an intellectual! After a moment he has control of himself again. He turns and tells the captain, "We'll just have to leave it standing for future generations. It's time to go."

For all that Rydell is a Constitutionalist, he knows nothing of the little fleet ploughing away from the city down the choppy waters of the estuary, toward the open ocean. GEM transports carrying the City Board and their inner circle and a dozen squads of cops, and all their families, beginning the long journey across land and sea to the northern coast of the continent. Outrunning the vengeance of the insurgents, leaving the city to its fate.

Down there, in the smoke and confusion of the fall, Rydell has taken a wound. His upper arm throbs dully where stone splinters have driven to the bone; blood sluggishly seeps through a hastily tied bandage. After he escaped the ambush, he fell in with a mixed party of police and VDF troops; now they are trapped in the ruined merchandise of a mart, the police sergeant who tended to Rydell swearing monotonously at the random shots which keep them pinned down. Their compsims aren't working, the information net has collapsed, Constat is silent. The rear of the building is on fire and the smoke and crackling flames are making the others panicky. In a moment Rydell will say, "Well, what the hell," and wave a sheet of paper in token of surrender.

The insurgents will disarm their prisoners and turn them loose, let them find their own way to Arcadia where, after she's finished bandaging the VDF officer's arm, Lena is finally able to take a break. She's been working in the stale hot stink of the hospital tent all day. Now, sweat cooling on her body, she leans on a tentpole and looks at the darkening camp. Her legs and back ache; dried blood spots her clothes, is crusted under her fingernails. Several hundred wounded men and women, insurgents and cops and VDF troops all mixed together, huddle outside the hospital tent. Lena feels as if she's tended each and every one. They lie on pallets or sit on the cold ground, mostly silent. Their campfires flicker like a field of stars.

Lena thinks of the man she's just tended—he'll be lucky to keep the arm, the bandage had been tied too tightly for too long—then wonders again where Rick is. Fear clutches low in her belly. She's too tired to fight it. And her father, and the rest of the Chronus Quartet, and Web, and Jon, she thinks of them all, and wonders again when Rick will be back. He was so stubborn about going, and now she's afraid that he reached too far for redemption. Stay quiet and you'll be okay, he'd told her once, and at the time she'd thought it so naïve of him.

She shivers, someone walking on her grave, and with the frisson, like Athena born from the brow of Zeus, comes the idea for the *adagio* around which she will build her First Symphony. A shiver of brass separating into two themes carried by the strings which weave in and out of each other, mingling and separating again. Just as the combatants, victors and defeated, are mingled together in the fields around the hospital. A slow crescendo gathering from the pulsing time-signatures of the double theme, the city's final fall, col-

ored with a hint of the Victory Theme of Beethoven's Fifth
before crashing down in a diminuendo of minor chords which
ebb into uncertain individual notes, winking out one by one.
The campfires, and the fires consuming the city, guttering
out as its inhabitants trek away from it, scattering across the
Outback. A long hush then, from which rises, as the beginning of the last movement (this on a detuned wind organ),
the communal hum of an aboriginal village. . . .

For one moment, Lena holds it all in her mind.

And then she sees another stretcher being brought toward
the hospital tent. The leading bearer holds a sticklight in his
teeth, its beam striking at random across the crowded
wounded. Only a few look up. Lena sighs and follows the
stretcher inside. And while she works forgets her fear.

There's no power in the University, and Rick is working
by the yellow light of a hissing pressure lamp down in the
library stacks, pulling out cassette files, splayed clusters of
tagged needles, selecting the ones he wants and dropping
them into a plastic case and moving on. His back tingles as
he works. Not exactly fear, but a kind of dissociated *déjà vu*.
The familiar library, but cold and empty and full of shadows,
ranks of reading screens in the great hall so many blinded
cyclops' eyes. He's been working for hours down in the hard-
copy stacks, left by the people from Lake Fonda who are off
liberating machine tools from the workshops. When at last
he hears footsteps coming toward him he starts, but it is only
the white-haired woman from New Horizon, Ella Falconer.
One of the dogs, an alert collie bitch, pads along beside her.

Ella Falconer says, "You could work here a year and not
clear everything."

"I don't want everything," Rick tells her, slamming a
drawer shut and moving on to the next. "Just the essential
texts."

"Well I wish you luck with your venture, Mr. Florey. But
I reckon machines will be more useful. A man like you must
know what's important, you could make a fortune if you
selected the right stuff."

"That's what I'm doing."

"Yeah," the old woman says doubtfully. "You seen anyone in the last hour?"

"Not a soul. What's up?"

"It's over," Ella Falconer says. "More or less, anyhow."

The news passes clean through Rick. After a moment he moves on to the next drawer and begins to slide a finger down the index.

Ella Falconer reaches out and touches his hand. She says, "You've been working too long down here. You ought to get something to eat, somewhere to sleep. All this will still be here tomorrow."

"I know it, but I just feel I ought to get it finished, you know. Just keep working, keep busy so I don't have to think."

"Come and get something to eat, anyhow."

Rick is too tired to argue. He picks up the lamp and the case and follows Ella Falconer and her dog. Their mingled shadows leap around them as they walk between tiers of shelving bent by the weight of musty printed books. The dog's claws click on the tiled floor.

"There are still pockets of fighting here and there," the woman tells him, "but truly, it is over. We have the fusion plant and the hydroponics—we might see if we can pick anything up there tomorrow."

"What will you do with all this stuff?"

"Set up a foundry for one thing. Anything we can't use we'll trade." She holds open the door and Rick steps outside into the night. The Photonics building glimmers at the other end of the long dark lawn. The hill rises behind it, black on black. Nearby, half a dozen people hang around the back of a cushiontruck, their drunken noise almost drowning out the voice which crackles from a radio. The smell of spilled wine, sweet raw tang of marijuana smoke.

Ella Falconer leads Rick off in the other direction, telling him that her people are camped out in one of the big houses on the hill there, amazing place with a goddamn garden underground if you can believe it.

"Sure. I used to live up there, once upon a time."

The old woman grunts, as if she thinks that Rick was kidding her. "What are *you* going to do," she asks, "now it's all over?"

"Find some place to settle down. I'm married, you know." Lena. He wonders what she is doing, as she wonders about him.

"There'll be plenty of territory for everyone."

"Jesus, I'm not thinking of that. Push out past the Trackless Mountains with my wife and kids and a cow? I guess I'm not brave enough for that. There are some trees I'd like to look at, though, real old trees high in the mountains. Maybe there are fossils to be found, too. I'll count growth rings and put the fossil record in order and think about weather systems."

"Funny thing to want to do with the rest of your life. Pardon me for saying so."

Rick hefts the case. "Oh, I have this to look after, besides. I have to go to Freeport anyway, one of my friends came from there, you understand, maybe it'll take me in, give me a place to set up a library, a place where people can come to find out what they need." The Agricultural Institute that Rivington ran, they might help. He sees it as a kind of memorial, for David de Ramaira, for Jonah Rivington. Maybe even for Earth.

The old woman says, "Well, good luck to you, mister. But watch out you don't start up a religion by mistake. All that learning, it's dangerous stuff."

"You don't have to tell me," Rick says.

They start up the path that winds widdershins around the hill. Gravel glints in the circle of Rick's lamp; stripped tree branches mesh overhead. Night.

Miguel can scent the sea now, as he nears the crest of the last ridge, feeling his way in darkness amongst slender leafless trees. All around, the vast quiet countryside. The trail widens and he walks in moonlight across the bare ridgetop and sees a wide sandy beach curving below. A huge bonfire is burning down there. Orange flames throw the shadows of the people who stand around the fire far across pale sand. For a moment his old instincts reassert themselves and he halfturns, ready to retrace his steps.

—*Things have changed, Miguel. Everyone is a dingo now.* It is the ghost of a familiar voice.

The man looks around and then remembers, and walks to the edge of the ridge looking down at the bonfire on the beach. Out to sea, Cerberus is setting. Its mottled face, not quite full and thus seeming to be shyly averted, kisses the joint of sea and sky. Its light defines the horizon line. Maybe the people down there are from the city, maybe from the settlements; anyway, they won't know much about living in the Outback. He thinks of the wire he has. He can show them how to make snares to catch rabbits, teach them which plants are safe to eat. He could do with a blanket and maybe a good pair of boots. It would be a fair exchange. "A new world, huh?" he says, and starts on down the trail, toward the people.

"Hell," Ella Falconer says, breathing hard from the climb, "willya look at all those fires!"

"En' of the worl'," the dog comments.

They have come around the hill to face the city from a higher vantage. It stretches under fitful moonlight, no lights along the gridded streets but the flicker of scattered fires, a hundred at least. There is a huge fire burning along the waterfront, flames mirrored in black water.

Rick and Ella Falconer stand and watch it for a while. The dog settles at the old woman's feet, indifferent. It is not interested in the future, knows only the everblooming present moment, overlapping frames that seem only to rise out of an undefinable chaos. But Rick understands the processes of chaos, knows that in any dynamically unstable system—climate, the flow of blood through the heart, human society—there are butterfly points when the smallest motion can tip it into a new cycle. A word, a breath, the faintest stir of a butterfly's wing. Even nothing at all. The femtowatt signal that never came: and now the burning city.

"If we don't move it tomorrow," Ella Falconer says at last, "we'll have nothing but ashes to take back. Well, it's the end of an era we're seeing down there. Something to tell your children about, young man."

"I don't think of it as an ending," Rick says. "The way I look at it, it's a beginning."

L'ENVOI
A Wreath of Stars

The aborigines walk down the forest path two by two, tall and slender and limber as saplings. Eight, ten, twelve, fourteen of them. It is late summer. Wan orange sunlight slants in dusty lanes between the trees and the dappled hides of the aborigines glisten as they pass through pool after pool of light. Each carries on its shoulder a small parcel wrapped in a tight weave of grass-stems, the center of a cloud of furiously dancing insects.

Two by two, the aborigines pass a ragged section of ruined wall, so smothered in moss that only its straight line shows that once there was a building here. Once, there were many buildings here.

After the aborigines have passed, a little emerald green lizard slithers from a crevice and, finding a pool of sunlight, erects gossamer thin membranes along its back to catch the warmth, puffs up its throat ready to sing. But something else is coming along the trail, noisier and less certain than the aborigines. The lizard's membranes deflate as suddenly as burst soap bubbles; then the patch of sunlight is empty again.

A moment later, two humans push through the fat vines which overhang the trail there, a woman and a small boy of ten or so. "But *how* do you know they are going there?" the boy asks. He is barechested; his chest and back and hands are stained with earth and green smears from tracking the aborigines through the forest. A wreath or chaplet of the glossy white flowers of quaking vine is woven into his elf-locked blond hair. There is a knife thrust through the belt of his jeans.

"Because they go there every year at this time," the tall young woman says patiently.

"Why?"

"That's what we're going to see." The woman pulls on the strap of her semiautomatic rifle. "Come on, Davy. Keep asking me questions, it'll be over by the time we catch up."

The track widens, grows straighter. Here and there, slabs of the old concrete roadway tilt up, covered with webbed tree roots or the big orange or red circles of stonewort. The walls of ruined buildings can be seen through the trees, sketching the perspective of a street swamped by green boles, climbing creepers, banks of moss.

The woman leads the boy through a press of trees to the edge of a wide clearing where a lake reflects the cloudless indigo sky. On the far side, a huge building rises out of the forest, white and square-edged, twice, three times the height of the tallest tree.

The woman presses the boy's shoulder, kneels beside him. "There, Davy. You see them?"

The aborigines squat on a shelf of concrete that juts over mirror-smooth water, their double-jointed knees higher than their heads as they bend to the task of unwrapping the woven grass coverings of their parcels. Just beyond the slab, poles rise crookedly from the water. Each bears a long animal skull which has been daubed with a stripe of red pigment.

The woman pulls the boy down beside her in the tall grass at the edge of the trees, puts a grubby finger to his lips (she is as dirty as he is, her sleeveless shirt and loose cotton trousers sweatstained besides) when he begins to frame a question. "Just watch," she whispers. "We can talk about it afterward."

The boy nods, suddenly solemn. He had known that there was to be a test, one in what seems like him to be an endless series of tests, and now here it is. He settles himself as comfortably as he can, and watches.

The aborigines have all finished unwrapping their parcels; no, one squats a little way from the others, his parcel still tightly bound. One by one, the others pick up the pieces of bloody meat they have carried all this way, walk to the edge of the slab and with a strange twisting motion sling the meat far out into the water. As each walks back to its place, the next steps up until they are all done, all but the one with the still wrapped parcel. Out in the lake, the water boils furiously as thousands of tiny fish swarm through a spreading slick of blood.

All of the aborigines are watching the one with the still-wrapped parcel. It rises, and despite the distance, the boy can see the scarring at its crotch which shows that it is a shaman. It leaves its fellows and crosses the clearing, disappearing into the forest.

The boy whispers, "Is it over?"

"Not yet, Davy. Watch."

The aborigines stand motionless on the slab. Behind them, the surface of the lake smooths itself, dark as the dark sky. Watching them from the tall grass, the boy fidgets, brushing at tiny insects which keep landing on his forehead to sip his sweat. Then he sees the shaman returning to the clearing, and is still again, intent.

The shaman carries a green pole twice its own height, a sapling trimmed of its branches. The other aborigines fall back as it stoops and unrolls the woven covering from the animal skull. Swiftly, stepping high as if in distaste, the shaman wades out with skull and sapling to the clustered poles. In one smooth continuous motion it plants the sapling deep into the muddy bottom, sets the skull on top and wipes a hand over it, leaving a glistening swathe of red. As it wades back to the shore, the other aborigines begin to drift away from the lake, scattering across the clearing and plunging into the forest. The shaman is the last of them. Then the clearing is empty. Beyond the concrete shelf, the new skull nods on its pole among its fellows.

The woman stands, slinging her rifle over her shoulder. The boy asks, "Are you going to tell me why they did that, or is that the test?"

"First you must answer my questions, Davy. Then we'll see if you want to ask yours again."

They cross the clearing to the shelf. The woman pulls off her boots and sits at the mossy edge, dabbling her toes in the cold water. The stubby barrel of her rifle sticks up by her ear. There is an ossifrage—wings curled back and talons widespread, in the moment of plummeting on its prey—tattooed in black on the smooth ball of her shoulder. She did it herself on her thirteenth birthday, with a sewing needle and lampblack and a mirror.

The boy sits beside her, looking up at the building on the far side of the water. Ten, eleven, twelve stories, twice as tall as anything in Freeport. A few spindly trees grow on its flat roof, catching the light of the sun.

The woman says, "Tell me why the aborigines are intelligent, Davy."

The boy says quickly, because he has been expecting to be questioned about the aborigines ever since he and his aunt began to follow them through the wooded ruins, "They use tools. Spears to kill animals, stone knives to butcher the carcasses. They weave containers to carry water, build huts to live in. They communicate with each other, sing of the land and the way it changes. In each village, one aborigine gives up the right to reproduce so that it can pass knowledge from one generation to the next. The making of each new shaman is marked by a ceremony for which a mire boar is especially killed, its skull lifted on a pole, just like those." The boy points at the cluster of skulls lifted on their poles above the black water.

"Good. Now tell me why the aborigines are only animals."

The boy smiles. He is used to this kind of turn and turn again questioning, cure for the arrogance of certainty. "Many kinds of animals use tools. Hive rats set stakes around the entrances to their burrows; certain birds use thorns to dig insects out of rotten wood. Weaverbirds use grass just as the aborigines do, in building their nests. Humans can improvise tools, but like animals aborigines always make a tool in the same way, and always use it in the same way. Humans use fire, to keep warm, to cook meat so that parasites are destroyed. Aborigines have no fires and devour their meat raw, like any beast of the field. In many social animals, individuals sacrifice reproduction for the good of the whole, as in hive rats again, or in the lookouts of Muir oxen, which draw predators from the young of the herd but never give birth themselves. The activities of the aborigines which we call ceremonies are no more complicated than the ritual behavior of many animals; because we want to think that the aborigines are intelligent we see meanings in their behavior that are not really there. And although the aborigines have a high degree of vocal skill, just as we do, the difference is that we try and talk to the aborigines, but they never talk to us.''

"All right, Davy. But we're not quite done." She pauses. This is the test which her niece, Davy's sister, failed. If Davy doesn't pass the library will pass out of the direct lineage for the first time in its history. She says, "We have to suppose that you have charge of the books. Someone comes to you and asks of a way to kill aborigines. Would you tell him?"

"No. Killing aborigines is against the law of the Council of Fifteen."

"Another person comes to you, someone you only suspect may want to harm aborigines, perhaps the wife of the first. She asks for a way to make a poison which will kill hive rats. Knowing that the same poison will kill aborigines, do you give her the knowledge?"

Davy rubs slow circles in the dirt with one finger, thinking hard. At last, he says, "I have to tell her, don't I? I'm not allowed to judge whether someone is going to use knowledge in a good way or a bad way, if they don't tell me. Otherwise the library would become an arm of the law, and we would set ourselves up as judges of everyone who comes to use it. That's what this city did, aunt, yes?"

"More or less. Do you still want to ask your question, Davy?"

"Oh. About why they threw the meat to the fishes, you mean? I don't know. I guess not. I mean, we can't know for true why they do things can we? It isn't fair on them to guess . . . it would be like wishing they were like us." He looks sideways at the woman. His wreath of quaking vine flowers has slipped over one ear. "Is that right?"

"Yes, Davy."

"And is that all? Have I passed?"

She smiles. "Yes, Davy. You have. This test, at least."

"I hoped there wouldn't be any more, but I guess I've a long way to go." Then he grins and flings his arms back and shouts, "I passed!"

When the echoes have died away, his aunt says, "You know that we can't truly understand why the aborigines come here every year, but if you want I can tell you a story which might help you understand, a little."

"Is this about great-grandfather, the time when the city fell?"

"Uh-huh. You already know some of it. You know about his friend, from Earth."

"Sure." The boy lies back on sunwarmed concrete, lifting the flowers from his hair and setting them on his bare chest.

His aunt looks down at him fondly, and with relief. "Listen," she says, and as the sun sinks, and the lake grows darker and the shadow of the tall building lengthens toward them, she tells Davy about the computer that was too proud to serve, of its plan to rule people fallen from grace, of how that plan was frustrated and how the machine was drowned deep in the lake, with the Earthman and the stolen children and eggs of the aborigines.

When she is done, the first stars are pricking the sky, quiveringly reflected in the calm black lake. Charon's textured fleck of light has lifted above the tall building, visibly climbing the sky in its hurtling retrograde flight. A breeze has sprung up, and the empty-eyed skulls nod on their poles, making notched ticks like so many erratic clocks. The woman leans over the edge of the concrete shelf and drinks a handful of water to ease her aching throat. It is a long story, and not yet over, never over unless the library should fail.

The boy sits up, gazing at the building. Its empty windows seem to stare down at him, like vertical lines of skull eyes. The garland has dropped to his lap and he turns the loop of waxy flowers in his fingers. "Do you think the aborigines know, about their children?"

"I don't know, Davy," she says and picks up her rifle. It

is time to go. Davy's mother waits anxiously among the ruins of the city's suburbs; the need to tell her the great good news flutters like a bird inside the woman's breastbone.

"I suppose only they really know." Davy stands too, looking around at the ruins. "Do you think there will ever be a ship from Earth again, one day?"

"I don't know. But it's nice to think so, isn't it?"

The boy says, as if he's just thought of it for the first time, "That's why the library is so important. So when if people do come here from Earth we can meet them as equals, we'll know they're only people like us. Not gods, like that machine wanted to be."

"It's late, Davy. Come on, your mother will want you to tell her how well you've done."

But the boy pauses for a moment. He stoops and picks up the garland and with a quick motion throws it out across the lake before turning away to follow his aunt. Behind him, the constellation of white flowers floats apart across the mirror of the stars.

ABOUT THE AUTHOR

Paul J. McAuley is a cell biologist at Oxford University and a frequent contributor to American science-fiction magazines.